Claudia Carroll is a top ten-bestselling author in the UK and a number one bestselling author in Ireland, selling over 700,000 copies of her paperbacks alone. Three of her novels have been optioned, two for movies and one for a TV series on Fox TV. In 2013, her tenth novel *Me and You* was shortlisted for the Bord Gáis Energy Popular Choice Irish Book Award. Her latest novel, *All She Ever Wished For*, spent over 12 weeks in the Irish top ten. She was born in Dublin where she still lives.

Our Little Secret

Claudia Carroll

avon

This novel is entirely a work of fiction.
The names, characters and incidents portrayed in it are
the work of the author's imagination. Any resemblance to
actual persons, living or dead, events or localities is
entirely coincidental.

AVON

A division of HarperCollins*Publishers*
The News Building
1 London Bridge Street
London SE1 9GF

www.harpercollins.co.uk

A Paperback Original 2017

2

A catalogue record for this book is
available from the British Library

TPB ISBN: 978-0-00-814077-9
PB ISBN: 978-0-00-814076-2

Set in Minion by Palimpsest Book Production Limited,
Falkirk, Stirlingshire

Printed and bound in Great Britain by
Clays Ltd, St Ives plc

MIX
Paper from
responsible sources
FSC™ C007454

This book is warmly dedicated to three very special people, who between them make up the most extraordinary team.

For Ann-Marie Dolan, Mary Byrne and Tony Purdue at HarperCollins here in Dublin.
With love and thanks, for everything.

Prologue

With a slow, sickening sense of horror, Sarah found herself peering through the darkness of night, right into her own living room window. And there it was for all to see – the happy family tableau that was playing out inside, picture perfect in every way.

The roaring log fire? Tick.

The glasses of wine served out of the good crystal? Her good crystal goblets that had been a wedding present, thanks very much. Tick.

The whole scene looked like something out of an Ikea catalogue, right down to the daintily laid out plates of bruschetta and picky dippy things artfully dotted around the coffee table.

To Sarah's astonishment, both her ex-husband and her daughter had completely abandoned TV, iPhones and iPads and were actually playing Monopoly. (Christ, Monopoly . . . seriously?) All while *she* looked on, smiling happily and carefully noting down the score while the three of them laughed and joked, everyone in high spirits.

Just look at you, Sarah thought, as she stood in her own front garden, her eyes burning into the back of the woman she still thought of as her friend.

I've just been warned about you. I've been told you won't stop till you're actually living my life.

But by the looks of it, you already are.

*

Did it all start such a very short time ago? Has it really only been a year since I could call my life my own?

Here, for what it's worth, is how it all began. With a simple manicure on my lunch break, in the middle of a day, when I was stressed out of my mind. All I wanted was a snatched half-hour of time out, before heading back into the manic whirl of the Sloan Curtis offices. Nothing more.

But if I'd known then what I know now, then trust me, I'd have been a very distant speck on the horizon.

JANUARY

Chapter One

Sarah

'You have very good cuticles. Badly neglected though, I'm afraid. They just need a little bit of work,' my beauty therapist said, her head of thick, glossy dark hair bend low over the nail station, uttered focused on her work.

'I'm afraid I don't get a huge amount of time to take care of myself.' I smiled politely, flicking though that month's *Vanity Fair* with my other hand. There was an article about Kate Middleton's mother that I remember particularly wanting to read, for no other reason than to valet park my brain for the next half-hour. Exactly what I needed after that morning's conversation/screaming match with Darcy, my teenage daughter. Not to mention the snippy tone my boss had taken with me in a meeting earlier that day to discuss a legal brief I wasn't quite up to speed on. At least not yet, I wasn't.

A little half-hour of pampering on a Friday lunchtime before the weekend, that's all I was after. Something I hadn't indulged in for years. In fact I think the last time I spent a bit of non-essential cash on myself was long before Darcy hit secondary school.

'But it's so important to make time for personal grooming,' Lauren, my therapist, gently insisted with a sweet smile. 'These little things matter. My mother always used to say you can tell anything you want about a person just by looking at the state of their nail bed.'

'Yes, yes, of course,' I chimed automatically, completely absorbed by the article in front of me. Jesus, had Carole Middleton really made £30 million by the time she'd turned forty? And all from flogging little party bags? What was wrong with me anyway? Why couldn't I come up with a home-based cottage industry like that, which would go on to dominate the Forbes index and put an end to all of my money worries?

'Will you be taking any holidays soon?' my therapist asked, interrupting my thoughts yet again. Oh God, I groaned inwardly. Do we really have to have the holiday chat? Couldn't this one sense I just wanted to pull a Greta Garbo and be left alone to my thoughts?

'I wish. I can't remember the last time I took a proper holiday,' I replied, flashing her a quick smile.

'Going out tonight, maybe?'

'No, just back to the office shortly to catch up with a few things I need to sign off on, I'm afraid.'

'And any plans for the weekend?'

Not unless you count frantically playing catch-up with work, bickering with Darcy and trying my level best to be civil to Tom when he comes over to collect her later on, then no, I thought. As it happens, I was plan-free right through till the following Monday morning. If I was very lucky I might get to see an episode of *House of Cards* that I hadn't seen before on Netflix and maybe, just maybe, I might even chance a sneaky glass of Pinot Grigio when I had the house to myself.

As you could see, it was set be another wild weekend in the life of Sarah Keyes.

'No, just a quiet one for me.'

'Say no more,' Lauren smiled very sweetly. 'I get it. A romantic Friday night in with your husband, am I right?'

'A romantic night in with *who*?' I asked, looking up at her, confused.

'Your husband,' she said, two chocolate-brown eyes blinking innocently back at me.

'I'm not married,' I replied, just a bit too quickly. 'At least, not any more I'm not.'

'Oh, I'm so sorry, me and my big mouth,' Lauren said, blushing very prettily as she rubbed a dollop of cuticle cream in. 'It's just that you're wearing a wedding ring, so I assumed—'

'Separated.'

'Ahh,' she said, nodding. 'I see. Do you have children?'

'Just one. Darcy. She's sixteen.'

'I'm sure she's a wonderful girl,' Lauren said diplomatically.

Oh yes, a wonderful girl all right, I thought. *If you overlooked the sudden downturn in her school results ever since Tom and I broke up, the mitching off school, the sulkiness, the violent mood swings and don't even get me started on the amounts of cash that seem to disappear out of my purse on a daily basis.*

Back then my brain melted with the guilt of how badly Darcy had been dealing with the whole separation. And, of course, every time I tried gently to broach the subject with her, I'd either get the sulky silent treatment or else her bedroom door slammed square in my face.

'Absolutely,' I agreed, with as bright a smile as I could muster. 'Darcy's a terrific kid, thanks.'

A pause while I went back to my *Vanity Fair*, hoping that was us done with the chit-chat. No such luck though.

'So, whereabouts do you work?'

Oh please, if I tip you extra, can we just edit out the small talk?

'I work over at Sloan Curtis,' I said, taking a sip of the latte in front of me, resigning myself to the fact that I'd have to make conversation. 'That's a legal firm,' I added, a little patronisingly, now that I come to think about it.

'Yes,' Lauren nodded thoughtfully. 'Sloan Curtis, I've heard of you. You mostly concentrate on company and taxation law cases, don't you?'

At that, I looked up, my attention caught. But then you don't really expect your nail technician to be au fait with local legal practices and their individual specialties, now do you?

'You've heard of us?' I remember saying.

'Yes,' Lauren nodded, with a knowing smile. 'I certainly have.'

'I hope you don't mind my asking, but how?' Clients from the firm must come to her for treatments, I guessed.

'It's just that, well, let's say I'm very interested, that's all.'

'You mean you're interested in studying law?' I fished about a bit, wondering if that's how this one stumbled across the company name.

'Oh no, nothing like that,' she said. 'You see, I'm already a fully qualified lawyer. I'm a solicitor, in fact.'

At that, I put the *Vanity Fair* aside and really had a good look at Lauren, taking her in properly this time. The girl was twenty-five tops and stunningly pretty, with brown eyes like twin Cadbury's Buttons and a figure that Miss Universe might have wept for. She smiled a lot, and had a soft, gentle accent that was hard to place. From the West of Ireland, I wondered. Galway, maybe?

First impression? That this was a sweet, bright girl, albeit a little bit on the talkative side.

'So is the salon a part-time job for you?' I asked.

There was a pause while Lauren fumbled around with a selection of SHELLAC nail varnishes in different shades of beige.

'Blush or bashful?' was all I got by way of an answer though.

'Excuse me?'

'Which colour would you like on your nails? Blush or bashful? You did specify nude colours and these are the ones I think would probably work best with your pale skin tones—'

'Lauren,' I persisted gently. 'You didn't answer my question. Sorry if I sound nosey, but I'm just curious to know why you don't actually practice law.'

I remember hoping I hadn't caused the girl any offence, though it was clear what I was really asking. Why was a fully qualified lawyer working in a cut-price nail bar in a dingy salon, above an Indian takeaway in the middle of Phibsboro?

'Money is a little bit tight just now,' she said, pushing her hair behind her ears self-consciously.

'But wouldn't you earn much more if you worked for a legal firm?'

'Absolutely, yes,' she replied, focusing on my nail bed and not making eye contact. 'Of course I would. But it's so hard for someone like me to get started in that field. Almost impossible, in fact.'

'What do you mean, for "someone like you"?'

'It's . . . a little bit complicated,' she said, blushing.

'Complicated, how?'

'You work at Sloan Curtis,' Lauren answered politely, 'so you of all people must know how it is. The legal field is a pretty rarified one and it's tough to crack into. Particularly when you don't have a single friend or contact in that world. And I've been working hard to try and get some kind of a break, believe me. I've been trying so hard, you wouldn't believe it. But sometimes it really feels like I'm banging my head against a brick wall.'

Looking back, it was that one single sentence that caught me.

I thought for a moment, then nodded in agreement, absolutely chiming with what Lauren had said. Because it had been a huge struggle for me too, back in the day. I didn't come from a legal background, unlike so many in my class at college who had parents and relations practising as barristers and, in one case, even a High Court judge.

I remembered all too vividly how tough I'd found it to get a paralegal job – any kind of job, really – after I first graduated, all those years ago. How I'd had to graft away as a postgraduate, doing any kind of legal temping work that came my way. I had to shatter every glass ceiling I came in contact with all by myself, with absolutely no one to help me. Then eventually after years of that, an opportunity finally opened up for me at Sloan Curtis. It felt utterly miraculous to me that I'd managed to land an actual bona fide job there. I really couldn't – then or now – believe my luck.

'All down to my magic novena to St Joseph,' my mother had preached at the time, wagging a triumphant finger in my face. Yeah, right. More to do with the fact that I invested years practically battering down the door of Sloan Curtis before I could even get an interview in the place.

Because Lauren was absolutely right. The legal world was then and is now a virtual closed shop, and it takes grit and iron determination to get a foot in the door. And that's only if you happen to be one of the incredibly fortunate ones.

'So where did you qualify?' I asked, turning my attention back to Lauren, feeling guilty for not having engaged with her a bit more beforehand.

It struck me as strange that she didn't even attempt to answer my question. Instead she flushed red with a coy, embarrassed little shake of her head.

'Or did you study abroad?' I persisted, confused by the silence.

'It's a long story,' she said quietly.

I looked expectantly across at her, waiting on her to elaborate a bit but, no, there was nothing. Instead, she just kept her head bowed and her mouth firmly shut as she continued filing away at my nails.

So I let it drop. Was the girl exaggerating her qualifications? Possibly. Maybe she was doing some kind of night course in law and had decided to 'big' herself up a bit. Which happened all the time, by the way. We'd just been interviewing for an intern over at Sloan Curtis and some of the exaggerated fiction that prospective candidates adored their CVs with would almost be worthy of a book award.

A companionable silence fell and I went back to my *Vanity Fair*, while Lauren concentrated on applying a perfect layer of topcoat.

It was only as I was leaving that it happened. I remember

going to the till and paying what I owed to a surly looking receptionist who barely glanced up from the *Hello!* magazine she'd been reading as she took my money; instead she just growled at me to 'come back again – whenever'.

Then I made a point of going back to the nail station to find Lauren, so I could give her the fiver tip I had clutched in my hand for her.

'Thank you so much,' I said, shaking her hand and pressing the cash right into her palm.

But Lauren didn't respond with an automatic 'thank you', the way any other therapist would. Instead she locked eyes with me and stared at me for just a beat longer that you'd expect, almost like she was trying to communicate something unspoken. Then to my surprise, she handed the tip right back.

'Please don't,' she said. 'There's really no need.'

'Come on, Lauren, take it,' I persisted, gripping her hand and forcing it on her gently. 'Cash is cash.'

It wasn't much but still, I wanted the girl to have it.

'No, really,' she insisted, her voice wobbling a bit.

'Come on, you've earned it. It's just my tiny way of saying thank you, that's all.'

'Oh no,' Lauren said, 'I'm the one who should be thanking you. It meant so much to me that I got to talk to you. As one lawyer to another, that is. It's been a long time for me and it's so hard. You really have no idea just how hard—'

Then her voice cracked and I could have sworn the girl was getting a bit teary. But she'd turned away before I could properly see.

'Lauren?' I asked. 'Are you alright?'

'I'm OK,' she said quietly, head bowed as she cleaned up her nail station, almost as though she didn't want me to see how upset she was. 'But you know, if it's not too cheeky of me, I'd love to just chat to you properly over a coffee sometime, that's all. Just a coffee. That's all. I know you're busy and everything, but if you ever had the time – well . . . you know where to find me.'

I walked back to my car, went back to the office and gradually fell into my normal work routine.

But I thought about Lauren for the whole afternoon. Thought about her, and wondered.

Chapter Two

Darcy

'So would you do Josh Andrews?'

'Eughhh, no! He's got more zits than I have myself. What do you think I am, desperate or something?'

'I bet he's totally into you. Besides, you have to lose your virginity to someone, so why not Josh? And he'll definitely be at the party on Saturday night.'

'Abi, please, can we not talk about my sex life in the middle of Zara?'

'Sure, whatever you say. Virgin.'

Darcy shrugged it off and acted like Abi's taunts didn't get to her, but deep down she actually wished her pal would lay off her a bit. Not that she could ever say anything back. Abi was by far the coolest girl in her class and because Darcy was now officially one of her gal squad, she was able to bask in all of that reflected popularity.

Abi smoked freely, didn't give a shite who saw her and was dating Louis Ryan from 5B, by far the best-looking guy in their year. Not only that, but she was also an expert at siphoning off vodka from her dad's drinks cabinet into an empty bottle of 7UP before they went out, then

14

discreetly topping up their drinks for the whole night.

'The trick is to water up the levels so my dad can't see that there's any vodka missing,' Abi always said. Not that there was much point in Darcy's trying anything like that in her own house. The only booze back home was the occasional baby bottle of white wine that her mum allowed herself as a treat at the weekend, while sitting on her own in front of *Strictly Come Dancing* or some crap on the telly. Totally sad, middle-aged-woman carry on, Darcy thought. Pathetic. Not at all like how things used to be when her dad was still around.

'So how hot do you think I'd look in this?' Abi said, picking up a strappy, silver party dress from the clothes rack beside her; it was short, scarily short.

'Are you kidding me?' said Darcy, admiring it. 'Pile on a full bottle of Cocoa Brown tan and you'd be stunning!' Then she spotted the price tag and her smile instantly faded. 'It's €95 though, have you got the dosh?'

'Louis will be knocked out when he sees me in this on Saturday night, won't he?' said Abi, completely ignoring the question and holding the dress up to her in front of the mirror.

'May I help you, girls?' said a shop assistant, suddenly manifesting out of nowhere beside them. Darcy flushed red in the face and buried herself in a rackful of 'reduced to clear' items, terrified that their school uniforms would mark them out as mitching off school. But Abi, as ever, braved it out fearlessly.

'We're absolutely fine, thanks,' she said, smiling sweetly back at the shop assistant. 'But if we do need help, don't worry, we'll be sure to let you know.'

'No school this afternoon?' asked the assistant. Darcy

could have been imagining it, but did this one sound a bit suspicious?

'Half day,' Abi tossed back without a blink. But then that was another thing Darcy admired about her brand-new friend. Her uncanny ability to make a lie sound utterly plausible. It was an out-and-out whopper of a lie too; right now the pair of them were supposed to be sitting through a double biology exam, but instead they'd just skipped out through the school gates and no one even thought to stop them. It really was that easy.

The assistant nodded and moved off, as Abi rolled her eyes and give her the two fingers behind her back.

'Nosey bitch,' she muttered. 'Now, come on, Darcy, let's find you something to wear to the party on Saturday.'

'I wish you'd stop going on about Saturday night,' Darcy groaned back at her. 'It's pointless.'

'Pointless how?'

'Because I have to spend the weekend with my dad, don't I?'

'So?'

'He never lets me out of his sight,' said Darcy, working her way through the 'reduced to clear' rack. 'Always wants to do lame stuff like hang out in this shitty little flat he's renting and order in a pizza. He even gives out to me for being on my phone too much. Says it wrecks our 'quality time' together. It's a hashtag nightmare.'

'The trouble with you,' said Abi, completely absorbed in admiring her own reflection in the mirror and only half listening, 'is that you haven't a clue how to use the fact that your parents are separated. You should be manipulating this to your advantage and playing them off against each other.'

16

'How do you mean?' said Darcy, picking up a sexy black dress that would be perfect with her high, black, wedge sandals. Then instantly putting it back as soon as she realised it was €120.

'Just tell your dad that your mum says you're OK to go to the party and tell your mum that he said the exact same thing. Christ, you're thick sometimes.'

'Don't be daft,' said Darcy, flushing at being called thick. 'My parents actually *talk* to each other, that's the problem. I'd be found out in no time, then probably grounded from now till after the exams.'

'Maybe,' said Abi, with her eyes twinkling mischievously, 'but the chances are you won't get caught out till *after* the party, in which case it'll all have been worth it. Come on, Darcy, Tony Scott will be there and you know you totally want to do him.'

'Piss off,' Darcy protested weakly, though she was lying. Just about every girl in her year fancied Tony Scott and, as Abi said, the ones who didn't were a big bunch of lesbians anyway.

'And you could wear this little cutie with your skinny boyfriend jeans,' Abi said persuasively, holding up a scarlet red halter-neck top that was more of a glorified bra than anything else really.

'Yeah, right,' Darcy said, rolling her eyes. 'I'm smashed broke. I've just about got the bus fare home and that's it.'

'Who said anything about needing dosh?' Abi said, deliberately keeping her voice low while Darcy blinked innocently back at her.

'What are you getting at?' she asked, puzzled.

'Watch and learn, babes, just watch and learn,' Abi said knowingly. Next thing, she started scooping up dress after dress and top after top; she even helped herself to a gorgeous biker jacket that cost well over €150.

'For fuck's sake, Abi, what are you doing?'

'Just do exactly as I am,' her friend said bossily, 'and trust me. The more stuff you take into the fitting room with you, the less they notice. Just remember to grab a few things that don't come with tags. Jumpers and knitwear, they're ideal. Now come on, move your arse. What are you waiting for?'

'Abi!' Darcy hissed, panicking. 'Are you talking about shoplifting?'

'I might be.'

'Are you insane? You'll get us kicked out of here. And I actually *like* Zara, I want to be able to come back here again.'

'Just shut up and imagine yourself in that fabulous red top this Saturday,' Abi replied coolly. 'Your tits would look amazing in it and, trust me, Tony Scott will totally make a move on you. Besides, I've done this loads of times before and a store like this will barely even miss the odd thing that might accidentally go walkabout.'

'Are you actually being serious?' said Darcy, totally taken aback. After all, it was one thing to mitch off school and have the odd sneaky vodka every now and again – everyone she knew was at it – but the thought of out-and-out stealing left her with a sick feeling right in the pit of her stomach.

'Shut up and just do it!' Abi hissed.

Darcy wavered, but then saw for herself how confidentially Abi was pulling it off and so, for better or for worse, she decided to copy her pal. The funny thing was it actually felt good to indulge in a bit of fantasy shopping, to pick up clothes she could never afford and try them on anyway.

What the hell, it wasn't like she was doing anything wrong, now was it?

Not yet, at least.

And that red halter-neck top really was stunning. In her daydreams she could just see herself rocking up to the party on Saturday night in it. Maybe then all eyes would be on her for a change, and not on Abi, with her swishy long hair that she dyed blonde and her push-up bras that she claimed made her look a bit like a Kardashian.

While Darcy wavered, Abi, it seemed, was determined to take this right through to the finish line. She just sailed past the assistant at the fitting room door, and when asked how many items she was trying on, without a blink answered, 'eight, thanks.' Darcy shot her a nervous look, because she knew Abi had at least two more than that, buried deep under the mound of clothes she was laden down with.

So Darcy chanced her luck too. After all, why not? She hadn't had anything new in months and even if she did ask her mum for extra dosh to go shopping, all she got was a lecture about how lucky they were to still live in the family home since the separation and how her mum was working round the clock to make sure they could still hang onto it. #Boooring.

'How may items?' the shop assistant asked her.

'Emm . . . five please,' she replied, hoping the wobble in her voice went unnoticed. Because she actually had six, if you counted the red top that was secreted away under her pile of clothes, which by a pure stroke of good fortune came without a security tag.

Two minutes later, Abi came skipping into Darcy's little cubicle, hands on her hips as she showed off the silver party dress.

'So what do you think?' she demanded, sashaying in front of the mirror, admiring herself from all angles. 'How fucking hot am I in this?'

'Abi, it's a fortune! If you're going to shoplift, should you really take something so pricey?'

'Shh, you doofus! That dork of an assistant outside hasn't a clue. This baby is going into my schoolbag and that's me sorted for the party.'

'But the security tag . . . ?'

'There isn't one, you sap-head,' said Abi impatiently. 'What, you think this is the first time I've done this? Now you take my advice and nab that red top while you can too. And hurry the fuck up, the whole point of this is to do it quickly, then make a fast getaway.'

Darcy looked down at the top that was right in her hand, conveniently untagged. Who'd even miss it? she thought out of nowhere. Zara had piles more where this came from and, besides, Abi was right: it would really look sensational with her skinny boyfriend jeans, even if she couldn't get to the party on Saturday night.

In spite of her better judgment, she was completely swept up in the whole fantasy of not having to wear the same old boring clothes that everyone had seen her in already. So on Abi's hissed instructions, she stuffed the red top right down into the very bottom of her backpack, while her pal did exactly the same with the silvery dress.

The next challenge though was to sail past the assistant at the entrance to the fitting rooms. At that, Darcy broke into a cold, clammy sweat, but Abi coolly handed back the mound of clothes they weren't taking with a sweet smile, saying, 'I'm so sorry, it all looks great on the hanger, just not so great on me, I'm afraid.'

Meanwhile Darcy flushed red in the face, muttered the same and handed back the bulk of her stuff, her heart pounding so loudly that she actually thought she might black out.

Next thing she knew, she was trailing after Abi who breezed casually towards the exit. Darcy's eyes darted nervously towards the security guard standing right by the door; a huge, beefy looking guy with a walkie-talkie clamped to his hand, staring at a screen in front of him.

Supposing they were caught? It didn't bear thinking about what her parents would say. She could probably worm her way around her dad, but her mum was a totally different story. Her mum would give her one of her lectures about how disappointed she was and the guilt of that was nearly worse than an out-and-out screaming match any day.

Two steps more and we're home and dry, Darcy thought, actually short of breath by then as the blood pounded through her ears, while Abi sailed on ahead of her, managing to look the very picture of innocence. Then somehow, by a sheer miracle, the two of them were safely outside and no security alarms had gone off.

'Now stay cool,' Abi muttered under her breath, 'and whatever you do, don't say a fucking word until we're safely out of earshot. They could still be watching us.'

That didn't happen though. By the time the two girls got as far as Starbucks up on the mezzanine level, they'd erupted into loud squeals of triumphant giggles and they didn't give a shite who saw.

Best. Day. Ever, Darcy thought hours later, when she was safely back at home, in the privacy of her bedroom. Even if it turned out the red top didn't actually suit her that much at all.

Chapter Three

Sarah

'The thing was, she really seemed like such a lovely girl,' I said to Tom, my ex, back at my house later on that evening. 'And she's a fully qualified solicitor too, or so she says. Working in this dive of a nail bar for buttons.'

'Yeah, you already told me. Twice.'

'Wouldn't even take a tip from me, you know. Too proud.'

'So you said.'

'Lauren, that's her name.'

'I know.'

'And . . . well – I suppose she just reminded me of how tough it was for me when I was starting out too. That feeling of constantly battering down doors and getting nowhere. You remember, don't you?'

Tom said nothing, but then he hardly needed to. I could remember for both of us exactly what it was like when I first left college. How tough I found the legal profession to break into, while guys who I'd graduated with and who were far less qualified that I was seemed to sail effortlessly ahead. The law is nothing if not a misogynistic profession, as I'd learnt the hard way. And maybe as poor old Lauren was finding out for herself now.

'She wants to meet me for a coffee,' I said, aware that I was more or less talking to myself by then. 'And you know what they say. There's a special place in hell for women who don't help each other.'

'If you take my advice you won't,' was the only shrugged response I got. But then Tom was sitting at my kitchen table totally absorbed in the sports pages at the time, and I should have known of old that it was always impossible to get his attention whenever the Six Nations was in full swing.

'Still,' I said, lost in thought as I leaned up against the dishwasher and stared off into space, 'it just feels right to meet her again. I don't think I'd be able to live with myself otherwise.'

'You're stone bloody mad, you are. Totally insane. Asking for trouble.'

'And why does wanting to help another human being make me insane?' I said, looking at Tom, or rather, looking down onto the top of his head. Greying a bit now, I noticed. And was that a bit of male-pattern baldness I could see? You'd still class him as attractive though, in the unfair way that some men seem to look better the older they get.

'Because whoever that manicurist one is,' he replied, actually glancing up (shock horror) from reading about Ireland's imminent clash with England at Twickenham that weekend, 'you only have her word for it that she even has a law degree in the first place. She could be a complete fantasist for all you know.'

'No, I don't think she was lying. She didn't strike me as the type.'

'Trust me, Sarah, if you do get involved, you'll be sorry.'

'Yeah, but this girl really seemed smart and bright and . . . lovely. And she's struggling, just like I had to. Forgetting about her and walking away doesn't sit right with me.'

'Then on your own head be it,' he said, sitting back at the kitchen table and coolly folding his arms. Still proprietorial about 'his chair', I noticed, even though he didn't live here anymore. 'Just don't say I didn't warn you.'

'Warn me about what?' I said defensively. 'I'm just going to call the girl and meet her for a quick coffee, that's all.'

'Bleeding-heart liberal,' he sniffed, going back to the sports pages, the conversation clearly at an end as far as he was concerned.

It's funny, I remember thinking. When Tom and I first got together all those years ago, he used to love that about me. That I'd regularly volunteer free legal aid, and help out the homeless in my spare time. Back then 'bleeding-heart liberal' used to be a term of endearment he'd use to describe me. Whereas these days it's something that's flung back in my face.

Darcy came home just then, banging the hall door behind her and, unusually for her, clinging to her school backpack like her life depended on it, instead of flinging it onto the floor and abandoning it. Tom, of course, immediately changed personality with a bright, 'hey, there's my best girl!', as he went to hug her.

'How are you, Darce? Looking forward to the weekend with your old man?' he asked, as Darcy submitted to the hug, then pulled away as soon as she feasibly could, with a mumbled 'whatever'.

'So how was school today?' I asked, turning back to load up the dishwasher.

24

'Fine.'

I was long accustomed to the monosyllabic responses by then, and I persevered.

'Didn't you have a biology test this afternoon?'

A grunt was all I got as she buried her face deep into the fridge.

'So how did it go?'

'OK, I suppose.'

'OK good or OK bad?'

'I dunno.'

'Darcy, all I'm asking is how your exam went.'

'And all I'm telling you is that I don't know, OK?' she snapped back at me. I glanced over to Tom looking for backup, but as usual, I was wasting my time.

'Never mind about your exam, Darce,' he said, 'I'm sure you did your best and that's all that matters.'

'And do you have much homework to do over the weekend?' I persisted. 'Are you planning on finishing your history project about 1916?'

'Actually,' Darcy said, pulling a bottle of sparkling water from the fridge and unscrewing it, 'there's a bit of a get-together happening at Amy Irwin's house tomorrow night and I really want to go.'

Now when a sixteen-year-old girl tells you there's 'a bit of a get-together', what a parent actually hears is 'I've been asked to a drug-fuelled orgy that will probably go viral on Twitter when five thousand total strangers gatecrash it, trash the house and ultimately end up on the nine o'clock news as a cautionary tale.'

'And is Abi Graham going?'

'Course she is. All my friends are.'

Then that, as far as I was concerned, put the tin hat on

the matter. Abi Graham was a girl in Darcy's class and a very disruptive influence, as far as I was concerned. The two of them had only recently become friendly, and ever since then Darcy's grades had steadily been going downhill.

'No, is the answer,' I told her firmly. 'You're not going anywhere until that history project is finished; you're weeks behind on it now.'

'But I really want to—'

'Darcy, no means no.'

'Dad, tell her it's actually normal to want to go out on a Saturday night, not sit at home like some total loser!'

'Sweetheart,' said Tom, 'you can't speak to your mum like that. If she says no, then that's final. Besides I've been looking forward to spending the weekend with you and I've got lots planned. I even got Netflix installed so you and I can watch *Orange is the New Black* back to back.'

'I've already seen that,' said Darcy sulkily.

'Well, then we can go out to a movie or just maybe order in and have a bite to eat at the flat.'

'But I don't want to sit in your poky bedsit for a full weekend when Abi and the rest of the gang are over at Amy Irwin's house!'

'Your mum already said no,' said Tom, trying to keep his cool.

'So how come I never get to do the things I want? Why do I always have to do what you tell me?'

'Darcy!'

'Oh, just piss off the pair of you,' she half shrieked, as I looked on, shocked. 'For once I actually came home in good form today and I'm not in the door two minutes before you're on my case about some stupid exam, then telling me how I can and can't spend my weekend. Back the fuck off, can't you?'

'Darcy! It's not OK to speak to either of us like that . . .' I spluttered, but it was too late. She was already out the door and halfway up the stairs to her room, taking care to bang the door twice, just in case we missed it first time around.

'You'll have to speak to her,' Tom said to me, shaking his head.

'Why do I have always have to be the one to speak to her?' I said hotly. 'Why not you for a change? It's not fair that I'm the disciplinarian while you get to be Fun Dad.'

'Believe you me,' said Tom, looking right at me for the first time since he'd arrived, 'there's nothing fun about any of this. There's nothing fun about being a separated dad. And if that's what you want to think, Sarah, then you're kidding yourself.'

His accusation hung unspoken in the air between us.

You're the one who wanted this. You're the one who wanted me gone. So Darcy acting out like this is indirectly your fault.

I didn't even get the chance to make peace with Darcy before she headed off for the weekend. She and her dad left soon afterwards, with Tom and I managing a sort of *entente cordiale* on the doorstep solely for her benefit. He even grazed me lightly on the cheek, but our 'look at us, still a happy, coping family' little performance was utterly wasted on Darcy, who was glued to her phone, pointedly blanking out the pair of us. I gave her a tight hug goodbye, even though she was already pulling away from me.

'Have a great time with your dad, pet,' I told her, 'and I'll be over to pick you up on Sunday afternoon, OK?'

27

'Whatever,' was all I got though, as she brushed me off and stuck her earphones in.

'I love you,' I said to the back of her hoodie as she scrunched down the gravel path.

Minutes later they were gone, leaving me alone to my thoughts and to another lonely night in front of the *Late Late Show* with sod all else lined up for the entire weekend ahead, bar catching up on some work cases I was behind on.

Welcome to my world.

*

Saturday morning and with yet another long, lonely day stretching out ahead of me, I was out of bed early and stuck into work not long after. By eleven, I was fully up to speed on one case and by early afternoon, not only had I drafted a rough brief for our Defence, but I'd even got around to hoovering the entire house, changing the bed sheets and doing a perfunctory tidy on Darcy's room, which she'd doubtless crucify me for when she got home. ('Mum, you were AT MY STUFF!').

I can remember particularly wanting to get all the Saturday chores out of the way because that day, I was a woman on a mission. In spite of all Tom's forebodings, I still hadn't forgotten about Lauren, that lovely, sweet girl in the nail salon from the day before. I couldn't; she'd been on my mind all night.

So why not go back there, I thought? Why couldn't this be my good deed for the day? After all, it was firm and guiding principle of mine that we were all put on this earth to help each other. And maybe Tom was right and maybe the young one was completely fantasising about her legal qualifications, but what was so wrong with seeing her again and just hearing what she had to say? I'd be out and about anyway and it wasn't that far out of my way to go back to the salon.

So I drove to Mountjoy Street, found parking, then braced myself for the icy cold as I retraced my steps back towards the Indian takeaway, which was directly below the salon. Funny how it all came back to me, the smell of garlic and ginger that seeped out onto the street and the dingy looking bookies shop next door, where shouts of encouragement were being yelled at some horse race that was in full swing on the telly inside.

As it happened I shouldn't even have been there in the first place the previous day; Phibsboro wasn't in my neck of the woods at all. But I had a meeting with an inmate in Mountjoy Prison who needed my help with some free legal aid work, and I could only get parking on the same street where the salon was. Then while I was walking back to my car after the meeting, I noticed that the nail bar were doing SHELLAC manicures for just €20, ridiculously cheap for Dublin. I was on my lunch break, I'd a bit of time to spare, and I just walked in off the street, simple as that.

For the second time in twenty-four hours, I found myself tripping up that dangerously uneven staircase, with the paint peeling off the walls and an overriding stench of damp, all the way up to the salon above. When I stepped inside, the same surly looking receptionist who'd been there the previous day was still sitting behind the desk, looking bored and thumbing through *OK!* magazine.

'Hi there,' I said, 'I was in here yesterday having my nails done and I'd just like to—'

'Is there a problem?' she interrupted, eyeing me up and

down suspiciously as if I'd come to shut the place down. She was skeletally thin, this one, and middle-aged, with a headful of badly dyed orange hair, grey roots clearly on show.

'No, really, it's nothing like that at all.'

'So have you come back here to complain or what? Because, you know, love, the standard of hygiene here is very good. We even have a certificate hanging up in the loo. I can show you if you want.'

'There's really no need, thanks, Beryl,' I said, reading the nametag pinned to her black work overall. 'This isn't a complaint, nothing like that. It's just—'

'That's a SHELLAC you've on you,' Beryl said over me, casting a quick, professional glance down at my nails. 'Do you want it taken off? Are you sick of the colour already? I don't blame you, love, it looks very sludgy if you ask me. But there's an extra charge for removal. Fifteen euros. And we only take cash.'

'I've just come to see Lauren,' I told her firmly. 'If she's working today and if she's free, that is.'

'You want to see Lauren?'

'Yes.'

'*Lauren*?' she repeated, as if I was looking for an audience with Pope Francis.

'That's right. If it's OK.'

'Well, she's here alright,' Beryl said warily. 'But she's with a client now. Did you want to book in with her for another treatment? Maybe to get something done with them eyebrows of yours?'

'Ehh . . . well, not exactly . . .'

'And if you don't mind me telling you, love, your top lip could do with a bit of bleaching while you're at it. I could do the whole lot for you for forty euros, if you want? That's my best offer.'

'No, I'm fine, thanks,' I said, ignoring her dig at the state of my face. 'I just wanted to have a quick word with Lauren, that's all.'

'Then you'll just have to wait till I see if she can fit you in,' Beryl said, as if the place was heaving with customers all clamouring for treatments, when apart from the two of us, it was tumbleweed empty.

'OK then, in that case I'll wait.'

So I perched on a cheap, uncomfortable plastic chair in that drab reception area, and flicked through a copy of *Hello!* magazine so old that Zayn Malik was still in One Direction. I waited for a good twenty minutes and was just about to throw in the towel when, suddenly, I heard her voice. Funny, how clearly I could remember it; that soft, gentle West of Ireland accent. A beguiling voice; one that sucked you in.

'Thank you very much once again.' Lauren was smiling prettily at a sweaty-looking middle-aged man who looked old enough to be her grandfather. 'And if you've got any problems at all, just give the salon a call.'

He muttered gruffly at her, but the minute he went to pay up at the till, Beryl underwent a complete personality change, suddenly transforming into sweetness and light.

'Did you enjoy your treatment, sir?' she simpered, eyelashes fluttering.

A grunt was all she got in response though.

'So you had a bit of waxing done, didn't you? You went for the full back, sac and crack? The bad news is that'll be forty-five euros, please.'

The guy paid in cash and left, I noticed, walking uncomfortably, like he'd just got off a horse, and without leaving any kind of tip.

'Someone here to see you,' Beryl said curtly, nodding over in my direction before going straight back to her magazine. Lauren glanced over, then her big brown eyes lit up as she spotted me sitting discreetly in the waiting area. She was straight over to me like a bullet.

'Hey, you've came back,' she said delightedly, with a friendly, open smile. Perfect teeth, I noticed too. 'I hope everything was OK with your treatment?'

'Everything was fine,' I said, 'it's just that you seemed a little bit upset when I was leaving yesterday.'

'Oh God . . . I'm so sorry about that,' she began to say, but I gently interrupted her.

'Please, don't apologise. I was passing anyway and just thought I'd drop in to see if you were all right. You were on my mind and I was a little bit concerned about you, that's all.'

At that something flickered across the girl's expression, which instantly turned from warm and welcoming to something else that I couldn't quite put my finger on. There was a glint in her eye that hadn't been there before. Hard to say what it was, though. She didn't say anything, just looked back at me from under impossibly long eyelashes.

'Here's the thing,' I said gently. 'You said you'd like to have a coffee and a chat sometime? So how about now, if you're free?

She glanced over her shoulder towards Beryl, who I noticed was glaring hotly at the pair of us, clearly tuning in to every word. As luck would have it, just then the phone at reception rang and, while Beryl was distracted, Lauren grabbed her chance.

'Not here,' she whispered softly to me. 'I'm so sorry, but I can't talk to you here . . . I mean, I can't talk to you properly. I'll tell Beryl I'm taking my break now and maybe you and I could meet somewhere outside?'

'Emm, yeah, great. Why not?'

'There's a coffee shop just across the street,' Lauren said under her breath. 'I could meet you there in about ten minutes, if that's OK?'

'I'll see you there,' I said, getting up to leave.

'Oh, and ma'am?' Lauren added as I gathered up my bag and made for the door, 'thank you. Thank you so much for coming back. You've no idea how much it means to me.'

'No need to call me ma'am,' I told her. 'I'm Sarah. Sarah Keyes.'

And she smiled.

Chapter Four

Darcy

If only getting away from her mum was as easy, Darcy thought, as her dad dropped her outside the Dundrum Town Centre that Saturday afternoon. With her dad, it was a complete doddle. Ever since the separation she could play him like a violin. All she had to do was drone on about how hard she was working in school and how tired she was after a long week, then nine times out of ten the chances were he'd say, 'so is there anything in particular you'd like to do today, love?' In which case she had her answer all dressed up and ready to go.

Because Abi was dead right. There were few enough advantages to having separated parents, so why not milk the whole poxy situation for all it was worth?

'Don't suppose we could swing by the Dundrum Town Centre, could we, dad?' she wheedled, glancing hopefully over at him from the passenger seat of his car. 'Just for an hour tops, I promise, that's all.'

Always best, she'd learned from Abi, to go in looking for significantly less than you actually wanted, then work your way up from there. Aim low; you always got further. Because

Darcy had no intentions of staying in the shopping centre for just an hour; there was a gang from her class meeting in Starbucks, including Tony Scott, and wild horses wouldn't drag her away from any gathering that Tony was at the centre of.

'I dunno, Darce,' her dad said warily. 'Your mum already thinks you spend quite enough time there as it is.'

'Yeah, but Dad, this is only for a bit. Besides,' she added, trying to keep her tone light and breezy just like Abi always did, 'I need piles of stuff for my history project and I'll be able to pick everything up in Easons while I'm there. Come on, just one lousy hour, that's all I'm asking. Then you and me have the whole weekend to hang out, don't we?'

'One hour then,' Tom said, yanking the car off the M50 and taking the turn-off for Dundrum. 'But if your mum gets to hear about this, then on your own head be it, missy.'

'Thanks, Dad, you're a star,' Darcy smiled angelically, then immediately whipped out her phone to text Abi.

GOT AROUND MY DAD. YOU'RE RIGHT, SO EASY TO DO I'M LMFO. JUST DRIVING BACK TO THE SCENE OF THE CRIME, LOL. WHERE ARE YOU, HUN? YOU IN STARBUCKS YET?

The reply came back immediately.

JAMMY BITCH. WOULD KILL TO BE THERE WITH YOU, BUT MY BITCH MOTHER SAYS I HAVE TO GET MY HISTORY PROJECT DONE. FML.

Shit, Darcy thought. She'd been looking forward to seeing her pal and maybe even bragging a bit to the gang about how they'd literally got away with daylight robbery just the day before. Still though, everyone else would probably be at Starbucks by now, and maybe it wasn't any harm that Abi was grounded for the afternoon. She was always just a shade too flirty with Tony Scott for Darcy's liking, even though she had a hot boyfriend of her own.

Then a second text pinged through from Abi.

SEE YOU TONIGHT AT THE PARTY. AND FFS WEAR THAT RED TOP, YOU LOOKED SO HOT IN IT!

Tonight, Darcy thought, just as her dad pulled up outside the shopping centre. The big party at Amy's that everyone was going to. Well, everyone except her. How was she going to get her dad off her case so she could go too?

Baby steps, she thought, that was the only way to handle her dad. If she could get around him to let her shop for the afternoon, then she'd keep working on him so she could get to the party too. Or failing that, maybe she could even slip out the door when he was asleep. Because if he fecking well thought she was staying holed up with him in that freezing kip of a flat on a Saturday night, then he'd another thing coming.

'Alright then, love,' Tom said, rolling down the passenger window and leaning over to talk to her as she clambered out of the car. 'I'll nip up to the DIY store in Dundrum village to get some paint I need and then maybe you'd like to help me redecorate your bedroom later on? I've been threatening to do it for ages and now's as good a time as any.'

36

Darcy smiled through gritted teeth. FFS, is this really how he thought she wanted to spend her precious Saturday? Getting paint in her hair and trying to tart up that poxy little room that barely held a single bed? He was #deluded. Outwardly she said nothing though, just smiled sweetly and marked that down at yet another battle to be fought later on.

'So I'll see you back here, at this exact spot in one hour, OK?' he said.

'Sure, Dad,' she replied, thinking, as if. When the hour was up, she could always say her phone had run out of battery while she was still up in Starbucks and he started bombarding her with one ballistic phone call after another.

'Oh, Dad, wait I forgot!' she called after him, just as he was about to drive off.

'Yes, love?'

'Gonna need some dosh to cover everything I need to buy for my project. That OK?'

'Oh, right, yeah, of course,' Tom said, looking momentarily wrong-footed. 'Cash, of course.' Then he pulled his wallet out of his bag and peeled off a €50.

'That enough?' he asked a bit reluctantly.

It wasn't really, but it would just have to do.

Two minutes later Darcy was in the shopping centre on her way to Starbucks to meet the others, but when she got there, there was no sign of anyone. She texted Amy and a few other pals who'd faithfully promised her they'd be there, but every one of them got back to her, bailing out. A whole flurry of excuses came through to her phone.

SORRY HUN, GOTTA GET THIS STUPID PROJECT ON 1916 DONE.

*ANOTHER TIME, DARCY, AND SEE YOU TONIGHT
. . . TONY SCOTT DEFO GOING TO THE PARTY TOO
. . . LOL.*

And one last and final text from Amy, who was hosting the party tonight because she had a free house and an older brother in college who didn't give a fuck what she got up to whenever their parents were away.

*NOOOO . . . CAN'T MAKE STARBUCKS TODAY, TOO
BUSY MAKING VODKA-TINIS FOR TONITE . . . CU
LATER BABES!*

Darcy felt a sharp stab of hurt when she scrolled down through all the messages; FFS, her mates had all faithfully promised to meet her there. They had a solid, concrete arrangement. And her pals were all she had these days, so when they let her down, then she really had no one, absolutely no one else she could depend on.

Her mum? That was a laugh. All her mum did was work around the clock these days, constantly reassuring Darcy with pep talk like, 'I'm doing this for you, you know, pet.' Just so they could 'keep the roof over their heads and not have to move to somewhere smaller'.

Like Darcy gave a shit about mortgages and repayments and private school fees. At this stage, she was sick to the gills of her mum's standard issue lecture every time she asked her for cash, about how she had to make short-term sacrifices for the long-term good. Her dad was that bit easier to handle – but still, her friends were her real family now. Without them, who had she left?

Darcy wandered around the main shopping concourse

on her own, but by the time she'd bought mascara and a Cocoa Brown tan in Penny's, a new plunge bra and G-string set for tonight plus a few other bits and pieces, the €50 was long gone. Fuck this, she thought, kicking her way down a flight of stairs, bored out of her head. The January sales were still on, there were bargains everywhere, but still. Shopping on your own was no fun. To kill time, she wandered into H&M, then got into an irrational temper when she saw it was chock-full of clothes that she knew would look great on her, but that of course, she couldn't afford.

One in particular caught her eye. It was a sexy black thigh-high dress, with lace all down the back and long sleeves. And they had it in her size too. Quickly, she checked the price tag. €75. There was no way she could afford it, but what harm was there in just trying it on?

Five minutes later, Darcy was in the fitting room, swaying this way and that in front of the mirror, temporarily cheered up when she saw how fab the dress looked on her. Somehow it just clung to her in all the right places; it even made her boobs look bigger, which was probably no bad thing as rumour had it Tony Scott was a tit man. Plus Abi was always flaunting herself around the place in low-cut tops and it certainly didn't do her any harm.

Darcy was just about to reluctantly peel the dress off and put it back on the hanger when suddenly she realised something. There was no security tag on it. She checked and checked again, but there was definitely nothing there. It was made of a lacy, silky fabric, which would probably have torn if they'd even attempted to tag it. At that thought, her mind started to whirr into overtime.

Because she could, couldn't she? Just because Abi wasn't

with her didn't mean that she couldn't indulge in the old 'five-finger discount' by herself now did it?

She thought of the red halter-neck top she'd swiped from Zara just the previous day. And how easy it had been. FFS, that dopey sales assistant at the fitting rooms had barely even noticed and the security guard must have been half asleep. #Morons. And that top was only a cheapie, look at the dress that Abi had got away with – about three times the price. So why not chance it now?

Nervously, Darcy poked her head around the fitting room curtain and peered out. It was crazy busy; the place was packed to the gills with Saturday afternoon shoppers including a bunch of teenage girls around her own age, all giggling and messing as they ran in and out of each other's cubicles, demanding to know whether their arses looked big in whatever they were trying on. Just like Darcy should have been, instead of some complete saddo stuck here on her own. #Billynomates.

There was only one sales assistant at the entrance to the fitting room, busily scooping up discarded piles of clothes and neatly folding them back onto hangers again. She looked hassled and distracted, so without a second thought, Darcy grabbed at her chance. Back in the privacy of her little fitting room, she pulled on her own jeans and winter coat, then flipped open her backpack and stuffed the black dress deep down inside it, where no one would ever look. Would they?

Nah, of course not, she figured. Besides, as she and Abi had justified only yesterday, chain stores like this were huge global corporations that probably used little kids in Chinese sweatshops to make their stuff for a fraction of the price they charged for it. This was just a tiny way of getting back at them, that was all. Ripping off the system and not the individual.

She pulled her backpack up onto her shoulder and looked in the mirror. OK, so maybe she was a lot redder in the face then normal, but with any luck, the floor staff would be way too distracted to even notice her, just one teenage girl in a sea of so many, battling their way through the bargain rails on a Saturday afternoon.

She tried her best to act cool and breezy as she strode past the sales assistant at the fitting room door, even if she did slightly stumble over a discarded hanger left lying on the floor.

'Nothing to return?' the assistant, a girl not much older than herself, asked sniffily.

'Ehh – no,' Darcy improvised, caught on the hop. 'I was just in with my pals,' she added, thinking on her feet and gesturing vaguely in the direction of the gang of girls who were by now taking up about three fitting rooms between them.

'OK,' the assistant shrugged, getting back to the pile of jumpers she'd been sorting through.

The main exit back out to the concourse was just seconds away from her, Darcy thought, keeping her head nice and low so no one would clock her bright red face. She could almost feel the weight of the dress weighing down her backpack like it was made of lead, instead of just a bit of flimsy fabric.

Shit, shit, shit, she thought. As bad luck would have it, there was a security guard on duty, a big, square-headed guy with a fat arse perched on a high stool just inside the door. Which meant she'd no choice but to brave it out and breeze right by him.

41

Believe that you're innocent and all will be well, she told herself as she got closer and closer, heart hammering as the blood pounded through her ears. A cold, clammy sweat broke out all down her back and as the door loomed nearer, she vowed that if she could only get away with this, she'd never try anything as reckless ever again.

If I can just get away with it one last time . . .

Then by some miracle she was outside, right back on the main shopping concourse and it was suddenly like the weight of the world had been lifted from her shoulders. She could breathe properly again. An instant rush of euphoria came over her as she walked away, quickly, purposefully, just to put as much distance between her and the scene of the crime.

She'd almost made it as far as the escalators and was just about to allow herself a jubilant grin, when out of nowhere she felt a hand clamp down on her shoulder.

A man's hand, firm and sweaty.

She jumped around to see the security guard from H&M standing right beside her, his big, square face stony cold.

'Miss?' he said gruffly in an Eastern European accent. 'I'm going to have to ask you to step back inside the store please. We need to search your bag.'

'But . . . but I have to meet my dad . . .' Darcy stammered, clutching at straws.

'This way, please. Now.'

Chapter Five

Sarah

'Drugs?'

'No.'

'In that case, she's got a booze habit. Or else wait till you see, it'll turn out she has a boyfriend in prison who needs bailing out.'

'Liz, I promise you, Lauren isn't like that at all. She's a nice girl. A *good* girl.'

'Excuse me, this young one emotionally guilted you into coming back to the salon, so she could bend the ear off you. Believe me, she's only after one thing and that's cold, hard cash. I'm just trying to figure out why, that's all.'

'No,' I said hotly, 'you don't understand. I mean, if you could just see this girl for yourself. She's bright and intelligent and articulate. Besides, we can't know for certain that it's about money and nothing else. So what's wrong with giving her the benefit of the doubt?'

'Sarah, you utter dimwit,' my pal Liz sighed wearily down the phone. 'Thank God you have me in your life, so you don't get taken for a ride by complete chancers more often.'

I was sitting in a coffee shop just around the corner from

the beauty salon as I waited for Lauren. So in the meantime of course, I'd rang my pal Liz for a big gossip and to fill her in.

'It's not like that at all,' I told her, trying to sound as patient as possible. 'For starters, Lauren told me she's a fully qualified lawyer—'

'Yeah, right,' sniffed Liz, deeply unimpressed. 'Because as we all know, the first thing newly qualified lawyers do to keep their career options open is learn how to wax lags and apply nail varnish. Jesus, Sarah, are you really that naïve? If this one really is a lawyer, then excuse me while I go and polish my Oscar.'

'Look, I felt sorry for her, that's all,' I said defensively. 'And if you'd seen the state of the kip she works in, you would too. What's so wrong with doing one selfless, disinterested act of charity anyway?'

'Bloody do-gooder,' said Liz, to the cacophony of a Labrador barking in the background and Sean, her six-year-old, howling the house down because the dog just ate a bit of his Minecraft Lego set. 'If you really want to do a selfless good deed, just come round here and babysit for one hour, before I end up in the nearest psychiatric home. Or better yet, do me a favour and foster one of my kids until they're eighteen.'

Just then, I glanced out the window of the coffee shop and spotted Lauren crossing the busy road opposite, still in her neat, black, work overall and shivering against the sharp January wind as she scanned the road up and down for traffic.

While Liz refereed a full-scale fight on the other end of the phone, I turned towards the window to really have a good look at her this time.

Lauren was a lot taller than I'd originally thought, lean and graceful as a ballerina. Even with her luxuriantly long hair blowing away from her head in that awful gale, somehow the girl still managed to look vulnerable, fresh-faced and innocent. How old was she I wondered, about twenty-four or twenty-five maybe? In that moment, I decided I didn't give a shite about what Liz and Tom had said; I wasn't leaving until I'd heard Lauren out. That's all. Just one quick coffee and then I'd go.

'Liz?' I said, to the sound of her screeching at either the dog or the kids in the background, 'gotta go, here she comes. I'll call you back later. Darcy's spending the weekend with Tom, so I'll be able to chat to you properly for once, instead of talking in code all the time.'

'Better yet, I'll get a babysitter so I can drop around to you later on for an Indian takeaway,' said Liz crisply. 'Because if I don't get a break out of this bloody house I'll go insane.'

'Well, now you're speaking my language.'

'See you later then. Just do us both a favour and make sure there's a very large bottle of wine chilling in your fridge before I get there,' she said, before adding dryly, 'oh, and good luck with Amal Clooney.'

A moment later, Lauren was in front of me, smiling and shaking my hand again as she slipped elegantly onto the plastic bench opposite. Her hands were icy cold; cold and thin and bony.

'Thank you so much for this,' she said simply, her huge brown eyes focused on me as she kept her hands neatly folded on the table in front of her, like this was some kind of bizarre job interview.

'Can I get you a coffee?' I asked her, instantly switching

45

into Mammy-mode. 'Or maybe you'd like something to eat? A sandwich or something?'

'Just a glass of water would be lovely, thanks,' she said to a passing waitress, who'd come to wipe down the cheapie plastic tablecloth in front of us. I ordered a coffee then leant forward, all ears as to what this one could possibly have to say.

'You're an angel to meet me like this, Sarah,' Lauren began, then instantly bit her tongue like she'd gone a bit too far. 'I'm so sorry, is it all right if I call you Sarah? Is that a bit cheeky?'

'Of course not.'

'It's just that you were so lovely to me yesterday,' she said. 'I instinctively felt like you were someone I could talk to. Someone warm and approachable, who might even listen to me.'

'I'm listening,' I said coaxingly.

Lauren looked at me for a moment, as if weighing up whether or not she could tell me something she badly needed to get off her chest. Then decided that she could.

'I wasn't lying or even exaggerating, you know,' she said, looking right at me with the twin chocolate-brown eyes. A mesmerising gaze, I found myself thinking. 'I need you to know that right from the start.'

'You weren't lying about what?'

'When I told you that I was a fully qualified lawyer,' she said softly, so softly that it was almost a strain to hear her above the background clatter in the coffee shop. 'Because I'm sure you must have had your doubts when I mentioned it yesterday. Would I be right?'

I nodded, but said nothing. Because of course I'd taken that with a very large pinch of salt; my very first thought

46

was that the girl was just romanticising. And that if she did happen to have any kind of legal qualification hanging on her wall, it probably came from some online course whereby if you could string a sentence together, they'd hand you over some class of a Mickey Mouse law degree.

'And I think I could hazard a guess what you must be thinking now,' Lauren went on, correctly reading the silence. 'After all, why would a lawyer ever agree to do a gig like mine? A job in a cut-rate beauty salon wouldn't exactly be my first career choice, as I'm sure you can understand. This wasn't something I'd ever normally have chosen.'

'I do understand.'

'But then you of all people must know how tough it is to break into the legal profession,' she went on, with a tiny glance up at me from under those Bambi eyelashes. 'If I want to stay in Dublin and keep firing off my CV to law firms, then I don't have much of a choice. After all, I have to earn a living some way, don't I?'

'Of course you do,' I said, reaching forward to pat her hand encouragingly.

'And I'm so sorry for getting a bit upset with you when you were leaving yesterday,' Lauren said, sitting back and pulling her cardigan tightly around her thin little frame. 'It's just that – well, I suppose . . . these days I just feel so completely overwhelmed and frustrated at every turn. Then when you were with me, you just seemed so kind and sensitive, I hoped that maybe I could talk to you privately, outside of work. Because you know what? That's all I'm asking. Just in case you thought I needed money and that's what I was really after – you'd be so wrong and I'd be mortified. I'm only asking you for a few moments of your time, with absolutely no agenda on my part. Is that OK?'

She looked pleadingly at me, her eyes shining bright, then added, 'after all, you've come this far, Sarah. So maybe I could just bend your ear for a little bit longer?'

'Why don't you start at the very beginning,' I said. 'And tell me everything.'

'Tell you everything,' Lauren smiled wryly. 'Wow. So how long exactly have you got?'

'Well, for starters, I'm guessing you're not from Dublin.'

'You've a great ear for accents. Fair play to you,' she said with a tiny smile.

'So why don't you tell me what brings you here?'

'Well, I'm originally from Ballymeade, outside Galway, but you probably wouldn't have heard of the place,' she said, clocking the blank look on my face. 'Don't worry, it's such a tiny, remote part of the country, virtually no one has. To this day, there's nothing to it apart from three streets, two pubs, a chipper and a Centra. But that's where I was born and raised.'

'Why don't you tell me about your life back there?'

Lauren paused and took a delicate sip of water before going on.

'I'm an only child, you see,' she began, 'and my dad passed away when I was just a toddler.'

'Oh, Lauren, that's terrible,' I said gently as I could.

'My parents owned a small poultry farm and he had an awful accident with farm machinery – the poor man was killed instantly. I was just three years old and the awful thing is that, apart from a few photos I have, I've absolutely no memory of him at all.'

'I'm so sorry to hear that.'

'Then things really took a downturn for Mum and me after that,' Lauren went on. 'A lot of our farmland had to be parceled up and sold off to pay the death duties and my mother found it almost impossible to cope. She . . . well, after Dad passed away – I'm sorry to say she started drinking. Very heavily. So a big part of my childhood was spend taking care of her, instead of it being the other way around. I remember I'd come home from school and I'd have to do absolutely everything, from cooking and cleaning to the little bit of farm work I could manage. Anything, just to keep our heads above water.

'When I was younger, my friends from school would spend all their weekends going off to play dates. Then, as we got older, that gradually turned into parties or the movies – they all had a great time for themselves. Whereas I just worked and worked and lived in constant dread of being taken away from my mother and put into foster care.'

'Lauren, you poor girl,' I said feelingly. 'That's heart-breaking.'

'But through all that, I did learn one valuable life lesson,' she told me, with tears at the corner of her eyes. 'And that was that the only thing that would get me out of the cycle I was stuck in was to study for all I was worth and get the best grades that I possibly could. So,' she added, with a tiny shrug, 'that's what I did.'

'Good for you,' I said, almost wanting to applaud her.

'Thanks to a fantastic teacher I had in school, who really believed in me when no one else did,' she said, 'I'm glad to say – and I hope you don't think I'm bragging here but . . .'

'But . . . ?'

'But I did pretty well in the Leaving Cert.'

'How well?' I wondered aloud.

'Six hundred points, to be exact,' she answered with a modest little smile. At that I almost spluttered on my coffee.

Six hundred points is as rare as hen's teeth – that would put any school-leaver at genius level. If Darcy came home with grades like that, then I'd die a happy woman. Grades like that would almost guarantee you entry into the Oxbridge college of your choice.

'So they must have been flinging college places at you, with a result like that?' I said, seriously impressed.

'I was offered a place studying Law in City College, here in Dublin,' Lauren replied and I nodded along. City College was about the most prestigious college going.

'But in my case, there was a problem,' she went on. 'The same problem I'd battled with my whole life.'

'Money,' I guessed, finishing the thought for her.

'In a nutshell,' she shrugged. 'The course cost a fortune and not only that, but the price of student accommodation in Dublin is extortionate. Plus, I had to deal with—' she broke off there and had to pause for a bit before she could go on 'well, let's just say I had had more than my fair share of personal problems to deal with at the time.'

'Do you want to talk about it?' I asked her gently.

'This was about seven years ago and my mum was dangerously ill at the time. So much so that she had to be hospitalised. Cirrhosis of the liver is what her doctors said, along with some pretty serious renal damage too. The worst part of it all though was that it was mainly caused by years and years of alcohol abuse. So college was out of the question for me. Mum was sick and she needed me, it was as simple as that. Plus there were hospital bills to be paid. We ended up having to sell the farm for a pittance and pretty much all of the proceeds went on my mother's healthcare. Then, when she passed away—'

The poor girl broke off here and I had to pass her a

tissue from my pocket so she could dab at her eyes.

'Oh God, Lauren,' I said uselessly. 'There really are no words to tell you how very sorry I am.'

'Now, all I have left of my mother is this necklace, which she gave me when I left school,' Lauren said, touching a fine filigree gold necklace that was hanging at her throat. 'Mam told me she was proud of me, and that if I worked very hard that only good things could come to me. And I did just as she asked and yet here I am. I'm working day and night, all the hours God sends and yet . . . and yet I'm trapped in this awful cycle with seemingly no way out of it.'

Her voice wobbled just a tiny bit and I automatically leaned forward to grip her hand, which I noticed was trembling slightly. The poor girl was in bits and I didn't have the first clue what to say to her. How was it possible, I thought, for someone so young to have suffered so much?

'So now you see why I have to work,' she said, making an effort to compose herself. 'Once Mum was gone, I trained as a beauty therapist because I'd been told the tips were good and that over time I could gradually save up the cash to get to college. Which I did eventually, but of course by then, I had to enroll as a mature student.'

'Why don't you tell me about that?' I said, utterly riveted.

'Well, I certainly loved studying,' she said, dabbing at her eyes with the tissue I'd given her. 'And I discovered I really did have a deep passion for the law. Being a mature student isn't the easiest though; I was working day and night in a salon outside Galway, just so I could prioritise college work and get to all my classes. It was tough going, particularly when my classmates were all so much younger than me. 'All they ever wanted to do was go out and get trashed in the student bars, whereas I just worked and worked. But you know something, Sarah? When we graduated, even though I had no family there with me, I honestly think it was the proudest and happiest I've ever been. It was the best day of my life. By far.'

'You did well in college, I'm sure,' I smiled at her.

'Came top of my class,' she replied, blushing modestly.

And that was it. In that moment, I felt a huge maternal surge towards this brave, bright young woman. Suddenly, I knew I had to help her out in any way that I could. Lauren looked imploringly across the table at me and there was something in her gaze that made me melt.

'Can I ask you something?' she said. 'Do you ever take a look at your whole life and think: has it really come to this? Working day and night in a salon for a virtual pittance just to keep the roof over my head? Which I'm sharing with two other students by the way, both totally financed by the bank of Mum and Dad. And neither one of them seems to have the slightest interest in studying or – God forbid – in making the most of the privileges they've been handed on a plate. Privileges I'd nearly have *killed* for at their age. All they want to do is get wasted drunk or high as kites, sleep with as many fellas as they can, then trash the house whenever they feel like it.'

The more she went on, the more utterly humbled I was by her story. Because, yes, as it happened – in my own, comfortable, middle-class way – I could relate to exactly what Lauren was saying.

I graduated with a healthy second-class honours degree and I did all the things that you're supposed to do in life, thanks very much. Married a nice man who at the time seemed beyond perfect, had a gorgeous daughter who grew into the most adorable child you could imagine, and worked my way from a low-paid, humble apprentice in a respected solicitor's office right the way up to where I was, junior partner.

And yet there I was that icy cold Saturday afternoon, with another long, lonely weekend stretching out in front of me, a teenage daughter who was turning into a harridan from hell and who I could barely have a conversation with without it descending into slammed doors (her) and furious tears (me).

Throw in an ex-husband – the man I signed up to grow old with – who was now living in a rented flat and blaming everyone else except himself for how he ended up there and, yes, I knew exactly what Lauren was getting at. There were days when I looked at my life and wondered how in God's name it had all turned out that way.

Then I thought of Darcy. There were just a few short years between her and Lauren and yet when I thought of how much Lauren had suffered by comparison, it made the breath physically catch in my throat. The girl was reaching out to me and I knew I'd be the worst person in the world if I didn't at least try to do something for her, anything. After all, if Darcy ever found herself in this position, then wouldn't I want some kind stranger to help her?

'Sorry about this,' Lauren said, glancing down at the time on her phone, then gathering up her bag to leave, 'But I really better get going. Before Beryl starts wondering what's taking me so long. And I'm even more sorry for taking up so much of your time. But you've no idea how much of a relief it is to talk to someone who actually listens for a change.'

'Lauren, please understand that I'm not promising anything,' I said, making my mind up on the spot. 'But just leave it with me and I'll see what I can do for you. OK? Will you trust me?'

'Of course I will, Sarah,' she smiled, her eyes almost tearing up with gratitude. 'But right now, I better get back to work. And I know you've got a family of your own to get back to. I think you mentioned that you had a teenage daughter, isn't that right?'

'Yes,' I said. 'Darcy.'

'You must be so proud of her,' Lauren smiled. 'I'm sure she's wonderful.'

'I am proud of her, yes,' I said, thinking back to the days when I could use a sentence like that and actually mean it. 'She's a terrific kid.'

Just then, my mobile rang, but it was a number I didn't recognize. I made an 'excuse me, gotta take this' face at Lauren while I answered.

'Is this Sarah Keyes speaking?' came a gruff man's voice, with an Eastern European accent.

'Yes?' I said, puzzled as to who this could be.

'I'm calling you from security at H&M in the Dundrum Town Centre. I'm afraid it's about your daughter.'

'About Darcy?' I said, the breath catching in the back of my throat as sudden shock sent my heart hammering. 'Why? What's happened to her?'

'We've just taken her in for shoplifting and we need you to get here immediately.'

Chapter Six

Darcy
(The third worst day of her life)

It had been slightly over a year now, but if pushed to it, Darcy could still remember with searing clarity the third worst day of her entire life to date. She'd just turned fifteen back then and was bird-happy in school with great friends, an even better social life and grades that – although they mightn't exactly have set the world on fire – were certainly enough to keep everyone off her back.

Then her stupid parents had to go and break up, didn't they? Her pal Abi, whose mum and dad were separated too, had always said it was such a relief when her old pair finally did call it a day. 'I was fed up lying in bed night after night listening to the two of them tear strips off each other when they thought I couldn't hear. Like I was deaf or something,' she used to say.

When it came to Darcy and her parents, she'd almost wished for that, longed for it. Because anything was better than the forced politeness they'd started using towards each other whenever she was around. Young and all as she was, it wasn't difficult to sense the surface tension simmering away between her mum and dad, each wary of letting rip at each other until they were alone. And even then, from the privacy of her bedroom Darcy could still hear them bickering away, no matter how loudly she turned up her headphones to try and block it all out.

She'd spend hours fretting and worrying herself into a frazzle over it. Whenever she was out on an overnight sleepover, while the other girls giggled and gossiped and stuffed their faces with pizza, she'd sit silently in a corner, stressed out of her mind wondering what the hell was happening at home without her around to referee and to keep the peace. Once, to her mum's great worry, she'd even asked to be driven home in the middle of the night, claiming she was having a panic attack, even though it was perfectly obvious she wasn't. Her hostess wasn't a bit impressed, of course, and this carry on had worried her mum sick, but Darcy didn't care. If her physically being home stopped the rowing, even temporarily, then wasn't it worth it?

Second warning sign something was up? When they completely stopped doing things as a family, so Darcy had to spend time with her parents separately. Up until about a year ago, her family was the kind of tight-knit little unit that did everything together, to the point that her pals would often tease Darcy over it. But she'd just grin and say, welcome to the wonderful world of being an only child.

Back then she didn't particularly care what any of her mates said. Because even trips to the shopping centre on a Saturday afternoon were like an adventure whenever she was with her mum and dad. The way her mum would be pretend-y annoyed when her dad slipped her fifty euros and told her to buy herself something nice in Topshop. Then there was the way he'd groan and roll his eyes whenever she and her mum disappeared off into House of Fraser, while he sloped off to have nice, peaceful coffee and a read of his paper. But he'd always come out with something light and jokey like, 'ahh, would you look at the pair of you . . . if shopping were an Olympic sport, then my two girls would be world champions by now.' Which showed he didn't mind really, Darcy always figured.

Then maybe they'd all troop off to a family movie in the cinema afterwards, to munch on popcorn and watch some class of 'valet parking for the brain', as her mum would always complain afterwards. Even though Darcy secretly knew she'd enjoyed it just as much as everyone else. Often, she'd even catch the old pair holding hands whenever they thought no one was looking. Just the memory of those happy family outings was enough to make her well up, all the more so now that they were a thing of the distant past.

These days her mum was working so hard that Darcy really only ever got to see her over dinner. Only then, of course, she'd constantly get on Darcy's case about school and all the subjects she was supposed to be working on. Whereas with her dad, he'd either throw cash at her and let her go off to entertain herself, or else sit her down to share a pizza in that shithole of a flat, then bring the conversation around to her mum and what she was up to in her spare time. Did she go out much these days? Who was she friendly with? What were her plans for the weekend?

Fishing, Darcy thought. Pathetic really, because it was obvious what he really wanted to know, which was basically whether she was seeing anyone else or not. As if. Darcy almost puked at the idea. All her mum seemed to do these days was work, then come home, nag her senseless about school, then bury her head in legal briefs and free legal aid work for the rest of the night. And always with the same old excuse: 'Sweetheart, I just have to get on top of this deposition for tomorrow's hearing, but you know we'll spend proper quality time together very soon, yeah?'

Yeah, right. Darcy could barely bring herself to look at her mother these days. She blamed her full on for the separation and still couldn't bring herself to forgive her for throwing her dad out. Because her mum was the one who'd called a halt to the marriage; that was plainly obvious. And as for all that crap about 'spending time together soon', Darcy saw right through it for the load of bollocks that it was.

After all, her mum had no problem doing her ten-hour workdays, did she? And even going to Mountjoy Prison in her free time, to help out some convicts with legal aid. As far as her mum was concerned, everyone and everything else were her top priorities in life.

Everyone and everything except Darcy.

*

It was just before Christmas the year before last when the shit really hit the fan at home. Darcy hadn't a clue what was going on between her parents, all she knew was that – whatever had happened – they were barely speaking by then and that Christmas dinner had been so tense, she'd thought she'd end up on a therapist's couch for years afterwards reliving it.

Her mum had cooked for her whole extended family, including Darcy's granny, her auntie Lil and her twins daughters, aged six and as cute as buttons. It should have been a happy family occasion, but Darcy just sensed something was up by the pointed way her mum refused to speak to her dad, or to even make eye contact with him, for that matter. It was all, 'ask your father to pass the mince pies', while her dad would snap back faux politely, 'I'm not deaf, you know. I'm right here, in the room. It's actually OK to address me directly.'

Darcy tried her best to busy herself with the twins, somehow sensing that her Auntie Lil was well clued in to whatever was going on. Over that whole miserable Christmas, Lil would have hours-long, hushed chats late into the night with Darcy's mum at the kitchen table, when they thought everyone else was asleep.

What the fuck was going on between her parents was all Darcy really wanted to know. How come they'd seemed as happy as Larry together not that long ago and yet now all they could do was snipe at each other? But from what she could glean through snippets of shameless eavesdropping, there was trouble afoot, and her mum was firmly blaming her dad for whatever had happened.

'Will you for God's sake just tell me?' Darcy had begged her Auntie Lil during that God-awful New Year's Eve. 'I'm not thick you know, I can tell something's up. And as usual, I'm the last to know anything. All I'm asking is to be treated like an adult here.'

She knew she could trust her Auntie Lil, who never talked down to her and who insisted on paying her full babysitting rates for taking care of the twins, even though Darcy adored the girls and would gladly have done it for free.

'You really want to know?' Lil had asked, sitting down at her dressing table in the spare room and abandoning her packing so she could give Darcy her full attention. Darcy nodded back, steeling herself for the worst.

'Well, do you know what a mid-life crisis is? Because it

seems that's what your dad is going through and now that's what poor Sarah's having to deal with.'

As it happened, Darcy hadn't a clue what a mid-life crisis was, but when she conducted a straw poll among her pals, it seemed that lots of their dads had been through it too. Getting a tattoo featured largely, as did pulling insane stunts like heading off to climb Kilimanjaro for three months.

Then things happened in such quick succession Darcy barely had time to even react. Before she knew it, her whole life had flipped over like a pancake, without her having the slightest say in the matter.

First of all, her dad lost his job. He'd worked in IT for a software design company and one day he had a job, the next day he didn't, simple as that. Her mum's reaction was to purse her lips, declare herself the sole breadwinner and hand her dad a list of household chores that had to be done everyday, so she could continue working. 'This way, at least we can keep the roof over our heads,' as she kept on reminding him.

Her dad though, Darcy couldn't help noticing, seemed to spend far more time on Facebook and Twitter than he ever did hoovering and grocery shopping. Which of course only led onto more rows when her mum came home, to the point that if Darcy had to listen to her saying, 'so I'm expected to work my arse off, then come home and take care of everything here, am I?' she thought she'd scream. Worse though was her father's unfailing response: 'have you any idea what it's like for me to feel so emasculated?'

Darcy had looked up the word in the dictionary and didn't like what she saw.

Next thing, out of nowhere, her dad had decided to set up a start-up online recruitment agency. Her mum had agreed to invest their savings in it and for a brief window of time all was well. With Dad busy and Mum at the office most of the time, peace reigned.

Until her dad turned fifty, that is, and went out and treated himself to a brand-new motorbike, a Harley-Davidson. Her mum was typically tight-lipped about it, but Darcy was able to tell that, deep down, she was practically spewing fire.

Not long after, her dad joined a biker club that met up every week and went roaming around the Wicklow mountains at weekends. Course it didn't take long before he started disappearing every Saturday and not reappearing till all hours that night, usually after a few drinks with Spud and Gerry, his two New Best Friends.

'You and your bloody penis extension,' she'd once heard her mum snipe at him, as a precursor to yet another row in hissed tones. At this stage, Darcy had taken to sleeping with her iPod plugged into her ears to block out the awful sound of their near-constant bickering.

But then came the very worst day of all. When she came home from school one afternoon and was puzzled to see her mum's car parked in the driveway; she normally wasn't home till well past 7pm most nights.

It got worse. The minute Darcy opened the hall door, she could just feel that something weird was up. There were all sorts of pictures missing from the hallway, family snaps like the one of Darcy making her Communion and a lovely one of the three of them the time they all went off to EuroDisney.

She could still remember the smell of baking from the kitchen – yet another early warning sign. Her mum never, ever baked; it was a family joke, in spite of all the magi-

mixers and cake tins she'd been given for various Christmases and birthdays. She always claimed she intended to learn, but just never seemed to have the time. Yet there was no mistaking that distinctive smell that hit Darcy the minute she let herself in through the front door; cinnamon and cloves, smells that to this day could still turn her stomach to ash.

When she went into the kitchen, her mother was standing over by the oven, wearing an apron and with flour halfway up her arms.

'Hello, sweetheart,' she said, just a degree too brightly, coming over to kiss Darcy and leaving flour on her cheek. 'Just thought I'd make a little treat for us. Cup cakes . . . your favourite!'

They weren't Darcy's favourite at all, as it happened, and she instantly sensed that this was a weak attempt to soften some kind of blow. So she forced herself to endure tea and buns, (rock hard, with dribbly, watery icing sliding off the top) before her mum finally got to the point.

'Anyway, pet,' she began tentatively, flushing red the way she always did whenever she had something awkward to say and didn't know how. Then came the words Darcy had both suspected and dreaded for the best part of a year. Coming to Darcy in fragments that she could still recall with pin-clarity all this time later.

'There's no easy way to say this Darcy,' her mum said, 'so I'll just come straight out with it . . . your dad and I love you so much, but we both think it's better if we just take a little bit of time apart . . . now it won't affect you in the slightest though, we're both so anxious to make sure your life goes on as normal . . . we just think this is the best thing all round for us as a family, for the moment at least . . .'

'No!' Darcy had yelled back, mashing that disgusting cupcake into her plate with her fork. 'The best thing for us as a family is to stay together, so why can't we do that?'

'Because sweetheart, your dad and I . . .'

'This is all you,' Darcy had said savagely, getting up to her feet, even though her legs felt wobbly underneath her. 'You don't think I hear you night after night giving Dad a hard time? Picking on him non-stop, even worse than you pick on me? It's not his fault he lost his job! And it's not his fault that he has to start out all over again, is it? You drove him out of this house and I'll never forgive you for it, not as long as I live!'

Darcy had long thought that no matter what else life held in store for her, she could never possibly live through a day as horrendously awful as that one. Not as long as she lived.

Until today, that was.

Chapter Seven

Sarah

It surely didn't get any worse than this. It couldn't possibly. There was a place in hell reserved for mothers whose children went off the rails and on that bleak, miserable January day, I felt like their poster girl.

'Jesus, Tom, what happened?' I half-snapped, out of my mind with stress, when Lauren and I finally met him outside a tiny, cramped little office right at the very back of H&M in the Dundrum Town Centre. I couldn't even find the words to introduce him to Lauren properly, or even to explain what she was doing there in the first place, instead I just launched straight into a row.

'I don't know,' he said tightly, with just a quick, curt nod in Lauren's direction. He looked ghostly white and his fists were clenched deep inside his pockets, the way he always did whenever he was quietly furious. 'I got the call from security same as you did, so I just dropped everything and ran here. I'm as much in the dark are you are, Sarah.'

'But I left Darcy with you!' I hissed, hot tears of frustration and worry stinging at the corners of my eyes. 'You were supposed to go straight around to your flat and spend the weekend with her there. What was she even doing in a bloody shopping mall in the first place? She was supposed to be safely back at the flat with you studying for her history project!'

'I know, I know, but she just wanted was to swing by here for an hour tops. And that was it, honestly. I thought, what was the harm in that, when she and I had the whole weekend ahead of us?'

'Our daughter could end up spending this weekend in a prison cell, thanks to you!'

'Oh, so this is my fault, is it?' Tom said, turning the full focus of his anger on me. But then, misdirected anger was always where he and I excelled ourselves.

This was just on the verge of escalating into a full-on flare-up, as poor Lauren looked on silently mortified, not having the first clue where to look. Next thing an inner door to an office beside us opened and out came a woman in her thirties, thin as a pin, stressed looking and dressed in a neat, black suit. She introduced herself as Tanya, general manager of the store and shook hands briefly with each of us.

Through a chink in the opened door behind her, I could see Darcy, sitting at a desk inside, looking red-eyed, white-faced and so ridiculously young that I just wanted to grab her, hug her for all she was worth, then spring her out of this kip and get her home immediately.

'You're Darcy's parents?' Tanya asked briskly, sounding like a woman who had two thousand other places to be and two thousand better things to do. Tom and I both nodded.

'Well, in that case, it's my duty to tell you that we take all cases of shoplifting here very seriously. Now I've spoken to your daughter at some length—'

'Please, I really need to see her,' I said to Tanya, wanting nothing more than to brush past her and get to my daughter. To my little girl, who needed me. Before Tanya could answer though, Darcy spotted us and ran straight over. Tom got to her first and bear hugged her, saying over and over again, 'don't worry Darce, this is all going to be OK. We'll make it OK.'

Then I yanked her away from him, hugging her so tightly I thought I'd squeeze the kid to death, before I burst into a flood of uncontrollable tears.

Without Lauren, I don't know what we'd all have done that awful day. As Tanya sat us down and explained at length the store's strict policy on shoplifters, mentioning the word 'prosecution,' just a bit too many times for my liking, Lauren effortlessly seemed to just take control.

'It's a first offence,' she said calmly, the only voice in that stuffy, overcrowded room that actually sounded reasonable and measured, 'so with the greatest respect, I'd ask you to consider letting Darcy off with a caution. Isn't that standard procedure in cases like this? As established in Guinness versus Williams in 2014?'

'Who's your woman anyway?' Tom hissed from beside me. 'Some junior from the office?'

'She's . . . emm . . . oh, look, I'll explain later,' I whispered back, unsure of what to answer really. 'She and I were just having coffee together when I got the call came to come here. So, of course, Lauren came with me.'

Truth be told though, I think I went into total shock as I sat in that dingy coffee shop with Lauren, the moment the call from security at the shopping centre came through. But Lauren just seemed to take over, acting decisively, making helpful decisions for me on a minute-by-minute basis, thinking on her feet and always, always two steps ahead.

'Do you have your car with you?' she'd asked as I'd scrambled to pull my coat on, before racing to the shopping centre. I'd nodded yes, scarcely able to remember how to even drive, I was that shell-shocked.

'Then maybe you'll let me drive you there?' she'd offered. 'You're in absolutely no fit state to and, besides, at least this way you won't waste any time trying to find parking.'

It made sense, so I said yes and was bloody glad that I did. My hands were trembling badly and I could barely fumble around my bag for the car keys. So Lauren gently helped me, running with me to the car and slipping into the driver's seat while I phoned Tom, without fear of getting yanked over by the police.

Then before I even knew how it happened, Lauren had followed me into the security guard's office and was coolly taking control of the whole God-awful situation, pleading with Tanya and making a clear-cut case to let Darcy go. All while Darcy snivelled, and with me borderline hysterical by then.

'I'm sure you're very sorry, aren't you Darcy?' Lauren prompted her gently.

'It was all just a stupid mistake,' Darcy muttered in a tiny little voice that made her sound exactly like she did when she was about five years old and was in trouble for not tidying away her toys. 'I didn't mean to do anything wrong. Honestly.'

'What you fail to realise is that H&M have a very strict policy when it comes to shoplifting,' said Tanya, utterly unmoved. Like this was the kind of thing she dealt with a dozen times a day with a dozen different sets of neglectful parents and their wayward kids. 'Now we have crystal-clear CCTV footage of you taking a garment valued at €75 into the fitting rooms, then exiting without it.'

'Is this true?' I asked, but Darcy said nothing, just stared at the floor, red-eyed by way of a reply.

'I'm happy to show you the CCTV footage if you don't believe me, Mrs Keyes,' Tanya said crisply.

'Jesus,' said Tom, running his fingers though his greying hair, so it stood up in tufts. 'I don't believe this. Shoplifting. Seriously, Darce? I mean, if you'd wanted new clothes so badly, then all you had to do was ask. I'd gladly have bought anything for you. But to do something senseless like this—'

'Tom, please, this isn't helpful,' I snapped at him, still in a total state of shock. 'Can't you see she's upset enough as it is?'

'I can appreciate that no one likes hearing their child is a shoplifter,' Tanya went on, 'but I'm afraid we have concrete proof that's the case and we do intend to prosecute.'

'She's only sixteen!' I said. 'And she's never done anything like this before in her life, have you, Darcy?'

'We don't look on that as any kind of exonerating factor,' Tanya replied.

Tempers were on the verge of flaring by then and I was pathetically grateful to hear Lauren's crystal clear, articulate voice speak out.

'Could I just interrupt you all for one moment?' she asked calmly as all eyes swiveled towards her. 'It's just that, as you can see, this has been a huge shock to both of Darcy's parents and it would be a great help to us if we could have a little time to process this. Could Darcy possibly ask for a private moment with her family? Please, Tanya? Just five minutes, that's all we'd ask.'

As luck would have it just then Tanya's mobile rang, so she agreed to leave the room while she took the call, cautioning us all as she did that she'd be back 'in five minutes, max'.

Then the minute she was out of the room, Lauren just seemed to take over while I squeezed Darcy's trembling hand and Tom looked on, grey-faced.

'Darcy,' Lauren said, 'I really do think that they're serious about prosecution and that's the last thing that you need at your age. It would mean a possible court case in a juvenile court and although it's unlikely you'd be sentenced, it would still be there on your permanent record, for all the world to see.'

'Oh God, Mum, I feel sick,' Darcy said weakly, gripping onto my hand tightly.

'It's just that if the store has CCTV footage of you walking into a fitting room with a garment then leaving with nothing,' Lauren went, never raising her voice and being all the more authoritative for it, 'then you can see how it weakens our case. So we've got to find some exonerating circumstances here. Some reason we can give them to explain why you acted the way you did. Do you understand me?'

'I'm sorry, but – who is this again?' Darcy asked me, unable to grasp that a complete stranger seemed to be in charge of her case.

'Shh, I'll explain later,' I hissed back at her. 'Now just try to answer the question, love. Your dad and I won't be annoyed, we promise. All we want is to get you out of here.'

I could still see Darcy staring at Lauren and taking her in, wondering what the hell was going on as Lauren spoke coolly and clearly, looking and sounding exactly like a lawyer. And suddenly in that moment, I knew everything she'd told me about herself was true. That she had indeed come first in her class at City College, qualifying with top marks. That she was a fully qualified solicitor, one that could kick-ass when she needed to. Here was proof, if I needed any.

'Darcy, please,' Lauren insisted. 'We don't have much time and I really need you to work with me here. I know you and I have never met before, but you have to trust me. I'm on your side.'

'It's utterly out of character for her,' I suddenly said, kicking myself for not having thought of it any sooner. 'Darcy has never been in any kind of trouble before, and her dad and I can both vouch for that. Can't we, Tom?'

'Ehh . . . yeah, yeah, of course we can,' Tom chimed in.

'I'm afraid that won't be enough,' said Lauren, her head swiveling sharply back to me. 'Do we have anything else to go on? Anything at all? Any exonerating circumstances?'

I didn't get a chance to answer because next thing Tanya bustled importantly back into the room with a beefy-looking security guard behind her and a disc in her hand, which I could only presume was the CCTV footage she kept harping on about.

I gripped Darcy's hand in mine and watched in awe as Lauren effortlessly took control.

'Thank you so much for allowing us a brief moment to ourselves,' she smiled at Tanya, the very essence of polite-ness. 'I've spoken with both Darcy's parents as well as with Darcy herself and we're all agreed. Firstly, that Darcy has never been in any kind of trouble before, we hope that we can respectfully ask you for a small degree of leniency here.'

'Secondly,' I piped up as Tanya stood with her arms folded, listening intently, 'it goes without saying that Darcy

70

won't be allowed within two miles of this shopping centre as long as she lives. I give you my word on that. As her mother.'

Tanya didn't react, so I kept on arguing, finding my voice the more I spoke.

'And on top of that,' I added, 'I'd just like to point out that Darcy has been under huge stress recently, as a result of her dad and me splitting up.'

'As you probably know,' Lauren chipped in, almost like she could second-guess the point I was making and was trying to back me up, 'an unfortunate side effect of any family breaking up is that the kids of newly separated parents sometimes act out a bit.'

'Exactly,' I said, 'so they're not fully in control of their actions. It kills me to say it, but for any teenager in Darcy's situation, behaviour like this is not uncommon. But as her parent, I will of course make sure that nothing like this ever happens again.'

'Darcy is deeply sorry about this,' Lauren went on, 'but we do feel that the fact she was under undue stress at home, coupled with intense pressure at school—' she added hopefully, with a quick nod from Darcy to back her up.

'Yes, absolutely!' I said. 'Exam stress coupled with her parents' break-up certainly had a direct effect on Darcy's actions today. Ordinarily my daughter would never countenance doing anything like this. Not in a million years.'

'To be perfectly honest,' said Lauren, 'I think this was nothing more than a vulnerable young girl's cry for help, that was all.'

'And of course I'm prepared to pay up,' Tom chipped in from where he was sitting beside Tanya's desk. 'Whatever the dress cost, I'll give you cash for it right here and now.

I'll pay double if it'll mean you'll just drop this and let us out of here.'

'Well, store policy is that all shoplifters should be prosecuted,' said Tanya, wavering a bit.

'But maybe in this case, we might plead with you to make an exception?' I asked hopefully.

Our four anxious faces turned to look up at Tanya, as she chewed her lip and twiddled with her disc in her hand.

And we waited.

Chapter Eight

Liz

I'd been friends with Sarah Keyes for well over twenty years by the time all of this started. All the way through college, where she and I first bonded over a mutual love of seriously unhip nineties bands, heavy fringes and way too much blue eyeliner. (Ahh, the nineties, aka, the decade that taste forgot.)

She was the one who held my hair back when I puked up in the streets after our graduation party. And she was the one who held my hand right the way through my very first childbirth. We've seen each other through thick and thin; Sarah was my bridesmaid when I married Harry over seventeen years ago, and is godmother to my eldest, Rosie. And for my part, even though I didn't get to do the bridesmaid honours at Sarah's wedding (she and Tom ran off to Vegas, told no one, then came home and announced it to their shocked family and pals), I did at least throw them both one helluva post-wedding bash.

And OK, so it was far from the joyous, celebratory affair I'd wanted it to be, mainly because Sarah's mother was so unimpressed with her new son-in-law Tom, that she'd point-blank refused to show up, which did put a bit of a dampener on things. But then that's a whole other story for a whole other day.

I was Sarah's very first visitor to the hospital when Darcy bounced into the world, one sunny September morning over sixteen years ago, just two months ahead of my own daughter, Rosie. And just as Sarah's been there for me ever since, I'd like to think that I've been there for her too, through our kids' first steps, first words, first day at school, first lost tooth, all the way up to now, when suddenly our kids aren't children any more, but young adults who want to fight with us, tear strips off us and basically spend their time as far away from us as they can physically get.

Sarah Keyes is the kind of friend who was right at my side throughout a terrifying breast cancer scare (which thankfully turned out to be perfectly benign), and, for my part, I've been there for her at probably the lowest ebb in her life to date: when she was finally forced to call time on her marriage to Tom, to predictable 'acting out' from poor Darcy and a chorus of 'I told you so' from her family.

In all that time, the woman has been a rock for me. A guiding light, a sort of moralistic North Star. To the extent that whenever I have a difficult decision to make, all I need do is ask, 'what would Sarah do?' And time and again, that'll always be the right thing. Not necessary the easy thing, but always the right one. Souls like Sarah, you see, don't come into this world all that often. Conscientious and kind; the kind of person who'd do anything for you and drop everything just to help you .

'She's all heart,' as Harry, my other half, often says about the two of us. 'Whereas you're all head. So between the two of you, you make a perfect whole. It's the main reason you've stayed pals all these years.' And Harry would know; he's worked as a legal partner alongside Sarah at Sloan Curtis for years now and has nothing but the utmost respect for her.

He's dead right too; Sarah really is all heart. I've seen her on top of the world and I've seen her when that whole world fell apart. But I'd never seen her as down and out as she was that horrible, grey Saturday night in January, the day Darcy was caught red-handed shoplifting.

'It's all my fault,' she kept on saying, over and over again, as she and I sat at her kitchen table while I poured Sauvignon Blanc down her throat. Anything to try and calm the woman down a bit.

'Jesus, Liz, have I really reared a shoplifter? Did I take my eye off the ball so much that I didn't notice my only daughter was acting out like this?'

'For fuck's sake Sarah, how is any of this your fault?' I told her firmly. 'You've done everything for Darcy, particularly since the break-up.'

But predictably, of course, Sarah was having none of it. Nothing would do her but to take the full brunt of the blame on herself: she'd been working too hard; she was too focused on making her mortgage repayments and keeping the roof over their heads 'to minimise the effect of the separation on Darcy'. Not only that, but according to her, she'd been spending too much time sorting out testimonies for repeat offenders in Mountjoy to even notice what was going on under her own roof.

'Now you just listen to me,' I said. 'You've done nothing but be an incredible parent through probably the worst upheaval in Darcy's short little life. She's a teenager. And she's acting out, just the way teenagers do. For feck's sake,

75

only the other day Rosie said she wanted a tattoo for her seventeenth birthday. Harry nearly vomited.'

Sarah said nothing, but then she didn't have to, I already knew what she was thinking. Whereas my Rosie had always been a relatively easy kid, normal and ordinary, lately Darcy was prone to getting into trouble and now, by all accounts, she was hanging around with a bad crowd. Worse, the two girls had always been quite pally until Sarah and Tom broke up. Then almost overnight, Darcy suddenly seemed to morph from a happy, easygoing girl into a moody, hormonal teenager.

'Darcy's all in with Abi Graham and that gang now,' Rosie confided to me one day after school. 'And all they talk about is sex and boys and how many Jaegerbombs they can put away at the weekend. They think it's cool, but it's actually really boring.'

I was lucky with my Rosie and I knew it; she was just one of those quiet, bookish kids who wasn't really inter-ested in boys or partying, at least, not then. I was still waiting on her teenage hormones to kick in, but in the meantime, she was a girl who just got on with life and rarely gave me any hassle, unlike my two boys who were a totally different story. Yet time and again, Sarah would look at Rosie and say to me, 'do you know how lucky you are to have a teenage daughter who doesn't hate you and blame you for everything?'

So she and I sat at her kitchen table that miserable night, but instead of it just being the two of us, Sarah and me, taking the world apart and stitching it all back together again as we'd done so many times in the past, this time we had company.

'Only for Lauren today, I don't know what I'd have done,'

Sarah said, looking gratefully up at her, as Lauren busied herself making a pot of tea without even being asked to.

Ahh, Lauren.

So how did it all start? All I know is that the minute I got the call from Sarah to tell me what had happened, I raced around to her house, but instead of Sarah or a shame-faced Darcy opening the front door, there was this fresh-faced, strikingly pretty girl, dressed in a neat, black, work pinafore and already acting like Sarah's unofficial PA.

'You were fabulous today, Lauren,' Sarah said, smiling warmly up at her. 'I really have no words to thank you.'

'Seeing Darcy safely back at home is all the thanks I need,' Lauren smiled, wiping down the kitchen counter, almost like she worked there. I swear to God, by the time she was done, the kitchen surfaces were so pristine, you could practically have performed an autopsy on them.

'Well Lauren, I'm certainly impressed,' I said to her. 'And maybe when you're finished on those worktops, you'd come around and make a start on my pigsty of a house?'

'Sure there's no harm in making myself useful, now is there?' She grinned back at me.

'Jesus, where did you find this young one?' I asked Sarah jokingly, 'because I could seriously do with a Lauren in my life to sort me out.'

'It's nothing!' Lauren insisted, as she bustled about the place with wet sponges and tea towels.

She eventually left, to a warm hug from Sarah and a polite 'nice to meet you', from me. As she was leaving though, I noticed that Sarah insisted on giving her the taxi fare home.

'No . . . please, there's really no need,' Lauren said, looking mortified as she handed the cash right back.

'You saved my daughter's bacon today,' Sarah told her firmly, 'so the very least I can do is make sure you get home safely. I'd drive you myself only—' She broke off there, indicating the empty glass of wine she'd just drunk.

'It was absolutely nothing,' Lauren smiled modestly. 'I was happy to help out in any way I could. It was the very least I could do after you were so kind to me earlier.'

'You'll stay in touch, won't you?' said Sarah, hugging her goodbye.

'You won't get rid of me that easily!' was the laughing response. 'But before I go, I'll just pop upstairs and say goodbye to Darcy first, if that's OK?'

'Of course. And Lauren?'

'Yes?' said Lauren, with her coat on, halfway out the door.

'Don't worry, I'll find some way to pay you back. And that's a promise.'

As soon as we had the kitchen to ourselves again, I took care to top up both of our wine glasses.

'I have to say,' I said thoughtfully, 'it seems I was wrong about that girl.'

'Wrong how?'

'Well, I thought Lauren was only trying to get in with you so she could wheedle a few quid for herself. But she seems really lovely. Kind of like a Rose of Tralee type. Put a sash on that young one, stick her in the Tralee Dome and you've got the perfect candidate for the "Lovely Girls" competition.'

'She's an angel,' Sarah smiled. 'She was completely wonderful this afternoon. My brain just turned to jelly in that security room, and I was so grateful that Lauren was there to help me out. I hate to think where Darcy would be tonight if things hadn't worked out the way they did,' she added with a shudder.

'In that case,' I said, raising my wine glass in a pretend toast, 'here's to Lauren.'

'To Lauren,' Sarah said, clinking glasses with me.

And the two of us laughed.

Hard to believe looking back, but it's true.

Back in January, when Sarah and I spoke about Lauren, we actually bloody well *laughed*.

Chapter Nine

Darcy

So now Darcy was grounded for the rest of her natural life, according to her dad. And never allowed to go within a ten mile radius of the Dundrum Town Centre, forevermore into eternity. In fact his exact words as he dropped her home that evening had been that apart from school and hopefully college, she wasn't to step outside of the front door till she turned forty.

'And until then,' he'd added, 'every man that sets foot under this roof will be related to you.'

The official result? H&M had let her off with a strict caution, even though that Tanya one practically read her the riot act. Threatened her with court and everything. But there was this younger woman with her mum and between the two of them somehow they'd managed to take charge of absolutely everything and everyone.

Lauren somebody. Attractive-looking, skinny, dark-haired type. A colleague from the office, Darcy figured. Typical of her mum; you get a call to say your only child has been caught shoplifting and your first call is to the office to yank in some work colleague to defend her.

But even Darcy had to admit, they'd all have been lost without that Lauren one, whoever she was. It was like she was Darcy's unofficial barrister and when they finally got home, her mum insisted that she 'say thank you to Lauren. She's been incredibly good to us today. And to you in particular, Missy'.

Darcy muttered her thanks, then dragged herself up to the privacy of her room and flung herself onto the bed. One small mercy; they'd forgotten to confiscate her phone, but as she scrolled down the screen she instantly wished she hadn't. Abi and all the gang were Instagramming her non-stop with photos of themselves getting ready for the party that night. The party she was so looking forward to, the party she should have been at.

WHERE ARE YOU, BABES? THERE'S A VODKA-TINI HERE WITH YOUR NAME ON IT!

Abi texted her, along with an Instagram shot of her posing in that silver dress she'd just nicked the previous day. Pointless Darcy asking if she could go to the party now; she was under lock and key and would be doing well if she was allowed to go to school without an armed Garda escort from then on.

She texted back immediately.

I GOT CAUGHT IN DUNDRUM TODAY. SECURITY, COURT THREATS, THE WORKS. GROUNDED FOR LIFE NOW. FML.

Abi was straight back to her.

YOU FUCKING IDIOT! WHAT KIND OF A SAP-HEAD GETS CAUGHT? HOPE YOU DIDN'T TELL THEM ABOUT ME YESTERDAY BTW. FOR FUCK'S SAKE, KEEP YOUR MOUTH SHUT!

Darcy had to read the text twice, so she could really take it in. Weren't friends meant to rally around when you'd had a shit day? Was it really friendship, she wondered, to make her feel even worse than she already did after the day from hell? Just then, there was a gentle rapping on her bedroom door.

'Come in,' Darcy said in a low voice, too depressed to even haul herself off the bed. The door opened and in came Lauren, with her scarf and coat on, like she was ready to leave.

'I only came to say goodbye to you,' she said softly, standing in the shadows at the doorway. 'And of course, to check that you were OK.'

'Oh, I'm on top of the world here,' Darcy muttered sarcastically. 'Can't you tell?'

She hadn't meant to sound like such a bitch. Those Instagram pictures from Abi had just made her snap, that was all.

'Is it OK if I come in for a minute?' Lauren asked. Darcy shrugged 'whatever' as Lauren stepped inside, closing over the bedroom door behind her.

'Look' she began, 'I know today was a total nightmare for you.'

'That's putting it mildly—'

'So I just came to make sure that you weren't about to fling yourself out the window or anything.'

'Right now, I actually feel like it,' Darcy said, almost to herself as she glanced over at the window. As it happened, there was a tree right outside, a fine, sturdy oak that could take an adult's weight easily. When she was a kid, she used to be able to scale up and down it like a monkey, much to the despair of her mum. It was how she got the neat little scar on her left arm, remembrance of a fall she'd had from the tree when she was about twelve years old.

Darcy found herself looking longingly over at the window again and for a split second, thought why not? Why not just get the hell out of there and run? Who'd even miss her? Certainly not her mum, who was in the kitchen at that very moment, downing wine with her pal Liz and no doubt lamenting what a sad disappointment she'd turned out to be. Snippets of their conversation kept filtering up the stairs to her and they were enough to turn anyone's stomach.

Liz had a foghorn of a voice, the kind of mum you could hear yelling from the far side of a hockey pitch and right then Darcy could hear her loud and clear.

'Just be thankful you don't live in the Gulf States,' Liz was saying. 'The girl could have got her hand chopped off for a lot less, you know.'

'Darcy?' said Lauren, interrupting her thoughts and gently reminding her that she was still standing expectantly in the doorway.

'Look,' said Darcy moodily,' I know I should be thanking you for today and everything, but right now, you're in my private space and I'd really rather be left alone.'

'Say no more,' said Lauren, turning on her heel to leave. 'I only came to ask how you were feeling before I left, that's all.'

'You really want to know how I am?' said Darcy, slumping back on the bed again and staring up at the ceiling.

'Yes, of course I do.'

'Well you know those prisoners my mum goes to visit? Right now I feel like one of them.'

'You're seriously comparing yourself to a prisoner?' Lauren asked, slightly incredulously.

'Yeah, as it happens, I am. I made one, stupid mistake today and because of that, I'm probably locked up here till I leave school. All my friends are out at a party tonight and more than anything else, I just want to be there too. And do you want to know something else, Lauren – or whatever your name is?'

'What's that?'

'I didn't even want that stupid dress I got caught stealing today. I only took it because I had this fantasy in my head that I'd be able to slip out of Dad's flat tonight and get to the party somehow. So if you're asking whether or not I'm OK,' she added sarcastically as the full brunt of her frustration bubbled to the surface, 'then the answer is no I'm not. In fact right now it's a big, fat FML from me.'

'Fuck my life,' said Lauren thoughtfully. 'That's what you mean, isn't it?'

Darcy looked at her, her attention caught, but then she hadn't expected someone Lauren's age to be fully au fait with teenage text-speak.

'Look is it OK if I sit down for a minute?' Lauren asked her. Darcy shrugged 'whatever', then patted the edge of the bed for her to sit there.

'I know you and I have just met,' she went on, perching as prompted, 'but can I tell you something?'

'If it's another lecture, then I'd rather you left it out. I've had enough of being lectured for one day.'

'It's not a lecture. For God's sake, I'd be the last person to lecture anyone.'

'Then what is it?'

'Lauren looked thoughtful for a moment, glancing

around her and really taking in the room around them. The pretty floral bed with matching curtains, the deep-pile carpet in a bang-on-trend creamy colour, the desk piled high with schoolbooks and a wardrobe that seemed to be bulging apart at the seams. 'Do you seriously think of this place as a prison?' she asked. 'Because if you do, then fine, go ahead. But let me tell you one thing. What you think of as prison, plenty of other people would consider to be paradise.'

'Like who, for instance?'

'Well, like me for one.'

Darcy pricked up her ears, intrigued in spite of herself.

'Come on, just take a look at your life!' Lauren went on. 'You've got two parents who love you to bits. And OK, they're upset at what happened today, who wouldn't be? They want the best for you and I for one can only envy that. I wish I had someone out there who genuinely wanted nothing but the best for me too.'

'They want a perfect daughter,' said Darcy. 'And I'm far from that. Right now, they probably hate me and you know what? That's absolutely fine by me because at this moment in time, I hate both of them right back.'

'That's not true and I'm sure you don't mean it,' came the calm reply.

'Oh yes it is and if you don't believe me, then just wait until I turn eighteen so I can get the fuck out of school. Because I'm planning to get as far away from both of them as I possibly can. San Francisco. Or Sydney maybe. Somewhere I can escape to and do what I want and live life on my own terms for a fucking change. '

There was a long, long pause before Lauren eventually spoke.

'You don't need to tell me about escaping,' she said quietly. 'I already know all about it. It's a lot of the reason why I came to Dublin in the first place.'

'I don't get it,' Darcy said, looking at her more closely. 'You're escaping from what exactly?'

'From a whole lot of things back home,' said Lauren thoughtfully.

'But it's not the same,' Darcy said. 'You're an adult, you can do what you want, whenever you want.'

'You'd think, wouldn't you? But I'm afraid life isn't that easy for some of us.'

'Mum says you're originally from Galway,' said Darcy, slowly starting to engage a bit more with this total stranger who, if nothing else, at least wasn't snapping the face off her like everyone else this evening. 'Some tiny town that I can't even remember the name of. Sorry,' she added apologetically.

'That's right,' Lauren nodded. 'And let me tell you something. If you think you have it rough here, you're living the life of a Disney princess compared with how things were for me at your age.'

'How do you mean?'

'You're, what, about sixteen years old?'

Darcy nodded.

'Well, when I was your age,' Lauren went on, 'there was just me and my mother, living on a farm that it was almost impossible to make any money out of, we owed so much on it. Then my mum got sick – very sick – so ill that she had to go into hospital. So not only was I more or less supporting myself and struggling to keep up with my schoolwork, but as well as that, I was shuffling in and out of the hospital day in, day out. And the longer my mother stayed there, the sicker she seemed to get. At your age Darcy, all I could do was count the days till I turned eighteen, just so social services wouldn't take me in.'

'So what happened then?' said Darcy, in a small little voice.

'The same year I left school, Mum passed away.' Lauren told her calmly. 'Then not long afterwards the bank foreclosed on our farm, which of course meant I had to leave. So in a frighteningly short amount of time, I'd lost everyone and everything I'd ever loved. And just like you're probably feeling right now, I wanted to run away, to start over. But do you know something?'

'What?' said Darcy, temporarily forgetting her own woes.

'I've learned that running away doesn't solve anything. All you really do is substitute one set of problems for another.'

'You mean your life isn't any better for you now?'

'It's certainly an improvement, yes. As you say, I'm a grown woman and I don't have to answer to anyone. But am I living the dream? Definitely not.'

'Why's that?'

Lauren gave a wry little smile. 'I'm a qualified lawyer. I had to work my way through college and that was the toughest thing ever, but somehow I still did it. And now I'm lucky to get work as a beautician at a cut-price salon, in a part of town you and your friends probably wouldn't dream of setting foot in, because it wouldn't be trendy or cool enough for you. So while you sit here in this beautiful room feeling like you're locked up, I'm on my way home to share a shoebox of a flat with two students, one of threw up in the kitchen sink last night, by the way, while I'm convinced the other one is a drug user.'

'So you can feel as sorry for yourself as you like,' Lauren

went on, sounding more assertive, like a good dose of tough love was what Darcy really needed. 'Lie here on your comfortable, patterned bedclothes in this gorgeous home surrounded by great people who love you to bits, in spite of the fact that you messed up big-time today. Go on ahead and have a good wallow. Just know that there's plenty of others out there who'd kill to swap places with you, with me at the top of that list. And maybe, just maybe, it's time you got over yourself. You want your parents to stop treating you like a child? Then I suggest you stop acting like one.'

Darcy had no answer to that. Instead she just hugged her knees tightly to her chest, feeling more and more humbled by the second. Lauren's tough talking felt like it was getting through to her far, far more than all her dad's lecturing and her mum's teary, disappointed silence.

Then her attention wavered as another picture message pinged through to her mobile, yet again from Abi at the party. This time, it was a full on shot of her in that slinky silver dress sitting on Tony Scott's knee holding up a vodkatini, with the caption JUST KEEPING TONY'S KNEE NICE AND WARM FOR YOU, BABES!

Darcy said nothing, just looked in disgust at the photo, then cast it aside. But Lauren must have caught sight of the offending image because just as she gathered herself up to leave, she turned back to Darcy.

'And I hope you don't mind me saying,' she said quietly, on her way out the door, 'but friends are supposed to make you feel better about yourself when you've had a rough day, aren't they?'

Darcy nodded mutely.

'So ask yourself. Is that photo something that a friend would send? I mean, a real friend?'

FEBRUARY

Chapter Ten

Sarah

'We can't go on like this.'

'You've got to do something.'

'And by that, we mean actually DO something, Bernie. Not just faff on about it, before you bugger off on some class of a river cruise for the next fortnight.'

'I'll have you know that river cruises are the in thing right now,' Bernie, our boss, protested weakly, not letting the jibe slide as per usual. But then everyone in the Sloan Curtis office knew Bernie's modus operandi of old.

'Never ask me to put out a fire before the weekend,' was his catchphrase as he'd skedaddle out of the office, generally at around lunchtime on a Friday afternoon. Then he'd bolt off to the airport to meet his wife before jetting off with their gang of actively retired pals to see a West End show, or maybe to go wine tasting in Bordeaux, with his phone firmly on airplane mode for the entire weekend.

I was with my colleague Harry – Liz's husband – for this conversation as it happened. The two of us had just collared Bernie, our boss and senior partner, on his way into the conference room for a meeting, which, by the way, was the only feasible chance you got to have a one-on-one chat with Bernie: grabbing him on a corridor in between meetings, if you were very lucky. On the rare occasions when he was actually in the office, that is.

Bernie, you see, had just turned a white-haired, perma-tanned sixty-five and had clearly decided that life was for living and that the only thing he and his wife, both empty-nesters, were really interested in were walking tours of the Lake District, Caribbean cruises for the actively retired, and generally acting like Lotto winners.

As you do.

He inched away from where Harry and I had cornered him, just outside the door of our conference room, but neither of us was budging.

'Come on, Bernie,' said Harry wearily, rubbing at his chest the way he always did whenever his ulcers were at him. 'For Christ's sake, Sarah and I have been on at you about this for months now. We're at the end of our tether here. You've got to line up a new intern for us, or else we're really up shit creek.'

Not the most formal way to speak to your boss, I admit, but then Harry had been at the firm as long as I had myself and there was an unwritten shorthand between us and Bernie. Or 'the elusive Pimpernel', as we referred to him behind his back.

Harry and I were roughly about the same age, in our mid-forties, and we'd known each other ever since our college days, thanks to my friendship with Liz. Not only that, but we were both were parents to unruly kids (he and Liz have three, God bless their patience). Which in situations like this could actually work to your advantage, that unique ability living with a recalcitrant teenager gives you to not to take any shite from anyone, no matter who they are.

'It's getting to the stage where we're both falling way behind on casework and it's going to end up costing us,' I pleaded, knowing that this was probably the surest way of appealing to someone like Bernie, who was all about the money. The kind of absentee boss who'd be hard pressed to know how many court cases we had slated for hearing, but who knew to the letter exactly how many billable hours were due to each individual client.

'For feck's sake, we're only talking about a new intern,' Harry said, backing me up, now that we had the ear of God. 'That's it. Someone who, with a bit of luck, we can groom to take over as soon as Caroline goes off on maternity leave.'

Caroline was our resident junior but, as she was due to have her first baby in a few weeks' time, the pressure was on to replace her.

'Sarah and I are drowning in casework here,' Harry went on, still rubbing away at his ulcer, 'and we're already scarily behind on the McKinsey brief as it is. We need to start looking for someone good and reliable—'

'Just to take the heat off us,' I said, finishing his sentence for him. 'For Christ's sake, Bernie, we're a small little firm and we've absolutely got to have a replacement for Caroline lined up. Only yesterday, I lost two hours down at the circuit court chasing up case records. We can't afford to tie ourselves up like that any more. Just do as we ask and we'll all be in much better shape. Harry and I will be able to work harder, better and faster.'

Bernie looked at each of us and read the seriousness in

93

our faces. Then after an excruciatingly long pause, he reluctantly nodded.

'Right then, have it your way,' he shrugged.

I smiled. 'You won't regret it. And what's more, I'll even interview the candidates myself. I'll have the right person all groomed to start work the minute Caroline goes off on maternity. Trust me.'

'Just make sure they'll work for cheap,' was Bernie's parting shot as he turned his back to us and made his way into the conference meeting.

'You know, we're not asking for the sun, moon and stars here,' Harry said to me, when it was just him and I alone in the corridor. 'It doesn't have to be someone straight out of UCD or Trinity who came top of their class. All we need is a graduate with a semi-decent law degree, someone young and hungry who'll do what they're told, blend in with the wallpaper and who's not above making the odd mug of coffee when the need arises. Not exactly a job description that's going to set the world on fire, now is it?'

'You needn't worry,' I smiled confidently back at him.

'Why's that?' he asked, looking at me with two exhausted, bloodshot eyes, even though it was only a Monday morning and we still had the whole week ahead of us to battle our way through.

'Because I think I may just have the perfect person in mind.'

*

Later on that day I texted Lauren and asked to meet after we'd both finished work for the day. She texted me back almost immediately.

I'D LOVE TO SEE YOU TOO, SARAH. HOW ABOUT 7PM? TELL ME WHERE WOULD SUIT YOU TO MEET AND I'LL BE THERE. I DON'T WANT TO PUT YOU OUT IN ANY WAY. HOPE DARCY IS OK AND THAT YOU ARE TOO?

Typical Lauren, I thought, smiling as I scrolled down through her message. Never thinking of herself, always putting others first. I texted her back and asked her if she'd like to swing by my house for a bite to eat later on and she readily agreed.

I was delayed in work though, held up on a transatlantic conference call that ran well over time. So in spite of my best intentions, it was well past 8pm by the time I finally did fall through the front door, laden down with a mound of legal briefs that went clattering to the floor while I fumbled around with the door keys.

To my astonishment though, as soon as I let myself in through the hall door, I heard voices coming from the kitchen. And laughter. Actual *laughter*.

Which took me utterly by surprise, but then I was hard pressed to remember the last time anyone had really belly-laughed in this house. Not only that, but there was a gorgeous smell wafting back at me, garlicy and oniony. Delicious.

'I find the trick is not to chuck in the bulk of the mixture until the very last minute,' I could hear Lauren saying in that soft-spoken voice. 'Otherwise it'll just caramelize the butter and end up looking like . . .'

'A pig's mickey?' Darcy giggled.

'I wouldn't be much of an authority on pigs' mickeys, but if you like that analogy, then yeah, absolutely,' Lauren said, laughing.

I opened the kitchen door to find the pair of them elbow deep in just about every ingredient there was at the back of the baking cupboard, looking like they were having an absolute ball. Lauren even had one of my tea towels wrapped around her waist and was gently demonstrating the proper way to fold flour into a cake tin.

'Hello you,' I said, hugging her every bit as warmly as I hugged Darcy when I came in. 'It's great to see you, and thanks so much for coming over.'

Truth was, I hadn't actually seen Lauren since that nightmarish incident in H&M just a few weeks beforehand. We'd stayed in touch via text and the odd phone call, but the bulk of my time in the interim had been spent dealing with Darcy, trying my very best to get her back onto an even keel after the almighty shock she'd given us all.

'We can't exactly lock her up till she's eighteen,' as Tom pointed out, 'much as I'd like to. But until then we can at least keep a close, watchful eye.'

Darcy was grounded, of course, but I was doing everything I could to make it as easy on her as possible and to cut the poor kid a bit of slack. I was trying my level best to get home from work as early as I could, so I could cook dinner for her and hopefully spend some real quality time together.

In practice though, this usually involved me racing back from the office with a mountain of case work still to do later on that night, then sitting in stilted silence with Darcy trying to make small-talk and getting precious little in the way of a reply, unless you counted the odd grunt. Or the occasional 'whatever,' hissed at me, on the rare occasions when she actually – shock horror – glanced up from her mobile phone.

'Thanks so much for asking me to dinner,' Lauren said politely, immediately rushing to the kitchen table and handing me a bunch of flowers she'd bought which were so expensive looking, I was mortified. Had the girl really spent her hard-earned cash on me, when she was only earning buttons to begin with? For God's sake, I should have been the one giving her flowers and not the other way around.

'Wow, they're gorgeous,' I said. 'You really shouldn't have.'

'It's nothing. Just a tiny thank you for having me over, that's all,' she smiled shyly.

'And look, Mum,' said Darcy, 'Lauren is showing me how to make a ricotta and spinach pasta bake, with these gorgeous oatmeal seed cookies for desert. At least, they're meant to be gorgeous, if they end up even remotely looking like they do in this recipe,' she added wryly, indicating the open cookbook on the kitchen table front of her. 'And Lauren used to work in a vegan restaurant too, isn't that cool?'

'Fantastic,' I smiled, delighted to see the two girls getting on so well, even though Darcy's veganism had started exactly two weeks ago. Mainly influenced I think, by that new pal of hers, Abi, who she seemed to be inseparable from.

'I was telling Darcy that I used to work in a Lebanese restaurant to support myself back when I was in college,' said Lauren. 'And you know how it is, you pick up a few little chef's tips along the way.'

'I can't believe I asked you for dinner and you ended up cooking it yourself!' I laughed, grabbing an apron so I could at least give them both a hand. Instead though, Lauren just smiled and shook her head.

'It's my pleasure, Sarah,' she said. 'Now you just sit back and let me take care of everything. Look, I've got a terrific sous chef here in Darcy and between us we have it all under control, don't we?'

Darcy glowed and I couldn't help but grin at seeing her almost back to her old self again. And of course the dinner was divine, but then as I was to learn in the months to come, just about everything Lauren did was sheer perfection. Normally, when it was me behind the cooker, Darcy would rearrange the food around her plate and only reluctantly swallow down a tiny bit of it if I nagged her enough.

Not that night, though. To my astonishment, Darcy not only licked her plate clean, but even passed around second helpings for us all to tuck into. And we had a conversation around the table, an actual, proper, adult conversation about politics, Brexit and Donald Trump's hair. It was a joy to see my daughter really come into her own and to hear her speak knowledgeably and confidentially about her social science class and how much their teacher encouraged them to talk about world events.

Lauren didn't talk down to her as I was sometimes inclined to do, falling into the old trap of thinking that she was still my little girl. Instead, Lauren treated her like an adult and Darcy responded accordingly.

Later, as we tidied up and cleared away with everyone in high spirits after such a fabulous meal, I wondered had there ever been a Saint Lauren?

Hard to believe, but back then, that really is what I thought.

MARCH

Chapter Eleven

Darcy

It was all because of that bloody A1 in English.

To explain, ever since she got caught at H&M, Darcy had been under effective lock and key, not only when she was at home, but when she was over at her dad's flat too. Which meant there was basically shag all else for her to do but study.

And she liked English, even though Hamlet was fairly boring as plays went. But after a school trip to see Benedict Cumberbatch take on the title role in one of those 'live events' where you watched a link-up of the show while munching popcorn in the cinema, she was a convert. Anyone who could make those long, boring soliloquies sound as exciting as Benedict Cumerbatch did automatically had her attention.

So while Abi remorselessly taunted her for turning into 'such a bloody swot', Darcy would coolly answer that she was still paying the price for the whole shoplifting episode, which left her with feck all else to do but study. So that's exactly what she did. Then by her Easter exams, to her complete shock, she'd actually done the unthinkable and come home with the most perfect report card ever seen in their house.

'I couldn't be more proud of you, sweetheart!' her mum had beamed, practically doing a happy dance around the kitchen. 'Now come on, grab your coat, I'm taking my little genius out for dinner. Anywhere you like, pet, it's your treat and you've earned it the hard way.'

'Actually, Mum, if you don't mind, I'd sort of planned on doing something else to celebrate. If it's OK with you, of course,' Darcy took particular care to add politely. Baby steps and all that.

The thing was, it was the official start of her Easter holidays that Friday evening and there was a party on that she just HAD to get to. It was an absolute matter of life or death. Tony Scott's parents were away at a fiftieth birthday, leaving him with a free house for the whole night. His two older brothers had been left in charge, but according to Tony both of them were in college and neither particularly gave a shit who he had around, providing they didn't trash the place.

By then, Tony had been sort-of flirting back and forth with her in school for weeks and as Abi had pointed out 'all you need to seal the deal is to get drunk, flirt a bit and let nature take its course. Simple as that, babes. Just learn from the master'.

Abi had been going out with Louis Ryan for almost a year, so whenever she deigned to dole out relationship advice, you made damn sure to listen.

'Please can I go, Mum?' Darcy begged. 'It's just that my whole class will be there tonight and I really need to let off a bit of steam. Come on, I've been working so hard for weeks now and you said yourself my results were as good as perfect. Don't you think I deserve a bit of a break?'

'Well, I suppose it wouldn't do any harm . . .' her mum had wavered.

Which was when Darcy had seized her chance.

'Amazing! Thanks so much, Mum, you're the best!' She grinned, hugging her tight. 'And you needn't worry about me getting home or anything, because Abi asked me to stay the night with her. That's OK with you, isn't it?'

That was an out-and-out lie, of course; there was no such plan at all. Instead the two girls had planned to get as trashed as possible at the party. 'We're not leaving until you've ended up in bed with Tony Scott,' as Abi had put it, 'or at least kissed him. You big virgin.'

Not only that, but Abi had somehow arranged to get hold of a fake ID card, so they could go for a pre-drink or a 'prink' beforehand. Which effectively meant a few vodkas in a dive bar in town called the Palace, the only place they knew of that turned a blind eye to teenage drinkers and didn't give you the third degree if they were a bit suspicious about your age.

To Darcy's utter jubilation, her mum nodded and smiled. 'All right then, love,' she'd said. 'You're absolutely right. You've really impressed your dad and me with the way you've pulled your socks up over the past few weeks, so you deserve a night out. I'll collect you from Abi's first thing in the morning and till then, you just stay safe. And enjoy.'

Not only that, but as great good luck would have it, her mum's pal Lauren had called around to their house again that night. Both of them kept going on about some intern's job at Sloan Curtis that her mum was determined Lauren should apply for. From what Darcy could gather though, there was going to be intense competition for the job, so the pair of them were holed up at the kitchen table with a mound of terrifying looking case documents and legal briefs as her mum coached Lauren through what she was likely to be asked at the interview.

Every few minutes, Darcy would interrupt the pair of them, prancing happily into the kitchen in one outfit after another, demanding to know which one looked better on her.

'I'd definitely go with the blue shirt and skinny jeans,' Lauren had said enthusiastically. 'With your lovely brown hair, blue is definitely your colour. And you certainly have the figure to rock those jeans.'

'Not my little black halter-neck top, then?' Darcy had asked hopefully.

'Definitely not!' said her mum, glancing up from a stash of papers, with her glasses perched comically at the tip of her nose. 'It's just a bit too revealing, love. Lauren's right, jeans and a crisp, plain shirt look far better on you. Far more age-appropriate too. The black top is way too ageing. You've the whole rest of your life to wear clothes like that, remember.'

Darcy was in far too good a mood to answer back, but the truth was she was determined to wear the black top whether her mum liked it or not. It had a padded bra incorporated into it, and with her boobs out on full display, she was good to go. Tony Scott wouldn't know what had hit him. Her plan was to wear the shirt and jeans out the door, but to have the black top on underneath, so that as soon as she got to the Palace Bar in town, she could whip off her shirt in the loo.

'Look at you, you're stunning,' Lauren had grinned at her. 'In fact, I've an idea, but only if it's OK with you, of course, Sarah,' she added, casting a quick, respectful glance in her mum's direction. 'It's just that – if you'd like – I could always do Darcy's make-up for her? It's something I do a lot at the salon and I thought, as it's a special night, why not? I've come here straight from work, so I've already got my make-up kit with me.'

Darcy let out an involuntary whoop at the idea, her mum beamed her approval, and a few minutes later, she was sitting upstairs with a towel wrapped around her neck while Lauren worked all kinds of magic with foundations, powders and eye-liners.

'You have such fabulous bone structure,' Lauren had said, giving her face a very professional sweep with a blusher brush. 'I have clients at the salon who'd kill to have cheek-bones like yours.'

'I can't believe my luck that you were here this evening,' Darcy grinned happily, loving the whole experience of being pampered in her own home. 'You can cook, you're a brilliant baker and now it turns out you rock at doing make-up too. How cool is that?'

Lauren smiled and moved on to applying MAC liquid liner to Darcy's eyes. 'Your mum has been so good to me,' she said, 'so this is the very least I can do in return.'

By the time she was finished, Darcy was stunned as she took in her own appearance in the bedroom mirror. Lauren had given her a smoky-eyed look, which was sexy and seductive looking, yet passable enough that she figured she'd make it out the front door without her mum reaching for the wet wipes to scrub half of it off. Not only that, but Lauren had applied some kind of liquid primer that gave her cheeks an apple-y, rosy glow and that along with just a tiny slash of natural lip gloss was all Darcy needed to make her feel on top of the world.

'Wow, I'm loving it!' She grinned as Lauren whipped off the towel from around her neck and revealed the finished product. 'You've made me look . . .'

'Beautiful,' said Lauren simply. 'You're a total babe. So go out and enjoy yourself. You deserve it.'

'I don't know how to thank you,' said Darcy.

'Absolutely no need,' Lauren insisted. 'But if you'd ever like me to do your make-up again, just call me anytime. It's a pleasure.'

Delighted with herself, Darcy made a point of adding Lauren's number into her phone contacts, then went down-stairs to show off the make-up to her mum.

'Wow, can this supermodel really be my daughter?' her mum said approvingly as Darcy swished around the kitchen.

Darcy smiled. 'Thanks so much for letting me go, Mum. You've no idea how much I need this.'

*

Half an hour later, her mum had dropped her outside a branch of Starbucks in town, where Darcy had told her 'all the gang were meeting'. Another whopper of a lie, of course; the truth was that all the others were meeting at the Palace Bar just a few streets away and the minute her mum pulled off, Darcy began to clip her way there in slightly too-high heels.

'There you are, bitch,' said Abi, who was already there ahead of her and standing outside, pulling on a cigarette and looking freezing cold against the icy March chill. She was dressed in a skirt that was more like an elongated belt really, with fake tan plastered all the way down her incon-gruously long legs and two guys were hanging out with her, smoking. Abi, however, made absolutely no effort to introduce either of them.

'Hey, did you get your make-up done professionally or what?' she demanded.

'Well, no, it's just that . . .' Darcy began to say, but Abi barreled over her.

'Whatever,' she said, eyeing her pal a bit enviously. 'If you ask me though, you look a bit overdone for just a few scoops at the Palace. Looks to me like you're trying too hard.'

Darcy felt a short stab of hurt, wishing that Abi hadn't said that in front of two complete strangers, but all was forgotten a minute later, when her pal produced a half-drunk 7UP bottle from out of her handbag.

'Here,' she said bossily, unscrewing the bottle. 'Take a swig of this to get you in the party mood.'

'What is it?' Darcy asked.

'Bit of everything I could snaffle from my dad's drinks cabinet. Just knock it back, you'll soon feel no pain.'

Darcy did as she was bid, even though it tasted revolting. It burnt her on the way down and both Abi and the two guys with her laughed to see her coughing and spluttering.

'You'll have to excuse my friend,' Abi said. 'She's not used to this. A long weekend in Magaluf, that's what this one really needs, lads. That'd soon knock the corners off her.'

They went inside to the bar then, but if Darcy had thought this part of the night would be just some pals gathering for a few laughs before heading off to the party, then she was sadly mistaken.

For starters, the Palace Bar turned out to be a complete dive and although some of the gang from her class were there, there were also a bunch of total strangers, including two improbably blonde girls who were draped around Tony Scott. Neither of whom seemed in any rush to move.

'Hiya, Tony,' Darcy called across the table to him, but he just nodded back, barely even acknowledging her before turning his full attention back to the blonde with the slightly bigger boobs.

'Here, have another drink, then you won't give a shit about him,' Abi said, just a bit too loudly for Darcy's liking. 'Because if Tony thinks he's in with the slightest chance with either of those bitches, he's kidding himself. I heard they're both repeating their Leaving Certificate at Mount Anville. And that one of them was in a bar in Magaluf last year, when she was offered a free holiday if she gave ten fellas a blowjob. So she did and you know what? Turned out the "free holiday" was the name of a cocktail. Apparently some eejit filmed it and it was all over YouTube.'

Darcy tried her best not to think about the college girl and all the blowjobs she gave to total strangers in Magaluf and instead took another swig from the plastic bottle she was being offered.

And you know what? Abi was dead right. By the time she'd knocked the rest of it back, she didn't give a shite at all.

*

When they eventually made it back to the party at Tony's house, Darcy felt woozy and a bit nauseous, but Abi assured her that was a really good sign.

'Means you're properly pissed, for once in your life. Now don't waste it, for fuck's sake. Go and make your move on Tony now. Quick, before one of those blondey bitches nabs him!'

It was weird though; even though no one was friendly with either of the two blonde girls, it still hadn't stopped either of them tagging along to the party, automatically assuming that their looks and hot bodies got them asked anywhere they liked. Try as she might, Darcy couldn't seem to get a word in with Tony; he was constantly flanked by the two of them.

'Who's that kid with the face-full of make-up anyway?' the slightly taller one of them asked Tony at one point, as they all helped themselves to beers in the kitchen. 'She's been following you around all night like some kind of lost puppy.'

'Just some girl from my class,' Tony had said with a shrug, clearly within Darcy's hearing. She'd shriveled inwardly at that and was just about to skulk out of the kitchen and as far away from Tony as possible when a voice from behind stopped her.

'Pay no attention to him. He's just an arsehole.'

Darcy turned around to see Sophie Greene from her history class, a girl she knew, though not very well. But then Sophie hung out with the nerd crew and everyone knew they were just one degree above being a complete laughing stock.

'Trust me, the Tony Scotts of this world just aren't worth it,' said Sophie, taking Darcy by the arm and steering her towards the TV room, which was packed full of people all in semi-darkness. 'Come on, the rest of us are all hanging out in here,' she added, plonking Darcy down on the sofa beside her.

'Thanks so much,' Darcy said gratefully, glad that Sophie was being so nice to her. And equally thankful for the chance to sit down because the truth was, her too-tight shoes were pinching her and she was starting to feel a bit green around the gills by then. She hadn't had time to eat before she'd left home earlier and if she was being really honest, the home-brew of cocktails Abi had been pouring down her throat all night actually tasted revolting.

'If you ask me, that eejit Tony is so up himself, it's not true,' Sophie chatted away. 'You know, I actually kissed him once? The night of the Junior Cert results. You're missing nothing Darcy, trust me. He's all tongue.'

Darcy giggled and was just starting to feel like her evening was turning around when next thing Abi materialized beside her and yanked her up onto her feet.

'I'm going outside for a fag and you're coming with me,' she said bossily.

'I'm fine here, thanks . . .' Darcy began, but Abi was having none of it.

'For fuck's sake, I'm gagging for a fag and I need to talk to you. Now.'

Darcy made an 'I'm sorry' face at Sophie and allowed herself to be yanked off the sofa and out the front door into the biting cold night.

'What the hell are you playing at?' Abi demanded, as soon as the two of them were alone, taking a slug out of a bottle of beer, then handing the rest of it over to Darcy.

'I don't know what you're talking about,' said Darcy, taking the beer, but pointedly not drinking it. She felt woozy enough as it was and somehow felt that one more drink would be all she'd need to really send her over the edge.

'You're letting those two college bitches nab Tony from right under your nose! Meanwhile you're just sitting on the sofa talking to boring, nerdy Sophie.'

'Don't call her that, Sophie's all right.'

'And why aren't you drinking that beer?' Abi barreled over her. 'I went to loads of trouble to snaffle that for you, you fucking idiot.'

Darcy pretended to take a sip of the beer, but didn't really. It smelt vile and disgusting and it was actually starting to make her stomach heave.

'Drink properly,' said her friend bossily. 'Don't just sniff at it. You look like a total sap-head.'

'I'm OK, thanks.'

'Give me that then,' said Abi, snatching the bottle away from her. '*This* is how it's done.' Then a second later, she'd knocked the entire bottle back, even if she did spew out an awful lot of it onto the grass that lined the front porch.

'Now you just pay attention to me, you big virgin.'

'Can you please stop calling me that?' Darcy said defensively.

'Whatever,' she slurred. 'The thing is I figured you and Tony needed a bit of a catalyst. So I just had a chat with him and I told him straight out you were seriously into him. Like . . . *seriously*,' she added for emphasis.

'Abi! I wish you hadn't done that!' said Darcy, suddenly mortified. 'Now what's he going to think?'

'Don't be ridiculous,' Abi said, this time producing what looked like a half drunk bottle of water from the tiny clutch bag that slung dangerously low around her waist. 'If anything I was doing you a favour. So just take a few mouthfuls of this and then you should be good to go.'

'Is it water?' Darcy asked, taking the bottle from her.

'Ehh . . . yeah,' said Abi, just a bit too quickly. 'Water. Course it is. So just down it in one, get back in there, and I think you'll find Tony Scott will be looking at you in a whole new light. No need to thank me,' she added, before

111

turning on her heel with a bit of a wobble and disappearing back into the throng.

Quietly furious, Darcy made her way back inside, resolved to do nothing more than find Sophie again and with any luck spend the rest of the night chatting to her. Sophie wasn't on the sofa when she went looking for her though, but someone told her she'd only gone upstairs to the loo.

Darcy followed her upstairs, thinking it would do her no harm to pat a bit of cold water on her face in front of a mirror. There was a queue outside the bathroom though, so while she was waiting she took the water bottle Abi had thrust into her hand and without a second thought, knocked it all back, thinking that water was exactly what she needed right then.

But it wasn't water at all. It burnt going down and if anything, only made her feel worse, far, far worse. She coughed and choked, just as the bathroom door finally opened.

'Sophie, I was looking all over for you,' said Darcy. But it wasn't Sophie standing in the bathroom at all. Instead she found herself face to face with Tony Scott himself.

'Well, well, who we have here,' he said, eyeing her up in a suggestive way he'd never done before. Christ, Darcy thought woozily, what had Abi told him about her anyway?

'I was just looking for—' she began, but Tony interrupted.

'Oh, Abi told me exactly what it is you're looking for babes,' he said, yanking her by the arm, hauling her inside the bathroom and taking great care to lock the door firmly behind him.

Chapter Twelve

Liz

There was a time, not so long ago, when I actually used to look forward to a Saturday night. Hard to think back on it now that everything has changed so much, but as recently as last March, the thoughts of a Saturday night would actually propel me though the whole week.

Harry, my other half, and I would do date night as often as we could afford it, but more often than not, a weekend night would involve him peeling himself away from his family for a poker night with the lads, delighted to get a welcome break from his nearest and dearest for a few hours. Meanwhile, I'd book a babysitter and take myself off to Sarah's for a bottle of wine, a takeaway, a good old bitching session, copious mugs of tea and many, many family-sized bags of Cadbury's miniatures.

The thoughts of a cosy night in on Sarah's sofa with either *Strictly Come Dancing* or *Britain's Got Talent* on in the background while the two of us nattered the night away would actually propel me though a freezing cold day spent cheering my two boys on from the side of a soccer pitch before ferrying them off to playdates and school parties afterwards. It got me through all the rows with my eldest, Rosie, over the state of her room and with my boys over the fact that like it or not, playing soccer inside the house was a strict no-no.

Don't get me wrong. I love my family more that life itself, but every so often I need time out from the whole shower of them so I can get offside with my best friend. And that's been our routine for years.

Me and Sarah, contra mundum.

Till it all changed, as recently as last March.

'Come over anytime,' Sarah had told me on the phone earlier that day. 'Darcy's out at a party tonight, so I'll be here all alone.'

'You're seriously letting Darcy out to a party?' I asked her, astonished. 'I mean . . . after what happened and everything?'

'I know,' said Sarah dubiously, 'but her school report was terrific so I figured she'd earned a night off. To be honest, it won't do me any harm either. Lauren is upstairs with her now, doing her make-up.'

Ahh, Lauren. Where to start about Lauren?

As usual, I rocked up to Sarah's with a bottle of Pinot Grigio tucked under one arm and the takeaway menu from the Bombay Pantry under the other, absolutely gagging for a big de-briefing session.

It was been a particularly shit day; I'd had a blistering row with Harry on my way out the door, over money – what else? Plus I was convinced Jack, my middle child was pilfering cash from my purse while Sean, my youngest, had thrown a tantrum in class earlier that week, so now his teacher was gently but firmly suggesting 'we might take a look at whether this really is the right school for him'.

I badly needed to talk to Sarah; I wanted nothing more than a night of gossip and bitching with my best friend, that was all.

But it was Lauren who answered the front door to me that night.

'Hello, Liz,' she smiled brightly. 'It's so lovely to see you again. Come in, you're very welcome. Here, let me take your coat.'

All very bland really, but there was just something about the proprietorial way Lauren spoke that gave me the feeling this one was going nowhere. I'd only met her once before, that awful night Darcy was nicked for shoplifting, and in fairness, she'd initially struck me as being a perfectly innocuous girl. Since then, I knew she and Sarah had grown closer – a lot closer. Every time I spoke to her, it was all 'Lauren this' and 'Lauren that'. I just hadn't realised that Lauren now spent most of her spare time hanging out here.

'Where's Sarah?' I asked her dubiously, struggling out of my big, soccer-Mom puffer jacket.

'She's just dropping Darcy off in town to meet her friends,' Lauren replied. 'She'll be back in a few minutes. Can I get you anything?'

So Sarah's gone out, and yet you're still in her house? It's almost as if you work here, I thought. *It's like you've become Sarah's unofficial housekeeper/personal assistant.*

I can't even put my finger on why that bothered me so much; all I can say is that back then, I was beginning to get a bad feeling about Lauren. A bit like Harry whenever one of his ulcers was at him.

She and I made stilted small talk while we both waited for Sarah to come home. I was plonked at the kitchen table, while Lauren loaded up the dishwasher, without even being asked to.

'So how long have you been here?' I asked her suspiciously.

'Since earlier this afternoon,' she said, smiling at me sweetly. 'Sarah's been so good to me, so doing a bit of light housework when she's out is the least I can for her in return. It's no trouble at all.'

Nothing to take exception to there, so a silence fell as my busy mind whirred.

'She mentioned something about an intern job at Sloan Curtis?' I said, after a long pause. 'And trying to get you an interview for it?'

'That's right,' Lauren nodded, taking care to wipe the kitchen surfaces cleaner than I'd ever seen them before. 'It would really be a dream come true for me to get work in the legal profession. Even if it's only mundane stuff like answering phones and photocopying. Do you ever miss work, Liz?'

'Why do you ask that?' I asked her, or rather, I asked the back of her head as she whipped out Windolene and I swear to God, actually starting doing the insides of the windows. Jesus, I thought crossly. Who comes to someone else's house and starts cleaning the insides of their windows? I mean, who actually *does* that?

'Well, I know from Sarah that you've been taking a career break from Sloan Curtis to look after your family,' Lauren said innocently, scrubbing away at the glass surfaces. 'Still and all, though.'

'Still and all, what?'

'I can't imagine that running around after three children is quite the same as being at the centre of a busy legal practice, now is it?'

'Excuse me?' I said, wondering whether or not I'd misheard her.

'Sarah tells me that you used to be quite senior at the practice,' Lauren went on, calmly cleaning away without as much as a backward glance back in my direction. 'And that you gave it all up to be a homemaker. Which I'm sure was the right decision for you at the time. All I'm saying is that it can't be nearly as fulfilling.'

'So according to you, I'm just some stay-at-home house-wife then, am I?' I said defensively, but before she had time to answer the hall door burst open and Sarah came clattering in, full of breathless apologies for being late.

'No worries at all hon,' I told her, getting up to give her a warm hug as Lauren just stood by and watched, saying nothing but taking everything in. 'Can we get started on the wine now? I'm absolutely gagging for a dirty big glass of the old Pinot G.'

Then maybe Lauren would finally take the cue that it was time for her to get going, or so I hoped.

'Of course babes,' Sarah smiled, gratefully taking the bottle I offered her and opening up a drawer to root out a corkscrew. 'Don't know about you, but I've been looking forward to this all day. God, this kitchen is so clean! Lauren, have you been tidying up while I was out again?'

'Just a bit,' Lauren said, or, as far as I was concerned, simpered.

'What are you like?' Sarah said, pretend angry.

'Sure when I'm here, I might as well make myself useful.'

'Would you like a glass of wine?'

At that, Lauren gave a firm shake of her head. 'Thank you, but I never drink.'

Course you don't, Little Miss Perfect.

'So how does a takeaway from Bombay Pantry sound to you?' I asked Sarah, as she poured out the vino for the two of us. 'I haven't had a chance to eat since breakfast and feck the diet, I'm bloody starving.'

'Sounds great,' Sarah replied. 'But you know, I'm sure poor old Lauren must be hungry too,' she added, taking great care to include her in the conversation. 'You came here straight from work, didn't you, Lauren? And you probably haven't eaten a scrap all day. Would you like to join us for dinner?'

I said nothing, just looked silently over at Lauren, thinking angrily to myself, *say no. Please say no. This is my one and only night alone with my best pal, can't you just take the hint and leave? You've had the whole afternoon to chat about your internship and Sloan Curtis and all of that malarkey, surely now it's time you pootled off?*

'Are you certain I wouldn't be intruding?' Lauren asked hopefully.

'Of course not,' said Sarah.

Actually, yes, you bloody well would. I tried to telegraph, pointedly giving her no encouragement.

'Well, in that case, thank you so much,' said Madam Lauren, pulling up a chair and plonking herself down right in between us at the kitchen table. 'I'd love to join you both. Can't think of a better way to spend a Saturday than a night in with my two new girlfriends.'

*

I got no private chat in at all with Sarah that night. Instead, Lauren sat between us by the sitting-room fire for the entire evening, with nothing stronger than a glass of fizzy water in front of her, contributing very little to the conversation, but listening carefully to everything we said, I noticed. Nor at any point throughout the night did she leave Sarah and me alone so I could hiss at my pal, 'why is that one still here?'

Instead, the girl sat for four solid hours and never once even got up to go to the loo.

'So you see, I'm very hopeful that if I can just get Lauren an interview for the Sloan Curtis internship,' Sarah was saying, over a half-eaten plate of chicken tandoori and an abandoned side portion of saag aloo, 'then with her qualifications, she'd ace it. Now admittedly, it would hardly be the most glamorous job in the world and the pay is a pittance, but—'

'But it would still be a dream come true for me,' Lauren chipped in, with a smile so sickly sweet, it would almost give you diabetes. Mind you, I was well onto my third glass of wine by then and the past few hours spent in the girl's company had done absolutely nothing to endear me to her.

'If you were to land this job, Lauren,' I said curtly to her at one point, 'then you'd end up working alongside my husband, Harry. Of course, that's if you managed to beat all the other candidates competing for the gig in the first place.'

Suddenly, I saw storm clouds hovering over not just Sarah's immediate future, but my own too. That this pretty, malleable, ambitious slip of a thing could end up working all those long hours with Harry, while I slaved away at home, running around after three school-going kids? And this one had the cheek to run down what I did as mere 'homemaking'? Fun and games, I thought, getting more and more irrationally cross with Lauren as the wine took effect and the night wore on.

119

'Yes, so I understand,' she replied, reaching out to top up our glasses of wine, but taking care not to touch a drop of alcohol herself. 'I've no doubt your husband is a brilliant lawyer, Liz, and I'd be honoured to work for him. Though of course the main bonus for me would be getting to work with this wonder woman here on a daily basis,' she added, with a respectful little nod towards Sarah.

'Isn't she a dream?' Sarah said, glowing, while I just looked on, tight-lipped. Next thing Lauren was up on her feet and tidying away the remains of dinner, ignoring Sarah who told her to sit down and relax, that there was really no need.

'No, please,' Lauren insisted. 'Stay and finish the wine with Liz. You've been so kind to include me in your girls' night in. The least I can do is clear up.'

Sarah made a half-hearted attempt to stop her, but Lauren had the advantage of being sober over the pair of us, who between us had already put away a full bottle of Pinot Grigio.

'You want to know something?' Sarah said, stretching contentedly out on the sofa as Lauren busied herself in the kitchen. 'On the surface, you'd think I was the one helping out Lauren. But the truth is, it's really the other way around. You should have seen her with Darcy earlier – she was like a cool big sister with her. Styling her, helping her out with her make-up, the whole works. If it were up to me, I'd have Lauren here with me every spare minute I could get her.'

And I'll bet she'd only be too happy to go along with that, I thought. But I was careful to say nothing.

Lauren didn't seem in the remotest hurry to leave either.

'So it's a Saturday night,' I said to her at one point. 'Surely a young one like you has friends to go out with and parties to go to? Or a boyfriend, even?' I added, fishing a bit.

'No to all three, I'm sorry to say,' Lauren laughed lightly.

'No man on the scene for you then?'

'I only wish.'

'Ahh, you're better off without them,' said Sarah tipsily. 'Who needs a fella anyway? Trust me, Lauren. You don't want to end up like me, with a Tom in your life who's a constant drain on you. You're young and beautiful, you can do so much better.'

'So how long have you been separated for?' Lauren asked, sounding coldly sober in comparison with Sarah and me.

'Almost two years now,' Sarah said, sprawled out on the sofa, with a pile of cushions at her head. 'Isn't it, Liz?'

'Hmmm,' I said, tight-lipped. But then Sarah knew exactly where I was coming from on that subject; it was ground she and I had covered so often in the past. As far as I was concerned, Tom still loved her and Darcy needed her dad around, simple as that. Yes, he'd fucked up big-time, there was no denying that. But I'd spent month after month pleading with Sarah that the guy deserved a second chance. Didn't we all? Everyone messes up in a marriage, and the whole point of being married is to deal with problems, then put them behind you both and move on together.

But no, Sarah was having none of it. As far as she was concerned, it was over. End of story.

'You two still seem close,' said Lauren.

'Well, he and I stay on fairly good terms because of Darcy,' Sarah replied, 'but we'll certainly never reconcile after everything that went down between us. At least, not unless I have a lobotomy first.'

'Yeah, but nothing is irrevocable,' I began to say, 'and

who knows what'll happen down the line? You might change your mind in time—'

But Lauren cut over me. Whether she did it intentionally or not, I couldn't say, but she still did it anyway.

'If it's over,' she said firmly. 'Then it's over. Stay strong, Sarah. In my own small way, I can relate to what you're going through and, for what it's worth, I know I'm certainly better off on my own. For the moment, at least.'

'Were you married?' I asked her, taken aback. Lauren seemed too young to have been through not only a marriage, but then a marriage break-up on top of that.

'Long story,' she smiled, looking up at me from under those impossibly long Bambi eyelashes as she cleared away the debris of our takeaway. 'Now can I get either of you two ladies a nice mug of tea and a chocolate biscuit while I'm on my feet? It's absolutely no trouble at all.'

*

It got to past midnight and we were still there, the three of us, me determined to outstay Madam, mainly so I could gossip about her when she was finally gone. Meanwhile poor old Sarah grew more and more heavy-lidded with deep exhaustion, the combination of a tough week at work and a few glasses of vino really starting to take their effect.

'Sorry, girls,' she said apologetically. 'I'm afraid I'm no company anymore. I'm so bone tired, I can barely keep my eyes open.'

'Maybe it's time we all called it a night,' I said, getting up to ring for a taxi.

'Don't kill me, Liz,' Sarah yawned sleepily from the sofa. 'I'm just a pathetic lightweight who can't even hold a few glasses of wine any more.'

'Shhh,' said Lauren protectively, pulling a cashmere throw that was covering the back of the sofa down over Sarah's legs, then tucking her in like a little baby. 'Why not stay and snooze here, in front of the fire? Liz and I will let ourselves out. Won't we, Liz?'

Jesus. Whatever you say, I thought furiously.

We switched out all the lights, locked up and left Sarah snoozing gently on the sofa. I whispered to her that I'd call her first thing in the morning, but she was sound asleep by then. So I pulled on my coat, just as the Hailo cab I'd ordered pulled up outside and the driver texted me to say he'd arrived.

I was halfway out the hall door, with Lauren following behind, when her mobile rang. She answered it quickly and quietly I noticed, taking great care to cover her phone, so I couldn't see who it was that was calling her.

'Yes? Yes, speaking,' she said clearly. 'OK. I understand. Well, the main thing is not to panic. I need you to say nice and calm for me, OK? Now just give me the address of wherever you are and I'll come and get you right away. No, I won't say a word to anyone, I promise.'

'What was all that about?' I asked suspiciously as soon as she'd ended the call.

'Oh, nothing for you to worry about,' Lauren replied calmly, giving absolutely nothing away.

'Didn't sound like nothing to me.'

'Like I said, it's personal,' she said firmly, in such a totally different tone of voice that it caught my attention. She sound flintier and more hard-edged; far from the simpering, obliging 'lovely girl' act she'd kept up all night. 'Now look, your taxi is here. You'd better not keep him waiting.'

'Can I drop you off anywhere?' I asked on my way out the door.

'There's no need, thanks. I'll get a late bus home.'

'Well, I could at least drop you off at the bus stop.'

'It's absolutely fine,' she said with great finality, pointedly waiting at the hall door for me to leave. 'There's just something I need to take care of first, that's all.'

'You're a real girl of mystery, aren't you, Lauren?' I said right to her face as I gathered up my bag to leave. Which sounded a bit catty I know, but by then the wine had dulled my senses to the point where I was beyond giving a shite.

'I think you've had quite a lot to drink tonight, Liz,' she replied coolly. 'And it's probably rude to keep your taxi driver waiting for very much longer.'

I couldn't think of a smart enough answer to lob back at her though, so Madam waited and watched while I walked down the driveway, clambered into the taxi and zipped off. I swear, I could actually feel her eyes burning into the back of my head, making doubly sure that I was really on my way.

What Lauren didn't know though was that pissed and all as I was, I was still a step ahead of her.

'I know this sounds a bit unusual,' I said to the driver, 'but would you mind just driving around the block, then coming back to this house again?'

'What did you say, love?' said the driver, looking at me through the rear-view mirror, mystified.

'Please,' I insisted. 'There's just something I need to check on, if you don't mind.'

He must have thought I was insane, but he still did as I asked. One lap around the block later and there it was, the concrete proof that I needed that Lauren was far from the innocent little ingénue she seemed.

By the time we drove back, she was climbing into the driver's seat of Sarah's car, starting up the engine and quickly zipping off.

I saw it clear as day, with my own two eyes.

I shouted at her, yelled, even got my taxi man to follow her for as far as he could. For all the good it did me. She was just too fast for us. After three streets, we lost her. Gone, just disappeared clean into the night.

Chapter Thirteen

Darcy

Darcy couldn't quite remember what happened next or in what order. Everything seemed to be moving at speed and suddenly she found herself on her own with Tony Scott, wedged up against the bathroom wall, with the door locked firmly from the inside.

'You look hot tonight,' he started to say, but even though her head was pounding, Darcy could sense the lie. Tony had barely looked twice at her for the entire evening; was she really expected to think he was suddenly interested in her now, out of nowhere?

'Look,' she began, trying to shove him away from her. 'I don't know what Abi has said to you, but—'

'She told me you were totally up for it,' he said, kissing her sloppily and clamping his hands onto her boobs. But there was absolutely nothing gentle or romantic about it, like Darcy had imagined in her head so many times. Instead he was rough and coarse and he tasted like stale beer.

'Tony, please stop it . . .'

She really didn't feel well. Whatever concoction had been

in that bloody water bottle Abi gave her earlier was seriously tipping her over the edge.

'Oh now, come on,' he said, moving his hand lower down, fumbling at her jeans and pressing her tightly up against the bathroom door. 'No one wants to be a virgin, not at your age. Just relax for fuck's sake and enjoy.'

'Tony . . . no . . . stop it . . . *please!*'

Just then, there was a loud, insistent hammering on the door outside.

'Hurry up in there, would you? Some of us are bursting for a pee out here!'

'Coming! I'm just coming,' Darcy yelled back, grabbing at the chance to shove Tony off her, unlock the door and make her escape. She felt wobbly, woozy and dangerously close to throwing up. But to her utter relief, when she opened the bathroom door, there was Sophie's pale face looking worriedly back at her.

'Jesus,' Sophie said, taking her in from head to foot. 'What the hell was going on in there anyway?'

Darcy turned back to Tony, who was standing unsteadily on his feet by then, with his zip down and the front of his jocks clearly showing. Her vision was starting to go a bit blurry, but glancing down at herself she saw that her own jeans were undone and her knickers were clearly on view.

'Sophie,' she said, leaning forwards to grab onto her pal's arm and almost losing her footing. 'I don't feel very well—' she tried to say, but it was too late. Next thing, she'd slumped down on the carpeted floor and thrown up all over herself.

*

Memory blackouts. She must have been having actual, proper memory blackouts, that was the only explanation for it. Fragments of snippets of conversation kept filtering back to her, with one constant at the centre of it all. And that was Sophie's voice, rising in decibels the more panicky she became.

'Shit, Darcy? Darcy, can you hear me? Come on, open your eyes!'

'Don't know what that prissy little virgin is play-acting about,' she could hear Tony saying, clear as a bell. 'One minute we were having a bit of fun, next minute she was acting like I was trying to rape her or something. Fucking idiot.'

'You're the idiot, Tony Scott!' she heard Sophie yell back at him. 'Now just help me get her downstairs!'

Then Darcy felt herself being lugged all the way down the stairs, each and every bump bringing on a fresh wave of nausea. More pulling, more tugging, more panicky voices filtering back to her.

'Jesus, Abi, what did you give the girl!'

'Look at the state of her—'

'Will somebody get her out of my parents' house, for fuck's sake . . . she's already vomited on the carpet upstairs and now I'll have to clean it up!'

Then came Abi's voice, clear as crystal.

'I don't know what you're all looking at me for. She only had a few vodkas, that's it. It's hardly my fault if some people can't hold their drink, now is it?'

'I think we need an ambulance,' someone else said, sounding completely freaked out.

'No, grab her phone!' Sophie cried out as Darcy felt herself being hauled out to the front garden. 'There has to be someone in her contacts list we can call for help!'

It was freezing outside, and the sharp Spring chill seemed

to sober Darcy up a little and snap her back to reality again.

'No,' she groaned weakly, suddenly aware that they'd put her stretched out on the grass and that the wetness of it was beginning to soak through her jeans. 'Don't call my mum, whatever you do,' she pleaded with Sophie, in between fresh waves of nausea. 'She can't see me like this.'

'Listen to me,' Sophie said, gripping both her shoulders. 'We need to get you out of here and get you sober. Have you any money for a taxi? I spent all mine in that shagging bar.'

'Will you check in my bag?' Darcy croaked, slumping back against the grass. Sophie did, but there wasn't a single euro left. Served her right for buying a round of those revolting cocktails in the Palace Bar earlier with a borrowed fake ID.

'Then we need someone to come and collect us,' said Sophie, thinking on her feet. 'Someone who won't go squawking either to your mum or to mine. But who? Who can we trust?'

'What about your older brother?' said Darcy feebly, remembering vaguely something Sophie said earlier about having a brother studying medicine, whose high grades she was expected to live up to.

'Not a hope,' said Sophie. 'He's away at a college ball tonight and he'll be more trashed than you are. No offence.'

There was none taken. Darcy was far too grateful to have someone here by her side, actually helping her. Unlike her so-called best friend Abi, who seemed to have disappeared back into the party the minute she'd made a show of herself.

'I know,' said Darcy, the thought striking her from out of nowhere. 'Lauren.'

'Who the hell is Lauren?' asked Sophie, puzzled.

'She's . . . well . . . she's sort of a friend of Mum's . . . at least, my mum is helping her out at the minute. She's pretty cool. At least, I think we can trust her.'

'Do you have her number?'

'In my phone,' Darcy said, suddenly remembering that she'd added Lauren to her list of contacts earlier that evening.

*

Exactly twenty minutes later, Lauren pulled up outside the front garden in Sarah's mum's neat little Nissan and both girls clambered in.

'You're a lifesaver,' Darcy slurred at Lauren, making a silent vow never, ever to get herself into a state like this again.

'If your mum gets to hear about this . . .' Lauren said warningly.

'Did you say anything to her?' said Darcy, as panic shot through her. 'Because if she ever finds out—'

'Relax,' said Lauren firmly. 'I left her snoozing peacefully on the sofa at home. She's out for the count and she knows absolutely nothing about any of this. Because if she did—'

But Darcy interrupted.

'You wouldn't, would you? You wouldn't tell on me? Not if I faithfully promise this will never happen again?'

Lauren didn't answer though, just pulled the car up at a set of red traffic lights.

'The question now is, ladies,' she said, 'where am I going to take you?'

It was unspoken between the three of them, but going back home was out of the question.

'If Mum sees the state I'm in,' Darcy groaned, feeling a

fresh wave of bile rising at the back of her throat, 'I can kiss goodbye to getting past the front door till I'm at least forty.'

'My house,' Sophie piped up from the back seat of the car. 'Why don't we go back to mine? Think about it,' she added, as both Darcy and Lauren's heads pivoted around to her. 'That way, you can sleep it off, sober up and then be good as new tomorrow morning when your mum comes to collect you.'

'What about your own parents?' Lauren asked.

'They should be sound asleep by now,' said Sophie. 'But as long as we don't wake them up when we go in, I promise they should be OK about this. Oh, and they might drag us both off to Mass first thing in the morning, but right now, that's the least of our worries.'

'All right then,' Lauren said, sliding the car into gear. 'Give me your address, and let's go.'

As it turned out, Sophie's wasn't too far away, and within half an hour, Darcy was tiptoeing up the stairs and climbing into the spare bed in Sophie's room, while Lauren made her gulp back two paracetamol she had in her bag along with a large bottle of water.

'I don't know how to thank you,' Darcy croaked at her, feeling a bit better already, more like herself. 'This is the second time you've saved my bacon.'

'Happy to do it,' said Lauren.

'And you faithfully promise me you won't say a single word to Mum?'

'I faithfully promise.'

'Is that a deal?'

'You can trust me,' said Lauren, with a smile that was hard to read, although Darcy couldn't figure out why.

'It'll just be our little secret.'

APRIL

Chapter Fourteen

Sarah

Last Spring, there was very little I couldn't have told you about the ins and outs of Ireland's recent case-law history and all manner of legal judgments I'd barely looked at since leaving college myself. By Easter, I could almost have taken a test in it. I'd insisted on prepping Lauren so thoroughly for the intern's job at Sloan Curtis that at one point I actually went to bed dreaming about corporation tax law and you name it versus whoever, 2009.

'You know, you're going to an awful lot of bother over this beautician mate of yours, whoever she is,' Harry sniffed at me over the top of his computer one day in the office. 'For feck's sake, Sarah, we've got our pick of Trinity and UCD graduates to choose from.'

'I know.'

'So why are you so insistent that this Lauren one get the gig? You know as well as I do that all she'll end up doing is photocopying and making coffee.'

'Harry, I'm asking you to trust me,' I told him firmly. 'Believe me, this girl really is something special. She just needs a helping hand right now and think of how great you'll feel knowing that you'll have changed a young woman's whole life for the better?'

'If you ask me,' he said, shrugging and turning back to the screen on the desk in front of him, 'she'd make more money working in that kip of a beauty parlour you found her in. At least she's getting cash tips in there.'

'Oh ye of little faith,' I said mockingly, smug and secure in the knowledge that Lauren would knock this job interview right out of the park. Besides, I thought, the only reason why Harry was prejudiced against the girl was because by then Liz had developed a right flea in her ear as regards Lauren.

It all dated back to that night a few weeks back when I'd let Darcy out to a party with some of her pals from school. Lauren was in the house too, when Liz called around for a takeaway and a big Saturday night gossip, as she regularly did. But when I conked out on the sofa after a glass of wine too many, it seemed Liz had got herself worked herself up into an irrational temper at what happened next.

Not wanting to disturb my girls' night in, and not having enough money on her for a taxi, apparently Darcy had called Lauren looking for a lift back to her friend's house. The following morning when all this came to light, I gave out yards to her for not ringing me first, but part of me could at least understand where the poor kid was coming from.

'But Mum, it was your Saturday night with Liz,' Darcy pleaded to me, 'and I didn't want to ruin that for you. So I called Lauren instead, thinking maybe she could take a cab to come and pick me up. What's wrong with that?'

Nothing, except that Lauren had taken it on herself to borrow my car. Liz had seen this happening right under her nose and had now 'taken agin' poor old Lauren over it.

'Please understand it's just that you were sleeping so soundly,' Lauren explained to me during the whole steward's inquiry that followed. 'And I was only gone for twenty minutes max. I'm so sorry, Sarah, but the last thing I wanted to do was either to wake you or worry you. I just didn't have the heart. So I acted on the spur of the moment, that's all. I dropped Darcy safely off to her friend's house, then left your car and your keys exactly as I'd found them, before I let myself out again. You'd had such a long week and you were snoozing away so peacefully on the sofa, I really thought it would have been a sin to disturb you.'

And when I collected Darcy at her friend Sophie's house the next day, all was well. True, Darcy was a bit fragile, but as she explained to me, 'it was just that the party went on a lot later than I'd thought, Mum. Plus I'm exhausted after studying so hard for the exams, that's all that's wrong with me.'

So what was the problem? Nothing, except that Liz had now decided that poor, well-meaning Lauren was the most insanely ambitious little thing to come on the scene since Madonna, circa her 1990's Blonde Ambition tour.

'You've done quite enough for that one as it is,' she told me darkly. 'So if you take my advice, you'll just walk away and let her find her own way in the world from here. Trust me Sarah, Lauren is one of those people that if you give her an inch, she'll take a mile. So I'm urging you to cut the ties now, because I have the most horrible feeling you'll regret it if you don't.'

I didn't understand her though or at least, I certainly chose not to. By Easter, as far as I was concerned, Lauren was a bright young woman who needed a leg up in life, and I was in a position to give it. So how could anyone with even half a heart possibly have a problem with that?

*

In the days leading up to Lauren's big interview at Sloan Curtis, I had taken to asking her over to our house on the evenings when she wasn't working late, so I could give her a mock interview at the kitchen table.

Easier said than done though, as generally Darcy would dance in and out demanding to know exactly how Lauren did smoky eye make-up or else begging for a proper, professional gel manicure. I'd jokingly chide her for disturbing us, but truth be told, it did my heart good to see both girls getting on so famously.

And Lauren was a super-fast learner. It was almost as though she had a photographic memory when it came to case studies and the intricacies of Company and Taxation Law. So much so that by the weekend before her interview, I honestly thought she was good to go.

'You really think I'm ready?' she asked, biting her lip worriedly. 'It's been so long since I studied case histories like this.'

'Lauren,' I told her, as I packed away the mountain of legal briefs and notes that were piled up on my kitchen table, 'your qualifications are top class, you're word perfect and as far as I'm concerned, the job is already in the bag. It's Bernie, the boss-man you've got to impress and win over at this interview, not me. To be perfectly honest though, I think Sloan Curtis will be the lucky ones to get you, not the other way around.'

'There really are no words for me to thank you,' she said

feelingly, getting up to her feet and tidying away the remains of the fork supper we'd just had. But then that was another thing I loved about Lauren. The fact that no matter how hard I tried, there was just no stopping the girl from constantly wanting to help out around the house. Like a very glamorous cleaning lady, albeit one I didn't have to pay.

Sometimes this involved cleaning away the debris of a cobbled-together late-night supper or sometimes she'd whip out a mop and bucket and insist on giving the floor a good going over. Once I even came home from a work meeting that ran over to find her mowing the lawn out the back.

Not only that, but it turned out Lauren was something of a maths whizz and, more than once, she'd give Darcy an unofficial grind if she was struggling with her homework. All while holding down a full-time, poorly paid job in a dingy beauty salon. Was there nothing this superwoman couldn't do?

The Saturday before her interview, however, I thought there was just one tiny little thing that I could do for her in return.

'Your clothes,' I said to her firmly.

'Oh. Right,' she said, blushing and pulling at the plain black crew necked jumper she was wearing along with a pair of leggings. It was an outfit I'd seen on her a hundred times and, to put it delicately, it had seen better days.

'You need something new to wear to the interview,' I told her. 'Something that will really impress.'

'I'm afraid money is a bit tight for me just now,' she said, biting her lip reluctantly, 'but maybe I could stretch the budget to a new blouse from Penny's.'

'Nothing against Penny's best,' I said, 'but I think we can afford to push the boat out a bit here.'

'Oh Sarah,' she protested, 'I really wish I could, but I just don't have enough spare cash.'

'Lauren, listen to me,' I told her, not taking no for an answer. 'You're going to be competing against the top graduates from all over the country. These people are the crème de la crème and they're going to swan into our office looking the absolute biz. And so, my dear, will you. I'm taking you shopping and that's all there is to it.'

'Makeover! Cool, can I come too?' Darcy chimed in, like an eager little puppy. 'If I say so myself, I'm really good at makeovers. I did my friend Sophie last week and everyone in my class said she went from looking like she just fell out of bed to an out-and-out Kardashian. Minus the curvy arse, of course, but then you can't have everything.'

So I drove the pair of them into Grafton St and we had the most blissfully fun, girlie afternoon, even if I did have to practically strong-arm Lauren into the more swish, upmarket stores like BT2's and Ted Baker. She kept insisting she couldn't afford a thing, but I wouldn't take no for an answer. Darcy worked tirelessly as her unofficial stylist and completely unprompted, managed to find a neat, gorgeous little work suit from Reiss in a beautiful shade of coral that according to her was 'so hot right now'.

Together we forced Lauren to try it on and when she came out of the fitting room, I'm not kidding, it seemed like every eye in the store turned around to gawp at this vision in red.

'Wow,' I said, as Lauren reluctantly paraded in front of us, her pretty face flushing the exact colour of the suit at the amount of attention she was getting on the shop floor. 'You're breathtaking! Just look at you,' I added, gripping Lauren by her skinny little shoulders and turning her around to face a giant, oversized mirror just behind. 'You're a goddess. Eat your heart out, Pippa Middleton.'

'You really need to have your gorgeous, dark hair to work a colour like that,' Darcy nodded approvingly, whipping out her phone. 'Now gimme a big smile, Lauren. I'm so Instagramming you right now. Just think, Mum, today could be the start of my whole career as a professional stylist!'

It really was the most magical afternoon, even if I did have to nearly arm-wrestle Lauren to the floor just so I could hand over my credit card to pay for the suit.

'I can't let you do this, Sarah,' she insisted, 'not after you've been so kind to me already. It would be wrong.'

'Think of this as an advance payment on your very first salary,' I said, crisply handing over my card.

'And think of all the times I let Mum buy me clothes and I never end up looking half as good as you do.' Darcy laughed. 'Besides, this can be like part-payment for all the free beauty tips you give me.'

'In that case,' Lauren said, with tears – actual tears – of gratitude shining in her eyes, 'you must promise to let me pay you back, Sarah. And with interest.'

'Just go into that job interview on Monday morning,' I told her, as the sales assistant wrapped the suit in crisp tissue paper, 'and nail it. Do it for me. Go in there and own the room. That's all I ask.'

We were all in such high spirits, that to make the day even more special, I treated Lauren and Darcy to a gorgeous lunch in Peploe's restaurant, just a stone's throw from us at the top of Stephen's Green. Feck it anyway, I thought. Days like that didn't come along very often and besides, that's what God made credit cards for.

'We're almost acting like you've got the job already,' Darcy giggled as the three of us slid into a banquette-style booth and ordered.

'Here's hoping,' Lauren smiled, with a shy little wink in my direction. Then raising nothing stronger than a glass of fizzy water, she added, 'and here's to your wonderful mother. The kindest, wisest and most generous lady I've ever met. I hope you realise, Darcy, just how blessed you are to have a mother like this in your life? So cherish her. Love her everyday. And appreciate what rare diamonds the Sarah Keyes of this world truly are.'

At her little impromptu speech, I found myself welling up a bit. This poor girl, I thought, who'd lost everything and everyone dear to her. Who had no mother of her own to mind her and to spoil her every now and then and even buy her a new suit when she needed one.

When, I found myself wondering, was the last time someone did this extraordinary soul a kindness?

Chapter Fifteen

Liz

Of course Madam Lauren not only went into her interview at Sloan Curtis, but, according to Sarah, absolutely aced it.

'Oh Liz, I only wish you could have seen her!' she gushed down the phone to me afterwards. 'Lauren absolutely batted it out of the park. I couldn't have been more proud of her. She strode into our conference room just brimming over with confidence and looking a million dollars—'

'In the brand-new suit you went out and bought for her, I suppose?' I quipped.

'Of course she was wearing the new suit,' said Sarah, a bit defensively. 'That's why I bought it for her. It's a *work* suit.'

'Hmmm,' is all I said in reply.

'Anyway, I think Bernie and Harry hardly knew what hit them,' she chatted away, oblivious to my tone, or at least, pretending to be. 'Lauren was just fabulous. She spoke so persuasively about what she felt she could bring to the firm and even had a few extra suggestions as to how we could get the most out of an intern here. And they were all ideas that she'd come up with herself, not just stuff that I'd spoon-fed her beforehand. She talked about the possibility of sitting in on case conferences so interns would automatically be up to speed without us having to brief them all the time. And not only that, but she was even fully prepped on some cases we've got coming down the line. Oh Liz, I couldn't have been more proud of my little protégée!'

'And what about getting her out of that dingy salon she works in? Will that be a problem, do you think?'

'A problem?' Sarah laughed. 'Are you joking me? It'll be a fecking pleasure. The happy day Lauren goes in there to tell them where to shove their job, I want to be there. I want a front row seat. She's such a hard worker, Liz, and she really *wants* this. We're lucky to have here at the firm. And I know she'll shine here. I can just feel it.'

I could feel something too, but it certainly wasn't gushing happiness for Madam Lauren, I can tell you.

Needless to say, I grilled Harry about it the minute he fell in through our hall door later on that night. I was in between refereeing a fight between Middle Child and Younger Child when he finally got home. (One of the joys of having two sons is that you realise how capable they are of having a blood feud lasting well into the next generation and beyond, over a single oven chip.)

'What interview are you talking about?' Harry yawned, loosening his tie and making straight for the leftovers of the kids' M&S fish pie dinner, eating it straight off the plate with a used fork.

'Harry! You know perfectly well what I'm talking about. The job for the intern that Sarah wants her New Best Friend to land.'

Pointless my trying to get a balanced answer out of Sarah; back then, she saw everything through Lauren-coloured glasses.

'Oh yeah, Lauren something,' Harry shrugged, with his mouth half full. 'The good-looking one.'

'You think she's good-looking?'

'She's OK, I suppose. Certainly she did a great interview. Full of ideas and suggestions. Seemed eager to learn.'

'And what about all the other candidates? Was there anyone else there who stood out?' Although what I really wanted to know was whether or not Lauren had any serious rivals for the job.

'Ahh, you know yourself,' Harry said, continuing to shovel food straight into his gob. 'We'd a gangload of graduates in, all the usual suspects. Jesus, is this really meant to be fish pie? It's disgusting,' he added, spitting out the remnants of the kids' dinner.

'And what were they like?'

'Who?'

'Harry!' I said impatiently. 'All the other people you interviewed! Surely there was someone there more suited to the job than Lauren?'

I can't quite put my finger on why I was so dead-set against her getting the gig. All I knew is that I had a bad feeling, a constriction around my chest, a tightness when I went to breathe. Like something very, very bad was about to happen and there was damn all I could do to stop it.

'I suppose the other interviewees were all much of a muchness, really,' he shrugged, bending down to cuddle Max, our Labrador and to feed him the left-overs straight off the plate. 'You know the type. All first- and second-class honours graduates who'd probably seen one episode too

145

many of *The Good Wife* and who thought they were on the brink of joining Lockhart/Gardner.'

I nodded, knowing exactly what he meant. It happened a lot with interns; I'd seen it for myself many times before. They do well in college, then can't understand why they're not working in the Supreme Court on high-profile criminal law cases immediately after they graduate. They may have first-class law degrees coming out of their ears but completely failed to understand that in some professions you have to start at the bottom and work your way up.

'At least that Lauren one is well aware of the limitations of the job in advance,' Harry went on, as the dog slobbered all over him, wagging his tail excitedly. 'Plus she doesn't seem above running out to the coffee shop and doing the odd bit of legwork for us when we need her to.'

'I see,' I said darkly. 'So in other words, you're saying Lauren's as good as got the gig, then.'

'If Sarah has anything to do with it,' Harry said, while the dog greedily licked his face, 'then the job is already hers.'

*

About a week later, my darkest suspicions were confirmed. Because of course Lauren landed the job; according to Sarah, it was a complete no-brainer. And not only that, but she even managed to wangle herself an invitation to the thirtieth-anniversary party too.

To explain, Sloan Curtis were celebrating thirty years in business and to mark the occasion, Bernie Curtis, my one-time boss and esteemed colleague was hosting a 'bit of a do' for all his clients and co-workers.

Bernie, however, was one of those employers who had absolutely no difficulty in splashing the cash on himself and his exotic holidays, but was well-known to be the scab-biest tight-arse since Scrooge when it came to his employees. So rather than go to the bother and expense of hosting a dinner in a posh restaurant like a normal person, instead he went for the more budget-friendly option of 'drinks and nibbles' at the office after work, one Friday evening.

'Looks like it'll be a lovely party,' Sarah told me over our usual takeaway feed/bitching session the previous Saturday night.

'Plus it looks like it won't cost old scab-arse more than a few hundred euros,' was my clipped response.

And naturally, Lauren was due to be there.

'Of course she's invited,' Sarah smiled. 'We'll be setting up a bar in one corner of the conference room and Lauren has very kindly agreed to circulate with some nibbly, picky things for our guests. Antipasti, you know, that sort of thing.'

'Hmmm,' was all I said, but it was enough for Sarah to pick up on.

'What's with the tone?' she asked innocently, as she played with a tendril of her fair hair.

'What are you talking about?' I blinked back.

'Whenever I mention Lauren's name, your whole face pinches up and you take on that narky tone.'

'Do not.'

'Yes you do, and you know it,' she said, sitting back at the kitchen table. 'Come on Liz, don't you trust me?'

'Course I do.'

'Well then, why can't you trust me about Lauren and just cut the girl a bit of slack? She's barely even started in the office and already I don't know how we managed without her. Nothing is too much trouble for her and no matter what I ask her to do, she does it with a big, bright

147

smile on her face. So come Friday night, I want to see you really giving her a chance. Deal?'

'OK,' I sighed reluctantly. 'Deal.'

*

And come the big night, there she was. Lauren. Front and centre.

Looking a million dollars too, though it choked me to admit it. She was dressed in a long, flowing maxi-dress in a vivid purple patterned colour, which really did look sensational against that flawless, deep caramel skin. All the other women there were dressed in various shades of black, navy, grey. Work colours, as most people had come directly from their own offices. So Lauren automatically stood out amongst them as she glided around the place, like some sort of exotic, colourful butterfly.

We were all stuffed into the Sloan Curtis conference room, which was packed to the gills with clients and their partners who'd just nipped in for a quick drink to kick-start the weekend. One of those functions where you never intend to stay for too long, but somehow by nine pm, it was still chockablock full of guests happily mixing and mingling as the Prosecco continued to flow.

Everyone seemed in high spirits, gossiping and chatting away while Lauren circulated with various trays of pecorino cheese, crudités with hummus and smoked salmon with goat's cheese crostini. I don't know how she did it, but the girl seemed to be everywhere at once, always smiling, always 'on', her energy never once flagging. Every now and then I'd spot Sarah whisper little words of encouragement in her ear. Not only that, but she was also busy introducing Lauren to just about every client the firm had.

'Lauren's just started here as our new intern,' I overheard her saying to Tony McGettigan, one of the firm's big corporate clients. 'And we're all absolutely thrilled with her. I think you'll be seeing and hearing a lot more from this girl in the future Tony, so you'd better watch out.'

Bernie Curtis, the boss-man was there of course, permatanned and glowing from his latest weekend away to God-knows where. In fact he was away so often, at one stage Harry and I had him pegged as some sort of tax exile.

'So Bernie,' I asked him, as a passing waiter topped up my glass of Prosecco, 'how are you finding her?'

'How am I finding who?' he asked absently, glancing down at his watch and doubtless wondering how soon he and his wife could reasonably slip off.

'Your new intern,' I said and on cue, Lauren, laden down with a tray of nibbles, weaved her way past a group of clients from Simpson Hotels who were all clustered together down the far end of the room. Bernie's eye automatically followed her, as did mine.

But then it was impossible not to stare at the girl, though it killed me to say it. There was just something about her poise and grace in that brightly coloured long dress that automatically drew your eye to her. For a moment or two Bernie and I just stood watching at her as she mingled and laughed, swishing her glossy mane of hair over her shoulders. At one point she offered to get some fresh glasses of fizz for a few clients who'd mislaid their glasses, even though there were plenty of bar staff on hand whose explicit job it was to take care of that.

'Oh, you mean *Lauren*,' said Bernie, as if he was really only noticing her now for the first time all evening. 'Sarah's new protégé. Lovely, isn't she?'

149

'Do you think she's working out here?' I asked him straight up.

'You know, it's a strange thing,' said Bernie thoughtfully. 'We've been through so many interns in the past and there's almost a law of diminishing returns with each and every one. The more highly qualified they are, the more they consider the job beneath them. Not this young lady though. She's only just started and yet it almost feels as if she's part of the furniture. Does that make sense?'

It did. Perfect sense. If there was ever anyone with a gift for inveigling themselves into their surroundings, it was Madam Lauren.

Then, not long after came an alarm bell that no one could miss, not even a blinkered optimist who only saw the good in people like my dearest pal, Sarah Keyes. It was about an hour later and I was just working my way over to Harry. I could tell by the expression on his face that he was slowly being bored out of his wits by one particular client well-known for only having one single topic of conversation – his golf handicap. I was squeezing through a group from Simpson Hotels, who were by then all high as kites after God knows many Proseccos. And as it happened, Lauren was standing beside them, ostensibly handing out canapés but taking great care, I couldn't help noticing, to tune in to their entire conversation.

'Hello there, how are you?' I said to Jim Simpson, chairman of Simpson Hotels and a long-standing client of the firm who I knew very well from my working days. At the office, we'd always had Jim pegged as a bit of a Lothario; he'd divorced years ago and was apparently now dating a string of glamour models and wannabe telly presenters. He was never out of the gossip columns – it was nigh on impossible to open a tabloid without a snap of Jim's Boris Johnson-blonde barnet looking back at you, generally with a babe hanging off his arm.

'Ahh Liz, great to see you again, how are all the family?' he asked, as we fell into an easy, relaxed chat. But then that was part of Jim's charm; he remembered things about you. Plus when he focused on you, he had the rare knack of making you feel like you really were the only woman in the room.

Next thing I was aware of, Lauren was beside me, hovering right at my shoulder with a tray of sausage rolls and seemingly in no rush to go anywhere. Standing there, just waiting to be introduced.

'Have you met Lauren?' I said to Jim, mainly because I had no choice; the girl was practically breathing down my neck by then. Jim politely shook her hand then eyed her up and down as she flashed him her biggest, brightest smile.

'It's a real pleasure to meet you, Mr Simpson,' she beamed. 'I've just started to work here and I've already heard so much about you. With all due respect sir, you seem to be a favourite client among the partners here at Sloan Curtis.'

Jim seemed flattered by this, but then who wouldn't be? A beautiful young woman, batting her eyelashes at him, Princess Diana-style? For a middle-aged egomaniac like Jim, he probably thought he'd died and gone to Heaven. At this point though, my stomach was starting to heave and I could take no more of Lauren. So I consciously turned away to chat to a few of the gang from Simpson Hotels, who I hadn't seen in years and who were full of gossip and chat and funny stories.

We had a great old catch-up and it must have been a good ten minutes later before I finally turned back to Jim and Lauren. What I overheard though, gave me an instant shiver right the way down my spine.

'So I understand you've got a big contract law case pending?' Lauren was saying intently. 'It's just that I had some thoughts about it I'd really like to discuss with you.'

'Feel free,' Jim smiled, barely able to lift his eyes off her boobs.

'The thing is, I'd really like to help, if I may. Because when I read up on the ins and outs of your case, I started to wonder if you're actually being given the best possible advice here.'

I froze right there on the spot. And yet that's exactly what I heard with my own two ears. Not only that, but I knew from Harry exactly what court case the little madam was referring to.

Simpson Hotels, owned by Jim and his family, had been represented by Sloan Curtis for decades and were being sued by a bride who claimed that her big day had been completely ruined by the hotel. She had cited myriad reasons via her solicitor: apparently there were no gluten-free options on the set menu, the power blew half way through the DJ's set during the reception and the happy couple had the bill for the entire shindig shoved under their door – at 5am the morning after the night before.

According to Harry, it was widely acknowledged within the firm that Jim Simpson would just have to dig deep into his pockets and settle at some point. But the way our legal system worked, it was all being drawn out via a mountain of lawyer's letters full of legalese, which might possibly go on for months, years even.

'Oh now, come on, Lauren,' said Jim, rolling his eyes.

'Please don't talk to me about work. You know, I'd far rather ask you what you're doing after we leave here. How about a late drink back at my club? It's just around the corner, if you were up for it.'

'I heard you're being encouraged to settle out of court,' Lauren smiled, ignoring the fact that the guy was plainly hitting on her.

'Well, yeah, but its not really a night to talk about work, now is it?' said Jim.

'The thing is you see, I completely disagree with the advice the partners here are giving you,' said Lauren quietly, but oh-so firmly. 'I don't believe you need to settle this case at all. You can fight this, Jim, and we can fight this for you. In fact I've been reading up on all your case files and I think I know exactly how you we can strategically argue a better, more solid defense for the Simpson Hotel Group.'

'Lauren,' I pointedly interrupted her, horrified at what I was hearing. 'Could I have a quick word with you, please?'

She looked directly back at me, unflinching.

'Can't it just wait for a moment?' she smiled sweetly.

'No, I'm afraid it can't,' I said, taking her firmly by the arm and steering her away from Jim and over to a quiet corner, where I was sure she and I wouldn't be overheard.

'Is there a problem?' she asked innocently, once she and I were alone, just outside the lift bank in the hallway outside.

'Lauren,' I said, folding my arms and deliberately trying to keep my tone cool. 'Are you off your head? Did I really overhear you giving legal advice to a long-standing client of this firm?'

'Yes,' she said calmly, smoothing down a non-existent

153

crease in the front of her dress. 'Because that's my job, isn't it? To give the best advice possible.'

'You as good as admitted that the advice Jim Simpson has been given to date isn't good enough. Advice he's been given from the very people you've just started to work for. Senior partners like Harry and Sarah, for feck's sake! Don't attempt to deny it, I heard you with my own two ears.'

'It's my considered opinion that Sloan Curtis can do better for Simpson Hotels, that's all,' she replied calmly.

'Have you any idea how out of line you are?' I half spluttered back at her, stunned at how unapologetic she was being about the whole thing. 'You're barely here five minutes and now you're undermining senior partners? Harry and Sarah have spent years working to build up a relationship with a client like Simpson Hotels! And you seriously think it's OK for you to just swan in and undercut all of that? Who exactly do you think you are?'

'I'm afraid I don't see what your problem is, Liz,' she replied, with an insincere little smile that never quite reached her eyes. 'My job is to represent clients to the best of my ability and that's all I'm doing. Surely you can't criticise me for that? For doing my job?'

'You're hired to work here as an *intern*,' I snapped back, actually wanting to smack her right across that smug little face. 'And now you're suddenly behaving like a senior partner who's been here for years! What in God's name gives you the right to do that?'

'That's not the case at all—'

'I think it's no harm for you to know your place, Lauren,' I told her with what I hoped was great finality, as I turned on my heel and moved away to rejoin the party.

I had to get away from her. If I'd stayed one more minute, I swear I'd have done the girl actual, physical harm.

'And I think it's no harm for you to know yours,' was her immediate comeback. I was halfway back into the buzz of the conference room with my back turned to her, but there was no way I misheard.

'Excuse me?' I said, turning around. '*What* did you just say?'

'Nothing,' Lauren said coolly, looking me straight in the face. 'I just feel that it's . . . let's just say inappropriate for someone who doesn't even work here to start telling me how I can or can't behave in an office situation.'

'May I remind you that I worked here for almost ten years?' I almost spat back at her.

'But you don't work here any more, do you, Liz?' she said. 'You were honest with me, so it's my turn to be honest with you in return. And I'd appreciate it if you didn't tell me how to do my job. After all, I don't come around to your house and tell you how to be a full-time homemaker. I don't hammer on your front door and start telling you how to pack school lunches and wipe your kids' bums, now do I?'

And with that, she smoothed down her hair before slipping back to the party to rejoin Jim Simpson and his cohorts. Cool as a breeze and with a smile on her face, like she and I had been having a chat about nothing more innocuous than the vegetarian vol-au-vents.

In a hot temper, I stalked off, nabbed Sarah away from a group of corporate clients then hauled her off to the privacy of the ladies so I could relay the conversation back to her word for word.

If I'd expected outrage and shock though, I was bitterly

155

disappointed. Instead, Sarah just folded her arms and looked at me worriedly.

'Oh, come on Liz,' she said wearily, rubbing her eyes, 'isn't this getting a little old? All this constant Lauren-bashing?'

'What are you talking about?' I fumed. 'The girl was unspeakably rude to me just now. So why aren't you as incensed as I am?'

'OK, so maybe she crossed a line,' Sarah went on, 'and I'll certainly speak to her about that. But she's young and she's hungry. Don't you remember when you and I were like that when we first started here? Come on, Liz, don't you remember what it was like to be young and hungry?'

*

After the crowd began to peter out, I was still in a righteous temper and wanted nothing more than to drag Harry back home and tell him everything. At least he'd listen to me. He'd understand; somehow he always did.

Instead though, Harry seemed determined to stay out as late as possible, taking full advantage of the fact that we had a babysitter on a Friday night, so he could actually enjoying a rare evening free of kids.

'How about we go on somewhere else, then?' he said to Sarah and me, his big red face flushed even redder from one glass of Prosecco too many. 'There's a new Italian restaurant just around the corner I'd love to try. Who fancies a late bite?'

'Actually, that's not a bad idea,' I said, welcoming the chance to talk to him and Sarah alone, outside of those four walls. I needed to vent, to rant and rave, to pick over everything that had happened and to hopefully bash some sense into Sarah once and for all, preferably with Harry's back-up.

But when the three of us did a final check of the now-empty conference room to make sure the place was cleared and to switch out the lights, wouldn't you know it, Madam Lauren was still in situ. We found her tidying away the debris of uneaten food and piling up dirty glasses for the caterers to come and collect.

'Oh, just look at you, Lauren,' Sarah said, shaking her head, pretend-annoyed. 'Still slaving away, when the party is long over and everyone's gone home.'

'It's nothing,' Lauren smiled, all back to sweetness and light now that her arch-protector was in the room. 'I'm just making sure the room is ready for Monday morning, that's all.'

'We were just off for a bite to eat,' said Harry. Then a silence fell as I pointedly didn't include Lauren in our dinner plans, just pulled my coat on and got ready to leave.

'OK then, so let's move,' I eventually said, aware that everyone was looking at me.

But then my lovable, big eejit Harry had to go and open his big mouth, didn't he?

'Of course, if you'd like to join us, Lauren, you'd be more than welcome,' he said politely to a furious glare from me, which he completely failed to register.

'I'm sure Lauren has far better things to do—' I began to say.

'I'm sure you haven't eaten a scrap all day, Lauren,' Sarah said at exactly the same time.

'In that case, thank you so much,' said Lauren. 'I'd absolutely love to join you.' Then with a sly little smile in my direction, she added, 'it's so sweet of you all to include me.'

MAY

Chapter Sixteen

Darcy

Something weird had happened and Darcy didn't know whether she should tell her mum or not. And what really annoyed her was that up till then, things had actually been going reasonably well for her.

Lately she'd taken to spending a lot of her free time hanging out with Lauren and her mum, just doing normal, girlie stuff together. Shopping for clothes maybe, or the odd movie. Which might have sounded totally lame on paper, but usually ended up being the best fun imaginable.

But then, that was the strange thing about Lauren. She almost felt as much Darcy's friend as she was her mum's. Whenever the three of them were together, the age gap between them didn't seem to exist. Her mum would lighten up on nagging her when Lauren was around and as for Darcy, it was beginning to feel like she had a cool older sister to hang out with. Someone who'd seen first hand the worst side of her, and yet who still wanted to be her friend in spite of it.

She could trust Lauren too, Darcy just knew it. Ever since the night a few weeks ago at that disastrous party in

Tony Scott's house, when she'd got trashed and ended up making such a mortifying show of herself, Lauren was the one who was there for her. Lauren and another gem of a pal who Darcy had grown a lot closer to in recent weeks: Sophie.

For all that she had a reputation for being Mrs Swotty Pants, Sophie really had shown herself to be a true pal in a way that Abi most definitely wasn't. In fact, after that horrible night at the party, not only had Abi more or less dumped Darcy, but she spent the next week in school taunting her over the state she'd got herself into. As if she herself had had absolutely no hand in it whatsoever.

'Here she comes, make way for the Virgin Queen,' Abi said quite loudly and pointedly in the Fifth Year Rec Room, as Darcy came in for lunch the Monday morning after that awful night.

It had taken guts on her part to even get out of bed that day, get dressed and somehow show her face back at school in the first place. And a small part of Darcy still held out hope that maybe Abi would go easy on her. Might even apologise for pouring what tasted like weed killer down her throat for the entire night. God knows, she might even have had the cop on to step up to the plate and recognise that she herself played a pivotal part in what had happened.

The auguries hadn't been good though. Abi had ignored all of her phone calls the day after the party and hadn't as much as texted to see how Darcy was feeling, where she was or how she'd got home.

'For God's sake Darcy,' Sophie had said to her the morning after the infamous night before. 'Just think of what might have happened! Supposing I hadn't got to that bathroom door in time? Suppose that arsehole Tony Scott had pushed you a bit further? Supposing you'd drunk yourself into a coma? Supposing we didn't have Lauren to come and bail us out, then what?'

Darcy knew only too well what might have happened next. She'd seen and read all the horror stories so many times before. Her mum had drummed it into her of old. 'Whether you like it or not, love,' she was always harping on, 'you've been born into a digital age. Things can go viral in a heartbeat. So just remember every time you're out and someone points a camera phone at you, you've absolutely no control over where your image will end up.'

But that awful Monday lunchtime in the Rec Room, the whole place went deadly, pin-drop quiet. It felt to Darcy like every head had swiveled around to look first at her, then at Abi, then back to her again. And all she could do was just stand nervously with her lunch tray clamped to her hands, reddening, not having a clue what to do or where to turn.

'Such a shame some people can't even hold their drink,' Abi said mockingly, to titters from the obedient gal-squad gathered around her.

Christ, Darcy had thought. Did I really used to be a part of that gang? Up until the previous week, she'd have been invited to sit with them. She'd have been just as much a part of Abi's squad. Probably, to her shame, taunting some other eejit who Abi had decided was to be the butt of her jibes for the day.

'Darcy?' came a calm, quiet voice from behind her. Darcy turned around to see Sophie's warm, smiley face patting an empty seat beside her. 'Here, look. I kept you a seat.'

'Yeah, go on then, sit with all the other nerds and virgins,' sneered Abi as Darcy gratefully slipped in beside Sophie. 'It's where you belong, isn't it?'

'Just ignore her,' said Sophie. 'It's the only way bullies like Abi Kinsella can get any attention. By giving everyone around her a hard time.'

'You were amazing to me at the party,' Darcy told her warmly. 'Like an angel. I've no words to thank you.'

'*De nada*,' shrugged Sophie. 'But to be honest, it's that friend of your mum's you should really be thanking. Lauren, isn't it? Only for her, God knows what would have happened.'

'It's our little secret,' Lauren kept saying, whenever Darcy delicately brought up the subject with her. She probably should have let well enough alone, but somehow couldn't. She just needed to be rock-solid sure that Lauren wouldn't go blabbing to her mum. Especially not now, when she and her mum were actually getting on for the first time since the separation.

'I won't tell if you don't,' was all Lauren would say though.

Then she added something that really gave Darcy pause for thought.

'Because who knows?' she threw in casually. 'Maybe someday I'll need you to repay the favour for me.'

*

Just a few weeks later, Darcy developed a slightly sick feeling in her stomach that nothing seemed to dislodge. She couldn't possibly talk it over with her mum either – that was out of the question. Which of course only made her feel even more 'eughh' about the whole thing.

It had been a regular, ordinary Saturday morning at home and her mum had just slipped out to get some groceries before Darcy's dad was due to call over later. The plan was he'd then whisk Darcy off for the day, as it was her turn to spend the weekend at his flat.

'We can all have breakfast together before you head off, sweetheart,' had been her mum's last words before she zipped off in the car. 'How do eggs Benedict sound to you? On some lovely, fresh ciabatta toast?'

'Go for it, Mum,' said Darcy, galloping upstairs to get her stuff organized, 'I'm starving'.

'Good girl. Now you just get yourself all packed, so you're ready to go when your dad calls. He should be here in half an hour or so.'

'I'm just going to jump into the shower first, before I decide what to wear.'

'Oh God, that could take weeks then,' her mum groaned with a wry little smile.

With the house to herself, Darcy hopped into the shower and washed her hair, then a little bit earlier than she'd expected, the doorbell rang. So she threw on her dressing gown, wrapped a towel around her dripping wet head and skipped downstairs calling out, 'hold your horses, Dad, I'm coming!'

Through the glass panel in the hall door she could make out her dad's silhouette, but the weird thing was he didn't seem to be on his own. Then she heard another voice, a woman's voice. Then laughter.

'Never mind what anyone says, if it's your thing, then you should just stick to it. If biking really is your passion in life, then you hardly need to apologise for it, do you?'

It was Lauren's voice, clear as crystal. There was no mistaking it, Darcy would have known that soft, Galway accent anywhere. Then she heard her dad speak again.

165

'This beaut is the very latest model, you know. It's called the Iron 883. Now I could have gone for the Harley-Davidson Road Glide, which a lot of guys in my bike club swear by. But to me, this just has more grip on the road.'

Darcy flung the front door wide open to find that the two of them had arrived at the house at exactly the same time and were now having a great chat together on the front porch. Her dad immediately went to give her a hug, and Lauren kissed her warmly too.

'Lauren,' said Darcy in surprise. 'We weren't expecting you – thing is, I was just about to head off with Dad shortly.'

'No problem at all,' Lauren smiled. 'I only called around to drop over the McKinsey brief for your mum; she left it behind her in the office last night.'

'She's just gone shopping for breakfast stuff,' Darcy said, 'but come on in, I know she'll be delighted to see you.'

Lauren looked particularly cool today, Darcy noticed. She was dressed in a simple pair of black jeans they'd bought together in Zara the previous weekend, along with a bright-yellow crop top, which really did look the biz against her shiny dark hair.

'You ready for a weekend with your old man then, Darce?' said her dad, taking off his bike helmet as the three of them clattered their way down the hallway to the kitchen. 'It's such a fabulous day,' he chatted away, 'and the forecast for the weekend is terrific. So I thought maybe you and me could take a spin on the bike later on? Brought the spare helmet with me and everything in case I could persuade you.'

He looked hopefully at her and Darcy gave a weak little half smile as she put on the kettle to make tea for everyone, but pointedly said nothing. The last thing she wanted to do was upset the applecart, but the truth was she bloody hated her dad's motorbike with a passion and dreaded the days he tried to coax her up onto it. She was petrified of the way it lurched terrifyingly in the traffic and always tried to have a good, cast-iron excuse to hand, whenever he suggested they take a trip on it together.

'Ahh, Dad,' she said a bit weakly, 'I'll end up with helmet hair and I've only just washed it. Can't you ride the bike yourself and I'll get Mum to drop me off at your apartment instead?'

'Oh,' said her dad a bit flatly, clearly disappointed as he sat down at the kitchen table. 'It's up to you, of course, love, but I just thought as the sun is actually shining for once, maybe I could take you up to the Dublin mountains? The fresh air would do you the power of good.'

He trailed off a bit, doubtless discouraged at Darcy's total lack of enthusiasm. Then Lauren piped up.

'I have to say,' she began, taking clean mugs out of the dishwasher for the tea, knowing exactly where everything was kept in the kitchen without ever needing to be told, 'there's nothing I'd love more than a spin on a motorbike. Especially a – I'm sorry Mr Keyes, did you say it was an actual Harley-Davidson? The Iron 883?'

'Sure is,' said her dad proudly, as if he were talking about a favourite child. 'Isn't she a beaut? And by the way, the name is Tom; Mr Keyes was my dad.'

'Tom,' Lauren said, smiling sweetly back at him.

'She goes from nought to one-twenty in under thirty seconds, can you believe it?' her dad chatted away, delighted to have an appreciative audience for once. 'Now a lot of guys in my bike club prefer the Harley Roadster, because it has to be said, first gear on the 883 can be a bit rough—'

Darcy tuned out at that point and instead focused on

making a good, strong pot of tea for everyone and sticking on the Nespresso maker for her mum. But then just about anything to do with her dad's bike bored her to sobs and once he'd got onto the subject, it was impossible to get him off it.

'And how is it on petrol usage?' Lauren asked, actually managing to sound genuinely fascinated.

This, of course, only unleashed another litany of facts and figures from her dad, about how fuel efficient the 883 was in comparison with some other models Darcy had absolutely zero interest in.

'You're a lucky man,' Lauren smiled, as she cleared and set the table. 'It's wonderful to find your passion in life. And even if you're only able to take the bike out on weekends, at least you get to indulge that passion. Now is the time to do it too, when you're still young.'

Her dad beamed at being referred to as young and there was a short, suggestive silence, punctuated only by the sound of the Nespresso percolating softly away in the background.

Then he spoke again.

'Don't suppose you'd fancy a quick spin on it?' he said lightly. At that, Lauren's whole face instantly lit up.

'Really Tom?' she said, 'do you mean it? I'd love nothing more – if you're sure that's OK?'

Bloody hell, Darcy thought. Was Lauren really just feigning interest out of politeness? Because if so, she was doing a fantastic job.

'Tell you what,' her dad said, getting up from the table and strapping his helmet back on, like he couldn't wait to get back up on the bike again. 'Why don't you finish getting ready, Darce, and I'll give Lauren a quick whizz around the block? Just to give you an idea of how well she runs,' he added, with an encouraging look in Lauren's direction.

'Be my guest,' shrugged Darcy, silently thinking 'sooner you than me'.

'Fantastic!' said Lauren. 'We won't be long, Darcy. Promise.'

So her dad and Lauren left together, as Darcy went back upstairs to dry her hair and get dressed. From out of her bedroom window she could see them zooming down the driveway, with Lauren clinging onto her dad's waist for dear life and squealing half in terror, half delight.

No more than ten minutes later, Darcy had finally decided what to wear and was just flinging stuff into her overnight bag, when she heard the roar of the bike's engine pulling back into the driveway. Zipping up her little wheelie bag, she was about to shut her bedroom window, when the sounds of laughter came wafting back up to her from the front lawn beneath.

'Wow . . . that was the most amazing experience,' she could hear Lauren giggling. 'What a rush!'

'Are you kidding me? That was nothing,' her dad was saying. 'Wait till you have a go of her on a mountain road, now that's when you really see what this baby is capable of.'

'You must feel so powerful riding her,' said Lauren, patting the pillion of the bike as she elegantly dismounted. 'It must be incredible to zip through the traffic on this.'

'It's a buzz alright,' beamed her dad proudly.

'It's sexy, that's what it is,' said Lauren and at that Darcy almost caught her breath.

'It's certainly empowering,' her dad replied, delighted with himself. 'And if you ever fancy taking a ride on her again, you've only to ask.'

'You know, I'd really love that,' Lauren smiled coyly, shaking her hair as she took off her helmet. 'Maybe as you were saying, up the mountains someday?'

'OK, then I'll hold you to it.'

There was a long, long pause while the two of them just looked at each other and suddenly the atmosphere seemed charged. Even from the bedroom window above, Darcy could sense it. Then, almost on cue, she saw her mum's little Nissan pulling into the driveway, with all the shopping done in perfect time for brunch.

Darcy had completely lost her appetite though.

Jesus, she thought, had she been hearing things? Was her dad – #passthesickbag – *flirting* with Lauren?

And even worse, was Lauren actually flirting back?

Chapter Seventeen

Sarah

It's a truth universally acknowledged that when every other aspect of your life is ticking over nicely, something you least expect is bound to go belly-up. And in my case, by the end of May it was my already precarious financial situation.

No matter where I looked, and believe me, I went through every household expense with the finest of toothcombs, I could find absolutely nothing I could possibly cut back on. Darcy's school fees? Forget it. I considered that money to be sacrosanct. She was actually doing well in school for the first time since Tom and I broke up. She was even hanging around with a lovely new friend, Sophie, who I liked enormously and, better still, who seemed to be a wonderful influence on her.

Not so long ago Darcy had seemed inseparable from Abi Kinsella who'd struck me as a troubled kid who trouble seemed to follow. On the other hand, this new pal Sophie was bright, intelligent and hard-working, but with the effortless knack of somehow making it all appear cool.

And, thankfully, by some miracle this was beginning to rub off on Darcy. Her grades were now as good as they'd ever been and she actually seemed happy to head off to school every morning, without my having to nag her out of bed, wrestle with her to eat a breakfast, then physically shove the girl out the hall door.

So yes, her school fees may well have been bloody extortion, but I'd rather have starved myself before ever cutting back on them.

The house was the other huge monthly expense that was now turning into a giant millstone around my neck. The mortgage payments were now a whopping €1500 a month and it seemed to gobble up most of my salary. To the extent that by the time that and Darcy's fees were covered, not to mention grocery shopping/car insurance/petrol, there never seemed to be a single bean left to actually live off.

By May, I was at my wits' end. All I ever seemed to do was work, I thought in frustration, so how come by the end of each and every month, I was left counting the days till my next payment went through?

The answer hit me sharper than a chilli finger in the eye one quiet weekday morning in work. 8am and, as usual, I was late into the office (traffic) to be greeted by a disgruntled eye-roll from Bernie, which I chose to ignore. (Always, always the best policy with Bernie.)

Meanwhile I plonked down at my desk and frantically tried to get up to speed on the McKinsey brief, before a big meeting we were due to have later on that morning with the mighty George McKinsey himself. Or as he liked to style himself, George McKinsey III. Almost as if he was a character from Shakespeare.

To fill you in, 'George McKinsey III' was a self-described businessman and entrepreneur at the top of his game: a player who headed up one of those spidery global corporations with offices that seemed to stretch from Birmingham to Belize and back again. But after an intricately thorough tax audit, he was now facing possible tax avoidance charges and that's where Sloan Curtis came in.

However, as you can imagine with a company that expansive, the legal end of it was a never-ending nightmare. So it was effectively left to myself, Harry and Bernie to somehow stich together a defense that would hold water in court under cross-examination. We'd all been slaving away on the case for months by then, and the more we uncovered about McKinsey's tax affairs, the more that seemed to lurk underneath.

I'd been working on it till all hours the previous night and had just whipped out yet another file from my briefcase to begin making further notes on it, when out of nowhere Lauren appeared at my desk, smiling brightly, with a big mug of coffee and a still-warm Danish pastry for me.

'I knew you wouldn't have had time for breakfast, so I took the liberty of buying you something to keep you going.'

'You utter superstar,' I beamed back at her, greedily taking a gulp of the coffee she'd offered: Black Americano, no sugar, just the way I liked it. How did Lauren do that, I marveled. How did she always seem to know exactly what I wanted, before I knew myself?

'If you don't mind me saying, you seem way too stressed out for this early in the day,' she added, looking at me worriedly. 'Is there anything you'd like me to help you out with? After all, that's what I'm here for.'

'Well, as a matter of fact, there is,' I said, explaining to her what we needed to be fully up to speed on before the 11am meeting with George McKinsey III.

Now strictly speaking, this was a little above and beyond what I should have asked of a humble intern, but I was desperately behind and Lauren seemed well up for it. Not only that, but unlike me, she had the knack of being able to whizz through vast columns of figures and instantly get to grips with them without having to constantly cross-reference her notes, as I had to. For a solid hour, she and I worked side by side together, all while I blessed the day a rare angel like Lauren crossed my path.

I can vividly remember sitting at my desk that sunny Wednesday morning as the sun streamed in and formed a perfect beam of light around her jet-black hair, while she sat painstakingly going through page after page of the most boring facts and figures known to man, never once complaining, barely even stopping to rub her eyes, as I frequently had to. I watched her silently as she worked away beside me.

Had it really only been a few weeks since she started working here? Already it seemed like she was part of the furniture. Always the first to her desk every morning and generally the last to leave each evening. Her dark head bent down low over her desk day and night had become a familiar sight by then.

By rights, we were working Lauren far harder than we should have been. Harry and I were forever foisting case-work on her, all the boring legwork that neither of us had time to deal with. It was always, 'Lauren, would you mind nipping over to the Four Courts with this document?' or 'Lauren, can you proofread this deposition, then make sure it gets faxed over to McKinsey's before end of play today?' Never once did she complain though and never once did she meet any of our demands with anything other than a bright, warm smile and a cheery 'no problem!'

Even Bernie had noticed. 'Jesus, has that young one moved in here or what?' he asked me once. 'No matter how early I get in or how late I stay on, you can be guaranteed that she'll still be here.'

It wasn't an exaggeration to say that everyone at Sloan Curtis seemed to like her. From Ruth, our young receptionist, to Lucy the legal secretary, none of us really knew how we'd ever managed without her. Ruth had already taken to grabbing lunch with Lauren on a daily basis, and since she and Lucy got on so well, Lucy had even invited her to her thirtieth birthday party.

And that's when the idea struck me, like a thunderbolt from the blue. The perfect solution to all my money woes. I was fairly certain she'd agree, but I just needed to gauge the temperature first.

'Lauren,' I asked her, whipping off my glasses as she looked up at me questioningly. Her two big, brown eyes almost seeming to say, 'the answer is yes. What is the question?'

'How would you like to have a lunch with me later on?' I said. 'There's something I need to ask you. In private, though.'

She smiled eagerly back at me. 'I'd love nothing more. But let's just get up to speed on this McKinsey brief first, and then we'll really have earned it, won't we?'

The meeting with McKinsey's, needless to say, was a huge success. Thanks to Lauren's help and with all her exhaustive prep-work, we nailed it. And all her figures were spot-on, just as everything the girl touched seemed to be perfect.

As per usual.

*

I can clearly remember wishing that our little lunch together had been somewhere fancy, with proper waiter service and bottled water. Because if Lauren agreed to what I had in mind, then this was hopefully something she and I could really celebrate. Sadly though, it ended up being nothing more than two snatched sandwiches in the coffee shop around the corner from the office, mainly down to lack of both time and money on my part.

'So, I'm guessing you need to talk about something sensitive?' Lauren said, as the two of us perched uncomfortably on metallic high stools at a tiny table, munching away on our lunch snacks. 'Something you can't mention in work? Oh God, I hope it's not Darcy?' she added feelingly.

'Darcy is doing great,' I told her, shoving away the remains of a hot cheese Panini, then taking a sip of coffee. 'But it's actually you I want to talk about, Lauren.'

'I'm all ears,' she said with the widest smile.

'Now you can tell me to mind my own business,' I said, 'but would it be very cheeky of me to ask about your living situation just now?'

Her face instantly fell and she abandoned eating the quinoa salad that she'd been picking at, her appetite wilted.

'Are you sure you really want to know?'

'Well, it's just that the last time we spoke about this,' I said tentatively, 'you'd mentioned you were sharing a flat with two other students who ... emm ... well ... you know ...'

176

I fished around as delicately I could for the right words to say, 'who regularly go out on the piss, openly use drugs and drag home a different fella every night of the week, so you never know what naked man you're going to bump into in the bathroom at 6am.'

Let's face it though, there wasn't really an easy way of putting it. And Lauren had never once complained; in fact her living situation was something she rarely discussed. Anytime I offered to drive her home late at night, she'd always thank me profusely, but insist that it was too far out of my way and that she was happy to grab either a bus or a taxi.

Funny thing, it never struck me as odd that Lauren rarely talked about this. It was as though she was so utterly focused on her work, little else in her life seemed to matter. She had a roof over her head and that, as far as she was concerned, seemed to be that.

'Yes, I do share a flat,' she said simply. 'With two other girls, but I think the less said about their lifestyle choices the better. We've been living together for about two years now.'

'And would you say you're happy there?' I probed.

'Sarah,' she said, the big brown eyes looking at me directly. 'What's this really about?'

'OK,' I told her, clattering my coffee mug down onto the metallic table, so I could really give her the full focus of my attention. 'Here's the deal. Darcy and I are living in a three-bedroomed house in a lovely posh area that realistically I can no longer afford. The mortgage payments are crucifying me and the fact is, the house is too big for just two people to rattle around in. It's impractical, it's unaffordable and it can't go on for very much longer.'

'So what are you saying?' she asked, puzzled. 'Do you want

to sell the house? And maybe you need me to help with packing everything up? Or with the legal end of things?'

'No, Lauren,' I said, and this time it was my turn to smile. 'I'm asking you if you'd be interested in renting out my spare room.'

'You mean . . .' she said, looking at me in total disbelief. 'That I could—'

'I'm asking if you'd like to move in with us,' I nodded, finishing the sentence for her. 'I can't think of anyone Darcy and I would love to live with more than you, and God knows I could really use the extra bit of cash.'

She fell silent and then, may I be struck down this minute, began to shed actual tears of gratitude.

'Oh, Sarah,' she said, as I passed her over a paper napkin to wipe her eyes. 'That would be like a dream come true for me! To get away from where I'm living now, and to actually be a part of your life and Darcy's? You utter wonder woman,' she said, getting off the high stool and hugging me so tightly that other lunchtime customers must have thought we were a lesbian couple making up after a big fight.

'Now be warned, my spare room room is nothing more than a shoebox,' I laughed.

She beamed back at me. 'I'd happily live in a cardboard box, if it meant getting away from the kip I'm in now.'

'So you'll move in then?' I asked her delightedly.

'First thing tomorrow, if you'll have me!'

*

Looking back, I should have seen the signs. Because they were all there, only I chose to ignore them. But at the time I was totally swept up in a tide of euphoria at the thought

178

of a brand-new lodger who'd put an end to all my financial woes.

To my surprise, though, Darcy seemed less than bowled over at the news when I told her.

'Oh, right. So Lauren's going to move in with us then?' she asked.

'Yes! Aren't you happy, love? I know how well you two get on.'

'Yeah, course I am,' she said, just a tiny bit flatly, I thought. 'I mean, if that's what you really want, Mum, then I suppose it's cool with me.'

The poor kid is just tired and exhausted from a long week in school, I remember thinking. That's the only reason why she seemed a bit unenthusiastic about the whole plan.

Worse eejit me for not reading the signs properly.

*

The next few days went by in a complete blur. I insisted on buying new paint, so we could redecorate the spare room to get it looking gorgeous for Lauren. Not only that, but I even took a trip out to IKEA one evening after work and filled two entire trolleys full of curtains, lampshades, a new matching bedspread and even a few pretty pictures to hang on the spare-room walls. Tom, in fairness to him, mucked in too, volunteering to help paint the bedroom before she moved in.

'You're sure you don't mind?' I asked, delighted with how supportive he was being about the whole thing.

'Why would I mind?' he asked, with paint-splodged hair, as he busily applied a base coat to the spare-room walls. The colour worked too; it was a vivid fuchsia pink that Lauren had picked out for herself. Personally, I thought it was far too strong a shade for such a tiny little box room, but when I saw it on the walls, I quickly changed my mind. Because it looked beautiful, bright and cosy – the perfect contrast to the creamy bedspread and lampshade that I'd bought in IKEA.

'I mean about my taking in a lodger,' I said, aware that Tom's name was still down as co-owner of the house and that whether I liked it or not, he was entitled to have his say in the matter.

'If you ask me, it's the best idea you ever had,' he said, as yet another droplet of pink paint fell onto the top of his head, making him look like he had psychedelic dandruff. 'Lauren's a great girl and Darcy seems to love her. Be fantastic to have her around that bit more often.'

'I'm glad you think so,' I said, delighted with how well things seemed to be working out.

'So when is she officially moving in?'

'On Saturday, I hope.'

'You know, my mate Spud has a van that I could borrow to give her a hand shifting her stuff. It's only a small one, but I could do a few runs over and back so she can get all of her stuff over in one day.'

'You're sure that's no trouble?' I asked him, surprised. Tom was very precious about his Saturdays. Either it was his day with Darcy or else his time to spend up the mountains with the biker club.

'No trouble at all,' he said, smiling.

Then he went back to painting Lauren's room for her, humming happily under this breath.

Like a man without a care in the world.

*

I was sure to pass on Tom's kind offer to Lauren when I saw her in work the next morning. To my astonishment though, she declined.

'I couldn't possibly put Tom to so much bother,' she said, looking up from her computer, where she'd probably been since 7am, knowing her.

'But it's no bother at all,' I insisted. 'Just think how much easier it'll be for you, to be able to load your stuff into a big van and get it all over in a few trips. Or possibly even in a single trip.'

'I have very little, you know, so really, there's no need, thanks.'

'Well, if you won't let Tom help you, then I can always load your things into the back of my car. It's not very big, but at least it's better than nothing—'

'Please, Sarah, no,' she said firmly. 'You've been so kind as it is. The last thing I'd ever want to do is put you out.'

'You're not putting me out at all, honestly. Just give me your address and I'll zip around to your flat and help you pile your things into the back of my car. It's no trouble at all, really.'

'I'm fine,' she said firmly. 'I'll manage.'

'Lauren!' I said, half laughing and half in exasperation at her stubbornness. 'Why won't you let me help you? And why won't you tell me where you live?'

'I'll see you on Saturday,' was all she said though, smiling enigmatically.

It took months before my question was answered properly. And then and only then did the penny finally drop.

JUNE

Chapter Eighteen

Liz

'I have no words to thank you.'

Oh, shut the fuck up, will you?

It's like there was no frigging escape from Lauren back then. If I called the office, Madam would invariably answer the phone, knowing right well I was ringing to speak to either my husband or Sarah and that I'd absolutely no time for her. But she'd still insist on doing the whole small talk thing, rarely, I might add, missing a chance to talk down to me as the humble homemaker she'd marked me down for.

'So how are the children, Liz?' she'd asked me once, faux politely. 'You must be run off your feet these days.'

'Fine,' I'd answered curtly, 'but can you please get Harry for me? He's not answering his mobile and this is really important. Urgent, in fact.'

It wasn't at all, I was just anxious not to have to deal with Lauren.

'I'm afraid Harry's in a meeting right now. But of course I'll tell him you called. He mentioned something about a cake sale at the boys' school later today that you're helping out with? Can I ask if that's what you needed to speak to him so urgently about?' she added patronizingly.

My tongue must have been raw red from the number of times I had to bite it back, purely to stop me from telling her to feck off.

Nor was there any escape from the little witch whenever I went over to visit Sarah at her house either. As ever, we had our little routine; I'd rock up to the front door on a Saturday night with a bottle of wine tucked under my arm, all set for a night of food, chat and gossip. Just like always.

But more often than not, Madam Lauren would answer the door with the fakest smile you ever saw plastered across that smug little face, instantly making me feel like I was as much a guest in *her* home as Sarah's.

'Come on in, Liz, we're just at dinner now, but you're welcome to wait in the TV room till we're finished,' was one particular beaut that's stuck in my mind. Or, 'Sarah's upstairs in the shower, would you like to wait for her in the kitchen? You won't be in anyone's way there.'

And of course all my grumblings and dire warnings to Sarah fell on stone-deaf ears. As far as Sarah was concerned, Lauren was the world's most fabulous housemate and I just had to give her more of a chance, that was all. In other words, I was the problem. Not Lauren.

Christ Alive, I thought, gnashing my teeth in frustration. Was I the only one who could see through Lauren? Was I the only one who could see past the put-on sweetness and the ever-obliging manner to the ambitious, manipulative little vixen that lay just underneath?

Yes, it seemed, was the answer. As far as either my husband or my best friend were concerned, I might as well have been

Cassandra from the Greek myths, correctly prophesising disaster, while everyone else just partied on regardless.

*

It was Harry who gave me my first clue as to what dramas might really be going on behind the scenes at Sloan Curtis. He and I were snatching a rare – a very rare – Sunday morning lie-in together, while the boys were glued to the telly downstairs in the family room and Rosie did her homework in the kitchen.

The two of us lay flaked out on our bed, enjoying the tiny window of rest, too far beyond exhaustion to do anymore than just crash out. I think we were both beyond actually having sex back then; thin walls and three wide-awake kids do not mix, etc. Not to mention that the sound of the *Horrible Histories* theme tune wafting up the stairs is a bit of a passion killer.

'So how was your girl's night with Sarah last night?' Harry asked me lazily, snuggling over to my side of the bed for a cuddle.

'Oh for Christ's sake,' I yawned sleepily. 'I was enjoying my snooze, and now you've gone and ruined the mood.'

'Why? What did I say? What did I do wrong?' he asked, at a complete loss.

'Well, if you must know, last night was fucking awful,' I groaned. 'In fact, I'm giving up going around to Sarah's at the weekends.'

'But you love your girls' nights in with Sarah,' he said, hauling himself up onto one elbow so he could look at me properly. 'You're always saying the break away from the rest of us keeps you sane. I try not to take offence,' he added dryly.

187

'Yeah, well, things have changed a bit in the last few months, haven't they?'

'What are you talking about?'

'These days you can't get Sarah on her own for a private chat, not for one single second,' I said, pulling the duvet tightly around me, 'because that bloody Lauren just clings to her, and never leaves her side. The girl completely fails to grasp that when someone says in a flat tone, "no, stay and join us, you're more than welcome" what they actually mean is "can't you just feck off and give us a bit of peace here?" It's all in the tone, you know.'

'You don't have a whole lot of time for Lauren, do you?' Harry said, wide-awake by then and staring blankly up at the ceiling.

'Sweetheart, take it from me,' I said, 'that one is a devious little she-witch, make no mistake. The type who'd live in one of your ears, and rent the other one out in flats. I mean, look at what she's managed to wangle for herself in the space of a few short months? It's unbelievable.'

'How do you mean?' he asked, as a row between the boys broke out downstairs. I couldn't quite catch the specifics, but it seemed to involve who had the remote to the XBox last.

'Only as recently as last January,' I went on, 'Lauren was working in some kip-hole of a nail bar and sharing a dingy, student flat with two drop-outs. Whereas now, not only has she got a job that plenty of honours law graduates would kill for, but she's living in a gorgeous family home in one of the swishiest ends of town. I'm telling you, love, that one's middle name should be wisteria, she climbs upwards so fast.'

'If you think that's impressive,' he said, peeling his

huge hulk away from me and heaving himself out of bed, 'it's nothing compared with the inroads she's making in work.'

Then he pulled on a dressing gown, presumably to go downstairs to referee the escalating fight. He was half way out the door by the time I hauled myself up onto one elbow and called him back.

'Harry, where are you going?'

'Ehh . . . in case you hadn't noticed, the Third Gulf War is about to break out downstairs. Plus, I thought I'd bring you up your cuppa tea in bed. I know, I know—' he shrugged 'Husband of the Year, that's me.'

'But . . . but you can't just come out with something intriguing like that, then leave me guessing! What did you mean about Lauren in work? What's going on in the office that you're not telling me?'

'Listen, love,' he said from the door frame, his big, broad silhouette almost blocking it, he's that chunky. 'You can say what you like about Lauren, and I know you don't have much time for her personally—'

'Understatement of the century.'

'But the fact is that she's a fabulous worker and a very gifted lawyer. Do you know how rare that is? She's seriously kicking arse on the McKinsey brief too. It's even come to Bernie's attention.'

'But the McKinsey brief is Sarah's baby,' I said slowly. 'We all know that. Jesus, even I know that much. She's spent months, no years, compiling all the evidence and she's been on it since day one.'

'Well, yeah,' Harry said sounding a bit doubtful. 'Of course Sarah's great and everything. But the thing about Sarah is that she has so much else going on in her life.'

'How do you mean?' I asked, as my still half-asleep brain tried to catch up.

'Come on, you know perfectly well what I mean, love. You know what she's like as well as I do. She's constantly being pulled in twenty different directions. And it's never her fault, of course, but the thing is, she's constantly late into the office because of some drama to do with Darcy, or else she has to skive off early, because she's off to Mountjoy or Wheatfield Prison to work on one of those free legal aid projects she's so committed to. Which is all well and good—'

'But she's on top of everything,' I said loyally, 'and isn't it wonderful that Sarah cares so deeply about her work? Plenty of top paid lawyers don't give a shite.'

'Yeah, but Lauren is always there for us, whereas Sarah isn't. And lately, Bernie and I have been leaning on Lauren an awful lot more than we ever did on Sarah. It's nothing personal, it's just that the McKinsey brief is make or break for a firm like ours and Bernie wants the best team on it. And its just at the moment—'

There was a horrible silence while we both just looked across the room at each other. The words were unspoken, but they hung there just the same.

And at the moment that might not include Sarah.

'Harry,' I said slowly. 'Sarah has slaved over that brief. She's practically sweated blood over it. You know as well as I do how devastated she'll be if she's taken off the McKinsey case.'

He didn't answer me though. Just shrugged and left the room, heading downstairs to sort out chaos and leaving me alone with my thoughts.

I had to talk to Sarah. I had to warn her. I had to get

190

her in a one-on-one situation preferably somewhere that was Lauren-free. Not the easiest task, given than when Sarah wasn't actually with Lauren you could be sure Madam would be calling and texting her non-stop about various crises that had cropped up in work.

But I was a step ahead and had it all worked out. It had been my birthday the previous Monday, and as no one ever wants to go out on a Monday night, I suggested that Sarah and I have a little dinner out together the following Friday.

'But don't you want to spend your birthday dinner with Harry and the kids?' she asked me, baffled.

'The best birthday gift I could ask for is a night off from my beloved family,' I told her firmly, not taking no for an answer. 'Besides, there's a gorgeous restaurant in town that's just got rave reviews and my mother gave me a voucher for it. So like it or not, babes, you're coming with me.'

I have to say, the thought of finally getting to spend some proper quality time with Sarah really did my heart good. It would be just like the old days, I remember thinking. Then when we'd both eaten and chatted the night away, I'd subtly introduce the subject of Madam Lauren and gently drop a hint that Sarah might just need to start watching her back in work. Particularly when it came to all matters relating to the McKinsey case.

The restaurant was called Rustic Stone, right in the heart of the city centre, and our table for two was perfect, in a lovely quiet little booth, so I could talk to Sarah in complete privacy. They even had pesto fries on the menu with Parmesan cheese and I've always thought it's impossible to be in bad form after a big feed of pesto fries with Parmesan cheese.

Sarah arrived a good twenty minutes late as per usual,

weighed down with heavy case files that spilled all over the floor the minute she went to hug me.

'Liz! I'm so sorry to keep you!' she said breathlessly. 'We had a late meeting about the bloody McKinsey case that ran over, wouldn't you know it? And on top of that, Joe Simpson and all the team from Simpson Hotels are calling into us first thing on Monday for a settlement briefing, so it's all hands on deck for that. Honestly, only for Lauren I don't know where I'd be.'

Jaysus, I thought. She wasn't in the door two seconds before the subject of Lauren had already reared its ugly spectre.

I smiled, waving at her to grab a seat. 'Never mind, you're here now. So why don't we start off by ordering a gorgeous bottle of wine? My treat, so let's really push the boat out.'

'Brilliant, Sarah smiled, sliding down into the chair opposite and whipping the reading glasses off the top of her head so she could scan down through the menu.

We were just about to order – tempura of salmon with crunchy broccoli for her and a filet of beef and mushroom for me with all the trimmings – when next thing, wouldn't you know it, her phone rang.

Lauren. Who else? I could see the name flashing up on the phone on the table between us, clear as crystal.

'Leave it,' I told her, clamping my hand down over hers.

'Oh, I really wish I could,' Sarah said, pulling an apologetic face, 'but I'm afraid it might be important.' So she answered, having to raise her voice slightly to be heard above the background restaurant clatter.

'Yeah . . . great . . . that would be amazing. Thanks, Lauren,' was the gist of the conversation. 'No, it's the section thirty-two file you need, subsection fifty, though you may need to double check that. Are you still in the office? OK . . . well, if you really insist on working from home tonight, then you'd certainly be doing me a huge favour. I shouldn't be too late home, so I'll be free to help out then. No, I'm out for dinner with Liz at the moment. OK, well, call me back if there are any more issues. Thanks, Lauren. Byeee.'

'Tell you what, why don't you switch your phone off?' I told her a bit bossily. 'Then you can really relax.'

'Sounds good to me,' Sarah smiled. She was just fiddling about with the phone, trying to find airplane mode, when it rang again almost immediately. And yet again, she answered.

'Lauren, hi. No, we haven't started eating yet; we've just ordered. Oh shit, you have got to be kidding me . . .' she said, her whole face suddenly falling.

'What's up?' I mouthed silently across the table at her. But Sarah just pulled a face, gave me a thumbs-down sign and kept up the conversation.

'Shit, shit, shit,' she was saying, 'in that case we're rightly screwed unless . . . no, hold on . . . now I'm just thinking aloud here . . . but unless we can argue tax alien status against that particular protocol? We'd really need to go through that whole section with a fine-tooth comb though. No,' she added, glancing over at me where I was sitting, I'm sure, with a face like a bag of spanners by then. 'Not really. Like I said, I'm out to dinner now . . .'

I'm sure she must have caught something in my expression that more or less conveyed 'you'd want to get off the bloody phone now and stop being so rude' because she said a hurried goodbye, hung up, then leaned across the table to give my hand a quick little squeeze.

193

'Jesus, Liz, you've the patience of a saint,' she said apologetically, just as our wine waiter arrived. 'Not only do you have poor old Harry chained to his desk day and night, but now you've got to deal with me and my awful manners too. I faithfully promise I'll switch my phone off and there'll be absolutely no more interruptions.'

I ordered a gorgeous bottle of Sauvignon for us both from the waiter as Sarah looked at me worriedly.

'Are you still speaking to me, Liz?' she asked but this time, I smirked back. Impossible to stay cross with Sarah for long; she's just too bloody *nice*.

'It's just – oh, you know how it is in Sloan Curtis,' she sighed deeply. 'Every single time something crops up, they expect all hands on deck. Honestly, you should have seen the filthy look Bernie gave me when I slipped off half an hour ago to meet you. You'd swear I was skiving off having done nothing all day – whereas I've been at my desk since 7.30 this morning trying to sort out this bloody McKinsey case for him. Talk about a thankless task.'

'I know how it is,' I said quietly.

'So now, let's talk about you,' she said, catching something in my expression and quickly changing the subject. 'How is everything in your world this week? How are Rosie and the boys?'

'As a matter of fact, work is kind of what I wanted to talk to you about,' I said, pointedly changing the subject back again.

'Oh really?' she said, looking genuinely puzzled.

Just then her phone rang. It was sitting on the table right in between us so I could clearly read the caller ID on it.

And, of course, it was Lauren.

'Oh rats,' said Sarah, biting her lip. 'I bet she's having

trouble with sourcing those tax alienation documents we were just talking about . . . Liz, I'm so sorry about this, would you think me the worst in the world if I answered? Just this very last call, then I promise, I'm all yours for the whole evening, I faithfully promise—'

I doubt it would have made a difference what I said; Sarah just went ahead and took the call anyway. Meanwhile I sat back, drummed my fingers off the edge of the table and stared crossly into space.

'Lauren, hi, what's up now?' she said. 'No, like I said what you're looking for is sub section fifty, I think. It's the bit about how many days you've got to be resident in the country. Oh, it's something like one hundred and eighty days, but there's loads of loopholes and exemptions that we really should be looking at a lot more closely. Yeah, great that would be fantastic, thanks so much, I really owe you one. Well, I'll see you back home later on then. You're an utter lifesaver.'

And just like that, I snapped. I reached across the table, snatched the phone from Sarah's ear and spoke slowly and clearly down into it.

'Lauren?' I said crisply. 'It's Liz here. I know you're obviously trying to put out some fire in the office and I know it's a matter of life or death, as everything in that bloody office always is, but Sarah and I are out to dinner now and we'd appreciate it if you didn't disturb us any more than you already have done. Whatever emergency you're dealing with will still be there tomorrow and you can both pick up the pieces then. Got it? Good.'

With that, I hung up the phone to a horrified look from Sarah.

'Liz,' she said, 'that was really rude! You just hung up on her!'

'To hell with Lauren anyway,' I said, taking a sip of the gorgeous Sauvignon Blanc that had just been poured out for us. 'In fact, it's Lauren I expressly wanted to talk to you about tonight.'

'Look,' Sarah said, shoving her glasses up into her hair, 'I know there's nothing more annoying than a phone that keeps ringing non-stop, but this really is an emergency—'

'It's *always* an emergency in there,' I said waspishly. 'You think I don't know that?'

'Lauren is working late tonight, picking up the slack for me, and she was only calling because she had an urgent question, that's all. She's doing me a huge favour here and you just hung up on her!'

'Jesus, Sarah,' I said, trying and failing to keep my cool, 'that one can't let you out of her sight for two seconds together! She's been calling you ever since you set foot in here – you don't see Harry or Bernie going on like that, now do you? And they're both senior partners! When are you going to cop the fuck on and see what's really going on here?'

'What are you talking about?' asked Sarah slowly, looking at me in a way she never had before.

And then, there was a silence, with nothing but the sound of the restaurant Friday night chatter in the background.

'OK then, I'll just say it straight out,' I said.

'I wish you would,' she replied coolly. 'Clearly you have a bee in your bonnet about something, so just get it off your chest and have done with it.'

'It's Lauren,' I said.

'Now why doesn't that come as a surprise?'

'She's moving in on you, Sarah, literally as well as figuratively,' I said, leaning across the table to her. 'So just open your eyes and take a good look around you. Not only is the girl living in your house now—'

'Excuse me,' Sarah interrupted. 'May I remind you that I was the one who invited Lauren to move in? I was short of dosh and the extra cash she pays me really goes a long way. Besides, when it comes down to it, how is this really any of your business?'

'I'll tell you how,' I hissed back, dimly aware that other diners close by were starting to give us puzzled looks. 'It's very much my business when Harry comes home and casually drops it into conversation that Lauren is starting to eclipse you in work. According to him, she's kicking ass on the McKinsey case and the general feeling seems to be that she's the horse to bet on for the future. And not you.'

As long as I live, I don't think I'll ever forget the horrible, withering silence that followed.

'You're suggesting Lauren is some kind of threat to me at work?' Sarah said, her voice low and dangerously calm.

'I'm not suggesting it. I'm warning you straight out that you'd want to start watching your back.'

'Because what?' she said sarcastically. 'Because Lauren is poised to take over my job and, according to you, I'll end up out on my ear?'

'She's young and she's hungry, you said so yourself,' I said, as calmly as I could, given that my hands were actually trembling. 'And in all my days, I don't think I've ever seen ambition like it; that one would take your eye out for an office with a corner view. Lauren, let me tell you, is all about furthering her own ambitions and, now that you've given her a platform to do that, there's no stopping her.'

'Liz, do you know how ridiculous you sound?' Sarah

spluttered furiously back at me. 'This is a twenty-five-year-old intern we're talking about here! I have decades of experience under my belt whereas Lauren's only just starting out.'

'Yeah, well, for someone who's only starting out, she's come a remarkably long way in a frighteningly short space of time. And all, I might add, at your expense.'

'You know what?' said Sarah, sitting back as her eyes started to well up at the corners. 'I actually think that you're jealous. I never would have believed it of you Liz, but you're jealous because I've got a brand-new friend and you don't like it.'

'Oh, will you stop being so bloody puerile. You're reducing this to playground politics now and we're far from that. All I'm saying – as a friend – is that you'd seriously want to wake up and smell the Nespresso.'

'No, let me finish!' she said crossly. 'You've been down on Lauren ever since day one. No matter what she says or does, you seem to have a problem with it. You hate the idea of her living in my house and now apparently just because she's a hard worker in the office, that's a big issue for you too. Just listen to yourself, Liz! When did you get to be so hard-hearted and cynical?'

'And when did you get to be so bloody naïve?' I batted back, folding my arms and glaring at her.

'Can't you just accept that this is a young woman who's only trying to do her best in life?'

'I only wish that were true,' I answered coolly.

'You're completely paranoid.'

'And you're bloody blind if you can't see what's going on here.'

Just then the waiter arrived with our main courses.

Sarah said nothing. Just picked up her bag and phone

and walked out of there, leaving me all alone at a table for two, full of smart-alec indignation with all the great lines I should have come out with, but somehow couldn't seem to find the words.

Chapter Nineteen

Darcy

Darcy would often fantasise about how it was all supposed to go and this was the rough gist of it.

OK, so her mum and dad happened to be spending a bit of time apart then, but that was fine. It was strictly temporary though, everyone knew that. Just while her dad worked through whatever mid-life crap he was wading through.

Her parents would get through it though, she was sure of it. Because they absolutely had to. Sooner or later, they'd both come to their senses and realise that by far the best thing all around was for the pair of them to get back together again. Time apart, Darcy hoped and prayed, would make them realise just how much they actually depended on each other and even missed being part of a couple.

Then, once the two of them were happily reunited, they'd be a family again. A proper family. Like her pal Sophie's family, who spent most of their weekends together and who went on holidays and who actually seemed to enjoy each other's company. For fuck's sake, they even went *camping* together. Because that was what Darcy craved more than anything, really. To be part of a real family once again.

What was particularly upsetting was that up until a few months ago, the straws in the wind had been pretty good. For a start, her dad seemed to be getting increasingly fed up with living the life of a separated single parent; Darcy could smell it a mile off. Maybe the freedom of having his own flat and his own space was initially a buzz for him; maybe once he'd enjoyed being able to hop up on his bike and head off to the Dublin mountains with his biker crew without having to answer to anyone. But now, it was as though the hard, cold reality was finally setting in and Darcy fervently hoped her dad was finally beginning to see himself as others did. Which was as a sad, middle-aged fifty-something with a receding hairline, living in a grotty little flat devoid of any home comforts, which she herself had come to dread spending the night in.

On the weekend nights when she had to stay there, she'd lie awake in that miniscule single-bedded room that was more of a cell really, staring at the ceiling and pulling a cheap IKEA bedspread around her, wondering what it would take for her parents to come to their senses and to get back together.

After all, she reasoned, when they broke up, there was no third party involved and both of them were still single. Her mum barely had time to wash herself, she was so overstretched in work, and the thoughts of her actually – ughhh – getting a new boyfriend were so ludicrous it almost made Darcy want to laugh. Or vomit, whatever.

The only sort-of obstacle that Darcy could see on the horizon was Lauren. Had her dad actually started flirting with her? Or had Darcy just been imagining things?

The logical part of her mind instantly dismissed the thought. For fuck's sake, Lauren was half her dad's age, if anything she was closer in age to Darcy. On the other hand though, she was a complete hottie. Even Sophie thought so. Last time she was around in the house, Sophie had made a point of saying, 'wow, your new flatmate really knows how to rock a pair of skinny jeans, doesn't she? Hey, do you think there's any chance she'd give me a gel nail manicure, just like yours?'

Lauren, of course, had obliged with a smile just like she always did and had sent Sophie home primped and preened to within an inch of her life.

'You're soooo lucky and I'm soooo jealous,' Sophie said to Darcy in school the next day.

'Why?' Darcy asked, baffled that anyone would actually be jealous of her.

'Are you kidding me? It's like you've got your own private beauty therapist on tap, twenty-four hours a day.'

And most of the time it was cool sharing the house with Lauren, Darcy had to admit. Lauren was so easy to talk to and she instinctively 'got' everything that was going on in her life. Darcy really did feel like she could tell her anything and that she wouldn't be shocked, or worse, try to judge her. She could talk to Lauren about school, about what an out-an-out bitch Abi was being to her, particularly since she'd got pally with Sophie. She could talk about Tony Scott and what an asshole he'd turned out to be, relentlessly teasing Darcy about 'still being a virgin', and always in public, when there were gangloads around to hear.

But how could she talk to her about what was really playing on her mind? What were the right words to say, 'I want my mum and dad to get back together again but I'm afraid that my dad is sort of flirting with you? And that – eughhhh – he might even fancy you?'

#Cringefest.

Nothing further seemed to happen between them though, and for a while Darcy allowed herself to draw breath. Her dad continued to drop her off at the house and pick her up as normal, and if Lauren did happen to be around, she always seemed to have her nose buried in work. So far, if she and Dad did make small talk, then that's as much as it ever amounted to.

So far.

Maybe it was all in her imagination, Darcy quietly hoped, allowing herself to heave a big sigh of relief after a few weeks of this. After all, if nothing else, Lauren was so far out of her dad's league that the notion of the two of them dating each other was laughable really. So gradually over time she allowed that particular worry to slip away and thought no more of it.

Until that miserable, rainy Friday night back in June.

Ordinarily her mum should have been home, but that particular night she was out to dinner with her pal Liz. Apparently it had been Liz's birthday during the week and the two of them were having a girlie night out together and, knowing them, a few glasses of wine along with it. Darcy was home alone, packing up her overnight wheelie bag, as her dad was due to call for her later on that evening so she could spend the weekend with him.

She was looking forward to seeing her dad, but given the choice she'd infinitely have preferred to spend time with him at home, where it was warm and cosy. Anything rather than another night in that horrible, pokey little flat. Preferably when her mum was around, so Project Reconciliation could continue. Or get started. Whatever.

It was one of those stormy summer nights where it's more like November than June and Darcy was upstairs in her room, throwing her trainers, jeans and warm fleece into an overnight bag, as the rain pelted against the window and it actually started to thunder. Next thing, she heard the key in the lock downstairs, and peered over the bannister railing to see Lauren downstairs in the hallway, having just let herself in.

'Hey, there you are,' Darcy called down to her, 'you're so late home – what happened to you?'

'Just a last-minute emergency I needed to sort out at the office,' Lauren smiled back up at her, peeling off her trench coat, which was completely soaked through. 'Nothing to worry about. What a night! I've never seen a storm like it. I swear to God, it's actually raining sideways out there.'

'Everything OK in work?' Darcy asked.

'Oh, it's just that McKinsey case your poor mum's been so stressed about,' said Lauren, carefully hanging her coat up to dry. 'It seems there's something we overlooked, which I need to get sorted as soon as I can. It'll be a busy weekend for me, that's for sure.'

'Mum isn't home yet, she's still out—'

'—having dinner with Liz,' said Lauren, running her fingers through sopping wet hair in a way that made her look completely sensational and not like a drowned rat, as anyone normal would have done. 'Yes, I know, I just called her.'

'At least you were able to get away from the office,' Darcy called back down from the upstairs landing.

'Well, I was working away in the office and security were

204

trying to lock up for the weekend. So I figured I could just as easily work at home,' she replied, taking off her sopping wet jumper. 'Then I thought, I bet anything Darcy won't have eaten, so—'

'So . . .?' Darcy asked hopefully, suddenly aware that all she had was a tub of yoghurt earlier at lunchtime and that her tummy was actually rumbling. She also knew right well there'd be nothing at her dad's flat only crappy take-out pizza and frankly, there was only so much stodgy pizza one person could deal with. She was craving something healthy and knew she could always rely on Lauren to come up trumps.

'Anyway, rain or no rain, I stopped off at Tesco and picked up the makings of a yummy dinner for us,' Lauren said, holding up two plastic shopping bags with French baguettes sticking out of them. 'So what do you say, Darcy? Fancy coming down to the kitchen and being my sous chef?'

A complete no-brainer as far as Darcy was concerned. Not only was Lauren the most incredible cook, but working in the kitchen alongside her was actually a bit of a giggle too. Her dad wasn't due to call over for ages yet, so Darcy knew she'd have time to grab something to eat first. Anything to avoid having to eat a rubbery takeaway back at that awful flat while sitting in front of *The Late Late Show*.

#Getmeoutofhere.

*

Half an hour later, she and Lauren were working away side-by-side in the kitchen, happily chopping vegetables and peeling carrots as Darcy learned how to make something called Pad King, a Vietnamese dish that Lauren said she'd learned how to cook when she was waitressing her way through college. Darcy had never heard of Pad King, but it smelled delicious; a mouthwatering combination of ginger, oyster mushrooms, spring onions, babycorn, peppers and a tiny bit of lean chicken too. #Divine

Darcy grinned, as she set the table for the two of them, even producing her mum's good crystal glasses, mainly because this was a meal that seemed to demand all the trimmings.

'We've made so much food,' she beamed. 'Wow – you've even made bruschetta! This is going to be more like a banquet than a casual supper. Such a shame Mum is missing out on it.'

'Don't worry,' said Lauren, busy doing all kinds of magical things with soy sauce and lime juice over at the wok on the cooker. 'There'll be enough leftovers to feed us all for a week.'

'Do you really have to work later on?' Darcy asked sympathetically, noticing the stuffed briefcase that had been abandoned on the kitchen floor.

'I'm afraid so,' Lauren shrugged. 'In fact I'll have to pull a few all-nighters to get up to speed for Monday. But it's always much easier to work on a full stomach, don't you think?'

Twenty minutes later, Lauren had lit the fire in the living room so she could work in there later on, even dotting the bruschetta around on tiny serving dishes. 'Because I get so hungry when I'm working late,' as she explained. Then, just as she and Darcy were sitting down to a dinner so beautifully presented that it almost looked worthy of a Michelin star, there was a sudden, unexpected knock at the door.

'I'll get it,' said Darcy, springing to her feet to answer it. It couldn't be her dad, she thought; it was still too early for him to collect her. But even from the hallway she could clearly make out his familiar short, stocky silhouette through the glass of their hall door. Her tummy instantly tensed up a bit and she instinctively knew she had to get him out of there ASAP.

'Dad!' she said, letting him in and kissing him on the cheek.

'Hey Darce!' he said, warmly hugging her back. 'Jeez, what about this storm! You'll be delighted to know I didn't take the motorbike tonight.'

'Good to know you don't want me to drown,' she said, pulling a face.

'But maybe tomorrow you and I could take a scoot up the mountains,' he added hopefully. 'If the weather clears up a bit, that is?'

'Lauren's here and we're just having dinner,' she said, deliberately side-stepping the question as he followed her into the hall. 'Just give me two minutes, that's all, and I'll be ready to go. Do you want to wait in the TV room? The fire's lit in there.'

'Why would I want to wait in the TV room?' said her dad, puzzled. 'Take your time, and finish your dinner. I'm happy to wait in the kitchen with you and Lauren.'

'In that case,' Darcy said, thinking on her feet, 'I'll wolf this back as quick as I can and then we're out of here. That OK?'

As they came into the kitchen, Darcy couldn't help but see her dad's craggy, lined face light up the minute he saw Lauren sitting at the kitchen table, looking, as ever, beyond fabulous. Jesus, even after the soaking she'd got earlier and with absolutely no make-up on. How the feck did she manage to do that?

Suddenly it was even more important to get her dad out of there very, very fast.

'Ahh, there's Lauren. How are you doing?' her dad said, grinning at her, and flushing red in the face, Darcy noticed. Like a bloody schoolboy with a crush. #Mortifying

'Hi Tom, good to see you,' Lauren smiled warmly back at him.

Was she always this friendly to everyone, Darcy tried to think, paranoia raging. Or was she being especially nice to her dad? Like nice, bordering on flirtatious?

'Well, something smells good,' said her dad, pulling out his usual chair at the top of the table as he always did.

'It's called Pad King,' said Darcy, wolfing it back as fast as she could. 'But don't worry, I'll be out of here in a flash. I'm all packed up and ready to go – thirty seconds, Dad, that's all I need. Max.'

'Don't eat so fast, Darce,' he said, stretching his legs out under the table. 'You'll only get indigestion. Besides, what's the big hurry? I'm in no rush.'

'In that case, here's a thought,' said Lauren, and Darcy's bowels clenched, sensing exactly what was coming next. 'Maybe you'd like to join us for dinner, Tom? There's tons left over, isn't there?'

'Ummm,' mumbled Darcy, with her mouth stuffed.

'Well now, I can't remember the last time I sat down to a proper home-cooked meal.' Tom grinned, patting his tummy and looking absolutely delighted with himself. 'Thank you so much, ladies. Dinner with two beautiful women? Now there's an offer no man could refuse.'

And of course after dinner there was no budging her

dad no matter how hard Darcy tried. He even suggested they all move into the living room, where it was cosier by the fire and then insisted that they all play a game of Monopoly. Christ Alive, Darcy thought, wondering if she'd have to physically sandblast him out of there. Where was this all going to end?

Chapter Twenty

Sarah

'Why do you do it?' people would often ask me. 'You've quite enough going on in your life as it is. Why use the little chunk of time left over to volunteer for free legal aid?'

Because of the reality check it gave me at times like this, was my inevitable answer. Days when my best friend wasn't on speaking terms with me. Liz, who I as good as grew up with; Liz, my 'sister from another mister'. In twenty plus years of friendship, we'd never once had as much as a cross word until that awful night at the restaurant when she and I bickered over Lauren.

I stormed home that night, firing her off a text on the way to say I was sorry for abandoning her, but not in the least bit sorry for what I'd said. Not long afterwards, I came home soaked through to the skin to the sound of loud laughter and giggles from the living room and when I went in, there were Darcy, Lauren and Tom sitting around the fire, picking at bruschetta and actually playing a board game that hadn't been touched since Darcy was about ten.

All three of them looking perfectly happy, like they were

all having a rare old time of it, until I walked in like a drowned rat and ruined everyone's night.

'Mum, are you OK?' said Darcy, hopping to her feet the minute she saw the state of me.

'Jesus, Sarah, what happened to you?' asked Tom.

'Is everything alright?' Lauren asked, instantly leaping to her feet to help me out of my soaking wet coat.

'No, it's not alright,' I told the three of them. 'I had a lousy night and—'

And suddenly it was all too much to take. So I just flopped into an empty chair and burst into tears. Big, snotty, gulpy tears; the kind I never allowed myself.

There wasn't a single response from Liz in answer to my text message either. Nothing, not a whisper. And to complicate things, I had to deal with Harry on a day in, day out basis at the office. Clearly, he knew exactly what had gone down, but just asked me if I was OK (no, was the answer), then told me that he was pleading the Fifth on the rest of it.

'Liz is my wife,' as he'd put it, 'and she's your best mate too. So, on this one, think of me as you would Switzerland.'

A great loss to the diplomatic corps was our Harry.

And that, in a nutshell is why I made a point of offering free legal aid in any spare time I had. Not just for the fulfillment, but for the sense of perspective I got from it during troubled times. It was the perfect antidote to the stresses and strains I seemed to be carrying around with me on a daily basis back then.

That week back in June, I remember going to visit a woman about my own age in the Dochas Centre, which is the Women's Prison Wing in Mountjoy. She and I met in the visitor's room, which might sound cosy and welcoming,

but the truth was that all visitors had to perch uncomfortably behind a metal grille on a swingy iron seat nailed to
the floor. Meanwhile the defendant I was supposedly
helping twitched nervously back at me from behind bullet-
proof glass.

The limited bit of time we had together was strictly
monitored by the prison guard on duty, who was watching
over us and listening in to every single word. In between
watching an old episode of *Masterchef* on a tiny, crackly
little overhead telly, that is.

'Can I ask your name?' I asked my new client as gently
as I could, reaching out for a notebook and pen.

'Sabrina Sparkle,' she replied, hugging two skinny little
arms around her gaunt, emaciated frame and pulling the
cardigan she was wearing even tighter around her knees.
The grey colour of the cardigan, I couldn't help noticing,
was the exact same pallor as this girl's skin. Jesus Christ, I
thought, suddenly cross. When were these women ever
allowed to see a decent bit of sunlight?

'I said Sabrina Sparkle,' she repeated. 'Why aren't you
writing that in your notebook, love? You're meant to be me
lawyer, aren't you?'

I sighed, took my glasses off and gave my eyes a good
rub.

'Sorry about this, but I'm afraid that for court, they're
going to need your real name.'

'Oh, right,' she shrugged indifferently. 'Then you should
have said. Me real name is Tina. Tina O'Neill.'

'Tina, it's good to meet you. I'm Sarah and I'm your free
legal aid volunteer.'

'Me wha'?'

'Your free legal . . . oh, look, it doesn't matter. The main

212

thing is that I'm here to help you in any way I can, OK? But first of all, I just need to ask you a few quick questions.'

'You need to get me outta here,' Tina said, suddenly becoming animated. 'I've two kids in foster care and they need me. You *have* to help me.'

'And that's exactly what I'm here to do,' I told her as placatingly as I could.

'Because I had another lawyer a while back and he was fucking useless, so he was. Told me if I pleaded guilty, I might get out of here in three years with good behaviour. Fuck that, I told him, I've two kids! I need to get out of this kip now!'

'Watch your language over there,' said the prison officer sternly from where she was watching us beadily from her perch in the corner of the visitor's room. 'There's no need for talk like that, Tina. Especially in front of your lawyer.'

'It's not Tina, it's Sabrina.'

'Whatever,' shrugged the guard, going back to the re-run of *Masterchef* on the tiny overheard TV.

'Look,' I said, whipping off my glasses so I could really focus on Sabrina/Tina, 'my job is to get you out of here as quickly as possible, but to do that I need to put a good, solid defence together. And I can only do that with your help, OK?'

'OK then.'

'So in your own words, tell me what happened on the night of . . . January 21st 2014,' I said, referring back down to my notes.

'I killed me partner,' Tina said, as casually as if she was saying she'd hoovered up a spider.

'Tell me what happened, in your own words,' I told her as encouragingly as I could. 'And try not to leave anything

213

out, because it could turn out to be very important later on.'

'Me daughter is only fourteen,' Tina went on, 'and she's a grand girl. Nice and quiet, do you know what I mean? She helps out with me son a lot.'

'And how old is your son?'

'He's three now, but he was only a babby then. He's me son with me partner. Me daughter's da is long gone off the scene.'

'I see. So tell me what happened, Tina.'

'For fuck's sake, it's *Sabrina*.'

'Sorry, I mean Sabrina.'

'Well, I found out the fucker was abusing me daughter, didn't I?' she said. 'So I ran at him with me good kitchen knife. And I'd have done worse to him, I swear to God.'

'I see,' I said quietly, taking off my glasses so I could give her the full focus of my attention.

'Do you have a teenage daughter?' she asked, two hungry little eyes looking flintily back at me through the metal grille. 'Do you ever feel you'd stab anyone who looked twice at her? Who looked at her – a bit funny, if you know what I'm getting at?'

'I do, as it happens,' I said. Well maybe not the stabbing with a knife bit, but apart from that, I could see perfectly well where Tina was coming from. The thoughts of anything like that ever happening to Darcy – well, my stomach muscles clenched tight just at the very thought.

The scary thing was that in her shoes, I'd probably have done the very same as Tina. Sorry, Sabrina. And not only that, but I'd have done it without compunction.

For another hour, I worked side-by-side with Tina, patiently transcribing every time, date and place that her

214

daughter, who I discovered was called Kim, had reported abuse by this new partner who'd moved himself into the family home.

I plotted and planned and mapped out the best defense that I possibly could for Tina, highlighting the fact that she herself had become a mum at the age of sixteen, that she'd done her very best to make the most of every disadvantage she'd been born into and that, no, we weren't denying the fact that she'd once been charged with possession of heroin.

'But you successfully completed a methadone programme, didn't you?' I asked her, noting down every word she said.

'Did a bit of it, yeah,' she Tina sullenly. 'Jaysus, there was more drugs in that clinic then I ever seen them dealing on the street outside. Grade-A gear and all, it was.'

'You're clean now though? And you were on the night of January 21st 2014?'

'Might have done a bit of hash, but apart from that – yeah,' she sniffed. 'I could stroll through the "nothing to declare" channel at the airport, I'm that squeaky clean.'

My best way forward, I decided, was to paint this woman as a mother tiger who was prepared to defend her cub to the death. So I combed through her whole backstory, painstakingly writing down every detail she gave me about her own drug addiction and the battles she'd overcome to get clean. How she met her partner, now deceased, and how he slowly enticed her back into the world of drugs she'd been brave enough to break away from. Most importantly of all I was careful to take note of how Tina just snapped, finally reaching break point when her daughter confided in her about the abuse.

'Time's up,' said the warden, yawning and stretching as

215

soon as *Masterchef* came to an end. So I said a confident, upbeat goodbye to Tina, assuring her that I'd do everything I could to fight her case. Then I went through all the 'exit' security checks visitors have to go through before you can get back out into the crisp fresh air and warm sunshine.

As I slipped into my lovely comfortable driver's seat, I offered up a silent prayer of thanks. There I was, driving to my gorgeous office, safe in the knowledge that my own daughter was happy, that she and I had a roof over our heads, that I had secure employment and that, thank God, we could afford all the little luxuries that life could give us.

Any problems I had, I thought, were just so First World compared with Tina's and the life she'd been born into. And women like Tina were the very reason why I'd never stop volunteering with the legal aid team. The reality check I'd just been given was beyond price.

*

I continued to think that right up until that afternoon back at the Sloan Curtis offices. It was well past two-thirty when I eventually made it back to work and I walked into a scene of understated panic. Lucy, our legal secretary, was faffing around, bright red in the face and visibly perspiring, but she froze dead in her tracks the minute she saw me stepping out of the lift.

'Sarah, there you are!' she blurted out. 'Where the hell have you been? I've been calling and calling you.'

'I was off doing legal aid work,' I told her, 'and I have to have my phone switched off while I'm at the prison—'

But Lucy just cut across me, which was most unlike her. 'That's what I figured, but Bernie is still having a total meltdown. It's this meeting with Jim Simpson from Simpson Hotels—'

'—which isn't until 4pm this afternoon,' I finished the sentence for her, refusing to join in with her wild panic, 'so I've still got loads of time.'

'No! That's just it,' she hissed, even redder in the face by then. 'The meeting had to be shifted at the last minute! I've been trying your phone non-stop and then I didn't know what else to do—'

'Lucy, calm down, take a nice deep breath,' I told her gently. 'Now just give me the last sentence first, OK?'

'I'm trying to tell you that the meeting started well over half an hour ago,' she exhaled, looking like she needed to breathe into a paper bag. 'Bernie and Harry were both going bananas because you were nowhere to be found. And they're all in the conference room. Now, Sarah, right now this minute!'

Suddenly feeling weak at the knees, I instinctively fished around the bottom of my handbag for my phone, switched it back on, and sure enough, there was the hardcore proof. No fewer than nine voicemail messages, all from either Lucy or Harry.

'Jesus Christ,' I muttered under my breath, immediately racing to my desk so I could try to unearth the mound of notes I'd already made on the Simpson case. My desk though, as ever, was a disorganised mound of clogged-up papers, files and memos, none of which were in any particular order.

'Quick, there isn't time!' Lucy stammered. 'The meeting has started, so you just need to get in there and try to wing it as best you can!'

'I'm on my way,' I said, grabbing my notepad and pen

and heading for the double doors of our closed conference-room.

'But at least Lauren is in there too,' was Lucy's parting shot. 'She'll give you a dig out, wait and see.'

Lauren? I thought, as I opened the door.

Lauren, did she just say? What business had the office intern doing taking a major meeting with an even more major client like this? And even more worryingly, what exactly had gone on when I wasn't there?

*

As it happened, this particular meeting had been slated weeks ago to discuss a case settlement with none other than the mighty Jim Simpson of the Simpson Hotel Group. But as far as Harry, Bernie or myself were concerned, it was likely to be little more than a formality that would take no more than an hour tops, or so we'd all thought. This was almost something that could have been done over the phone via conference call, with Bernie off on a golf course and me sat at home at my kitchen table.

The deal was this; the prosecution, a rival firm we'd sparred against many times in the past, were representing a newly wedded bride who claimed – and with pretty good reason, as far as I could see – that the hotel had completely ruined her wedding day. Her wedding day that had cost in excess of €15k, by the way.

There really was no other way out of it, but for Simpson's to bite the bullet and settle, as Harry and I had advised at great length over the previous few months. So, by extension, the whole meeting with Jim Simpson should purely have been to monetise the amount we'd eventually settle on the Plaintiff, a Mrs Shauna Kelly.

Mrs Kelly was looking for damages to the full amount her wedding had cost, and not only did I agree with her, but I knew that a large part of Harry did too. After all, the poor woman's dream wedding day was ruined and fair is fair.

Our only challenge, as far as I was concerned, was to get the legendarily bullish Jim Simpson to see that this amount was a tiny drop in the ocean to him and that if he wanted to avoid all the negative publicity a case like this was bound to attract, the only option open to him was to apologise, settle quickly and have done with it.

I raced upstairs to the conference room, taking the stairs two at a time, in a hot, sweaty panic. Why had the time of the meeting had been shifted at the very last minute? And even worse, why had no one thought to tell me, a senior partner?

As I pushed open the heavy oak doors and stepped inside, to my astonishment all representatives of Sloan Curtis were present and correct along with Jim Simpson himself. Bernie was there, Harry, and even Lauren.

Jesus Christ, I thought as my eyes fell on her. *She's actually sitting in my chair.* She gave me a tiny, supportive wave and looked sympathetically over at me with the big chocolatey brown eyes, but still didn't budge out of the chair, I noticed. Instead she just shuffled a sheath of papers in front of her and busied herself making copious amounts of notes.

'Ahh, here she is now, *finally*,' said a very suntanned-looking Bernie. 'Good of you to grace us with your presence, Sarah.'

Bernie didn't seem as relaxed as he usually did though; instead there was an unmistakable hint of ice in his voice.

But then the Simpsons were huge and longstanding clients of ours, so it didn't do to arrive late, hassled and sweaty, utterly caught on the hop as all heads swiveled my way, taking in the sorry state of me.

'I'm so sorry everyone,' I said breathlessly, 'I had no idea the meeting had been moved.'

'Which is the very reason why mobile phones were invented,' Bernie muttered under his breath. I heard him loud and clear though, as he no doubt meant me to. Meanwhile Jim Simpson, the old Lothario himself with the awful Boris Johnson barnet, was straight up on his feet to shake my hand, as charming and affable as ever.

'Sarah, lovely to see you again,' he said with that oily smile so familiar to me from all the countless gossip pages he was such a regular fixture in, generally with a 'glamour model' draped across his arm. Kind of like a younger version of Hugh Hefner, if Hugh Hefner had a receding chin and came from Thurles.

'Kept you from the gym, have we?'

Puzzled, I looked back at Jim not having the first clue what the guy was on about, then glanced down to see that I was still wearing the battered pair of trainers that I'd worn into prison earlier.

Shit, shit, shit, I thought, as drops of sweat started to work their way slowly down the small of my back. I'd forgotten to change back into the usual court shoes I wore to work, which of course were still sitting on the passenger seat of my car. Jesus Christ, I thought, perching on a free chair at the very edge of the table. Could the afternoon possibly get any worse?

Yes, it seemed was the answer.

'To fill you in on what we've been discussing,' Harry said,

while I fumbled around my handbag to find my glasses, then plonked a notepad in front of me and madly tried to play catch up. 'As you know,' he patiently explained, bless him, 'this was originally designated to be a settlement meeting.'

'I'm sorry – why are you saying "originally designated?" I interrupted. 'This *is* a settlement meeting. We've already discussed it and agreed on it. All of us.'

I just caught a tiny, barely perceptible eye roll from Jim Simpson, but it was enough to alert me. Somehow it seemed, the goalposts had shifted since I'd been out of the office. And yet again, no one had thought to keep me informed.

'If I may just say something here for a moment,' said Jim, before helping himself to a sip of sparkling water from the bottle in front of him, 'as the client who's actually paying for this meeting, then, yes indeed, Sarah, your initial advice was that I should settle. I recall that meeting quite clearly.'

'And as I already pointed out to you back then, Jim,' I piped up, desperately trying to claw back lost ground, 'the reason we gave you that advice is because the bride who's suing you, Mrs Shauna Kelly, just happens to have a far stronger case than we do. The facts here speak for themselves. Her legal team sent us a whole litany of complaints that she's made against the Simpson Hotel Group, including the fact that—'

'I'm already aware of all this,' said Jim with a dismissive wave of his hand. 'Because the gluten-free meal option wasn't available for her guests at the wedding dinner, that we were short of vegetarian options, that the wedding band failed to turn up, blah, blah, blah . . .'

'And let's not forget that a bill for the entire shindig was shoved under the door of the Bridal Suite at 5am.' I went on, determined to have my say here. 'So after a whole catalogue of disasters, the first sight that greeted the new Mr and Mrs Kelly on their first day as a married couple was a bill for in excess of fifteen thousand euros, for what the Plaintiff has referred to as "the most horrendous anticlimax of my life".'

Sod this, I thought, suddenly cross. After all, I'd worked bloody hard on this case from day one. I'd done everything I could to placate Shauna Kelly and to reassure her that things would be settled in her favour, to keep her from blabbing about it on social media, if nothing else. Surely I was entitled to voice an opinion here.

'But then you see, something happened to change my mind,' Jim went on, addressing me in exactly the same tone of voice you'd use to speak to a dim-witted child. 'Or more correctly, my mind was changed for me,' he took great care to add. 'On the night of your party at Sloan Curtis, as it happened. Here, in this very conference room.'

'Excuse me?' I stammered, aware that my mouth had gone very dry and that my heart was hammering against my ribcage, cartoon-style. 'In that case, Jim, would you mind telling me what exactly happened?'

'I had quite an in-depth conversation about our case with this remarkable young lady here,' Jim smiled, indicating Lauren, who was sitting just across the boardroom table from me. 'And subsequently she and I had a number of follow-on phone conversations about the case, which I must say I found most enlightening.'

I turned to Lauren in total, white-faced shock but all I got in return was a tiny, embarrassed little shrug as if to say, 'well, what could I do?'

'Lauren?' I said, aware that the room was silent now and

222

that all eyes seemed to be focused on just her and me. 'Would you please tell me exactly what you've been up to?'

'You see what I mean?' Jim interrupted, speaking to Bernie, my direct boss and the man who paid my mortgage, who was by then shaking his head at me in sad disappointment. 'This is exactly what I was talking about. Your firm have represented my hotel group for years, but it seems to me as though your partners aren't as on top of important briefs as they used to be. And now here's your proof.'

'Excuse me, everyone,' I said, addressing the room, wanting to stand up, but uncertain as to whether my legs could take the weight of my body. 'I'm afraid I need a moment's recess, please. Lauren, would you mind stepping outside with me for a moment?'

'No, she can't,' Jim Simpson cut across me, quite rudely I thought. 'In fact, Sarah, you should be down on your knees thanking this young lady. She's single-handedly turned this case around for the Simpson Hotel Group. And possibly saved us a fortune in the process too.'

'I'm sorry, what did you just say?' I asked, flabbergasted.

'Sarah,' Lauren began, sounding calm, authoritative and utterly in control. So unlike me, I could practically see my colleagues thinking, as I sat there in a lather of sweat and worry, hopelessly unprepared for any of this. 'I'm absolutely aware that your strategy was to settle this case as quickly as possible,' she went on, as Jim sat there beaming at the girl. Actually bloody well beaming, the lascivious little shit, I thought crossly. 'Before it began to leak to the papers or social media,' she took care to add carefully.

'Yes,' I said briskly. 'And that's more or less what I signed off on. So would you kindly tell me what's been going on since, that you didn't see fit to tell me about?'

'Well, in the meantime,' she said, looking me straight in the eye, 'I spent some of my spare time really combing through all of the finer details on the case.'

'Which is not in your job description, Lauren,' I interrupted.

'Hardly the point,' Jim Simpson piped up. 'And if you ask me, you should be delighted to have an intern on board who's prepared to go the extra mile for her clients.'

'Of course I completely understand how you feel, Sarah,' Lauren said gently. 'The last thing I'd ever want to do is to overstep the mark. It's just that I couldn't help noticing that the Plaintiff in this case only ever had a verbal agreement with Jim's events manager.'

Jim? I thought, actually wondering if I'd been hearing things. What the fuck was this? She was on first name terms with him now?

'So I contacted the Plaintiff, Mrs Shauna Kelly, and took a detailed testimony from her, purely to save you all the time and bother,' she added, looking at me contritely. 'I know how busy you are right now and I so was anxious not to overload you.'

'It's my job,' I retorted. 'Besides, I already took testimony from the Plaintiff, Mrs Kelly. Many, many months ago, long before you started to work here. Naturally it was the first thing I did. As any competent lawyer would.'

'Ladies, ladies,' Harry interceded. 'Is this really the time or the place?'

'Maybe you could save the cat-fight till you're in private?' Jim added a bit snidely.

'If I may just finish what I was about to say,' Lauren said, never once raising her voice and being all the more effective for it, addressing the whole conference room like she'd been doing it her entire life. 'It seems Mrs Shauna Kelly had temporarily employed the services of a wedding planner.'

A wedding planner? Jesus Christ, where had that come from? In all my dealings with her, Shauna Kelly had never once breathed a single word to me about a wedding planner.

'I'm so sorry, but I'm afraid I'm going to have to stop you right there,' I managed to say to the room as politely as I could, given that I was practically spewing fire by then. Clearly though, this nightmarish situation could go on no further. I had to call a halt, if nothing else, to make myself look marginally less like a complete idiot than I already did.

So that's exactly what I did.

'I need to ask for a brief, five-minute recess, please,' I said in a wobbly voice that sounded absolutely nothing like my own. 'And Lauren, I'd like you to step outside with me.'

'Handbags at dawn,' I heard Jim Simpson mutter, doubtless as I was meant to. But I was past caring.

Instead, I stumbled out of the room, somehow managing to spill over a big pile of legal briefs that had been neatly laid out on the conference table, just in case I hadn't made enough of an exhibition of myself.

But I didn't care. I was beyond it at that stage. Beyond politeness, beyond concern, beyond the whole damn lot of them.

Chapter Twenty-one

Liz

TONY AND STELLA

REQUEST THE PLEASURE OF YOUR COMPANY
AT A CELEBRATION OF THEIR WEDDING
ON SATURDAY, THE FIFTEENTH OF JUNE
TWO THOUSAND AND SEVENTEEN AT 2PM.
RATHSALLAGH COUNTRY HOUSE HOTEL, CO. KILDARE
R.S.V.P.

I'd been looking forward to this wedding for weeks and had been on a diet since approximately last February, just so I could fit into my brand-new outfit courtesy of ASOS. To explain: Tony and Stella were long-standing pals of ours; we'd all been the best of buddies ever since we were at college together, all those long years ago.

It was our little six-some against the world in those halcyon days; Tony and Stella, Harry and myself, and, of course, Sarah and Tom too, back when they were still together. We'd all gone our separate ways after college but we stayed in touch and, now, to everyone's astonishment,

Tony and Stella had announced out of the blue that they had finally decided to tie the knot. That's after twenty-five years and two kids together, by the way. Two kids who were now at college-going age themselves.

Stunned and overjoyed at this wondrous news, I remember asking Stella, 'but why now? After all these years of being perfectly happy together, what was it that made you both want to tie the knot?'

'Because he *asked*,' is all she said, simply. Point taken.

As you can imagine, with neither the bride nor groom in the first flush of youth, this was to be a fairly low-key affair with no more than fifty guests, mostly family and close pals.

Still though, I was as almost as ridiculously excited about this wedding as I was about my own. There was just something so heartening about a couple who'd been through absolutely everything that life had to throw at them: births, marriages, deaths, bereavements, the whole shebang. And in spite of all that, they were still taking the time out to make this vow and say to the world, 'actually, I really do love this person just as much as I did when I was twenty and I finally want to make it official. Here and now, in front of my nearest and dearest.'

Harry and I had jokingly christened the whole wedding the 'Better Late Than Never' stakes and, as the countdown to the big day approached, it was all any of us could talk about.

Well, that and the whole ongoing situation with Sarah. Because surprise, surprise, she and I had barely exchanged two words since our row in the restaurant that horrible night. The Sarah I knew of old was stubborn, but so was I and throw two stubborn women together and, as Harry always says, that's how World Wars start.

So now, if Sarah needed to speak to Harry directly about something work-related, she just called his mobile, full stop. Time was when she'd have made a point of asking to speak to me afterwards, 'just for a quick natter and a gossip'. But that had all stopped, and, I can't deny it, it hurt like fuck.

One night she even called Harry while we were out to dinner with the boys, which might sound posh, but trust me, it was purely down to the fact there was nothing food-wise in the house the two little brats didn't turn their noses up at, so I hauled us all down to our local Pizza Stop for much face-stuffing there. Rosie, my daughter, was going through a whole phase of lacto-ovo-vegetarianism, so she'd elected to stay home and eat brown rice with a few lumpy bits of tofu clinging to the side of the bowl. Quite wisely, as it turned out.

The four of us were squished into a tiny little booth in the pizzeria: me, Harry, Sean, my six-year-old, and Jamie, aged eight. We were about to eat when Harry's mobile rang, just as four Sloppy Giuseppe pizzas were unceremoniously plonked down on the table in front of us.

Harry immediately picked up the phone, not before I had the chance to read the name flashing up on the mobile screen in front of me.

Sarah, Office Phone.

Harry gave me a swift, apologetic glance, then answered with a cacophony of noise in the background and a brewing row between the boys over the fact I wouldn't allow them to have Diet Coke.

'Yeah, hi, what's up?' Harry said, mouthing 'sorry about this!' at me. For the next ten minutes, he then kept up a one-sided monologue about the increasingly labyrinthine 'McKinsey nightmare', as he referred to it.

Meanwhile I tried to keep law and order around the restaurant table as Sean and Jamie decided they'd no interest in their pizzas and that it was far more craic instead to have a game of chasing around the tables. Scrambling up onto empty booths, screeching their heads off, the whole works. Every parent's basic nightmare.

'Sit down and eat your dinner, will you?!' I hissed at the pair of them, while other disgruntled diners shot filthy looks my way – something you get surprisingly used to as the mother of two energetic boys, believe me.

'Sean! Jamie! Do as you're told right now! Remember, Santa is *always* watching!'

I signaled to Harry to get off the shagging phone and to come and help me deal with this. But then typical of him – fancying himself as a bit of a peacemaker/UN-roving ambassador – he had to go and stick his big size eleven feet in it, didn't he?

'I'm sure you can hear all this bloody racket in the background, Sarah,' I heard him saying, just as Jamie decided it would be a great laugh to rip down all the menus from the hostess's station at the front of the restaurant and start playing Frisbee with them. 'Yeah, yeah, sure you know how it is with my pair,' he went on, while I chased after Jamie, 'I'm just out for a bite with Liz and the kids – and I know it sounds like bloody mayhem, but this is actually quite normal behaviour for the lads.'

As I scooped up a wriggling Jamie, I waved frantically at Harry to grab Sean who by then was jumping up and down on the seats in an empty booth. But my lovely, gorgeous gobshite of a husband went and misinterpreted me, didn't he?

'Actually Liz is here too and she's waving at me,' he said,

beckoning me over. 'I think she might want to say hi to you? About time too, if you ask me. This stupid bloody feud between the pair of you has gone on long enough.'

I mimed a gesture of slitting his throat, but it was already too late.

'Oh, OK then, Sarah,' Harry said, his big, hopeful face falling as his chance to be Kofi Annan and broker a peace deal between his wife and her best friend suddenly evaporated. 'Don't worry, I'll explain it to her. No, of course not, don't be daft. Liz will understand.'

He hung up to see me glaring back at him.

'Liz will understand what exactly?' I demanded.

'Sarah says she was . . . just really busy. In work. She didn't have time to say hi. Sorry love,' he added dolefully.

'Hardly your fault,' I said, bending down to mop up a half-drunk glass of Diet Coke that Sean had sent sloshing all over the table. 'In fact, half of me doesn't even blame Sarah. This is all down to that manipulative little witch Lauren, isn't it? She's the only one I really hold responsible for all this.'

'Jesus,' Harry muttered, while arm-wrestling both boys back into the booth and desperately trying to restore order. 'Why is everyone so down on Lauren? She's playing a blinder in work and if you ask me, we're bloody lucky to have her.'

'I'm not down on her. I just don't like her and I certainly don't trust her.'

'What is it with you women anyway?' Harry said under his breath, as the boys finally settled and began to eat their pizzas. 'Could it have anything to do with the fact that she's young and gorgeous-looking? Are you really sure there isn't a hint of the green-eyed monster here?'

So that was it. The end of what was supposed to be a relaxed family meal out. End of what was supposed to be a fun night for all of us. And if Harry hadn't had the wit to grovel later on that night, it would have been the end of him sharing a bed with his loving wife for the foreseeable future.

*

Then, not two days later, things took a turn that not even I could have predicted. I met up with Stella, my college pal and the bride-to-be herself, for a fitting at Brown Thomas in town. None of your frou-frou, twenty-something bridal showrooms for this gal though. No, as she said herself: 'I'm a middle-aged bride who doesn't give a shite what I wear. I just want to be comfortable and to enjoy my day.'

I went into the changing rooms with Stella as she paraded out in a simple, elegant, cream shift dress with sensible-looking flat shoes and a gorgeous little cashmere shrug, just in case it pissed rain on us. Highly likely during an Irish summer wedding, believe me.

'So whaddya think?' she said, eyeing herself up and down critically in the mirror, messing about with her pixie-cropped blonde hair. 'You know I'm not trying to be Kate Middleton here; I just want to be able to breathe after I've stuffed my face with the five-course meal we've ordered. Tell me the truth now, Liz.'

'Oh, Stella, you're utterly gorgeous,' I said, genuinely meaning it. 'A total princess, if you ask me.'

'Can you see my knickers through this fabric?' she said anxiously. 'Because over my dead body am I wearing a G-string for the day. Dental floss for the lady garden? I think not, thanks.'

'A decent pair of Spanx and you're laughing,' I said, taking a photo of her in the dress, so she could see for herself how terrific she really looked.

For all that she was acting the part of a low-key, no-fuss bride, I could tell that that day still meant a lot to Stella, as it would to any bride-to-be. So to celebrate the fact that we'd successfully bought her wedding rig out, I whisked her off to the nearby Peruke and Perriwig cocktail bar for a lovely big margarita each, to really mark the day and to make a big fuss of her.

It turned out to be the perfect spot too; not too packed, so we could really chat, yet trendy enough that it was suitable for a 'special occasion'. You know the type of bar cum restaurant: fancy, with a lot of red velvet upholstery and deep-purple swag curtains going on. Kind of like an English gentleman's club circa 1850, if it were transported to present-day Dawson Street, with all the deafening Luas works outside.

'This is the equivalent of a Ryanair wedding now,' Stella warned me as we nabbed a cosy table for two and scanned down the menus that an impossibly good-looking waiter handed us. 'So if tonight turns into a fecking hen night with women I haven't seen in twenty years jumping out of the woodwork to say "surprise!", I swear to Christ, Liz, I'll crucify you.'

'Just you and me, babes,' I reassured her, as we ordered drinks and settled down for a chat. 'But even though this is a low-key wedding, am I allowed ask how the planning is coming along?'

Stella had successfully managed to dodge any questions along those lines over the past few weeks, claiming that I was to line her up at dawn and shoot her if she dared turn into a bridezilla. But given that it was less than two weeks to the Big Day, I didn't think my question an unreasonable one.

'Don't talk to me,' she groaned, kicking off her too-high shoes and rolling her eyes. 'The actual getting married part is the easy bit. Where it gets tough is trying to keep all your guests happy. Where to even seat people, for a start. Jaysus, it's a bloody social minefield. You've no idea.'

I winced a bit at that, but then of course Stella was a good pal of both Sarah's and mine. I'd already filled her in on our big row and she knew only too well that the two of us weren't even on speaking terms by then.

'Look,' I said, pre-empting what was coming, 'you really don't need to worry. Sarah and I are both adults and after all, this is your day, babes. I faithfully promise you it's absolutely OK to put the pair of us at the same table without fear of a cat-fight.'

'No, no, it's not that,' Stella began to say but I just barreled over her.

'Trust me, we'll both be on our best behaviour, and you can take that to the bank. So just relax, and put all sorts of rubbishy crap about seating plans to the back of your mind, OK?'

'Liz, I don't think you fully understand—'

'Of course I do! But just remember this is meant to be your day, and nothing is going to change that. I just want you to be perfectly happy and chilled out for the day and I know Sarah wants the very same for you—'

'You're not listening to me,' Stella said, just as our cocktails arrived at the table. Served in big, flowery teapots – all très chic, if you don't mind.'

'Why? What's wrong?' I asked, suddenly concerned when I clocked the strained look on Stella's face.

'The problem I have isn't you or Sarah,' she said, slumping back into the deeply cushioned chair. 'In fact, the pair of you and whatever feud you have going on is actually none of my business.'

Like Harry, Stella had a strict policy of acting like Switzerland in my whole falling out with Sarah. A wise policy and one I was particularly grateful for. Sarah was my closest pal and no matter what had gone down between us, the last thing I'd ever have done was run her down in front of a mutual friend. End of.

'So what is it then?'

'Actually, it's Tom.'

'Tom? Sarah's Tom?'

'Sarah's ex, Tom,' she corrected me.

'So what's up with him now?' I asked, worriedly. But then I'd always been fond of Tom and, in spite of everything, I still harboured hopes that he and Sarah might yet come to their senses and reconcile.

'Well, it's just that he called over last night,' Stella tripped over herself to say, 'and he sort of took me by surprise, really.'

'Why? What did he do?'

'It's more what he's planning on doing.'

'Which is . . .?'

'He's all on for the wedding—'

'I should bloody well hope so—'

'But he asked if he might bring a plus one. A date, Liz. His first proper date since he and Sarah broke up. And he's taking her to our wedding. Right under his ex-wife's nose.'

'Did he say who he's bringing?' I asked in a very small voice, utterly shocked at what I was hearing.

So then she told me.

And, in that moment, I saw everything.

Chapter Twenty-two

Darcy

The restaurant was her first giveaway that something really serious was up. On a Friday lunchtime too, after a school half-day when Darcy had the whole afternoon free.

It was the fact that her dad had taken her somewhere fancy, somewhere you needed an actual reservation to get into in the first place. Normally during Darcy's time with him, he did nothing apart from gripe on about money and the lack of it. Darcy was even convinced her mum was giving him cash handouts to tide him over till payday. Generally they ordered take-out food whenever she was staying over at his flat, pizza featuring strongly. And if he did take her out for something to eat, it was always somewhere cheap and cheerful, like that bagel place in Dundrum, or else maybe Butler's café.

But she didn't mind though, and never moaned. After all, her sole goal was to get her parents back together again, and as quickly as possible, wasn't it? So maybe all it would take was a bit of acceptance on her dad's part that her mum was the primary breadwinner, and probably always would be. By then Darcy had convinced herself that financial troubles and nothing else were at the whole root of her parent's break-up. So as soon as her father realised how much he really needed and depended on her mum, then the sooner they could all go back to being a happy family together. Couldn't they?

So why, Darcy racked her brains to try to figure out, was he splashing out on taking her to the trendy Greenery restaurant for lunch that Friday afternoon? A pay bonus in work, she wondered? Hardly a Lotto win, she knew straight off. Her dad was such an impulsive type that, if that were the case, he'd probably have rocked up to the house to collect her from behind the wheel of a Ferrari, then announced they were all off to the Caribbean on a five-star cruise the following day.

She glanced down through the menu, but just as she was about to order, she suddenly noticed him tense up. You could always tell with her dad, because he got all twitchy – never a good sign. In fact the last time Darcy could remember him acting weird as this was the first weekend she'd spent with him at the flat, just the two of them, right after the separation.

'Dad?' she asked, putting the menu aside for the moment. 'Are you OK?'

'What? Oh yeah, great,' he said. 'Fantastic. Never been better. You?'

'Fine.'

'Good.'

Then an awkward silence, punctuated only by the restaurant clatter in the background. It was a busy lunchtime and this place was a hotspot, so it was fast filling up.

'How's school?'

'OK.'

'And that new pal of yours, Sophie?'

'She's great, thanks.'

'And everything OK in school?'

'Dad! You just asked me that!'

'Oh, did I? Yeah. Sorry, love. Right.'

With that, she put the menu aside and sat forward, looking him right in the eye. Just the way her mum always said she did whenever she was working with one of her prisoners on legal aid. 'If you ever need to get a straight answer out of someone,' she'd always cautioned Darcy, 'then be sure to make direct eye contact. It's far harder for anyone to lie when you're looking right into the whites of their eyes.'

'Dad,' she began tentatively, 'is everything OK with you?'

'Yeah. Absolutely. Why do you ask?'

'Because you're acting weird. And you haven't stopped drumming that fork off your glass ever since we came in here.'

'Well, actually there kind of is something I wanted to run by you,' he said, looking at her a bit shiftily.

'Yeah?' she thought, thinking – as she always did whenever he gave a long preamble to big news – just tell me in a single sentence.

'The thing is Darce,' he went on, waving the waiter away when he came to take their order, with a quick, mimed, 'give us a minute here, OK?'

'Spit it out, Dad, will you? You're starting to make me antsy.'

'Right then, here it is, love,' he said, leaning forward on his two elbows, looking directly at her and keeping his voice good and low, so they wouldn't be overheard. 'Your mum and I have been separated for – how long is it now, would you say?'

'Almost two years,' Darcy told him, although she could have given him a far more accurate tally if he'd wanted. Because it was actually nineteen months, three weeks and two days since that nightmarish Friday evening, when she'd bounced home from school without a care in the world, only to find her mum at home with her 'there's something I need to tell you, love'.

'Well, I won't deny it to you, Darce,' her dad went on, 'it's been challenging at times. For both your mum and me. And I know you found it that way too, but I just wanted to say that I really think you've been amazing throughout all this. You've been so grown-up about the whole thing, so mature and I'm really proud of you.'

Darcy's head started to work overtime. Where the fuck was this going anyway?

'But you know, I'd be lying if I didn't admit that this was really taking its toll,' he went on, as some kind of Spanish guitar music played softly in the background. 'Living on your own isn't easy, you know. Particularly when you're used to being one half of a partnership, as your mum and I always were. As we're all meant to be, I believe.'

At that, Darcy caught her breath. Could this be THE conversation? The one she'd waited for all this time? The one where her parents finally told her they were reuniting?

'Go on,' she said hopefully, unconsciously gripping the edge of the table and inching her chair in closer. This she had to hear loud and clear.

'I'll be honest with you, Darce,' her dad went on, 'I'm rubbish at being on my own. Look, you're old enough now that I can be totally honest with you. And the truth is that I like having a partner in my life, it's how I function best.'

'You're dead right, Dad,' Darcy said, as a tidal wave of relief flooded over her. They were getting back together! They had to be! Finally, after all this time. And she'd been right all along. All her parents needed was just a bit of time out, that was all it took for them to realise just how stupid this whole separation lark had been.

Course if they'd even bothered to ask Darcy in the first place, she could have told them ages ago that they really belonged together and saved them all months of anxiety and heartache. But what the hell, she thought, suddenly feeling warm and benevolent towards the world. Better late than never.

'I can see how crap it's been for you living on your own, Dad,' she said generously, even reaching across the table to take his hand, something she hadn't done since she was about five. 'You always seemed so much happier when you were with Mum.'

'That's exactly it, love,' her dad went on. 'Although, mind you, I think it's a bit different for her.'

'Different for her – how exactly?' she asked, puzzled. What exactly did he mean by that?

'Well, she's got so many other things going on in her life,' he said, 'you know what I mean. Between all her legal aid work and then the hours she has to put in at Sloan Curtis just to stay on top of things. Your mum is a fabulous lady, but—'

Darcy didn't like the sound of that 'but'. Not one bit. Her stomach clenched up and whereas she'd been starving when she first got to the restaurant, now the garlicy smell from the kitchen was making her want to heave.

239

'But what, Dad?'

'But she's also a very independent lady, isn't she? I mean, you can see that for yourself, love. The two things that fuel her in life are number one, you, then secondly, her passion for the law. It's like a vocation with her. Most people we knew in college who went on to become lawyers only did it for the dosh. Not Sarah though. She did it because she genuinely wants to help people and to make a difference. I sometimes think that even if she never got paid, she'd still do it all for free. Come on, Darce, you know that as well as I do.'

But Darcy didn't. Nor did she properly understand where this long, meandering preamble was headed.

'So . . . what are you getting at?' she asked, with a horrible, sour feeling at the back of her mouth.

'I think it's time for me to move on,' he said softly, leaning across the table. 'But of course, only if that's OK with you. You're number one in my life too, you know that, love. And I'd never, ever want to do anything that might hurt you or upset you in any way at all.'

'And what is it that you want to do, exactly?'

'The thing is,' he said, awkwardly shifting about in the chair under him, 'as you know Stella and Tony's wedding is coming up.'

'Yeah?' said Darcy. Of course she knew about the wedding. Stella and Tony were her godparents, for fuck's sake. She hadn't been invited herself, as it was to be a small, low-key affair, given that the bride and groom were both about a hundred years old. But both her parents were going and Darcy knew how much her mum had been looking forward to it. She'd even booked to get her hair done beforehand and everything.

'And I'd like to take someone with me. But as I said, pet,

only if that's absolutely OK with you. You've got the veto on this, I want you to know that.'

'Jesus, Dad,' she said, the nausea she'd felt curdled her tummy. 'Are you talking about . . . taking a date to this wedding with you? An actual *date*?'

'Well, yeah,' he replied, flushing scarlet red, 'I am actually.'

Darcy thought she'd throw up.

'Who? *Who* is she?'

'It's fine, love,' he said, making a 'shush, calm down' gesture at her, and it was only then Darcy realised she'd been raising her voice.

'It's actually someone you already know. Someone you're already very fond of. That's why I'm hoping you'll be OK with this.'

Then he told her, ending his doubtlessly rehearsed little spiel with a shrug and a 'so what do you think, love?'

Then silence. Long, deafening silence, as all Darcy's long-held hopes melted to ice in front of her.

'You really want to know what I think, Dad?' she eventually replied in a low, eerily calm voice, quietly furious now that she knew the very worst. 'Then here's what I think. I think how *dare* you? How can you do this to me? Or to Mum? And you've even got the balls to sit there and justify this by saying that it's OK for Mum to be on her own, just because she's devoted to her work?'

'Come on now, love, there's no need to overreact,' her dad said, but Darcy interrupted him.

'Fuck you anyway!' she said, raising her voice and not even caring, as other lunchtime diners threw worried glances their way. She flung her napkin on the table and got up to storm out, almost making it as far as the door, before she turned back to get the last word in.

241

'Darcy, please come back—' her dad was saying, but she drowned him out.

'Fuck you and fuck Lauren too!'

*

'Lauren?' Darcy said down the phone, as she ran down Dawson Street, then turned into a branch of Topshop on Stephen's Green, where she was fairly sure her dad wouldn't be able to find her. 'Are you avoiding my calls or what? This is, like, the third message I've left for you. It's me. It's Darcy. I think you can guess what I'm ringing about. And you can be sure that it's bloody well urgent.'

Her phone kept ringing, but it was her dad's number that flashed up, so she angrily clicked it off every time. He could feck right off with himself, she thought. And if he went through with this date, then not only would she never speak to him again, she'd make his life a living hell.

Lauren! Bloody *Lauren!*

It was disgusting. Beyond belief. OK, so she might have picked up signs that her dad was flirting with Lauren over the last while, but the fact that the bitch actually took him up on his invitation to that wedding, without a single word either to Darcy or her mum? When they were all living under the same roof together? It beggared belief.

Darcy wandered aimlessly around Topshop till she cooled down a bit, then, just as she was on the bus home, the call she'd been waiting for finally came through.

Up flashed the name on the screen in her hand, clear as day.

Lauren. Office number.

Darcy answered immediately, the phone fumbling in her hands as she did. Suddenly she felt angrier than she'd ever felt, and wanted nothing more than to be able to rattle off everything she'd rehearsed in her head, every insult and every accusation, all without getting emotional. 'The minute you get emotional in any argument,' her mum always warned her, 'is the minute you lose.'

'Lauren,' Darcy said as coolly as she could, given that her hands were trembling so much by then that she could barely grip the phone.

'Hi Darcy,' she heard Lauren saying down the phone. She could almost hear the smile in her voice too. Like nothing was up, like there was absolutely nothing out of the ordinary going on. 'Are you OK? I was a little worried when I saw all the missed calls and texts from you. Everything alright in school?'

'This isn't a social call,' Darcy said, trying to channel a particularly assertive teacher she liked and admired in school for her take-no-prisoners, spunky attitude.

'What's up then?' Lauren asked, brazen as you like, sounding like she genuinely hadn't a clue.

'Oh, I think you know perfectly well why I'm calling you,' Darcy almost spat down the phone, dimly aware of an old lady sitting on the bus seat right beside her, tuning in to every word.

There was a pause, but Darcy let the silence sit instead of rushing to fill it like she normally would.

'I'm in work right now,' Lauren eventually said. 'And I'm just on my way into an important meeting with the Simpson Hotels Group, which will probably take up most of the afternoon. Can this wait? Whatever it is?'

'No,' said Darcy. 'It can't wait. You see, I've just come from a lunch with my dad.'

'I see,' Lauren said calmly after a long pause. 'Tell you

what, why don't we speak about this later? After work? I could bring home the makings of a yummy dinner and we can cook together and have a chat then?'

'No, we'll bloody well talk about it now,' Darcy insisted. 'And the thought of eating dinner with you makes me want to vomit.'

'Look, my meeting is literally about to begin,' said Lauren, 'and I can't be late. Sorry about this, but I'm afraid I'm going to have to call you back.'

'Dad said he was taking you to this wedding that's coming up,' Darcy blurted out, determined to have her say. She was all fired up for this and there was absolutely no way she was letting this bitch get away with what she'd done. 'Dad told me just now; I heard it straight from the horse's mouth. And he said that you'd agreed to go. With my father. On a fucking *DATE*, Lauren!'

The old biddy in the bus seat beside her tsk-tsked under her breath at the language but Darcy didn't give a shit.

'And, as I said, I think you and I should discuss this later,' came the cool reply.

'Did you tell my mum? Because if you don't, then I bloody well will.'

Darcy had left a few messages for her mother already, but her phone was switched off. She knew her mum was doing her whole legal aid thing that afternoon and apparently they confiscated your phone at prison security.

'This is hardly the time or the place,' said Lauren.

'So when exactly were you planning on telling my mum and me? On the morning of the wedding, when Mum bumped into you on your way into the church? After everything she's done for you? After she went and got you a job and not only that, but then gave you the roof over your head? What kind of a *duplicitous fucking bitch* are you anyway, Lauren?'

There was an even longer pause this time before Lauren spoke again. Darcy held her breath, half-hoping to be soothed and calmed and reassured that this was just a big misunderstanding, nothing more. That her dad had got hold of the wrong end of the stick. That he might have had a bit of a sad-old-man crush on Lauren, but that there was absolutely no way in hell she was going as his date to this wedding. In front of her mother. In public, for all their mutual friends to see.

But that's not what Lauren said at all.

'You know, your father is quite entitled to move on,' came the calm, measured reply, as Darcy strained to believe her ears. 'And although you mightn't think it now, Darcy, he actually did the right thing in telling you first. In asking your permission, so to speak.'

'Well, it's not OK with me,' Darcy hissed back at her down the phone. 'It's weird and it's sick and it's freaking me out and Mum is going to go ballistic when she hears about this!'

'It really is such a shame you're taking that attitude, Darcy. Are you aware of just how childish you're sounding right now?'

'Are you aware of what a fucking bitch you're being right now?'

'You don't have to play your cards like this,' Lauren went on. 'After all, you're hardly in any position to tell me what I can and can't do, now are you?'

'And what's that supposed to mean?'

'Only that I did you a favour not so long ago, remember? That night you got yourself so disgustingly drunk at your friend's party that you passed out on the grass outside. Remember, Darcy? Because I certainly do. I got you out of that situation and you made me swear not to tell either of your parents, so I kept my word.'

'What the fuck has that got to do with this?' Darcy demanded, her head swimming, while the old biddy beside her glared hotly back at her.

'I did something for you,' came the unhurried response, 'and now, it would seem, it's your turn to do something for me in return'.

'Do what exactly?'

'Oh please, Darcy. Do I have to spell it out for you? Are you really as thick as all that?'

'Lauren, you're starting to scare me now.'

'What's really frightening is just how upset your parents would be if they were ever to find out the real truth about what happened that night,' Lauren went on, utterly unruffled. 'About the amount you drank. How you almost got raped by some complete idiot because you were stupid enough to get locked into a bathroom with him. If I hadn't been there, you could so easily have ended up as a cautionary tale on the six o'clock news. It would break your mother's heart if she were ever to find out the truth about her precious daughter. Surely even someone as self-absorbed as you can see that.'

'So . . . what are you saying?' Darcy said weakly, glad she was actually sitting down for this. If she'd been standing, there was a good chance she'd have keeled over.

'I'm suggesting that if you want Mummy and Daddy to continue to believe the myth that you're little Miss Perfect Daughter, then you'd be well advised to say and do exactly what I'm telling you. Otherwise—'

Lauren didn't finish the sentence, but then she hardly needed to. Darcy knew exactly what she was getting at.

All of a sudden, she felt violently sick just thinking about what had been left unsaid between them.

Because now this was it, the very worst. She was being blackmailed, simple as that.

'So are we cool?' came Lauren's voice from the other end of the phone. 'Because if you're finally ready to see a bit of sense, then I need you to listen to me very carefully. Do you understand?'

Chapter Twenty-three

Sarah

'I'm still waiting on your explanation,' I said, arms folded crossly as Lauren and I stood face-to-face right outside the Sloan Curtis conference room. Jim Simpson and half the board of Simpson Hotels were still inside, having a brief, tense five-minute recess with Bernie and Harry, while I insisted on hauling Lauren out of there so I could get to the bottom of this. There were a significant number of raised eyebrows and a lot of audible tut-tutting from Bernie as I called for the short break, but I was beyond caring by that point.

'You made me look like a complete and utter idiot in there,' I almost spat, as Lauren calmly stood in front of me, not saying anything, just letting me rant, rage and spew rings of fire in her face. 'What's all this about the Plaintiff employing a wedding planner anyway? And why am I only hearing about it now?'

'If you're quite finished,' she said softly, her brown eyes looking innocently back at me from under those eyelashes, 'I was just about to explain.'

'Well, I suggest you make it a good one,' I snapped.

'Because after the stunt you pulled in there, it bloody well better be.'

'I was working entirely off one of my own hunches,' Lauren said, careful to keep her voice good and low so that even Lucy couldn't hear from where she was sitting at reception. 'You have to understand that. Nothing more. And I had a strong, gut feeling that Mrs Shauna Kelly had been behaving like a bit of a bridezilla. Certainly in the run-up to her wedding.'

'So?'

'So, I followed up on it,' she went on calmly. 'In my own time, of course. Just to put my mind at rest. First of all, I contacted Mrs Kelly to pick over her statement with her a little more carefully. We had a long and exhaustive chat and she inadvertently revealed that she'd hired a wedding planner. A Mr Frank Skinner. Only for a very short time though.

'Reading between the lines, it seemed that she and Mr Skinner fell out fairly quickly afterwards. Something to do with a flock of doves being released outside the church as the happy couple came out after the service. I'd need to get back to my notes to confirm that with you, though. It might have been an issue over Shauna Kelly insisting the birds be dyed pink, to match her bridesmaids dresses.'

'I'm not interested in a flock of pink doves,' I said waspishly, 'I'm interested in what information this wedding planner brought to the case and why it never occurred to you to tell me.'

'If you'd just let me finish,' Lauren said, as coolly as if she and I had been having a natter about some movie we were planning to check out later that night and nothing more. 'I'm trying to explain. Rightly or wrongly, I contacted this Mr Frank Skinner. Turns out he's quite a flamboyant character and he spoke to me at great length. According to him, Mrs Kelly had been a complete nightmare to work with right from the outset, making all sorts of ridiculous demands that were impossible to follow through on. At the last minute, she decided she wanted the entire theme of the wedding completely changed, so that the inside of the hotel banqueting hall looked like Hogwarts. All this was with one week's notice, by the way. Mr Skinner claimed she was impossible to work with and walked off the job. I took a detailed statement from him, which I'd be happy to show you. I think his exact words were that Mrs Kelly's behaviour was 'more diva-like than Barbra Streisand and Cher put together'.

'Never mind about Barbra Streisand or Cher,' I interrupted briskly. 'What I'm interested in is how this relates to Jim Simpson and the settlement we were advising him to take.'

'Mr Skinner,' Lauren went on, 'has gone on record saying he was present at a meeting where it was clearly outlined by the Simpson's Hotels event planner that a lot of Mrs Kelly's demands just couldn't be met. So in other words—'

'In other words,' I said, thinking aloud, 'we now have an independent witness who can go on record and claim that Mrs Kelly was never once guaranteed any one of the items she's prepared to go to court over.'

'Of course, it's very shaky as a defence,' Lauren added, 'which is why I didn't want to bother you with this. It was nothing more than a shot in the dark for us, albeit one that might just work. But it is certainly enough for Jim Simpson not to have to settle this right now. If nothing else, it buys us some leeway, doesn't it?'

'Yes, yes, I suppose it does,' I said briskly, my mind busily working overtime. 'But you really should have come to me with this first. You had absolutely no right to announce this in front of our clients and make me look like a total dimwit in the process.'

'Sarah, you know I would never do anything like that to undermine you,' she said, sincerity burning from every pore on her face, putting me in mind of one of my mother's holy pictures.

'And yet that's exactly what you did, Lauren. Didn't you?'

'I was calling you all afternoon to try to tell you, but of course your phone was—'

'Oh save it,' I said, turning on my heel and heading crossly back into the conference room to face the music.

*

'Now I've something to tell you and I don't want you to overreact.'

'What? What is it? Is it Darcy?'

'Darcy is one hundred per cent fine so don't worry. Just hear me out, OK?'

I was back at my desk later on that evening and Tom had just called. My heart constricted in my chest when I saw his number flashing up on the phone, but then whenever Tom called me unprompted, the rule of thumb was that it was never, ever good news. I still hadn't fully recovered from the time he took Darcy rollerblading in the park and she ended up in the A&E with two broken ribs. And that was ten years ago.

And so he told me. Everything. In typical Tom-style, even managing to get a dig in at me right at the very end of the call. Just in case my day hadn't been sufficiently shitty enough.

I listened to him. I heard him out as calmly as I could, all while I waited on the time-delay for the shock to really kick in.

'You know, it's really not that big a deal, Sarah,' he'd said. 'Besides, can I remind you that this whole separation was your big idea in the first place? So what did you expect me to do? Stay celibate for the rest of my life? Darcy is fine with this, and as far as I'm concerned, that's all that matters.'

'But *Lauren*?!' I managed to say numbly down the phone; the only thing keeping my tone civil the fact that I was still in the office and could be clearly overheard. 'Of all the women in the western world, you had to invite *Lauren* to the wedding?'

'What's wrong with my asking Lauren?' came the cool reply. 'She's single and thanks to you, so am I.'

'She lives with me, that's what!' I hissed back. 'And she works with me. Not to mention the fact that she's young enough to be your daughter. Tom, this is weird and it's sick—'

'Don't be ridiculous, you know perfectly well it's neither of those things. Lauren's great, she and I get on well and I needed a date for the wedding. Frankly, if you've got a problem with it, then that says more about you than it does me. If Darcy has no issue with this, then I can't understand why you're making all this fuss over nothing.'

*

Darcy was up in her bedroom by the time I got home, so I raced up the stairs to her, desperate to see her, to talk to her, to know how she was really taking this.

'Sweetheart,' I said, bursting into her room without even

252

bothering to knock. And there she was at her desk with her laptop propped up in front of her.

'Are you OK?' I said, coming around to face her full-on.

'About what?' she said, deliberately not lifting her eyes off the screen.

'I just spoke to your dad,' I said, gently, perching on the desk beside her so I could really read her face. 'And he told me.'

'Oh yeah, right,' she said with a tiny shrug. 'You mean about Dad taking Lauren to this wedding, I suppose.'

'Of course that's what I mean! So are you sure you're OK about it, love? I mean . . . it certainly took me by surprise, I can tell you.'

A gross understatement, if ever there was one. Truth was, now that the initial shock had settled, I was starting to feel nothing but anger. A cold, white anger that the only woman in the northern hemisphere Tom could 'move on' with happened to be my house-lodger, who'd just pulled one over on me in work earlier that day.

'If it makes them both happy,' said Darcy, eyes still glued to the laptop, 'then I suppose why not?'

'Darcy,' I said, going to close down the lid of her computer.

'Ahh, Mum, leave that open, will you? I was just in the middle of posting a photo!'

'This is important,' I told her. 'So just look me in the eye, will you?'

She slumped back into her desk chair, folding her arms sulkily.

'Because I think this is a shock for both of us,' I went on. 'So if you're not OK with it, then now is the time to tell me, all right, love?'

253

Not that I'd have been exactly sure of where to take it from there had she said, 'no, this is ick on every level, make it stop, Mum, for the love of God, will you just make it stop?'

But what she said next actually stunned me.

'I think it's actually kind of cool,' she eventually said. 'I like Lauren and if Dad was going to move on with anyone, then isn't it better that it's someone you and I get along with?'

I looked right at her, scanning her face up and down, trying to find a telltale sign that the kid was lying. But then, the logical part of my brain said, why would she lie?

So, God forgive me, I took her at her word.

'As long as you're OK about it all,' I said doubtfully.

'Better than OK,' she said, a bit too brightly. 'I think this is really great. And I couldn't be happier for both of them. Honestly, Mum, you really don't need to worry about me. It's fine. It's good. I'm cool.'

Chapter Twenty-four

Liz

'And now, I'd ask you all to raise your glasses to my beautiful bride. Stella, you make me happier than I ever could have dared to hope, and there's not a day goes by that I don't fall in love with you just a little bit more. So thank you, my love. Thank you for being my soulmate. Thank you for being my life partner throughout all these years of happily unmarried bliss.'

'Yeah, because it's all downhill from here you know!' some smartarse from the back of the function room yelled out. I swiveled around to see who it was, but it was too packed to see properly.

'Thank you for putting up with me,' Tony, the groom went on, valiantly soldiering on with his speech, 'and for being such a fantastic mum to our gorgeous kids all these years. Stella, you're the glue that keeps our little family together, and I love you just as much, if not more than I did on the day we first met. I can't tell you what joy it gives me to be able to say that in front of all our nearest and dearest. I love you from the bottom of a very full heart. And today Stella, you've made me the happiest man on

255

earth. Ladies and gentlemen, will you please raise your glasses to my beautiful bride!'

There was a round of thunderous applause at that and not long after, the happy couple took to the floor for their first dance. Meanwhile, the rest of the guests, myself and Harry included, formed an impromptu circle around them, as bride and groom whirled away to their first dance.

Which was to *There May Be Trouble Ahead*, by Nat King Cole by the way, to gusts of giggles from the assembled throng. But this couple had already dealt with just about everything life can throw at any of us; the good, the bad and the ugly. What further trouble, we all wondered, might possibly lie ahead for them, that they hadn't already come shining through?

Harry's chunky hand slipped over mine as we stood side-by-side watching the bride and groom dance and I squeezed it back, really delighted that the day had gone off so well. Stella may have claimed to be a 'Ryanair bride' who insisted on no fuss or frills, but still. This was her wedding day and I knew she wanted it all to run smoothly. And by and large, it had.

It was coming up to 9pm but, amazingly, the sun had shone all day and it was still bright enough that smokers and anyone who wanted a gulp of fresh air could drift in and out to the gardens through the open terrace doors, without fear of getting hypothermia. We were in the gorgeous, uber-luxurious Rathsallagh House for the wedding and the staff had really excelled themselves. The banqueting hall where the reception dinner was held had been lovingly decorated in delicate shades of lavender and lilac, all to compliment Stella's bridal colours.

It looked so simple and understated, just as Stella had

wanted, yet there was a fun nod to Tony and his tastes too when the wedding cake was wheeled out. In the shape of a giant Manchester United football jersey, Tony's favourite team. The hotel's banqueting team had surpassed themselves too, with a wedding dinner of Tuscan garden salad, baby rack of lamb and melt-in-the-mouth strawberries and cream that just made me feel like I should have been sitting Centre Court at Wimbledon.

The happy couple have two teenage kids, and Josh and Charlotte both made beautiful, heartfelt speeches that left not a dry eye in the house. Charlotte even raised a huge laugh by promising her parents not to have any house parties when the bride and groom were off on honeymoon, then gave a dirty big wink to the congregation and hissed, 'and if the old pair believe that, they'll believe anything. So watch this space, folks.'

'I always know if there's been a party when we're away,' Stella interrupted, to raucous laughter from around the room, 'because whenever we get back home, the house is always *too* clean!'

So overall it had been a happy, joyous occasion, I thought, happily snuggling into Harry as the bride and groom whirled away on the floor in front of us.

There'd only been one fly in the ointment that day and that was Tom and his bloody 'date'. Sitting at a table directly opposite us, with Madam Lauren dolled up to the nines wearing a long, flowing maxi dress in a vibrant shade of scarlet, which, much as it choked me to say it, actually looked well on her. Tom, for his part, couldn't take his eyes off Lauren and almost burst with pride every time he got to introduce her as 'my date for the day'.

'So where's Sarah?' I made a point of asking him earlier,

just as we were all settling down into our seats for the civil partnership bit of the service. I pointedly ignored Madam Lauren and even gave Harry a sharp poke in the ribs when he greeted her with an over-friendly 'hi!' Not only that, but I made a point of telling all our mutual pals at the wedding exactly who the little she-witch was and how hurtful and insensitive her presence here was to Sarah.

Sarah, who as it happened, had chickened out of going to the wedding altogether, claiming that she had mounds of work to catch up on for the McKinsey case and that she'd see us all at the afters instead. I knew right well what was really going on though; the subtext was all too obvious. She didn't want to spend the whole day looking at Tom with Lauren, and honestly, who could blame the woman?

Sure enough, on the dot of 9pm, I glanced over to see Sarah's lonesome, petite little silhouette framed against the doorway of the reception room. She looked gorgeous too, in a neat, blue, floral dress with a jacket to match that I'd never seen on her before, which meant she must have gone out and bought it specially.

She stood in the doorway wavering, but I seemed to be the only one who noticed her coming in; everyone else was having too much fun either Instagramming the newlyweds having their first dance or else slagging them off about it. Harry's eye followed mine though and as soon as he clocked Sarah, he instantly released his big, firm grip from around my waist.

'You know what to do here, Lizzie,' he said simply. 'She's your best friend, the pair of you haven't spoken in weeks and just look at her. If ever she needed you, it's now. So go for it and remember, friends don't judge. And a real friend always forgives.'

Point taken.

'Sarah?' I said, approaching her gingerly, but then this was the first real face-to-face contact she and I had had in weeks.

'Hi,' she said, looking at me almost bashfully. 'It's good to see you, Liz. Lovely dress. You look gorgeous in that nude colour, it really suits you.'

'Bollocks, the dress makes me look like a walking bandage and you know it,' I quipped, and was rewarded with a tiny smile. 'I really needed you with me when I was dress-shopping, Sarah. You and only you could have saved me from looking like a giant Elastoplast.'

A tiny pause while we weighed each other up, each of us wondering who'd speak next.

'So how did the day go?' she eventually asked.

'It was mostly beautiful and you should have been here for it.'

'Yeah,' she sighed, 'well, you know, work. At least I got here in time for the afters though.'

'Stella will be thrilled you've made it,' I said, but Sarah just looked back at me with a strange, puzzled expression.

'Why did you say the day was mostly beautiful?' she asked, as if the thought had just struck her. 'I mean, why only "mostly"?'

'The reason for that,' I told her straight, 'is sitting at a table directly behind you to your right, at two o'clock.'

Her head swiveled around and in a flash she took it all in. Tom, with Madam Lauren. They were sitting side by side as he droned on about something, doubtless to do with that motorbike obsession of his, while Lauren was smiling politely back. If she was only feigning interest, I thought, then she was doing a bloody good job of it.

'Jesus,' said Sarah in a little voice, almost under her breath, 'I never thought either of them would actually go through with it. I genuinely didn't.'

'That Lauren one is a she-witch from hell,' I said crisply. 'And if it's any consolation, I've spent most of the day describing her as exactly that to anyone who'll listen.'

A tiny smile from Sarah.

'Plus, would you look at how overdressed she is?' I added. 'Totally unsuitable for a low-key wedding.'

'She could be going to the Oscars in that dress, all right,' Sarah joined in, even though we both knew we were lying. There was no denying the fact that, like it or not, Madam Lauren actually did look radiant.

'Covered in pimples,' I said cattily, starting to enjoy this. 'I mean, you can practically see the half pound of Mac concealer she's had to put on her zits from here. Just so people won't look at her and vomit.'

'And has no one told her that it's the height of bad manners to wear a long dress to a wedding? Looks like trying to upstage the bride,' Sarah added.

'And what about the state of that date of hers?' I went on. 'What a bloody lech! Old enough to be her dad and looking like a pimp beside her, if you ask me.'

I think I might have taken the joke a tad too far though because next thing Sarah changed the subject and asked where she could get a good, stiff drink. I needed no further cue, so I gripped her arm and steered her off in the direction of the bar.

'Now come on, Missus,' I said bossily. 'You're a brave lady to get this far, but I really do think you'll fare an awful lot better from here on in with a very large mojito in your hand.'

'I think I might just need one,' she said, meekly allowing herself to be led. Two minutes later, we were propped up at the bar having a pretend fight over who got to pay – at an open bar. Then we both giggled awkwardly and sat back onto bar stools, as two fresh drinks were plonked down in front of us.

'Just like old times,' I said after a pause and Sarah gave me a tiny smile. 'Now come on,' I went on, feeling flushed and delighted the pair of us were actually back on speaking terms again, 'don't you think this daft feud between us has gone on quite long enough? I can't tell you how much I've missed you. I've missed our chats, our nights out and our Saturday nights in front of the telly with a takeaway. I've missed it all so much.'

'Oh, me too,' she said feelingly.

'The past few weeks have been shite without you and when I think of what we fell out over in the first place? Seriously, can you think of anything more stupid?'

'No, I certainly can't,' said Sarah, putting down the mojito on the bar in front of her so she could really give me her full attention. 'You know what? It's me who should be apologizing to you, Lizzie. After all, all you did was try to give me a friendly warning about Lauren. And I jumped down your throat and just left you in that restaurant high and dry. Can you ever forgive me?'

'Don't be so bloody daft.' I smiled, clinking glasses with her. 'Course you're forgiven. Sure what are friends for?'

'If it's any consolation,' she added, 'I'm starting to see where you were coming from, with regards to Madam . . . I mean, to Lauren.'

261

'Wow!' I said. 'Sarah, this is a bloody breakthrough moment for you, babes! I think that's the first unkind thing I've ever heard you say about another living creature.'

'I suppose I never really thought that she and Tom would go through with it,' she went on, sounding a bit sad, which melted my heart even more. 'Knowing full well that I'd be here. Knowing that Stella is an old pal of mine going back decades and knowing that there'd be a roomful of our mutual friends here too. I mean how could he do that? How could either of them . . .?'

'I hear you, sister,' I nodded, as we both automatically turned to look at the now deserted table where just Tom and Lauren sat alone. Everyone else was up dancing to *Bad Romance* by Lady Gaga, so there was just the two of them left there.

'After everything I've done for her?' Sarah said.

'Couldn't agree more,' I nodded sagely. 'And now it's my turn to make yet another apology.'

'What for?'

'For all the times I encouraged you to get back with Tom. For all the times I told you that Darcy needed her dad around and that you should seriously consider it. Because I'm looking at him now without the friendship goggles and thinking, Christ alive, you had a lucky escape.'

'I'll drink to that,' said Sarah, taking a tiny sip of the mojito in front of her.

'But on the plus side,' I said, 'it doesn't exactly look as though either of them are enjoying themselves, now does it? If you ask me, he looks like he's boring her to sobs, doubtless going on about the merits of a Harley Roadster versus a kick up the arse, whereas she . . .'

'. . . she looks like she's only feigning politeness,' Sarah finished the sentence for me. 'And that she'd actually far rather be scanning down through all the messages on her phone right now.'

'So why do you think Tom went through with it anyway?' I asked, thinking aloud more than anything else. But then I was a bit woozy from one drink too many and it was pretty much all Harry and I had talked about for the day. 'To make a point to you? To rub your nose in it? Or is this just a case of Tom Keyes and the Mid-Life Crisis?'

'Oh God,' Sarah groaned. 'As far as I'm concerned, let him. He's certainty done a lot worse, hasn't he?'

I nodded, knowing exactly what she was referring to.

'But it's her I can't get my head around,' Sarah went on, her eye drifting back to Lauren.

'Believe me, you're preaching to the choir here,' I said, trying hard to keep the poison out of my voice. 'Plus you're sharing a house with the bitch,' I added, taking great satisfaction from the fact that Sarah didn't leap to Lauren's defense, as she automatically would have done. A very good sign, I thought. 'So how has the little minx been acting around you since it came out she was coming to this wedding?'

'We've been carefully side-stepping each other,' Sarah said, 'which is surprisingly easy to do these days. Lauren seems to live in the office and by the time she's home at night, Darcy and I have long since gone to bed. And you know what, Liz?'

'What's that?'

'I'm bloody glad of it. And the sooner I can get her out of my house, the better. Don't get me wrong, I'm relieved that Darcy doesn't have an issue with Tom moving on, but still.'

'Still . . . what?' I said hopefully.

'If you ask me, Lauren just pushed her luck a bit too far this time. And maybe this is just the catalyst that I finally needed to see what you've been warning me about all this time.'

She put her drink back down on the bar counter and really looked at me, even though I almost had to strain to hear her over the band belting out that old wedding staple, '*Sweet Caroline*' by Neil Diamond.

'Because I think you've been right all along,' Sarah eventually said. 'Lauren is trouble. Big, big trouble. I think she's been using me from day one and, although I barely noticed in the early stages, now the stakes are suddenly a whole lot higher.

'The girl is a game-player, Liz. And a brilliant one at that. She doesn't care what she has to do to get exactly what she wants. Which she always, always does. Isn't tonight all the proof I need?'

And if she's capable of doing something like this, I thought darkly, then what else is she capable of?

Chapter Twenty-five

Sarah

'Oh, excuse me, I thought you were finished in here.'

'Five more minutes is all I need.'

'Fine. Sorry to have interrupted you.'

'That's OK.'

'I'll just wait back in my room then. Till you're finished, that is.'

'Yes. I think that's probably for the best, Lauren.'

Seven a.m. in my house and this was the charade that was playing outside the family bathroom first thing on a Monday morning. My own bedroom did have a tiny en suite, but it was just a glorified loo really, so whenever I needed to shower I always slipped into the main family bathroom on the landing outside, to veiled threats from Darcy about staying well away from her good shampoo.

And having successfully avoided each other the whole of that Sunday after the wedding, now it was Monday morning and, like it or not, I'd have to face the little madam back in work. So right there on my upstairs landing was a good dress rehearsal for what lay ahead, if nothing else, I figured.

Lauren hadn't said as much as two words to me about the wedding, nor I to her. On the day, we acted like two distant acquaintances and nothing more, which actually couldn't have suited me better. It was as much as I could do to even turn up there with a smile on my face, and only for Liz I'd never have got through it.

In spite of that though, there was so much I was burning to know, but determined not to ask. Like had anything happened between Lauren and Tom after the wedding? I was pretty certain the answer was no; the two of them had left long before Liz, Harry and I did, and Lauren's bedroom door was firmly shut when I crawled in hours later.

Did she plan on seeing him again? Pointless asking Tom, I knew; he looked so besotted with the girl, as far as he was concerned the answer would be a very obvious yes. Lauren, I instinctively knew, would be the one holding all the aces here. If they were to date again, it would only be because she chose to and precious little to do with Tom, no matter how much of a ladykiller he considered himself to be.

But the Sunday morning after the wedding, Lauren was out of bed and gone, mentioning something to Darcy about her plans to spend the whole day in the office getting fully briefed on the McKinsey case.

The best of luck to her, I thought silently, as Darcy and I sat down to breakfast, just the two of us. Besides, I reminded myself. The only person who really mattered was sitting right in front of me. If Darcy had the slightest problem with any of this, then I would have unleashed merry hell. But as long as she was being so cool about the whole thing, then how could I possibly feel entitled to voice my own concerns?

Then directly after the wedding, my darling daughter, who'd been doing so well for so long, suddenly stopped acting like herself. Nothing solid that I could put my finger on, and outwardly it was business as usual. I just got the feeling that there was something preying at the back of the girl's mind, that was all. Call it a mother's instinct, if you will, but something was up, I could sense it. When it came down to it, I began to wonder, was Darcy really OK about the whole Tom/Lauren thing? Or was there something else going on that I didn't know about?

By the Monday morning after the wedding, Darcy seemed slightly withdrawn, then complained that she hadn't been sleeping properly for the previous few nights. So I dropped her off to school and as she and I sat side-by-side in the car, I fished around a little deeper to see what the matter was. But no joy, nothing.

The beginnings of an eating disorder maybe, I fretted, as the two of us sat in silence, stuck at traffic lights while my worried mind raced.

No, I thought, immediately discounting the idea. She may have only picked at a dinner the previous night, but that certainly didn't stop the girl putting away two slices of toast and half a jar of Nutella for breakfast earlier that morning, while Lauren was upstairs in the shower. Bulimia? Similarly unlikely. Darcy definitely wasn't loosing scary amounts of weight and I could personally vouch for the fact that she didn't peel away from the table to use the loo the minute she was done eating.

Then suddenly my heart stopped. Self-harming maybe? I'd read so much about it and it was always a constant worry at the back of my mind – or that of any parent to a vulnerable teenage girl. Apparently kids cut themselves at body parts that aren't necessarily visible; the top of the thigh for instance. Or around the tummy area.

'Darcy,' I asked her as we were stuck in never-ending traffic. 'Pet, is there anything you want to get off your chest? Anything at all that's troubling you? Because you know, your old mum is un-shockable. There's nothing you can be going through that I didn't have to deal with myself when I was your age.'

'I'm good. Thanks, Mum,' was the only shrugged response I got though.

'So there's nothing you want to talk to me about?'

'No.'

'You're sure?' I said, glancing worriedly over at her. She looked pale and stressed, not her usual, robust self.

'And it's not this whole thing with Lauren and your dad getting to you, is it? Because if it is . . .'

'It's definitely not that, Mum,' she said, turning her head away sharply. 'I told you, I'm completely cool.'

'So what's up then, love? Come on, you can talk to me.'

'It's nothing.'

Now rule one of parenting is this. When a teenager says 'nothing', then what they actually mean is the exact opposite.

But what could it be? That was what I was racking my brains trying to figure out. So I said no more, and made a silent resolve to speak to Darcy's class tutor as soon as I could feasibly get an appointment.

One thing was for certain though; whatever was up, it definitely wasn't 'nothing'.

*

I was late getting into work again that morning and had the bad luck to bump into Bernie in the lift on the way up to the office, so my unpunctuality was well and truly noted.

'Bernie,' I said breathlessly, squeezing into the lift beside him, as usual laden down with a disorganised mound of files and briefs. 'So sorry I'm a bit behind today, I had to drop Darcy off at school and you know how the traffic is on a Monday morning.'

'That's quite all right, Sarah,' was his shrugged reply, which caught me completely off guard. Usually Bernie was always the first to tick me off about my perpetually bad timekeeping skills.

'I will of course make up the time later on,' I hastened to add, but he cut across me just as we arrived to the top floor and the lift doors pinged open.

'That's OK. We've got everything under control here.'

Again, odd. Normally Bernie would come out with some snide comment along the lines of, 'too bloody right you will', and I'd bite my lip and that would be an end to it. I put it out of my head though and made my way to my desk, which was in complete Monday morning chaos with a stuffed inbox and a teetering pile of legal correspondence that I somehow didn't find the time to get to over the weekend.

But something was up, I could sense it. Normally Monday mornings here had an atmosphere of low-level panic; everyone would be at their desks bent down over laptops, madly trying to get a head start on the week ahead, before the office filled up with client meetings.

Not that Monday though. Instead there were a lot of empty desks, which again was odd for that time of day. I glanced around to see if I could make out the top of Harry's fuzzy head, because if I could rely on anyone to fill me in on what was going on, it was him, but there was no sign of him. Another early warning sign that something was amiss.

Next thing, Lucy swished past my desk, but instead of her usual bright, cheery 'good morning!' she looked at me strangely, almost like she was seeing double.

'Hi Lucy, how was your weekend?' I began, but she cut over me.

'Sarah?' she said, puzzlement writ large all over her face.

'What? What's up?' I asked her.

'Well, you tell me. You're the one who's sitting out here when the meeting is just about to start.'

'Oh Jesus, Lucy, not this again!' I said, as sudden electric shockwaves ran right through me. 'What meeting? With who?'

'You didn't know? With George McKinsey III himself. He's just arrived and right now he's having coffee with the team outside the conference room.'

'But how can he be with the team if I'm here? And knowing absolutely nothing about any meeting?'

'Well, Lauren is already up there, so I assumed you'd sent her in your place?' Lucy stammered. 'Maybe because you were going to be out of the office all morning, or something?'

Fuck, fuck, fuck, I thought as a cold, clammy panic clutched through my ribcage and gripped at my heart like a vice. What the hell was going on behind my back? How had the goalposts shifted so much over a single weekend? I fumbled around my desk for the McKinsey briefs I'd practically been sweating blood over, but could only find approximately half of them.

Christ, I though furiously, ripping drawers open and half tipping the contents out onto the floor in my search for the right files. Why had no one thought to tell me about this?

There was one vital file that for the life of me, I couldn't find. The Belize brief, which painstakingly unraveled all of McKinsey's corporate holdings in South America. I'd spent bloody weeks working on it and now, at the exact moment when I needed it, do you think I could find the effing thing? Thinking fast, I abandoned the mound of papers on my desk and went to my laptop instead, because I knew there was a copy there which I could use as back-up in an emergency. And by Jesus, this really was an emergency.

'Sarah, hurry!' hissed Lucy from beside me, in a worse panic than I was myself. 'You don't have time for this!'

'Just one second, there's a file here I just need to make sure I've got hold of!'

'Take your computer with you and just go, will you?' she said urgently. 'I'm sure you'll find whatever you're looking for on your laptop during the meeting – now come on, move!'

I didn't need to be told again. I scooped up my briefcase, files and laptop and raced for the lift, not having the first clue what lay ahead.

As it happened, everyone was gathered in the tiny foyer area just outside the conference room when I finally got there and by that, I really do mean everyone. George McKinsey III himself had even deigned us with his presence, the first time I'd actually met the man face-to-face.

He looked younger than I'd have thought, a sprightly octogenarian looking for all the world like a cut-price version of Prince Philip, right down to the deck shoes, navy blazer and signet ring; the whole 'off-duty guards officer' look.

McKinsey's seem to have brought a huge team along with them and there were a lot of unfamiliar faces buzzing around, but I could still make out Harry at the far end of the room, his frizzy mop of curly hair as usual, clearly visible a good head and shoulders above everyone else.

'Harry,' I whispered, angling myself in beside him, 'would you please tell me what the feck is going on here?'

'Oh, you know how it is with these high-flyers like George McKinsey,' he shrugged benignly, but then Harry rarely got fazed about anything. 'He decided he'd be in Dublin this morning, so this meeting only got scheduled at the very last minute.'

'It couldn't have been as last minute for you as it was for me,' I hissed back. 'I found out about this exactly four minutes ago.'

'You mean you didn't get that email memo last thing on Friday evening?' he said, looking puzzled.

'I certainly didn't,' I told him stoutly. 'I think I'd have remembered something as important as that, don't you?'

Nor had Harry mentioned any meeting at the wedding on Saturday. Mind you, that was hardly his fault nor mine. Truth was, we didn't discuss anything to do with work at all. But then it was a wedding, a night off, why would we have talked about work?

'But I think I did refer to it,' Harry said, 'when Liz and I were dropping you home in the taxi after the wedding. I might have been pissed as a fart, but I'm pretty certain I said something to you about it.'

'You didn't say a word! All you said was see you on Monday morning bright and early, or words to that effect.'

'Yeah, well, I meant at the meeting, of course,' he said, looking completely caught off guard just as Lauren drifted past us to join Bernie.

'Well, I just assumed you meant—'

'Hey Lauren,' Harry interrupted, 'how come Sarah never knew anything about this meeting?'

'I've no idea,' Lauren replied smoothly.

'Apparently you sent out an email memo on Friday evening?' I prompted her. 'Which everyone else in the office seems to have received except me, for some mysterious reason.'

'What's this?' said Bernie, pricking up his ears at the earliest strain of conflict.

'You're absolutely right, Sarah,' Lauren smiled sweetly back at me. 'I didn't forward you on the email about this morning's meeting. For the excellent reason that I told you about it myself. Personally.'

'Excuse me, Lauren?' I said, flabbergasted. 'What did you just say?'

'As you may know,' Lauren said, turning to address Bernie, who stood beside her, all ears. 'Sarah and I are sharing a house right now. So of course I didn't bother emailing her; not when I knew I'd see her personally over the weekend. So I could tell her to her face about this meeting.'

'But you did no such thing!' I said, aware that I'd raised my voice a bit, but too shocked to care.

She turned back to look at me, her face a study in cool composure.

'Oh, but I did, Sarah. More than once, in fact. I even reminded you first thing this morning, just to be on the safe side. Don't you remember? It was just over two hours ago.'

Mother of Jesus, I thought, too shocked for speech. All I could do was stare at her, open-mouthed. *So now you're a barefaced liar on top of everything else, are you?* I actually was starting to feel light-headed as I looked at her; at the thought that her innocent, angelic expression could harbour such a manipulative little witch just underneath.

'Lauren,' I eventually said, aware that Bernie and Harry

were right beside us, and that at all costs I needed to hold it together. 'You know perfectly well that you told me nothing whatsoever about this meeting. So just drop the act right now, OK?'

'Maybe you were a little bit distracted?' she said calmly. 'I know you were rushing to drive your daughter to school this morning and maybe it just slipped your mind?'

'You're lying!' I spluttered. 'This is all complete bollocks and you know it!'

'Oh, for God's sake, Sarah,' said Bernie, 'you're the one who's making a complete song and dance out of nothing.'

'It's not nothing to me, Bernie,' I told him. 'I've slaved over the McKinsey brief and I need to be here.'

'But as I told you when I bumped into you in the lift earlier,' was his suave reply, 'we have it all under control here, thanks to Lauren. So does it really matter how or when you got to hear about this meeting? The fact is that we're in good shape and that, as far as I'm concerned, is that. So now, without further ado, I suggest we all get started.'

*

Lauren, needless to say, didn't just wipe the floor with the rest of us during the meeting; she aced it right out of the park. In spite of all the months-long preparatory work that Harry and I had both put in, Lauren always seemed to be five steps ahead of both of us. That and that alone was my one consolation; at least I didn't seem to be the only one utterly floored by her sublime efficiency.

Every labyrinthine trail of figures that we needed to discuss at that meeting Lauren had right to hand, seemingly summoned out of her head, like she was some kind of maths whizz on top of everything else.

Literally, I'd still be fumbling about on my laptop, telling the room, 'no hang on, gimme just a sec, I have the Belize figures right here . . .' when Lauren would come in on top of me with a crisp, clear statement along the lines of, 'the exact figure you need is that in 2014, during the first quarter of the tax year, the company wrote off 13.7% in fixed assets, and declared a net profit of $47.75 million clear of tax, which goes down to a total of $41.78 million when we factor in corporation tax rates at 12.5%.'

Time and again she trumped me, until it almost go to the point where I honestly felt like throwing in the towel. Not only that but the white hot rage that flooded through me every time I looked into that innocent, pretty face was affecting me. Every time I tried to address the room, it came out as a semi-coherent stammer and every time I rummaged around for the correct file to back up a module that was being discussed, my fingers, physically shaking with anger, would betray me.

After two hours of this, even I could see that it was pointless. God knows I'd busted a gut doing my homework on the McKinsey brief, but Lauren was way ahead of me. And not just ahead of *me*, by the way; I could even see Harry look on in dumbfounded shock as she effortlessly rang rings around him too. It was as though the girl had a photographic memory for the most boring facts and figures known to man, so that when the entire boardroom would be twiddling away on computers double checking long columns of figures, she'd have it all done in her head way ahead of anyone else.

I thought the meeting would never end, but eventually it did. And the outcome was a foregone conclusion. Even the mighty George McKinsey III seemed bowled away by

Lauren's sheer brilliance, and as for Bernie? Well, as we all congregated outside for a coffee break after such a grueling few hours, I could clearly see him gazing proudly at Lauren, in much the same way that a horse trainer looks at a jockey whose just steered one of his horses towards victory at the Gold Cup.

'Jesus,' said Harry, shuffling up beside me, red in the face as he undid his top shirt button and loosened his tie, 'that Lauren one isn't even human if you ask me. She's a fucking machine.'

'She's a fucking machine who's walked all over me for the last time, Harry. The very last time.'

*

Not only could I have accurately predicted what came next, I could have started taking bets on it. Sure enough, later on that morning, I had a call from reception to say Bernie was upstairs in his office and wanted to speak to me right away.

Punch drunk and walking numbly, I made my way to the lift bank, aware that just about every eye in the office seemed to be following me. Dead Girl Walking. I got a lovely, encouraging wink from Harry, bless him and lots of my co-workers glanced up from their desks to give me the thumbs up sign, which bolstered me a bit.

It was notable though, that the only person on the whole office floor who completely blanked me was Lauren, but then she seemed far too engrossed in her computer screen to even look upwards.

I tapped on the door of Bernie's office and as I stepped into the inner sanctum, I saw that he was clearly a bag of nerves about what he was going to say.

Very Bad Sign.

'Sarah,' he said, just a degree too brightly, 'sit down there, take the weight off your feet. That's it, good woman.'

That alone was a giveaway – the fact that he was being so nice to me.

'Bernie, about this morning's meeting,' I began, pre-empting him, or so I hoped. 'Look, I know I didn't seem to be as on top of the McKinsey brief as I'd like to have been, but—'

'Hey, that's not a problem at all!' he said, over-enthusiastically. 'You're a busy lady, Sarah, you've got a whole lot of other stuff going on. So how is that daughter of yours, Daphne, isn't it?'

'Darcy. She's well, thanks.'

'Yeah, yeah, Darcy, that's it. She must be about twelve or thirteen now, is that right?'

'She's sixteen actually.'

'Really, that old, yeah? Wow, time flies, doesn't it?'

'Bernie! You're making me nervous,' I said as lightly as I could, hoping to jolt him to the point.

'Well, here's the thing, Sarah,' he eventually said, easing his portly bulk down onto the heavy oak chair behind his desk and steepling his fingers. 'You've been here a very long time, haven't you? I even remember you coming into work when you were pregnant.'

He's going to fire me, I thought, my mind racing into panicky overdrive. Jesus Christ, he's actually going to do it.

'And I've worked hard for you and always done my best,' I somehow found words to say in my own defence.

'Your best, yes,' he said, swiveling his chair to and fro. 'Yes, yes, you see, that's what I want to talk to you about, Sarah. You're a smart woman. Now, do you honestly think that you were at your best in that meeting this morning?'

'No, Bernie, I certainly don't, but you have to remember, I was unprepared and completely caught off guard.'

'Ahh, but a good lawyer is always prepared. Look at Lauren, and how well she handled this morning's meeting. The girl was *superlative*. In fact, George McKinsey's last words to me before he left earlier were that he wants her to take charge on his accounts from here on in. Which of course means I've got to drop someone from the McKinsey team. And as you yourself just admitted, Sarah, you hardly brought your A game to the table this morning, now did you?'

*

Ten minutes later I didn't so much as walk as stagger out of the lift and through the main office back to my desk.

Harry caught up with me, gripping my arm and steering me into a tiny side annex where we kept all the tea and coffee, so we could talk privately without being overheard.

'Jesus, you were up there for ages. You OK?' he said, urgently scanning my face up and down, as if he was afraid I might burst into tears at any minute. He needn't have worried though, I was beyond tears by then.

'Which do you want first, the good news or the bad news?' I said flatly.

'The good, always the good.'

'The good news is that I'm not fired. At least, not yet I'm not.'

'That's better than good, that's great,' he said encouragingly. 'And the bad?'

'The bad is that I'm officially dropped from the McKinsey case. Effective as of now.'

'Ahh, jeez, Sarah, that's rough,' Harry said, shoving his

278

fists deep into his pockets. 'After all your months of hard work? That's overly harsh, if you ask me.'

'It wasn't even up to Bernie in the end,' I said numbly, feeling like someone who'd just lost a limb. In no pain, but knowing it would kick in soon. 'Apparently this came directly from the top, from George McKinsey himself.'

'May he be inflicted with a severe dose of double diarrhea with immediate effect,' Harry quipped and I silently blessed him for attempting a joke, however lame, at a time like this.

'You haven't heard the best part yet,' I went on. 'I'm out and Lauren is in. Just like that. The woman is barely here a wet week and I'm not kidding, Bernie is already talking about her being "partner material".

As soon as I invoked the name, I glanced around the office and, at that exact moment, happened to catch Lauren glancing up from her desktop. Just as before though, she blanked me out like I didn't exist. As if she'd successfully sucked all the usefulness out of me and was now moving on to bigger fish she had to fry.

When I first met you, I thought, deliberately holding eye contact, *you were painting nails in a dingy cut-rate beauty salon. And just take a look at you now. So who exactly are you? Why are you putting me through this, when all I ever did was try to help you? You're living my life. You're actually living my life. But now I want it back.*

Chapter Twenty-six

Darcy

'During the period 1871–1914, how did one or more of the following contribute to international tensions: colonial rivalries and/or the naval policy of Wilhelm II; Serbia and its neighbours?'

There was an audible groan from around the classroom, but Darcy was too tuned out to notice. She was sitting right by the window and was gazing out over the school hockey pitch, completely wrapped up in thought. Or worry, rather.

'So who'd like to elucidate us, please?' Miss Grey, sharp-nosed and eagle-eyed as ever, said as she sniffed the air to convey how unimpressed she was with the total lack of enthusiasm from her class. ('That one has a face like a bulldog sucking a wasp,' as Sophie quite accurately described her.)

'Let's see now . . .' Miss Grey went on, referring down to a class list in front of her. 'So how about you, Darcy? We haven't heard from you in a while. May we have your thoughts on the subject, please?'

Darcy froze in her seat, aware that everyone in her whole

class was staring at her, thanking their stars that she'd been picked, not one of them. And, of course, on cue she went completely and utterly blank.

'Darcy?' Miss Grey went on. 'Come on, don't keep us waiting. Just give us the key and salient points about the Arms Race, that'll do for now.'

Darcy tried to speak, but couldn't. The words just wouldn't come out of her mouth, no matter how hard she willed them to. And what was even more frustrating was that she actually *knew* this. History was one of her good subjects, and she'd learned off the Arms Race ages ago.

'Say something,' Sophie, who was sitting right beside her hissed urgently. 'Anything at all, just don't sit there like a mute, or you're dead.'

'Darcy,' said Miss Grey slowly, worriedly, 'we've covered this at great length. You know the answer to this, you did an essay on the subject for me not two weeks ago. Now come on!'

More silence. Horrible, bowel-withering silence.

'Darcy?' Miss Grey insisted. 'I'm speaking to you. What's the matter with you?'

What's wrong with me? Where do I even start? Darcy thought, flushed scarlet in the face from the red-hot mortification of being so publicly humiliated in front of everyone.

Same thing in her maths class later on that day. She hadn't done her homework and when Mr Devlin, who was usually easy enough to get around, asked her a direct question, yet again she completely clammed up.

Not only that, but then the gobshite arsehole tried to make a holy, mortifying show of her in front of the whole class, insisting on dragging her up to the whiteboard to write out a theorem that stated that 'if opposite sides and angles of a parrelellogram are equal, then the opposite angles of a convex quadrilateral are . . .' blah, blah, blah.

It might as well have been written in a foreign language as far as Darcy knew. Or cared.

'Come on, Darcy, you're normally on top of all this,' Mr Devlin said, shaking his head sadly at his once-star pupil. 'What's happened to you?'

'I'm sorry, sir,' said Darcy weakly. 'I'm just . . . not feeling very well today.'

'Go on outside then and get a bit of fresh air. Sophie, you can go with her, in case she feels weak.'

So the two girls slipped out of the stuffy, overcrowded classroom, but whereas ordinarily they'd have been giddy and skittish about the bonus of an unexpected free class, this time Darcy was in no mood to care.

'You should have seen the look on Devlin's face when you said you weren't well,' said Sophie, as they sat side by side on an empty park bench out in the school grounds. 'I think he was terrified you were about to tell him you had women's problems, and that's why he was so quick to spring the pair of us out of class.'

Darcy couldn't answer her friend back though. Instead she pulled her knees up tight to her chest on the park bench and concentrated really, really hard on breathing.

'Some water, hon?' Sophie asked, passing her over a bottle of sparkling water. Darcy just shook her head; then the thought of either food or drink was physically turning her stomach to ash. Instead she started out over the school hockey pitch, where the third years were practising for a match. They were all leaping around and madly waving hockey sticks in the air and even from the bench where she and Sophie were sitting, you could still hear the sound of their giggles and high, good humour wafting back.

I used to be like those girls, Darcy thought forlornly. *There was a time when I didn't have a care in the world, just like them.*

'Darcy?' said Sophie gently, from beside her. 'Is everything OK? I mean, clearly it's not or else we wouldn't be here, would we? But you know, well . . . oh look, I'm shit at this sort of thing. All I'm saying is that if you need to talk to me, I'm here.'

'I know,' was all she got though, by way of a shrugged reply.

'Is it that arsehole Tony Scott again?' Sophie probed. 'Or is it Abi and her gang giving you hassle? Because we've got lots of options, you know. We could talk to Miss Grey or one of the staff. There's all sorts of procedures put in place for bullying in schools now. They take that kind of thing really seriously.'

'And what if the bullying isn't necessarily coming from someone in school?' Darcy said slowly. 'What if it's actually happening a whole lot closer to home than that?'

'What are you talking about?' said Sophie, looking at her with huge, mystified eyes.

Darcy sighed, taking a long look across at Sophie.

I've got a true pal here, she was quick to remind herself, and a worry shared is always a worry halved.

'OK, look, so here's the thing,' she began slowly, formulating the words as she went along. 'You remember that night a few months back? The night of Tony Scott's God-awful party? And how trashed I was and how he locked me in the bathroom and . . . well, you know the rest.'

'Did you have to remind me?' Sophie groaned mock

283

playfully, trying to lighten the situation, bless her. 'I'm still having therapy to recover from that shitty night.'

'Then take a look at this,' said Darcy, fishing about in her pocket for her mobile. There was an utter blanket ban on phones during school hours, but right now she didn't give a shite. She produced the phone, clicked on her password, then brought up the offending messages – and for fuck's sake – even the photos that came with them – passing them over to Sophie, who took the phone gingerly, not knowing what to expect.

'Oh Christ, you've got to be kidding me,' she said, as her eyes took in the first few texts, the colour draining away from her the more she read on.

'Just keep scrolling down through all the messages,' Darcy said, staring blankly ahead at the hockey match in the distance. 'Trust me, they get a whole lot worse.'

As Sophie scanned down through them, Darcy rewound them all in her mind's eye, fresh waves of worry sweeping over her as she did.

REMEMBER TO KEEP YOUR MOUTH SHUT AND I'LL DO THE SAME FOR YOU was one text. A pretty mild one at that. But they got worse, far, far worse. Some even had photos taken that night, of Darcy lying comatose on the grass in the front garden outside Tony Scott's house while Sophie fussed over her, neither of the girls having a clue their photo was being taken.

REMEMBER THIS? The sickening caption read. *THINK OF HOW DISAPPOINTED AND UPSET MUMMY WOULD BE IF SHE WERE EVER TO SEE THE STATE HER DARLING DARCY GOT HERSELF INTO.*

Then there was an even worse one of her with her jeans zipped open, knickers on full view as she lay unconscious on the grass, vomit running down the front of her top.

THINK OF WHAT YOUR DAD WOULD SAY IF HE WERE EVER TO SEE THIS, DARCY read the message underneath.

'I do not believe what I'm seeing,' Sophie said, very slowly. 'Who'd do this to you? Who'd be that callous and cruel? Not Tony, or Abi surely?'

'Guess again,' said Darcy.

'Not . . . not Lauren?' said Sophie, horrified.

'Who else?' said Darcy with a shrug. 'Look, she clearly took that photo from the car, when she pulled up outside the party to collect us that night. So there I was like a complete eejit, actually thinking of her as a friend who was doing me a favour, whereas the truth was she was collecting dirt on me all along.'

'I can't believe it,' Sophie said, sounding utterly shocked as she kept scanning down through the phone. 'Lauren, who did our make-up for us? Lauren who the two of us actually thought was pretty cool?'

There were even more photos though. Including one of Darcy crashed out on the spare bed in Sophie's house, then being sick into the plastic bucket Sophie had placed beside her.

'I can't get my head around this,' Sophie said. 'That photo was taken in my *parents*' house. I must have just slipped downstairs to get you some water, I was probably only out of the room for a minute or two. But to think that when you were throwing up, Lauren was there snapping away, taking photos of you on her phone? For fuck's sake, this is scary stuff!'

'It's sick. She's one manipulative bitch. And now it's getting worse.'

'Getting worse how? How could it possibly be any worse?'

'Because now Lauren's holding this over me, like a whip,' Darcy said, the words spilling out now that she'd actually begun to talk about it. 'She's started dating my dad and I hate it and I hate her for it and I want it to stop and yet there's absolutely nothing I can do. Lauren keeps sending me all these vile texts and photos and threatening to tell Mum about what happened that night, unless—'

'Unless you smile and act like you think she and your dad are the greatest couple going,' Sophie said, finishing the sentence for her. 'Jesus, Darcy, this is intolerable. How long have you been putting up with this?'

'Long enough that I'm now at breaking point.'

'She's a fucking psycho for doing this!'

'I know.'

'But you can't keep on letting her get away with this.'

'What else can I do? What other option do I have?'

'Listen to me,' Sophie said decisively, turning to face Darcy and gripping her by the shoulders. 'This is blackmail, pure and simple. And the one thing we know about black-mailers is that the minute you take away their power, they've got nothing left. Absolutely nothing.'

'So what are you suggesting?' Darcy said weakly.

'Well, it's obvious, isn't it? You've got to go to your mum and dad before she does and tell them everything. All about the night of the party and how Lauren came to rescue us, or so we thought. Show them both every revolting photo and tell them how Lauren is now using this against you and driving you to the brink of a breakdown with it. Because if you don't,' her pal went on, 'one thing is for certain.'

'Which is?'

'Which is that it'll get a whole lot worse. If Lauren is

prepared to go this far to get what she wants, then there's no telling what she might pull on you next. She's got to be stopped. Now. And by you.'

'So I have to tell my parents then?' Darcy said feebly, sick to her stomach at the very thought.

'The truth, the whole truth and nothing but.'

*

Darcy spent a tense few hours on her own at home, waiting, waiting, waiting on her mum's key to turn in the lock. She didn't know what to do if by any chance Lauren came home first. In all probability, she'd just run to her room and hide away from the scheming bitch. But then the chances were remote; the one saving grace in all this was the fact that Lauren genuinely did work such long hours at the office.

Darcy's stomach was in a knot of tension and every time she heard a car pull up on the busy road outside, she almost thought she'd black out with nerves. *It's only Mum,* she had to keep reminding herself. And yes, the actual telling her was going to be excruciating, but then as Sophie wisely pointed out, as soon as she'd got it over with, in that one fell swoop, she'd take all Lauren's power away.

Just after 8pm, Darcy heard the familiar sound of the key in the front door lock. She raced out of her room as a wave of relief flooded through her, taking the stairs two at a time and flinging the hall door open.

'Mum? Thank God you're home, I really need to talk to you—'

She broke off though, mid-sentence.

Because it wasn't her mum who stood there at all. There – in her neat little work suit with her still-immaculate hair and make-up and an important-looking briefcase tucked under one arm – was Lauren.

Darcy froze. Then braced herself.

This is my house, she reminded herself. My life. And this bitch has walked over me for the very last time.

Chapter Twenty-seven

Sarah

'I know it's a cardinal sin to want a glass of wine in front of your teenage daughter,' I said, letting myself in through the hall door and throwing my briefcase down with a loud clatter, 'but trust me, love, after the day I've just had, your mother needs to spend a bit of time with her old pal Pinot Grigio.'

Instead of the usual two-second delay when I normally came home, during which I'd try to guess which room Darcy was in and whether she was glued to either her phone or iPad, this time I could clearly hear voices coming from the direction of the kitchen.

Raised voices, there was no mistake.

'Darcy,' I heard Lauren saying, crisp and clear, 'I thought I made it perfectly clear to you that my private life is absolutely none of your concern.'

'Oh yeah,' I could hear Darcy yelling back at her, 'you've made it clear all right. You've only blackmailed me with all of your poisonous texts and bombarded me with photos that you'd no right to take in the first place!'

'It's hardly my fault if you're just a spoilt, stupid little girl who doesn't even know how to behave properly in public.'

'And it's certainly not my fault that you're a fucking psycho!'

Jesus Christ, I thought, as sudden horror flooded through me. What was going on under my own roof? What fresh hell was this? I raced down the hall and flung open the kitchen door to find Darcy and Lauren in the throes of a full-on screaming match.

'Mum, you're home . . . oh, thank God!' said Darcy, running over to me and flinging herself into my arms so forcefully, she almost knocked me over.

'What's this?' I said, cradling her and glaring at Lauren accusingly. 'What exactly is going on here?'

'I can't take it any more, Mum,' said Darcy, bursting into tears as I held her tight. 'I can't be around this fucking lunatic for one more day. So go on then, Lauren,' she said, twisting around in my arms and glaring over at where Lauren stood calmly by the fridge, 'Mum's here now. Go ahead, do your worst. Tell her everything. Because you know what? If that's what it'll take for her to see you for the fucking head-wreck you are, then that's all I need!'

'Darcy, please calm down, love!' I told her. 'Now Lauren,' I said coldly, 'I suggest you start talking.'

'If that's what you really want,' said Lauren so calmly it was almost frightening, as she opened up the fridge door and scanned down through the contents, like she could actually eat at a time like this, in the middle of Armageddon. The true hallmark of a sociopath, I remember thinking. 'But I warn you Sarah, it's not very pretty.'

'Do it,' Darcy half snarled. 'Go on, you stupid bitch. Do your fucking worst.'

*

Almost twenty minutes later, I'd put Darcy to bed with a hot cup of tea and a buttery muffin, the only 'dinner' I could get her to eat. But when I came back into the kitchen there was Lauren, calmly frying up Spanish potatoes and tossing a light couscous salad together for her own dinner. Not a bother on her, like this was just another regular day in this house. She just looked so proprietorial that I actually had to remind myself that this was my house and my kitchen and that I had a perfect right to say what I was about to.

Lauren didn't even consider me worthy of looking up from the cooker for. Instead she just blanked me out, but continued to use my frying pan on my cooker with all my utensils and served it all up onto my crockery. Christ, I thought, as what felt like ice flooded through my veins.

You can do this. You can actually wreak havoc on the life of an innocent young teenager and then calmly eat dinner, like nothing at all happened. But Darcy is wrong about one thing. You're not a psycho at all. You're the bloody Ice Woman.

'I want you gone,' I said, taking great care to close the kitchen door behind me. Poor Darcy had been through quite enough for one day, I figured. Last thing she needed was to overhear any of this.

'Excuse me?' said Madam, not even glancing up from the frying pan.

'Oh, you heard me, Lauren. I'm giving you till the end of the week to get your stuff out of here and that's final,'

I said, frightening myself at how even tempered I was managing to sound.

'Well, now you're just being ridiculous,' Lauren said calmly, taking more leftover couscous out of the fridge and doling out an even bigger portion of it for herself. I watched dumbfounded as she grabbed herself a knife and fork from the dishwasher and calmly took a seat at the kitchen table. Like she and I were having the most relaxed, benign girlie gossip going and nothing more.

'For a start,' she continued, munching away on the couscous, as I looked on dumbfounded, 'may I remind you that I have rights here?'

'Not as far as I'm concerned, you don't,' I snapped back.

'Tenants have rights,' she barreled over me. 'I need hardly remind you of that. Legally, you're obliged to give me at least a month's notice. Everyone knows how tough it is to find accommodation in this city. So I strongly suggest you play fair.'

'Lauren, I want you to listen to me very carefully,' I told her evenly, 'because I'm only going to say it once. Either you clear out of here by the end of the week, or else you'll come home to find all your stuff in black bin liners dumped on the road outside, with all the locks changed. Oh, and I wouldn't try calling my bluff on this either,' I added, on my way back upstairs to Darcy. 'I've never been so deadly serious about anything in my life.'

'You're overreacting, Sarah,' she said, munching away on her plate of dinner. 'And as usual, you're not fully thinking this through.'

'Excuse me? What did you just say?' I said, turning back to her as I stood in the doorway.

'Well, for a start, just think how this is going to play out in work. Just because I happen to be outscoring you when it comes to the McKinsey case, just because I've replaced you on the brief, next thing you're turfing me out of your home. Hardly good for optics now, is it?'

'You want to sit there and speak to me about optics?' I spluttered back, hardly able to believe what I was hearing. 'Then how's this? You've spent the last few weeks sending the vilest and most abusive text messages to a vulnerable teenager. Blackmailing her about a night that happened months ago, all behind my back. And for what? So you could get to date my ex-husband who I can guarantee you will have nothing more to do with you when he hears about this? When I did nothing all along but show you friendship and kindness? When I went out of my way to help you?'

'There's absolutely no need to gild the lily here, Sarah,' she said coolly. 'You know perfectly well that I'd eventually have got a decent post in a legal firm with or without your help. I'm fantastic at my job and you know it. In fact deep down, that's what you can't really handle. This whole outburst of yours is little more than misdirected anger.'

'You're quite wrong there, Lauren,' I spat back, quivering with rage, unable to rein it in any longer. 'Because there's absolutely nothing misdirected about my anger. I'm perfectly clear about where to direct it.'

'Then I strongly suggest you start looking in a mirror.'

'Excuse me?'

'Well, you're the one whose completely neglected a growing teenage girl to the point where her natural default setting is either to go out shoplifting, or else to get so wasted drunk that she's incoherent and vomiting. Nice work, Sarah. They really should make you a candidate for Mother of the Year.'

I was too stunned to even answer her back. It was the exact same sensation as someone slapping me across the face.

You're a psycho, I thought. *I'm sharing my home with a fucking psycho.*

And I don't think I've ever been so frightened in my life.

*

'Do you really have to tell Dad?'

'Shhh, you know I do, sweetheart. He has to know.'

'But, the photos. Those awful photos. Mum, they turn my stomach just having to look at them. Does he have to see them? Really?'

I thought about it, then shook my head 'no'. Poor Darcy had been dealing with quite enough without that much hovering over her.

'No, pet. Of course not. But I do need to tell him everything that Lauren's been putting you through. He has a right to know.'

'Suppose,' said Darcy, pulling the bedclothes tighter around her. She'd got into bed beside me, probably for the first time since she was about five years old. And she just sounded so frail and little-girl-lost and battered by the whole thing, that all I wanted was to wrap two strong arms around her and keep her safe. I mightn't have done that good a job with her up till then, but by God, that was all about to change.

'You should have told me, pet,' I said through the darkness, knowing she was still wide-awake and listening, 'because I think that's what's breaking my heart more than anything. That you felt you couldn't come to me the minute she started harassing you.'

294

I couldn't even invoke Lauren's name just then. 'She' would just have to do. Even from my room at that time of night she could still clearly be heard, tidying up in the kitchen, loading the dishwasher, acting like this was just a normal night for her after a perfectly normal day.

'I suppose . . . well, I think I was hoping for a miracle really.' Darcy sighed deeply, turning to lie flat on her back, so she faced up to the ceiling. 'That's what I was holding out for. Then that lunatic bitch came along and scuppered everything, didn't she?'

'What do you mean, you were holding out for a miracle?' I asked through the pitch-black room.

'That you and Dad might . . . you know,' said Darcy.

'Do you mean that your dad and I might reconcile?' I asked gently.

She gave me a tiny nod back.

Oh God, I thought. I'll have to tell her. The timing couldn't be worse after the day we'd both had, but if there's one lesson I'd learned by then, it was that honesty and directness were always, always the best policy.

'Pet, you do know that's not going to happen, don't you?'

'I think I do, now at least,' she said softly, so softly I had to strain to hear her properly. 'Seeing Dad move on with Lauren, even though it hurt like hell to think about it, at least it made me realise that he wasn't going to stay single forever. No matter how much I wanted him to get back with you. But it's not going to happen, Mum, is it?'

Astonishingly, given what she'd been though, my little girl didn't seem upset or even wobbly about this. Instead, she amazed me by sounding mature and adult-like. I thought for a moment, and wavered.

Did she really need to know the full truth about why

295

Tom and I broke up? The real catalyst that meant the final whistle on our marriage? After everything else she'd been dealing with that hellish night?

No, I thought, finally making up my mind. Darcy loves her dad so much. She looks up to him, she needs that firm father figure in her life and the last thing I'd ever want to do is tarnish that for her.

There were some secrets that, for better or worse, were actually worth keeping.

Chapter Twenty-eight

Liz

'Jesus Christ, Sarah. Are you being serious?'

'You think I'd joke about something like this?'

'You sound so calm. I think if it were me, I'd want the bitch's head on a spike.'

'I have to be calm for Darcy. Because if I lose it, then so will she.'

'And did you tell Tom? About Madam Lauren's horrible texts to poor old Darcy?'

'Course I did. He was utterly shocked, and as upset about it as I am myself. He's calling over later this evening to see Darcy and to make sure she's OK.'

'And are you on your way into Sloan Curtis right now? Are you calling me from the car?'

It was just after 9am, so a reasonable assumption, I figured.

'Are you kidding me?' Sarah groaned. 'I can't. Couldn't do it. Couldn't face it. I've just dropped Darcy off at school and I'm in the car on my way back home. Feck them in work, feck the whole bloody lot of them. Except for Harry, of course,' she quickly added.

'But you *never* take sick days. For feck's sake, you never even take holidays.'

'Oh, Liz, come on,' she said, having to raise her voice over the sound of the traffic outside her car window. 'How could I sit there at my desk like nothing has happened? How could I look at that psycho working away and then have to listen to Bernie rave on about what an exemplary employee she is? Jesus, even the thought of it makes me want to vomit.'

You needn't worry about Madam Lauren hanging onto her good name and reputation for too much longer, I thought to myself, but I said nothing out loud. Truth was though, I'd been waiting for a moment like this for a very long time. So the minute Sarah filled me in on Madam and her machinations, I made full sure not only to brief Harry, but gave him firm instructions to spread the news like wildfire all around the Sloan Curtis office. I might as well have written the poor guy out a script, I had him briefed so thoroughly on the whole thing.

'Ahh here, you know I don't like gossiping,' he grumbled, as I dumped down a bowl of Special K on the kitchen table in front of him earlier that morning.

'Sorry to tell you, love, but that's where you're very much mistaken,' I said, in between peeling Sean away from the kitchen wall, where he was scribbling a picture in crayon and steering him towards his breakfast. 'Because this isn't just any old gossip, I'll have you know. This is actual, hard-core proof that that little B I T C H,' I said, taking care to spell the word out in front of little ears, 'is an out-and-out sociopath. Trust me, everyone in the office needs to hear what she's been putting Darcy through. And that's just the tip of the iceberg.'

'It's horrendous, I know,' said Harry, horsing into the breakfast cereal, 'but I'm crap at office gossip. You know that, love.'

'In that case, just tell Ruth at Reception,' I told him bossily, knowing of old that Ruth had the biggest gob this side of the Grand Canyon. Literally, if you told her you had a heavy cold in the morning, by lunchtime, you'd be getting concerned questions from co-workers about your terrible dose of TB.

'Mummy?' Sean piped up, in between mouthfuls of Ready Brek. 'What does B I T C H spell?'

'Never you mind.'

'Fine. If you won't tell me, I'll just ask our teacher instead.'

*

Two hours later with the kids safely in school and Harry packed off to work, I pulled up outside Sarah's neat little driveway and hammered on her front door.

'Hey!' she said, hugging me as she answered. She looked drained, I thought, completely wiped out by what she'd been through. 'Come on in and have a coffee. God, it's good to see a friendly face.'

'Not a social call, babes,' I said briskly, not brooking any argument. 'I'm taking you on a little mystery tour and I won't take no for an answer.'

'Oh, Liz, do we really have to?' she groaned. 'I'm just so tired, I hardly slept with all the drama last night.'

'I'm giving you exactly five minutes to haul your arse into the shower. And I wouldn't push my patience on that either. I'm a mother of three. Believe me, I know all about brute force and coercion.'

Twenty minutes later, I'd successfully bundled Sarah into

the passenger seat of my Mammy Wagon and we were heading for an address close to the Four Courts in Dublin's city centre.

'You might at least tell me where we're going,' Sarah said exhaustedly, glancing at her reflection in the mirror above the passenger seat, then snapping it shut when she saw just how red-eyed and banjaxed she looked in harsh daylight.

'I'm taking you to see an old acquaintance,' I told her. 'Someone who, with any luck, might be able to help us right now.'

I pulled into the car park just at Wood Quay and steered Sarah across the busy quays and up onto Chancery Place, directly opposite the Four Courts.

'Oh Liz—' Sarah said slowly, as she read the name plaque on the wall beside us and realization slowly began to dawn on her. 'Please tell me you're not serious. I'm too tired for this, I haven't the energy.'

'Mal is the top guy in his field,' I told her crisply. 'He's loyal, he's a hundred per cent discreet and, what's more, he's going to help us.'

'A private detective, Liz? Seriously? Do we really need to take things that far? Lauren will be gone out of my house in a few days, so even though I'm stuck working with her, at least I don't have to spend any more time in her company than absolutely necessary. Do we really have to do this?'

'Sarah, that woman was prepared to hang not just you, but your daughter too. So like it or not, it's time to call in the big guns. Trust me. Back when I was still practising law, I called on Mal loads of times and he really is amazing. He was always at the other end of the phone for me if I needed him. If anyone can help us now, it's him.'

She wavered on the doorstep for a moment, so I roped in the big guns.

'Lauren completely shafted you, babes,' I said, raising my voice so I could be heard above the traffic. 'And in an astonishingly short space of time too. So is there any harm in finding out as much as we possibly can about her? If nothing else, so the she-witch can be stopped in her tracks before she almost destroys someone else's life.'

Turned out that was all it took. Next thing, with grim determination Sarah and I were tripping up the swishy Georgian staircase that led up to Mal's office. This was no gumshoe's hangout though; instead the office was one of those tastefully modernized period offices, all chrome coffee tables and lovingly restored wooden pine floors with sash windows.

'Pretty impressive, huh?' I said to Sarah as we sat in the waiting area, where even the magazines were bang up to date, I couldn't help noticing.

'Well, I suppose I didn't expect this anyway,' she said, half smiling.

'What did you expect? The Spanish Inquisition?'

'Well, whenever I hear the words "private detective",' Sarah said, 'I immediately think of suspicious husbands and wives trying to dig up dirt on a spouse they're about to divorce. I always picture seedy, smoky, disheveled PI's who spend half their time scouring around pubs in the daytime and smoking stale cigarette butts.'

'Yeah, I get that quite a bit actually,' said a man's voice. 'You'd be surprised.'

We both looked up sharply to see Mal himself standing in the doorway, clearly having overheard every word. Thing was, though, he looked so far removed from the scruffy gumshoe Sarah had in mind that it was almost comical. If this God-awful situation were any kind of laughing matter, that is.

Did I tell you about Mal? He's only a few years older than Sarah and me, and immaculately dressed in a well-cut suit that I'd have sworn at a glance was Hugo Boss. He's also tall and lean with slightly greying dark hair and twinkly brown eyes; one of those men who always seemed to have a light suntan on the go, regardless of the weather. The type of guy who could nearly sit beside a light bulb and take a colour. Wearing a light blue shirt and those trendy, square-ish glasses that you only ever see on architects in interiors magazines.

'Liz, it's good to see you again,' he said, coming over to kiss me lightly on each cheek. 'And you must be Sarah,' he said, instantly going to shake her hand.

'Yeah . . . and emm . . . sorry about my lousy preconceptions,' she stammered, caught off guard.

He smiled back. 'Not a problem at all. Now come on through to my office, ladies. Liz has already phoned ahead and filled me in briefly on, well, let's just say the matter in hand.'

'Delicately put, Mal,' I said dryly, 'well done.'

But then was there a polite way to say 'we're dealing with a lunatic bitch here and we want as much dirt dug on her as possible so she can be stopped?' Somehow I think not.

'OK, well, first of all,' Mal said, with a warm, open smile as he went behind his desk and whipped out a notepad and pen, 'let me begin by assuring you that you've come to the right place. Now grab a seat,' he added, 'and I suggest you start at the very beginning. Lauren, I think you said her name was. So what's her last name?'

302

And we told him. Everything. Right from the very start. Mal said nothing at all, just sat back, scribbled down pages and pages of notes and listened patiently. One of the things I'd always really liked about the guy – he was a Grade-A listener.

Then, after a very, very long pause, Sarah spoke.

'Can I be honest with you here?' she asked Mal, a little hesitantly.

'Of course, fire ahead. In fact, I wish all my clients were honest,' he quipped, with a tight little smile.

'We're all in agreement that Lauren has walked all over me,' Sarah went on. 'There's no question about her moral character here. She's proven herself to be sly, manipulative and, above all, a user.'

'Who had no problem in blackmailing your daughter,' I added, lest anyone forget the main reason we were all there in the first place.

'That too,' Sarah said, nodding at me. 'But it's just . . . and please don't take any offense here, Mal—'

'I wouldn't dream of it,' he said politely.

'It's just that when we first interviewed Lauren for the job at Sloan Curtis, the most thorough background checks were run on her. The company has already checked out her qualifications and followed up on her degree. We even got references from a few tutors at the university she went to.'

'So?' said Mal, sitting back and looking at her quizzically.

'So my question is this: what exactly is it that we're hoping to discover here?'

'You mean you're afraid this will all turn out to be a wild goose chase?' he replied with a tiny smile.

'Well . . . yes, actually,' said Sarah.

'Then this is the part where I tell you to relax. My job

303

is to find out exactly what Lauren *doesn't* want us to know. And you don't need to worry,' he added. 'I've got a fairly good track record in this field, as Liz, I'm sure, will testify.'

'They don't come any better than you, Mal,' I said stoutly.

'Remember,' Mal said, 'we're already fully up to speed with everything Lauren wants us to know about her. But my job is to find out what it is that she's trying to keep secret. And there's always something. Believe me.'

Chapter Twenty-nine

Darcy

Darcy's mum had pretty much given her a 'get out of jail free' card when it came to school that day, but Darcy was insistent. She'd been shaken to the core after the previous few days and craved nothing more than to get some semblance of normality back in her life again.

For better or for worse, she forced herself through the school gates that morning and was actually delighted she did, particularly when she saw Sophie's wide-open, friendly face keeping a seat for her in the fifth year common room, smiling warmly, asking how she was doing; basically the kind of pal that was a dream come true at testing times like that.

Not only that, but her dad had called Darcy just before school to see how she was holding up. Over the phone at least the two of them had somehow managed to skirt around the issue. They'd even successfully avoided invoking the name 'Lauren', which was easier said than done, considering her dad had just taken the bitch out on an actual date.

He'd asked to meet up with her after school, 'for a little bite to eat, maybe, Darce? Just so you and I can maybe . . .

well . . . you know . . . catch up with each other. After everything that's gone down. You know what I'm getting at here, love.'

After everything that's gone down, Darcy thought dryly, was about as subtle a way of putting it as anything. So after school she said goodbye to Sophie, then ambled out through the school gates on Stephen's Green and took the ten-minute walk to Le Petite Parisien, a particularly cool French coffee shop on Wicklow Street, where they'd arranged to meet. Darcy was the one who'd picked the venue mainly because they did the most divine cakes at Le Petite Parisien, more like confections really, and given what she was determined to ask, she figured they'd both need industrial quantities of raw sugar inside them.

It was unusually quiet when she finally got there, given that it was late afternoon. But Darcy was actually glad of it. What she was about to ask required privacy, that was for certain.

'Hey, there's my girl!' her dad said, spotting her and rising to his feet the minute she battled her way though the door, laden down with a heavy backpack and a hockey stick.

'Hey,' Darcy said, submitting to the tight hug he gave her and flinging her overweight schoolbag down at her feet.

'So do you want to order something?' he asked lightly.

'Come on, Dad, you know I do, that's the only reason I suggested we even meet here in the first place.'

They ordered two Americanos and a tarte aux pecan for him, while Darcy herself plumped for Le Fraisier, which was essentially Génoise mille-feuille sponge with strawberries and vanilla cream – to die for.

'So . . .' he said a bit awkwardly, after the waitress swished away with their order, leaving them in peace.

306

'OK, Dad,' said Darcy, grasping the bull by the horns. 'In answer to your unspoken questions, yes, I'm OK. At least now I am. Mum's already spoken to me about – well, you know—'

'Let's just say the night of the party that Lauren picked you up from,' he said softly.

'And all I can tell you now and keep on telling you is that I've learned my lesson. Well and truly.'

'It's just the thoughts of what you've been through since then, pet. That you kept it all bottled up.'

'I know.'

'It makes me sick to think that woman was actually using what happened against you, holding it over your head like that.'

'You don't need to remind me—'

'But what breaks my heart most of all is that you felt you couldn't come to me about it. That's what's really been eating me up more than anything. That you could have been spared so much worry and angst over all this.'

'Dad,' Darcy said, leaning across their tiny little table for two, 'as far as you were concerned, you didn't do anything wrong. You came to me and asked me if I was cool with you seeing Lauren. And I told you I had no problem with it, so what more were you supposed to do? You're not a mind reader after all.'

'Oh, I don't know,' he said quietly, just as their coffees and cakes arrived, 'there's lots I could have done. Maybe not asked a complete lunatic out on a date for a start. Certainly won't happen again love, you have my solemn word on that.'

'You weren't to know what she was playing at behind your back. She took us all in. Every one of us; you, me,

Mum, not to mention just about everyone Mum works with.'

'Still,' her dad said slowly. 'When I think of—' he broke off, unable to finish his sentence.

'Well, the good news is that she's moving out,' Darcy said, changing the subject as she helped herself to a tiny forkful of the strawberry-and-cream confection in front of her.

'Well, now, that is good news. The best news I've heard all day, in fact.'

'Mum's given her till the end of the week to clear all her stuff out.'

'Sooner the better if you ask me.'

'Otherwise we've threatened to fling her stuff out the bedroom window in black bin liners.'

'Fantastic idea. I'll even give you a hand myself.'

A silence fell as they both ate and sipped coffee. Meanwhile, Darcy cast around in her mind for the best way, the most tactful way, to ask the question that was really burning her up. She'd rehearsed it over and over in her head on the walk there and was so anxious for it to come out right.

Her father though could read her like an open book.

'Come on, Darce,' he eventually said. 'Out with it. There's something else on your mind, I know that look on your face of old.'

'Well, there sort of was something I wanted to ask you,' she said tentatively. 'Only because I tried to bring it up with Mum, but you know how she is. I mean, you know how loyal she is. She'd never say a bad word about any of her family. She's almost loyal to a fault.'

'What is it, love?' he asked. 'You know you can talk to me about anything.'

Just say it, Darcy braced herself. *After all, information is a wonderful thing. And this seems to be a time in our family for truth-telling.*

'OK, well here goes then,' she said, taking a deep breath. 'I'm all ears.'

'So . . . I think a lot of the reason why I was so upset about you taking Lauren to that wedding was because I didn't particularly want you bringing anyone. On a date, I mean. Oh, look, you know what I'm getting at here, Dad.'

'I think so,' he nodded slowly. 'You mean, it wouldn't have mattered who I'd asked. The fact was, I gave you this big speech about moving on, and that's not necessarily something that you wanted to hear.'

'But there was a reason for that,' Darcy went on. 'Because deep down, I suppose I was really hoping—'

'Hoping that what?' he asked, confused.

'That if you were going to start dating anyone again, it would be Mum. And no one else.'

There was a long pause while her dad sighed deeply and sat back, utterly wrapped up in thought.

'I wanted our little family back together again,' Darcy went on, finding her voice more and more as she finally got this off her chest. God, it felt like such a relief, having kept it bottled up for such a long time. 'A proper family again, just the three of us, like we used to be. I wanted it so badly. And I wanted Mum to be happy. I mean, just look at her. All she does is work and work and do her legal aid stuff and then run around after me.

'So I suppose what I really want more than anything is to see her smile again. I want to hear her laugh. Like she used to when we were all together. Do you know, it's weird, Dad, but I can't remember the last time I actually heard Mum laugh.'

'We're still a family, Darce,' he eventually said in a very small voice. 'Nothing will ever change that. But as for your mum and me ever reconciling—'

'Yeah?'

'Well, the thing is I don't think that's something that she'd want. Not after – after what went down between us.'

'You see?' said Darcy, puzzled. 'This is exactly what I don't get. Neither of you ever explained to me the real reason why you broke up in the first place. All I was told was that you were going through some kind of mid-life thingy, nothing more.'

'Jesus, Darce, you should have talked to me about this sooner,' he said feelingly. 'It's eating me up to think of how long you've been carrying this around with you.'

'So why not tell me the now?' she said, actually surprising herself by how calm she sounded. How grown-up and mature she was being about the whole thing. 'Mum won't say a word, but then I think she's protecting you. And I've got a right to know. I mean, come on, I'm not a child anymore. Haven't we had enough secrecy in this family? I'm so done with people keeping secrets.'

There was an even longer pause, while he looked absolutely anywhere except at her. In those few excruciating moments, Darcy's mind raced till her very worst suspicions came to the forefront of her mind.

'The thing is,' he eventually said, 'it's pretty rare in any marriage break-up that you can look at one spouse and say that they were completely blameless. But in the case of me and your mum, that's actually the honest truth.'

'So . . . it was you, then?' Darcy said, madly trying to piece together this final bit in the jigsaw.

'All my doing, I'm afraid,' he said, barely able to look her in the eye.

'Come on, Dad. The truth and nothing but.'

'OK,' he began, 'so do you remember when I first got the motorbike and joined the club up in Wicklow?'

Darcy shuddered, but realised that she was actually able to date all the problems her parents started having ever since then. That was when the rows started, the long silences, the unbearable tension about the house. It could all be dated squarely back to when her dad first came home with that ridiculous bike that she'd gladly have shoved into the canal, given half the chance.

'Dad,' she prompted him as the awkward silence wore on, 'I've got a right to know.'

'Let me put it this way,' he said, sitting forward and eyeballing her. Did he look a bit red-faced and bashful or was Darcy imagining it? 'Your mum is well rid of me. So well rid of me, it's not true.'

'Go on.'

'You see, around the same time I joined the biker club,' he said, 'I met someone. A friend of Bash's called . . . oh look, it hardly matters what her name was now. But the fact was that . . . that . . .'

'Jesus, you were unfaithful to Mum?' Darcy said, correctly second-guessing him. Surprising herself at how cool she managed to sound, once she'd actually said the words out straight.

'It was just once, just that one time, I swear to you,' he said, wiping tiny droplets of sweat off his forehead. Darcy could register what he was telling her, but somehow couldn't tear her focus from those tiny little droplets of sweat.

'But I came clean to your mum because I felt that I couldn't *not* tell her. I didn't want to and, believe me, I think it was the hardest thing I've ever done, but I knew it was the right thing. Your mum is such a principled woman and she deserved to know the truth. So that was the catalyst that drove us apart really. We both tried hard to make it work afterwards, but in the end . . .'

'In the end you were probably better off apart,' said Darcy, lost in her own thoughts. 'So really if you hadn't moved on with Lauren, then the chances are it would have been with someone else, wouldn't it?'

'Sweetheart,' he said, 'you know how much your mum and I both adore you and want you to be happy. But she and I ever getting back together again just isn't going to happen. I don't think either of us would want it and, to be perfectly frank, your mum is in a much better place without me.'

'I understand,' Darcy nodded, realising in that very moment that her little girl fantasy of them ever being a tight-knit little unit of three again had evaporated for good.

The weird thing was, though, that somehow it didn't seem to matter as much any more. All that mattered was that everyone was happy. And this way, she could actually see for herself that her mum would only ever find the happiness she deserved if she were to forge her own path from here on in.

'So are you OK with all this, Darce?' he leaned forward to ask her tentatively.

'More than OK,' she answered truthfully. 'I think deep down I always knew that the chance of a reconciliation between you and Mum was a long shot. But now there's only one thing that I want more than anything.'

'What's that, love?'

'I still want to hear Mum laugh again. Really throw her head back and belly laugh, like she used to. I want to see her smile. I want that for her more than anything. And I know you do too, Dad. She's been through so much lately. Doesn't she deserve at least that?'

Chapter Thirty

Sarah

'Remember, the more information you can supply me with, the more I can find out for you in return.'

Mal Evans, that was his name. Liz and I had just left his office on the quays with those words burning in my ears.

'So you know what you've got to do now, babes,' Liz said, as she dropped me off at the house not long after.

'I certainly do. Although I've got the most awful, sinking feeling that it could amount to little more than a wild goose chase.'

'Look,' she said, doing a nifty three-point turn on the road outside my house before I hopped out of her car, 'I know you think that Sloan Curtis ran pretty thorough background checks on Madam Lauren when they first took her on, but, like Mal just told us, there's always some sliver of information that could just have slipped through the cracks. Something that might stop her in her tracks, and who knows? Maybe even prevent her from shafting someone else the way she tried to shaft you. So isn't it worth taking the chance? I mean, come on, Sarah; what have you got to lose?'

'You're absolutely right,' I said, even managing a tiny

smile back at her before we said goodbye. 'Anything that prevents her from doing this again can only be a good thing.'

I just wasn't particularly looking forward to what lay ahead, that was all. So I said a warm goodbye to Liz, thanking God for small mercies and for the blessing of having her back in my corner once again. The last few weeks had been tough enough to get through without having my best friend on the other end of a phone. And it was entirely to Liz's credit throughout all of this mess that never once did she wag her finger at me and say, 'I told you so.'

Anyway after all that drama I needed to clear my head, so I hopped straight into my own car and zipped over to Mountjoy Prison to catch up on some free legal aid work I'd fallen behind on. But then you know how it is. Sometimes you need to have a half-hour of face-to-face time with a woman convicted of killing her partner in a drug-frenzied attack to put your own troubles into perspective. Sloan Curtis may have unceremoniously turfed me off the McKinsey brief, I figured, but at least my legal aid clients were still grateful to have me.

Darcy had called me on my way back to the house to say she was having a bite to eat with her dad and would be a bit late home. I told her to enjoy herself and not to worry about a thing, then as I hung up the phone, an idea struck me out of left field.

Because I could, couldn't I?

It was only about 5pm; I had hours and hours before Lauren would get back to the house. Those days, it was regularly past 10pm before I heard her key in the lock, which couldn't have suited me better. Mal's last words came back to me; 'remember, the more information you can supply me with, the more I can find out for you in return'.

In that moment, I made up my mind, jumped back into my car and headed for home. Minutes later, I pulled my car into the driveway and with the whole house to myself, tripped up the stairs to the bedrooms then let myself into Lauren's room. Exactly what I was hoping to find I couldn't say, but as Mal had said, anything, however insignificant, might be useful to us.

As you'd expect from someone like Lauren, her room was spotlessly tidy with not as much as a single spec of dust anywhere. I felt a momentary flash of guilt for being such an out-and-out snoop, then quickly snapped out of it. After all, this was my house and I was entitled, I figured. Besides, after what Lauren had done to me, she really didn't deserve to be treated any better, did she?

I began at the tiny little desk at her window, the one that neatly overlooked our front garden. I didn't even know what I was looking for; something, anything that might help us out, even a little. As it turned out though, she'd left her laptop behind, a MacBook Air. So I flipped it open, knowing it was a huge violation, but then reminding myself exactly what it was that Lauren had put my family through in the first place. But of course, wouldn't you know it? The laptop was password protected and I knew I hadn't a chance in hell of stumbling on her password off the top of my head.

I abandoned that as a bad job, then began to fumble through the drawers of her desk, but couldn't find a single thing. *Nada. Rien.* Just some immaculately compiled receipts, for her annual tax review and a load of printouts of email correspondence from Sloan Curtis, all to do with various other cases we had on the go. Nothing out of the ordinary.

Little that told me anything more about the woman than I already knew.

So then I moved away from her desk and threw open her wardrobe. Neat as a new pin, as you'd expect. Not only that, but all of her t-shirts and sweaters were colour co-ordinated and had been painstakingly laid out on top of each other in orderly piles, so even looking at them felt like being locked inside a Benetton showroom . . . literally; the darker-coloured cotton T-shirts were at the bottom, ascending in gradual order up to the lightest, which she kept right at the very top.

Jesus, I thought, taking the whole wardrobe in from left to right, who even does that? Quite apart from anything else, who has the shagging time? It was all I could do to get Darcy to pick up her clothes off the floor – or her 'floored-robe' as I'd christened it. Yet here were Lauren's clothes, so crisply ironed and starched, it was almost scary looking.

I glanced up and down the wardrobe and was just about to give up and admit defeat, when some sixth sense possessed me. Maybe, just maybe there was something at the top of the wardrobe that I couldn't see? Chances were slim, I reckoned, but then I was in blood stepped thus far, etc., and there was no harm in being thorough. So I hauled the chair by the desk over to the wardrobe and clambered up on top of it, so I could have a really good gawp.

There was a long horizontal shelf at the very top of the wardrobe, again with neatly folded away winter clothes, heavy jumpers mainly, all tidied away till the colder months came around again. I rummaged through them all, taking particular care to fold everything back carefully so it wouldn't look like I'd been fishing around. But after a few minutes I realised I wasn't going to find the Holy Grail up there – it was a complete waste of time. I was just about to clamber down off the chair I'd balanced on when my hand accidentally hit off something.

What exactly, I couldn't tell; it was buried too deeply at the back of the wardrobe and I couldn't see up that high. So I rooted around a bit under a pile of sweaters. No mistaking it though. Right underneath the clothes pile, buried tightly in at the very back of the wardrobe, I could feel a small-ish package.

I fumbled around and was just about to whip it out, when the mound of jumpers it had been carefully buried under went tumbling to the floor, scattering everywhere. Not that I cared; I was a woman on a mission by then. So I hopped up on tiptoe, and stretched until I got a firmer grip on whatever it was.

And that's when I heard it. The unmistakable sound of a key turning in the front door downstairs.

Darcy, I thought immediately. Then I stopped dead in my tracks. It couldn't be. At least, not just yet. She had texted to say she and Tom were having a bite to eat in town – surely it would be hours before she got in. Wouldn't it? Unless she wasn't feeling well and had decided to come home early?

But then that didn't make sense, my worried mind raced. If that were the case, Tom would have come with her. And they'd have called me first, wouldn't they?

'Darcy, is that you?' I called out, still on tiptoe fumbling about the top shelf of the wardrobe. 'I'm up here!'

No answer though. Instead I heard the sound of footsteps on the wooden hall floor downstairs. Heels, click-clacking their way down the hall.

Jesus, I thought, suddenly panicking. Lauren? Home now? At this time?

Move faster, quickly, quickly, quickly.

I kept on with my frantic fumbling and somehow just about managed to get a reasonable grip on the package so I had a chance of being able to slide it out. Next thing I heard footsteps padding up the carpeted stairs one at a time and briskly moving across the landing just outside.

Shit, shit, shit I thought, almost clinging to the wardrobe shelf for dear life. I'd just managed to grab hold of the package and slide it out towards me, when the bedroom door opened.

And there stood Lauren, coldly surveying the chaos; her winter clothes scattered all over the floor, her desk drawers wide open and me red-faced and flustered, standing up on a chair at her wardrobe, caught red-handed.

'Sarah,' she said in an icily calm voice, 'would you mind telling me what you're up to?'

I had the package though. I had it safely in my hands and I'd discreetly been able to shove it deep down into the waistband of my jeans a millisecond before she came in, praying that she wouldn't notice. Was I in luck? Hard to gauge. Madam was giving absolutely nothing away, that was for certain.

'I was just . . . looking for something,' I said, trying my best to sound unflustered.

'Looking for what exactly?'

'Emm . . . an adaptor. For Darcy. That she thought she'd left in here,' I stammered.

'I think you know perfectly well that there's no adaptor in my wardrobe,' Lauren said, folding her arms and eyeing me up and down with deep suspicion. 'Besides, if that's what you wanted, then all you had to do was ask me. I could have saved you what looks like a considerable amount of bother.'

'I was hardly going to contact you when I thought you were in work,' I said, clambering unsteadily down off the chair I'd been perched on, so I stood face to face with her. 'Leaving aside the fact that you and I are hardly on speaking terms. Anyway, what are you even doing home at this time?'

'I left my laptop behind this morning,' she said, stooping down to pick up the jumpers off the floor. 'And I need it for a meeting late this evening. A meeting about the McKinsey brief, as it happens,' she added cattily, like there was any need to rub salt in the wounds. 'But really, Sarah, rummaging about through someone's personal belongings could be considered a major violation of privacy. Not to mention tenant's rights.'

At that, a wash of hot temper flooded through me. Who the fuck did this one think she was to tell me what I could or couldn't do in my own home? After all the havoc she'd wreaked both here and in the office too?

'I'll do whatever I like under my own roof,' I said, drawing myself up to my full height of five foot two and trying my best to sound impressive.

'It's my roof too,' came the swift retort. 'I've paid rent up to the end of the month and—'

'Either you're gone by the end of this week, Lauren, as I've already told you, or you'll come home to find your stuff on the street outside in black bin liners. And I'd advise you not to call my bluff on that either.'

Seconds later, I was out of there and safely locked in the privacy of the bathroom. I undid the top button of my jeans and slipped the package out. It was a neat, padded, brown envelope that had already been opened and was addressed to Lauren.

With trembling hands, I pulled out what was inside as from the landing outside I heard Madam slam her bedroom door shut, click-clack on her heels downstairs and then close the front door firmly behind her. I glanced out of the bathroom window and could see her in the front garden below, just about to step into a taxi.

She's gone, I thought. *I've got the house to myself. I'm safe, for now.*

Hurriedly, I glanced through what was inside the envelope, read what was there, and a minute later was downstairs rooting about on the hall table for my mobile phone. Breathing tightly and with my chest pounding, I fumbled through my contacts for the number I was looking for, then punched it into the phone.

He answered after the third ring.

'Mal? This is Sarah here. Remember you told me that if I found any new information at all, I was to come straight to you? No matter how inconsequential? Well, I might have just stumbled on something. And I think it could be important.'

Chapter Thirty-one

Liz

I rarely, if ever, went into the Sloan Curtis offices, in fact I made it a rule not to. But that afternoon was an exception. It was a perfectly normal day on the Mummy-run as I call it; I'd just collected the boys from school and taken the pair of them home, so I could start the daily grind of a) trying to bully them into doing their homework, and b) subsequently cajoling them to get their heads away from the XBox long enough for me to shovel a few chicken nuggets down their gullets.

But then that's parenting for you: forty per cent nagging, twenty per cent cajoling, thirty per cent worrying and ten per cent picking socks up of the floor.

Then out of nowhere, Rosie, my super-studious, never-put-a-foot-wrong sixteen-year-old phoned me in a blind panic.

'Mum, I need help!' she said, sounding so anxious it alarmed me, but then Rosie never panicked, ever. In our house she was always the cool, rational voice of reason, who kept her head when all around her lost theirs.

'Are you home now?'

'Of course love, what's up?' I said, just as the boys started to bicker over whose go it was to have the remote control.

'I actually can't believe I was stupid enough to do this,' she said breathlessly, 'but you know my economics project on Brexit?'

Of course I did. This was a huge deal for Rosie; something like twenty per cent of her overall marks for economics were awarded based on this project. She'd slaved over it, working day and night; the girl had even voluntarily suspended all her own Netflix privileges purely to get her project finished.

'What's up, love? What do you need?' I asked, waving threateningly at the boys to keep it down.

'The biggest favour ever, please, I'm begging you!'

Now Rosie was one of those kids who never asked for anything. It's like she was born utterly self-sufficient, almost like a human version of a self-cleaning oven. So whatever she needed from me, the answer was an automatic yes.

'I was working on it at home last night,' she said, 'because my teacher wants to see a rough draft later this afternoon. But my laptop just crashed on me and I don't know what to do.'

'OK, love,' I said, thinking two steps ahead. 'I'm sure you've got it safely backed up somewhere. Do you have a USB stick somewhere in the house that I can get to you?'

'Well, that's the thing,' Rosie said a bit hesitantly. 'No. No, I don't.'

'Oh, honey, you mean you didn't back up?'

'Don't give out to me!' she half wailed down the phone. Bear in mind this was a kid who never put a single foot wrong, ever. In fact the only other time I think Rosie messed up was when she was aged five and forgot the words to

'Twinkle, Twinkle. Little Star' while onstage during her end-of-term school concert. Rosie was as close to a perfect human being as either her dad or I had ever seen. So what was the point in me giving out to her?

'OK, just stay nice and calm,' I said firmly. 'Tell me how I can help and between us, we'll fix this.'

'Well, I was working on Dad's laptop all last night,' she said, sounding like she needed to breathe into a paper bag by then. 'And the most up-to-date version of the project should still be there, saved as a Word document. So if you could just get to his laptop at the Sloan Curtis office, print it off, then get it to me here in school, all would be well. I know it's a big ask, but I'm begging here . . . my back really is to the wall.'

*

It was an out-and-out nightmare, but somehow I managed to cajole my childminder to come around to the house, so she could keep an eye on the boys while I zipped out to do the needful for Rosie. First stop, of course, being the Sloan Curtis office on Harcourt Street in the very heart of the city. Where it was always impossible to get parking, but thankfully I had Harry's pass on the dashboard of the car, which meant I could legitimately park in the underground car park of the office block.

And that's when I spotted it. I was just about to pull the car down the sloping ramp that led to the private car park – and there it was. A discreet black people-carrier jeep, one of those giant yokes that you'd nearly expect to see US Presidents being swished around in. With an actual driver and blacked-out windows, the whole works. Parked at street level at the side entrance to the Sloan Curtis offices, directly across the road from the National Concert Hall.

Odd, I thought. Who was inside anyway? Some VIP? Then I found myself wondering who in hell would drive a monster like that around Dublin 2, in rush hour traffic?

Then two things happened, in very quick succession – which I only chanced to see because the traffic was so heavy and I was stuck in the thick of it before I could get near the underground car park entrance. There I was, deeply frustrated, drumming my fingers impatiently on the steering wheel as my eye wandered back to that jeep.

Next thing, the driver of the SUV hopped out, all sunglasses and a tan, dressed in an impeccably cut suit. He was on his mobile, like he'd just had a call from inside the building warning him that someone was about to emerge and to be on high alert.

He went to wait outside the SUV just as a window on the rear passenger seat slid elegantly down, so I could clearly see who it was sitting inside. Some famous politician, I wondered? Maybe on their way to or from a TV studio for an interview?

But that's when my heart stopped my mouth. Because it wasn't a politician at all in the back of the jeep. Instead, it was none other than George McKinsey himself, or George McKinsey III as apparently he liked to be referred to, which Harry always claimed was a measure of just what a colossal prick he was.

The traffic lights I was stuck at changed from red to green but the traffic was so heavy, I could only advance approximately four inches. Which gave me a chance to have a good stare and really take in the whole scene. The mighty George McKinsey seemed in absolutely no hurry to get out of his car, I noticed, nor did his driver particularly look like he was going anywhere. The two of them were just parked there, waiting.

Which didn't make any sense, I thought. After all, Sloan Curtis were his go-to legal firm, weren't they? Everyone on the team, including Harry, and up till the other day, poor old Sarah, were slaving round the clock on the McKinsey brief. So why was the mighty man himself just loitering around outside the side entrance to the office, looking like he was in absolutely no rush whatsoever to go inside?

And that's when I saw her, clear as crystal, with my own two eyes. The traffic lights had just changed and yet again my car was still stuck in traffic when I saw Madam Lauren herself emerge from the side entrance of the office. The discreet entrance, the one you used when you didn't want to be seen. There was absolutely no missing her; she was dressed in a vibrant, deep-purple work suit, and was carrying a laptop and a neat briefcase.

Could McKinsey possibly be waiting for Lauren, I wondered? And my question was soon answered. She looked up, spotted the waiting jeep and gave a quick, professional wave. She was moving fast too, like she was anxious to get out of there as fast as possible without anyone noticing her.

Well, too bad, because you've just been rumbled, Lauren.

No one will ever believe this I thought, so I'm bloody well going to video it on my phone, for no other reason than that later on, when Harry tells me that I must have been seeing things, or even more annoyingly, that 'there's probably a perfectly reasonable explanation for this', at the very least I'll have a bit of back up.

I whipped my phone off the dashboard of the car, went to camera mode and pressed record. I filmed and kept on filming as the driver held the back door open for Lauren as she clambered inside, perching herself on the seat beside McKinsey. I even managed to get a sideways shot of him turning to smile at her, before the blacked-out window slid smoothly up as the car joined the traffic and drove away.

*

'You know, I've just seen the most bonkers thing,' I said to Harry, when he came out to meet me at the Sloan Curtis reception area upstairs.

'What's that, love?' said Harry, giving me a light peck on the cheek and handing over the print-out that Rosie was in such a blind panic to get her hands on.

'Lauren . . . getting into a jeep with none other than George McKinsey himself. Can you believe it?'

'Ah, come off it, that's impossible,' he said.

'Why is it impossible?'

'Because I know for a fact that George McKinsey is in London all day, on unexpected business. You must have been seeing things. Someone who looked a bit like him probably.'

'Harry, I know what I just saw!'

'Pet, it's just not possible. We were due to have a meeting with McKinsey later this evening, but he cancelled on us at the very last minute.'

'In that case, the man appears to have mastered the art of bilocation,' I retorted, delighted with myself as I produced my iPhone with the incriminating video footage on it. 'I'm telling you, I saw him outside this very building not ten minutes ago. Waiting on Lauren, as it happened.'

'On Lauren?' said Harry, visibly taken aback.

'Did you just mention Lauren?' said Lucy, the firm's legal

secretary, as she swished past at that moment laden down with a mound of heavy-looking files. 'Did she tell you? About her tooth, I mean.'

'Her what?' Harry and I said together.

'Oh, nothing to worry about, I'm sure,' said Lucy, dumping the pile of files and important-looking legal briefs on her desk at reception. 'She just had to leave a few minutes ago. All very last-minute, I'm afraid, but then she did say it was an emergency.'

'What emergency?' I demanded.

'She didn't mention it to you, Harry?'

'She certainly did not,' said Harry, his jaw tightening.

'Well,' Lucy went on, 'all I know is that about twenty minutes ago, Lauren told me she had an abscess on her tooth that she thought needed immediate attention. So she'd rung her dentist and he'd apparently told her to get over to him right away.'

'Did she say anything else?'

'Only that it was nothing to worry about, and that if you or Bernie were looking for her, to say she'd probably be gone for the rest of the day.'

Chapter Thirty-two

Sarah

Half an hour later, I was in my car and zipping my way north of the city to Phibsboro, just a short distance from the city centre. I'd arranged to meet Mal at the address I'd given him and was anxious to find it in good time.

Wait till you see, this place will turn out be a complete kiphole, I thought. Probably some run-down slum apartment, with mildew growing on the walls and drug dealers openly trading methadone on the streets outside. The kind of address where I'd worry about leaving my car parked, in case I came back to find it nicked or else burnt out.

But when I eventually found the right address on Great Western Square, it turned out to be absolutely none of the above. To my shock, it was actually an elegant row of old Corporation railway cottages, Edwardian in style and design, and looking impeccably well maintained – from the outside anyway.

There was a tidy little window box on the ledge to the front of the house, full of bright red geraniums in full bloom. The front garden was tiny, just a short pathway with a wheelie bin and some gravel, but neat and well-kept.

Not for a moment would you think of this place as being a hangout for two student wasters who spent half their time strung out on drugs, as Lauren had told me. It looked way too expensive for a start; the kind of house that didn't sell for less than €300k these days. So how could a bunch of students possibly afford it? Unless they were being completely bankrolled by impossibly wealthy parents?

What else have you lied about I wondered, scouring left and right for a parking spot. It was a warm, sunny evening so the whole area really did look appealing, the sort of street that 'trader upper' homebuyers would snap up in a heartbeat. Again, categorically not what I'd been led to expect. I eventually found a parking space and pulled up on the curbside, then waited till my phone rang as arranged.

Which it did approximately two minutes later.

'Sarah?' came that friendly voice. A reassuring voice, I thought. 'Mal here. I've parked a few streets away and I'm just walking around to the house. You'll spot me any minute now, I'd say.'

I'd barely hung up the phone when sure enough I saw Mal's tall, lean shape ambling towards me from a distance. He was wearing a navy jacket over a pair of chinos and between that and the clever-looking, architect-y, Clark Kent glasses, you'd think he was an off-duty businessman to look at him. Never in a million years would you have him down as an actual private detective.

I hopped out of the car and clipped across the street to meet him.

'Good timing,' he said, giving me a quick little smile. Attractive, I thought, now that I could have a good look at him without Liz distracting me. Yet not in an obvious sort of way. Not in the way that Tom was. Or rather, that Tom had once been a long time ago, before he started to lose his hair and grow a middle-aged spare tyre.

'Thanks so much for coming all this way,' I said as he and I stood on the pavement together facing number twenty-seven.

'That's what I'm here for,' he said, smiling. A warm, crinkly smile too, one that actually reached the corner of his eyes.

'You know, this will probably turn out to be nothing.'

'Possibly it will and possibly it won't. But in my experience, absolutely everything is worth checking up on.'

'When I found that bunch of correspondence at the back of Lauren's wardrobe with her old address there in black and white, I thought there was no harm in letting you know, at least.'

'You might show me the actual letters that you found,' he replied. 'You never know what I might to be able to glean from them.'

'It was mostly just a pile of mobile phone bills,' I shrugged. 'That was all. But the critical thing was getting hold of her old address. Then I remembered back to how secretive Lauren was about where she lived before she first moved in with me – refusing to give me her address when I offered to help her move her stuff, all that kind of thing.'

'Didn't you get a bit suspicious when she wouldn't tell you where she lived?'

'I only wish I had,' I said, pulling a face as we walked towards the right house, with Mal towering above me, he was that long and lean. 'But at the time she insisted she didn't want to put me to any trouble. So I figured she was just a bit embarrassed about it, and left it at that. More fool me,' I added ruefully.

331

'Hey, come on now,' said Mal, holding open the tiny garden gate for me. 'You can't beat yourself up about these things. After all, I'm sure you did what you thought was the right thing at the time.'

'And now I'm just praying that this doesn't turn out to be a wild goose chase,' I said, slipping through the narrow little gate. 'I'd hate to have dragged you all the way over here for nothing.'

'Not a problem. That's what I'm here for. And remember, we're trying to put together the full picture about this woman. The more pieces there are in the jigsaw, the clearer that picture becomes.'

We both tripped down the tiny pathway to the front of the house and Mal knocked on the door.

And we waited. And waited. Knocked again, waited some more. I strained to listen out for the sounds of life inside, a TV or radio or similar, but there was nothing. Mal looked at me and I pulled an apologetic face as much as to say, 'sorry for wasting your time'.

And that's when we heard it. What sounded like a garden door opening to the very back of the house from inside. Then bright sunshine spilled out onto the inner hallway, as footsteps tripped lightly down the hall.

'Coming!' said a heavy accented woman's voice from the other side of the door. 'Just a moment please, I need to get my clothes on!'

Jesus, I thought, remembering vividly back to what Lauren had told me about her flatmates being two dope-head students. But moments later, the hall door opened and there stood a girl in her mid-twenties, stunningly pretty with a neat, cropped, blonde bobbed haircut, wearing a light, cotton, dressing gown with a swimsuit clearly visible underneath.

'Oh,' she said, taken aback as she took in Mal and I together. 'You must excuse me,' she added, again in the English of someone who still hasn't quite fully mastered the language. 'I was outside of the home in the rear garden, oh . . . what is the correct word? For when you lie in sun to get some little suntan?'

'Sunbathing?' I suggested helpfully.

'Sunbathing, yes,' she smiled back at me, flashing a set of teeth so perfectly white, they could almost have been the 'after' photo in an ad for cosmetic dentistry. 'Forgive my English. My friends tell me it is big rubbish.'

'Not big rubbish at all,' said Mal, offering his hand to her. 'Can I introduce myself? I'm Mal Evans and this is Sarah Keyes. Can I ask if your name is Elena Kowalski?'

'Yes, yes, that is me. Is correct name. Is there problem?' she asked, puzzled.

'No, there's no problem at all,' Mal said reassuringly. 'We're very sorry to disturb you, but we'd just like to ask you some questions and promise not to take up more than a few minutes of your time.'

Elena looked a bit mystified, but still waved us inside and led us down a small hallway and on through the kitchen then outside to a sundrenched little patio space. Again, all neat as a new pin and absolutely not the kind of place Lauren had described. She'd led me to believe – at great length – that you'd walk in her front door to find half-eaten pizzas in empty boxes covered in flies, discarded tins of beer and hypodermic syringes scattered over the floor, with an overpowering stink of cigarette smoke and a few stray fellas in their underpants sprawled out on a maggoty sofa.

But this place was immaculate. There was even an actual birdhouse in the garden, for feck's sake. And a washing line with underwear pegged out on it, of the comfy, M&S variety. All deeply reassuring, I thought.

Lauren had lied and lied again. Which meant we had to be on the right track.

Mal and I sat down on some rattan chairs that were scattered about as Elena perched her long legs on the sunlounger opposite, then looked at both of us expectantly.

'We're actually hoping to ask you about Lauren Cunningham,' Mal began, taking out a small notebook from his pocket and referring down to notes he'd made earlier.

'Lauren?' said Elena and was I imagining it or did her pretty face cloud over a bit when he said the name? 'Lauren Cunningham . . . who used to live here?'

'She was here for almost two years, I understand?' Mal prompted.

'Well . . . yes, that's right,' Elena answered in that broken English. 'Until a few months ago. She moved out, said she has her own house now, in Dalkey, she tell me.'

I shot a quick look over a Mal.

'After Lauren left here,' I explained, 'she actually moved in with me. And I certainly don't live in Dalkey, let me tell you.'

Dalkey is uber-posh and houses there cost the approximate amount of a small Lotto win. So why had she claimed to live out there?

'I know that *now*,' said Elena, rolling her eyes. 'I just wish I know this sooner.'

'Can you explain?' Mal prompted.

'Well, when Lauren first move out,' Elena went on, 'she owe me and my other flatmate some money. Over five hundred euros in rent and in bills, that she no pay. She promised to pay us as soon as her next paycheck from work come in, and say she post me a cheque. But she never did. So I went to the address she gave me in Dalkey and . . .'

'And . . .?' I asked, intrigued.

'And there's no such place,' Elena said, frowning at the memory.

'Lauren say she moving into apartment block called Kingbay View,' she went on. 'But I go there not long after she move out to get money she owe . . . and there is no such block! Nothing, not a thing. Even street name she give me no exist. She tell me she live on Citric Drive – and it no exist, not on Google maps, not anywhere.'

'So Lauren was lying to you,' I said, then turned to Mal, who was eagerly writing down notes, 'yet another blatant, out-and-out lie.'

Which of course only made me wonder what other whoppers she's told.

'Would you mind if I asked you just a few more questions about Lauren and her background?' Mal asked as Elena nodded yes. 'She says she's been in Dublin for about four years now,' he said, 'and that she came here from a small town in the west of Ireland, Ballymeade. Is that right?'

Again Elena didn't contradict him.

'Can you tell us anything else?' said Mal as I instinctively sat on the edge of my seat. 'We're just trying to fill in some gaps here.'

But then her face clouded over and she looked at the two of us questioningly.

'Why?' she asked. 'Why you come here and want to know all this? Who are you both really?'

'I'm actually a private detective,' Mal explained patiently. 'And I've been brought in to find out a little more about

335

Lauren Cunningham, your former flatmate. That's all. Nothing more.'

'Lauren now works at a legal practice in town,' I chipped in, 'and it was actually me who wrangled that job for her in the first place. But let's just say her behaviour recently has left a lot to be desired. And that's why we'd just like to ask you a few questions about her background.'

'All of which will be treated in the strictest of confidence, of course,' Mal rushed to reassure her.

'So maybe you could tell us a little about how you first came to meet her?' I prompted as gently as I could.

'Well, I first meet Lauren when we were both in final year at college,' Elena said, pulling her bathrobe tighter around her. 'We never were friends, but the one thing we did have in common was that we both needed a home to live in after graduation. I had found this lovely house, but have not enough money to pay rent on my own. I have job, I have very good job, but not enough to rent nice place like this. Rent is big money, very big money.'

'May I ask what you work as?' Mal asked, looking up from his notepad.

'I work for mobile phone company,' she said. 'Based in city centre. Is good job, I like it very much. But it's my day off today, so that's why I'm home sunbathing.'

Yet another lie Lauren had fed me, I thought, and an unnecessarily nasty one too. To portray her flatmate, who seemed like a lovely girl, as some class of Grade-A drug-taking drop-out?

'I needed other girls to share home with me, so I – oh, what is correct word? When you write on noticeboard so everyone sees it?'

336

'I think you mean that you advertised for a flatmate,' said Mal.

'Yes,' Elena smiled 'is correct. So I find other girl from Poland like me, name of Karolina, very nice girl. We are great friends now, even have boyfriends who are friends with each other. Karolina very nice girl. You like her.'

'And I assume Lauren answered your ad too?' I said.

'Yes,' she replied, but this time the smile withered from her face. 'Lauren seem nice at first, but then when we get to know her bit better – not so nice. Never pay rent or bills on time, so we row at lot. Even though she have no student loans to pay off, like Karolina and me.'

'No student loans to pay off?' Mal said, picking up on it instantly. 'Can you tell us why?'

'Because her mother pay them all off for her. She's wealthy widow, live on big farm in countryside. Have lots of money. Always going off to New York for shopping trips, Lauren tell me.'

'I'm sorry,' I almost spluttered. 'Did you say her *mother*?'

'Yes, is correct,' Elena nodded. 'I never met with the lady, but I know she pay for Lauren to go to college. And she pay lot of her rent here too.'

'What's up?' said Mal, clocking the look on my face.

'Oh, nothing. Except that Lauren told me her mum passed away years ago, that's all.'

Elena laughed out loud at that.

'Dead? Are you making joke? That's ridiculous!' she giggled. 'That is very big pile of . . . what is the right word? Dog poo. Mrs Cunningham often call here to speak to Lauren. They have arguments though, big arguments. I don't know about what, but then Lauren very, very easy person to fight with. As my boyfriend say, she is – what is correct word? Toxic person. Is correct?'

'It's absolutely correct. It's just not the story that Lauren told me,' I said, turning slowly to face Mal, with shock I'm sure written all over my face.

'What did she tell you?' he asked.

'That she was an orphan. That her father died when she was a child and that she nursed her mum through terminal cancer, right up until she passed away a few years ago.'

I'd never forget it. The way Lauren told it, she made her whole family history sound like something out of a Brontë novel, with her cast centre stage as Jane Eyre. Jesus, who'd lie about a thing like that? About their own mother?

'Again, not one single word of truth in this,' Elena went on. 'Lauren's mother is well-off lady. When she come to Dublin, she shop only in Brown Thomas and eat lunch in Harvey Nichols. Is – what is the word? Loaded.'

'You OK?' Mal asked me, seeing the look on my face.

'This beggars belief,' I said. 'I'm just sitting here totting up one lie after another. Lauren distinctly told me not only that she was all alone in the world, but that the family farm had to be sold to pay off death duties and mortgages after her mum died.'

'No!' Elena insisted. 'Her family have money. She come from wealthy middle-class people.'

'But when Lauren first came here,' I went on, 'she worked in a beauty salon close to the centre of town. A slightly . . . well, let's just say a salon that had seen better days. It's where I first met her.'

Elena nodded. 'Yes, Lauren work in salon close by, but only part-time and just because she needed cash. She row

338

with her mother and soon after her mother stopped paying all bills for her. But all along Lauren plan to work in law. That what she studied and that what she came here to do.'

'She only worked in the salon part-time?'

'Yes, rest of the time she spent here, sending out her CV to lot of legal firms. Many, many legal firms. So many, we use to make joke about it.'

'That makes perfect sense,' I said. 'I remember when I first met Lauren, she surprised me when I told her I worked at Sloan Curtis and she knew all about the firm, right down to what we specialised in. I remember being completely taken aback by that.'

But then I trailed off, lost in thought. Jesus, I thought, suddenly furious. How could I have been gullible enough to have been taken in by such a web of lies? Why didn't I see through her?

'Beryl, a neighbour who live close by, gave Lauren the job at the salon,' Elena went on to explain. 'It was very nice of her as it meant Lauren have some cash. But when Lauren left to start work for you,' she added, 'she just walked out on Beryl, never even bother to give her – what is right word? Correct notice. Nothing. And Beryl had been so very kind to her.'

'I'm actually losing count of the number of lies she's told,' I said numbly.

'In my experience,' said Mal looking up from the notepad on his knee, 'if someone is prepared to lie about a little thing, then they'll lie about a big thing without a second thought. But my job is to sift out exactly what's truth and what's fiction.'

'My English is not as good as it could be,' said Elena, 'but Lauren is – what's the right word? Patholog. . . pathetic

. . . when someone lies so much they start to believe it as truth?'

'I think the phrase you're looking for,' I said, 'is that Lauren is a pathological liar.'

'Yes, yes, that's what I mean. And if you see her soon, tell her I want the money she owe me. If she no pay, I come around to her office, now that you told me where she work and make – as you Irish say here – holy, mortifying show of her.'

'I almost wish you would,' I said and for the first time since Mal and I got here, the three of us actually shared a conspiratorial smile.

*

Not long afterwards, Mal and I said our goodbyes to Elena, thanking her warmly and promising that we'd be in touch if there was anything else we needed to know.

'I feel like such a roaring eejit,' I said to Mal as he walked me back to my car. I was still reeling in shock by then and was bloody glad of his support.

'Well, you shouldn't,' he said.

'But I actually *believed* Lauren. I swallowed every lie she fed me!'

'Tell you one thing,' Mal said, gently taking my car keys from my trembling hands and zapping it open for me, then holding the door as I clambered inside, 'it sounds to me as though Lauren played you. From the very minute you told her you worked at Sloan Curtis, she had you marked.'

'Yeah, but how could I have been so naïve? I'm a lawyer, Mal; I'm supposed to see both sides of everything I'm told.'

'The critical thing here,' he said kindly, 'is not to beat yourself up too much over this. Look at it this way. A more suspicious type might have dug deeper for holes in Lauren's story, but it's a sign that you're a caring, trusting person that you listened and then tried to help her.'

'A caring, trusting idiot,' I groaned.

'Believe me,' Mal said, as I started up the engine, 'in my line of work I've come across an awful lot of Laurens. And in a funny sort of way, it's heartening to realise that there are still a few Sarah Keyes left in this world, in spite of that. And don't worry,' he added with a quick little smile, before ambling back to his own car, 'now that I've got all this to go on, I'm sure I'll be in touch with news very soon.'

Chapter Thirty-three

Darcy

It had been a long, long time since Darcy could remember a day like that. A real breakthrough day. Where she'd actually had what felt like a proper adult conversation with her dad and where for the very first time, they'd actually spoken in detail about the whole marriage break-up. And more importantly, the real reason why.

Her dad dropped her back at the house and Darcy hugged him warmly goodbye.

'So you and me are OK then, Darce?' he said to her hopefully, just as she hopped out of the car.

She smiled back fondly. 'You and me are better than OK, Dad. We've finally had the honest talk that I really wanted all along.'

'Should have done it an awful lot sooner,' he said regretfully.

'Well, you know,' Darcy told him, suddenly feeling sage beyond her years, 'maybe I wasn't quite ready to hear what you had to say. I still had this fantasy that you and Mum would get back together, even though the longer you were apart, the more obvious it was that it wasn't going to happen. But . . . the weird thing is . . . somehow it doesn't seem to matter any more.'

'And we're cool?'

Darcy even managed not to wince, like she usually did whenever he tried to talk down to her in his misguided idea of what was teen-speak.

'Better than cool,' she grinned as she scooped up her bag from the car floor and made to hop out. 'You know that, Dad.'

'Do you want me to come in with you?' he asked. 'You know . . . just in case.'

'Lauren won't be home for hours yet,' Darcy reassured him. 'That much I can guarantee you. But when she does happen to get back, then she's the one who'll want to watch out for me and Mum. Not the other way around.'

'Atta girl,' he said, revving up the engine to go. 'So just ring me if you need anything and I'll see you at the weekend, yeah?'

'See you Saturday,' Darcy said cheerily. 'Although, maybe not for a spin on your bike!' she joked, as she waved goodbye and hopped up the driveway, fishing her door keys out of her bag.

The house was deadly quiet when she came clattering into the hall.

'Mum? Lauren?' she called out, though instinctively knew she had the house to herself. You could have heard a pin drop, the place was so calm.

And soon Lauren will be gone out of our lives forever, Darcy thought happily, as she headed into the kitchen and made for the fridge to grab a few leftovers for a light supper.

Then the landline rang, which took her by surprise. But then, in this day and age, whoever rang the landline?

'Just a bunch of cold callers ringing from call centres wondering whether or not we're "happy with our service provider",' as her mum always said, on the rare occasions when it did happen.

The answering machine in the hallway clicked in to take the call and clear as you like, the voice on the other end drifted back to Darcy.

'Hi Sarah, it's Ali here, from Simpson Hotels?'

Ali from Simpson Hotels, Darcy thought racking her brains, but then the answer came to her. Yes, her mum had mentioned that name loads of times. She always spoke very highly of Ali, as they'd worked so closely together over the years, that the two of them had grown quite pally.

Apparently Ali worked for Jim Simpson who was the big Alpha Dog at Simpson Hotels; Darcy could picture him and his big blonde head of hair very clearly. He was always in the gossip websites and he'd even been dating one of the TV presenters on *The Weekly Dish*, her favourite online magazine show. A girl about half his age, as it happened, which Darcy and her mates reckoned was seriously vom-makingly pathetic.

'I'm so sorry to call you at home,' Ali's disembodied voice reverberated down the tiny hallway to where Darcy stood listening in the kitchen, 'but I've been calling your mobile all afternoon and it seems to be switched off.

'It's nothing urgent Sarah; it's only about this bloody meeting in the morning. I've just got back to my desk and have found out that's it's been moved from your office, to our new hotel here in Ballsbridge. Anyway, as you'll be coming out this way anyway, I wondered if you and me could have lunch afterwards? We've got a gorgeous new Jamie Oliver restaurant that's just opened here and I thought what the hell, my treat. Be fab to see you. Sure let me know how you're fixed. Bye for now!'

Lucky Mum, Darcy thought, plonking down at the kitchen table and munching away on the leftovers of a casserole from the previous night. But then that Jamie Oliver place at Simpsons of Ballsbridge was always featuring in the gossipy websites that Darcy was so addicted to. It seemed to be a real celeb hang-out and Darcy only wished she'd been included in the lunch invitation as well.

*

About an hour later, she was upstairs at her desk, supposedly working on an economics project for school, but in reality checking up on The Daily Dish i.e, her go-to site for all matters Aidan Turner-related.

Then her mobile rang. Her mum.

'Hey,' said Darcy, bursting to talk to her, 'are you nearly home yet? I had the best talk with Dad and I've loads to tell you!'

'And I've so much to tell you too, love, I almost feel like the latest edition of something,' said her mum.

'So where are you?'

'On my way home, pet. I was just checking you were OK.'

'Never better,' said Darcy brightly.

'You're on your own, yeah? Madam hasn't come home yet?'

'I've got the whole house to myself and there's absolutely no sign of the psycho bitch,' Darcy reassured her.

'Great. Then I'll see you in about a half hour or so, yeah? And we'll catch up properly then? I'm just in traffic now, but I shouldn't be much longer.'

'Fab. Oh and Mum?'

'Yeah?'

'I'm so jealous! Guess what?'

'Give in.'

'There's the loveliest invitation here for you to have lunch in the new Jamie Oliver restaurant at that posh new Simpson Hotel tomorrow. From your pal Ali, who works there. She even says it's her treat. She tried you on your mobile, but she couldn't get you.'

'Oh rats, I had to switch my phone off for the afternoon. What did Ali say in her message, exactly?'

'Something about a meeting that's been moved to the Simpson Hotel out in Ballsbridge instead of it being held at your office tomorrow. Ali said she'll see you there and then take you to lunch afterwards. You're so jammy, Mum. Wish I could go too.'

'Sweetheart, just rewind for one second,' her mum said, her tone completely changing. 'Tell me word for word what Ali said about the meeting being shifted to one of the Simpson Hotels?'

Darcy stopped in her tracks, sensing the urgency in her mother's tone.

'Is it important?' she asked.

'Yes, it's vitally important, love. You have absolutely no idea.'

Chapter Thirty-four

Sarah

We had her. Finally, we had her, after so long. I really thought that Lauren's little Reign of Terror was coming to a close.

I saw Liz's text coming through on my phone, and as soon as I spoke to her, I knew she was thinking along exactly the same wavelength as me.

CALL ME THE MINUTE YOU GET THIS, her text read. *I'VE GOT BIG NEWS FOR YOU AND I'M ONLY HOPING IT MEANS WHAT I THINK IT DOES.*

Then after we spoke, I called Mal too and his response was even more encouraging.

'Now we're really getting somewhere,' he said. 'So all I need is access to Lauren's computer and that should give us some cold hard, concrete proof. Tomorrow, maybe? If you think there's a good time for it to happen, you might let me know?'

'The very minute.'

*

Hours and hours after, Lauren finally got home. But I was still up and waiting for her, even though it was well past 11 at night by then.

'There you are,' I said, as she came in the front door, neatly packing her briefcase, coat and handbag on my hall table.

'Oh, it's you, Sarah,' she sniffed, barely bothering to put her head around the sitting-room door, as I quietly sat there, waiting. Utterly unafraid of her this time. And armed with more information, I felt, than the FBI itself could have provided me with.

Don't give anything away, I said to myself. *Remember, timing here is critical.*

'Wow, it really has been an incredibly long day for you,' I said dryly, but if Lauren picked up on the sarcasm in my tone, she certainly didn't let on.

'Yes, well, you know how it is in Sloan Curtis,' she said, making to go straight upstairs. 'It's always busy. There's always something that needs dealing with.'

'So how's your tooth?' I threw at her, just as she was halfway out the door.

'My what?'

'Your tooth? We heard in work this afternoon that you had to rush off to make a dental appointment.'

'Oh,' she said. But if I'd thrown her a curve ball, she certainly didn't let it show.

What an actress you are, I thought coldly. Someone hand this woman an Oscar, quick.

'Yes. That. My tooth is fine now, thank you for asking. But if you don't mind, I think I'll just have a quick shower and then go straight to bed.'

*

Given what had happened between Lauren and me over the McKinsey brief, I knew I had to tread a very fine line here. On the one hand, I couldn't let her get away with

348

what she'd been plotting; Bernie had to be told, simple as that. He was the boss and he needed to know.

'But on the other hand,' as I said to Harry over the phone from my car, first thing the following morning, 'I don't want this to look like a case of sour grapes on my part either. You know, that I'm out to get her purely because she shafted me in work.'

'We're dealing with a very clever lady,' Harry had said. 'In which case, you and I just have to be a little bit more clever. That's all.'

'I need more proof,' I told him. 'If we're going to do this, then as Mal says, we have to have cold, hard evidence that we're right.'

Lauren had lied through her teeth about her private life and about her family, but as Mal had pointed out, that still didn't give us enough grounds to do what we needed to really see this through.

'There absolutely cannot be a single loose end that she can wiggle out of,' I went on, 'because you know what she's like.'

'Like bleeding Houdini,' Harry said and I could almost hear the accompanying eye roll that went with it.

'So where are you now?' I asked, 'almost there?'

'Just pulling up outside. Where are you?'

'About two minutes behind you.'

'The good news is that Bernie should definitely be home. He was due to go away this week, but not till Friday. So if we're lucky, we might just be able to put this to bed before then.'

'If we're very lucky,' I said, instinctively looking for wood to touch on the dashboard of the car, then making do with my own head instead.

Moments later, I was pulling up into a parking space on Dublin's swish Ailesbury Road, one of those tree-lined areas where that was known far and wide as 'Millionaire's Row'. From the outside, the houses looked like enormous two-storey-over-basement Victorian red-bricks, but guessing by the amount of heavy building work going on all along the road, I figured there were more than a few of the neighbours having subterranean cinemas and home gyms installed. As you do.

I stepped out of the car and spotted Harry's fuzzy head of hair coming towards me from the opposite direction. We met in the middle, just outside number eighty-one and buzzed on the electronic gates outside. I peered up the enormous graveled driveway to the grandeur of the house itself, hoping to glimpse any signs of life, but so far at least there were none.

I'd only ever been invited to this house once before, to a Christmas cocktail party as it happened, about ten years ago and I remember even then being stunned at how wealthy and opulent it was inside; all mahogany staircases, Victorian-rose ceilings that seemed to be about twenty-feet high and huge sash windows overlooking immaculately maintained lawns to the rear of the house. A mansion, a real palace.

'Remember the Christmas drinks do here, a few years ago?' said Harry, correctly reading my thoughts.

'Only too well.'

'You know the only reason that Bernie never invited the office staff back to his house again after that night is because he reckoned it cost him too much. He spent the next month moaning that people stayed way too late and that they drank everything in the house, bar a few bottles of bleach under the kitchen sink.'

I gave a tiny smile, but then that was Bernie for you. Impossibly stingy to the point where it was almost comical.

'Yes, who's there, please?' a woman's voice came crackling remotely over the intercom at the security gates.

'Please tell Bernie that it's Harry and Sarah from work. And that we need to speak to him as a matter of urgency.'

The gates swung obediently open and Harry and I trooped up the long, tree-lined driveway then made our way up the granite steps to the front of the house, where a housekeeper was waiting for us, smiling and holding the hall door open.

'If you wouldn't mind waiting in the drawing room,' she said, 'I'll tell Mr Curtis that you're here.'

Minutes later, Bernie joined us, as Harry and I sat stiffly side by side on repro Georgian stiff-backed chairs that instantly made you feel like you were in an episode of *Downton Abbey*.

'Jesus,' Bernie yawned, still in his dressing gown and looking bewildered as he took in the looks on our faces. 'It's not even eight in the morning yet. What are you pair doing here? Where's the fire?'

'Sorry to disturb you, Bernie,' I began to say, 'but this wasn't a conversation that either of us were prepared have over the phone with you.'

'So what's going on?'

Harry and I shot a quick, loaded glance at each other.

'I'd sit down for this, if I were you,' Harry eventually said. 'Trust me, you'll be glad you did.'

*

When we eventually got back to the office, I was on tenterhooks as I made my way back to my desk. My head was pounding with tension and I had to keep telling myself at all costs to act normal.

The minute that she starts to suspect that we're up to anything, Mal had warned me at length, is the minute that we've lost.

From my desk by the window, I could see Lauren at her own work station, deeply engrossed in whatever briefs she was reading through, and giving absolutely nothing away. Looking, in fact, like butter wouldn't melt in her mouth.

Come on, I telegraphed over to her. Make your move. It's almost time.

It got to 10am though and there still wasn't a budge out of her. A few minutes later, my heart leapt in my mouth as she rose to get up, but it turned out she was only going as far as the staff loo in the corridor outside. I glanced down at my watch again. Almost 10.15am. She had to make her move soon, didn't she?

A beeping from my mobile made me jump and I glanced down to see a text message had just come through from Mal.

AM STANDING BY. LET ME KNOW AS SOON AS THE COAST IS CLEAR.

Almost 10.40am and still nothing. By then I was finding it hard to concentrate, it was all I could do to focus on my breathing and stare out the window onto the busy street four floors below.

Next thing, I jumped to see Lucy from Reception materialise out of nowhere to stand right beside me.

'Sarah?' she said, sotto voce.

'Everything OK?' I asked her.

'You asked me to let you know if Lauren left the office?'

352

I nodded, as my stomach instantly clenched up.

'Well, she just did,' Lucy went on. 'Just this minute, in fact.'

'Did she say where she was going?'

'To the Legal Records Office in town, she said. To pick up some files that she needed to work on.'

'Excellent, good, good,' I said automatically, as my mind clicked into panicky overdrive.

This was it then. Finally, it was game on.

'Sarah?' said Lucy, wavering at my desk.

'Oh erm . . . yeah?' I said, fumbling on my phone for the number I needed to call. 'Sorry, I'm just a bit . . . distracted, as you can see.'

'Would someone please tell me what's going on?'

Mal was as good as his word. A few minutes later, he texted me to say he was already in the lift and on his way up to our offices. I raced to reception to meet him there and instantly felt a sense of relief when I saw his long, lean, bespectacled figure emerge from the lift. He looked cool and in control, exactly the opposite to how jittery I was feeling.

'Well good morning,' he said, even managing a quick smile when he saw me waiting for him. 'So the coast is clear then?'

'For now,' I said. 'But this is the thing, we don't know for how long.'

'I'd better be quick then, hadn't I?'

I guided him through the office and as we weaved our way in and around other desks, Harry spotted us and came over straight away. I didn't need to introduce them; it turned out that Harry and Mal had actually met before, back when Liz was still working here.

'I understand time is of the essence here,' Mal said, as we guided him over to Lauren's empty desk.

'We're so grateful to you for coming in,' I said, as Mal grabbed a chair and got straight down to work.

'If there's absolutely anything you find that might help us out here,' said Harry, 'then the pints are very seriously on me, mate.'

I texted Ali from Simpson Hotels. Which made about my tenth text to her that morning.

ALL OK YOUR END?

She was pretty much straight back to me.

ALL GOING ACCORDING TO PLAN HERE. DON'T WORRY, I'LL CALL THE MINUTE ELVIS HAS LEFT THE BUILDING.

Which bought us a tiny bit more time, I figured. Just how much time though was anyone's guess. A few minutes later, I brought Mal over a coffee and a pathetic-looking rubbery croissant from the office kitchen area.

'Not the most tempting, I'll admit,' I said, plonking the coffee and croissant on the desk beside him as he worked away. 'But I just thought you might be able to use the sugar hit.'

'That's really nice of you,' he said, glancing up at me from Lauren's desktop.

'Dare I ask how you're getting on?' I said hopefully.

'Well, her computer is password protected,' he said, taking a tiny sip of the coffee and mercifully not grimacing. But then the Sloan Curtis coffee was Bernie-style: done on the cheapo-cheapo and bloody awful.

'So . . .?' I began, but he finished the sentence for me.

'Not to worry, Sarah,' he told me with a reassuring smile. 'I'd have been astonished if her computer wasn't password protected, and I've come well prepared. I've got firewall technology to get around that, it just takes a little bit longer, that's all.'

'Oh,' I said, as my face fell a bit. I didn't like to say it aloud, but all I could think was, how much longer? Time was not a luxury we had going for us.

'But in the meantime,' he went on, 'I've just got my hands on something that might be of interest to you.'

'What's that?'

He didn't answer though, just stayed focused on the screen in front of him, as a whole bank of numbers popped up. Hundreds of them, like a digital address book. Mal scanned down through the screen, hit on one with a numerical prefix I'd never come across before, then whipped out his mobile and dialed the number.

'Oh, I'm sorry,' I said, a bit mystified. 'If you're making a call, I should probably give you a bit of privacy.'

'No,' he said in a low voice, waving at me to stay. 'This you might want to stick around for.' Then he turned back to the phone as someone obviously answered. Quickly, he switched to speakerphone and Facetime, so not only could I hear the conversation, but I could see who was on the other end of the phone too.

Not that either meant anything to me. Up popped an image of a smart-looking, middle-aged woman sitting in a hairdresser's chair, with a black gown on her having tin foil meche highlights put in. Clearly a 'well-maintained' woman, you might say.

'Who is this please?' she asked politely, in an accent that sounded eerily familiar. 'I don't know your face,' she added, squinting at the phone from sideways on. 'Are you one of that broadband crowd? Because I waited in all day for you yesterday, you know, and your technician never called. My broadband has been dodgy for several days now, I'll have you know.'

'Hi there, my name is Mal Evans,' Mal started to say, 'and I'm calling on behalf of Sloan Curtis solicitors—', but whoever this woman was, she just barreled over him.

'Never a good time for your broadband to crash on you, you know,' she said crossly, twisting her phone to a funny angle so that Mal and I got a great view up her left nostril. 'And I was right in the middle of *House of Cards* on Netflix too,' she added. 'Season 5. The *best* one.'

'I'm actually calling from a legal firm here in Dublin,' Mal ploughed on, 'and I just wanted to ask you a few questions about Lauren Cunningham, if you had a moment to spare?'

There was the longest pause, and all I could hear was 'Uptown Funk' by Mark Ronson playing on the salon's sound system in the background.

'Oh Christ,' this lady groaned as a hairdresser hovered into view and plonked what looked like a cappuccino in front of her, 'I was afraid of this.'

Afraid of what exactly? my mind raced.

'So what's she done this time?' this lady said with an exhausted sigh as she leaned forward to take a sip of the cappuccino. It left a foam moustache on her top lip and, for some inane reason, that was all I could focus on. 'Don't tell me, Lauren's looking for more money? Now why doesn't that surprise me?'

Then in the space of a heartbeat, I knew exactly who this woman was. That unmistakable west of Ireland accent.

356

Not that I looked properly, even the bone structure was uncannily similar.

Mal gave a discreet cough before continuing.

'May I confirm that your name is Irma Cunningham? And that Lauren is your daughter and only child?'

'Yes, yes, yes,' Irma said wearily. 'But I do warn you. If you're ringing on her behalf because she owes you money, then my answer is a very firm no. Not after what happened last time. And I might add, Lauren has a right cheek to pass on my number to you. Although after everything she's put me through, why am I even surprised? Not even a call on Christmas Day from that one, not a card, nothing. For her own mother! As far as that girl is concerned, I'm just an ATM machine.'

'It's nothing like that at all,' Mal said calmly. 'I'd just like to ask you when was the last time you heard from your daughter?'

'Oh, I can tell you exactly,' came the tart reply, without a scrap of hesitation. Almost like she'd been dying for the chance to rant about this for a long, long time.

'It was well over two years ago as it happens,' Irma went on. 'Lauren came to me wanting me to sell the family business, liquidate the shares, then hand her a large, cash lump sum, so she could get started in the legal business in Dublin. She was prepared to sell the roof over my head and to put me out of house and home – me, her own mother! My girlfriends still can talk of little else, and that was over two years ago.'

'Ask about the family business,' I hissed to Mal, but he was ahead of me.

'You own some farmland, is that right?' Mal said courteously. 'Outside Ballymeade on the Clare–Galway border?'

'It's a little more than that, actually,' said Irma snootily. 'We have one of the largest poultry farms in the county. Ballymeade Eggs are the third biggest egg supplier in Galway region, you know. We employ well over seventy-five staff at our production plant.'

Jesus, I thought, my head reeling from the sheer number of lies Lauren has spun me about her family and her life before she came here. I felt actual, physical shortness of breath and had to perch down on a chair beside Mal till the room stopped spinning.

'I have a feeling you may be hearing from your daughter a lot sooner than you think,' said Mal and Irma give a tight, quick smile.

'Well, of course, I'm her mother and my door is always open. But you can also tell her from me that she has a long way to crawl back from what she put me through. Unforgivable, you know. Utterly unforgivable.'

'I certainly will,' said Mal.

'Now if you'll excuse me,' Irma went on, 'my colourist Linda is anxious to get me rinsed at the basins. And I've got a lunch with the girls afterwards at the G Hotel, so I'm afraid I really do have to go.'

'In that case, thank you for your time,' Mal said politely, as the call clicked off.

'You OK?' he asked, instantly turning his attention to me, where I sat slumped on the chair beside him.

'I'm in total fecking shock,' I said in a tiny voice. 'That woman, Irma? That glamour-hammer on her way to have lunch with her girlfriends? According to Lauren, she died of terminal cancer brought on by alcohol poisoning seven years ago.'

Mal just nodded, listening intently.

'And the family business? The one that's clearly worth millions? According to Lauren, she grew up in a one-horse farm that had to be sold to pay off debtors! Sweet baby Jesus and the orphans, where will it all end?'

'I'll tell you exactly where it'll end,' he said grimly. 'It'll end with the truth coming out because it always, always does. Trust me, Sarah. What I'm finding out now is just the tip of the iceberg. She's lied about her background, but as you know, that's still not enough for us. We need to find out what she's lied about professionally because that's how we nail her. And try not to worry,' he added, before turning back to the computer. 'Whatever Lauren has in here that she doesn't want us to see, I can get my hands on. That's a promise. So trust me. I've got this.'

I gave him a weak smile and even managed a little thumbs up sign, then turned back to my own desk. But I made sure I had my back to him, so he couldn't see me biting my lip doubtfully as I made my way.

*

It was coming up to lunchtime and I'd had a uselessly unproductive morning, most of which I'd spent like a total bag of nerves, anxiously staring out the window, in between jumping about six feet in the air every time my mobile pinged.

Liz kept phoning and texting what felt like every hour on the hour, with all manner of positive cheerleading along the lines of *DON'T WORRY BABES, TODAY IS THE HAPPY DAY THAT MADAM LAUREN IS FINALLY OUTED!!!* Followed by a whole series of emojis of a horned devil, then a load of smiley faces.

I kept looking across the office floor to where Mal was

still deep in work at Lauren's desk, barely looking up. From where I was sitting, I could make out the top of his thick, dark hair bent double over the computer, hardly even coming up for air. I tried to interpret whether this could be construed as either a good sign or a bad one, but quickly gave it up as a bad job. Then with my stomach in a tightly coiled knot of frustration, I went back to staring stupidly out the window and down onto Harcourt Street below.

I was just trying to focus on a legal file in front of me, even though my head was pounding and my eyes were actually starting to blur a bit around the edges, when, next thing, I was aware of someone standing right at my shoulder. I turned around to see Mal standing there, to my surprise, with a tiny half-smile on his face.

'Well?' I asked him anxiously, heart hammering off my ribcage.

'I think we have her,' he said. 'You won't believe what I've got for you. I can scarcely believe it myself. But then if it's one thing I've learned after years in this business, it's to expect the unexpected.'

'Cold, hard proof?'

'Hard as concrete.'

Chapter Thirty-Five

Her meeting had gone brilliantly, there was no other word for it. Fan-fecking-tastically, as that idiotic little teenager she was forced to share a house with would doubtless have said.

Darcy. God, she thought, it would be such a joy to see the back of her. There was only so much teenage angst and self-absorption that a grown woman could take and this particular grown woman had long since reached saturation levels.

Of course there was still the vexing issue of where to move to, now that she was being unceremoniously turfed out of Sarah's house, but that was a whole other problem for a whole other day. Right now, she had far bigger fish to fry.

Besides, she reasoned. There was always Tom to fall back on, wasn't there? She always knew he'd have his uses one day, and maybe this was it. She could always fix it so she could move in with him. Strictly on a temporary basis, of course. Just till she found somewhere more suitable. Some-where more in keeping with what she was fast-tracking her way to be. An up-and-coming legal hotshot with a fast and ever-growing list of A-list clients to her name.

True, there was one slight problem with Tom, in that he'd doubtless been poisoned with a whole lot of nonsense about her in the past few days. He'd probably take a bit of getting around, but she felt confident it was nothing she couldn't handle. The Toms of this world were so laughably easy to win over, which was precisely why she'd targeted him in the first place. It was no harm for her to have someone in her corner, who'd do precisely as she wanted, when she wanted it. And she was bloody good at that. When it came to manipulation and getting around people, by God she was practically a master.

Mind you, she'd started young. She had barely any memory of her father, but by the tender age of eight had come to realise exactly how useful a dead parent could prove to be. If she was a bit behind on homework? 'Sorry, miss, it was my dad's anniversary.' Ditto if there was a PE class she wasn't in the mood for, she'd claim she was missing her dad so much that she couldn't possibly take part. Similarly with kids' parties; if she wasn't invited, then all she had to do was turn on the tears and just the merest mention of her father was enough to secure her any invitation, anywhere she wanted to go.

By the age of ten the man probably had about a dozen anniversaries a year. So much so that her own mother got wind of it and came down on her like a ton of bricks. To this day, her words still resonated. 'Is this what I've reared? A barefaced liar?'

But the main thing she learned was that lying worked. Always did, always would. And with lying came the effortless charm that she really needed to win people over. All the better to get around them. Feed them a sob story, play to their sympathetic side, then cash in. Worked like a dream, particularly when it came to her career. Because when it came down to it, 90% of people were so easy to get around it was a joke. They were in such a rush to be your new best friend that it was a doddle to manipulate things your way. If you were clever about it, that was.

Admittedly there was a price to be paid, in that people in the legal profession were famous for being heavy socialisers and expected you to be on hand to go to the pub with them at the drop of a hat, but generally she was a woman who could deal with that.

It was pathetic really, she often thought as she stood at bars with nothing but a sparkling water in her hand while some drunken idiot slobbered all over her. Or worse, while one of her legal colleagues bored her to sobs about his private life, after a glass of Merlot too many. Drinking and socializing were such a colossal waste of time, she'd always thought, while standing there with her jaw practically hard-wired into a grin. Honestly, how did these people expect to be taken seriously?

And as for Sarah?

She felt a tiny twinge of something akin to guilt when she thought of Sarah. Which was unusual for her, but then empathy wasn't something she usually allowed herself to indulge in. Regrets were for losers, after all. But then Sarah had been her key into all this, hadn't she? Right from the get-go, this woman had correctly identified Sarah for what she was: a do-gooder. A people-pleaser. One of those women who actually swallow all that nonsense about the sisterhood and there being a special place in hell for women who don't help each other.

An easy mark, in other words, she thought, as she stepped into the waiting taxi and gave the driver the address. But then she instantly brushed away any lingering feelings of regret or God forbid, remorse, when she thought of Sarah Keyes.

After all, when it boiled down to it, she was really the one who had been doing Sarah a favour, not the other way around. Their paths had crossed for a reason and from Sarah's point of view, it was clear that reason was that she had a lesson to learn. To stop being so trusting and taking people at face value. To use her wiles a little more, to start thinking like a lawyer, for God's sake; weren't they supposed to be trained to always be doubtful and to question all information they'd been presented with? Yet Sarah had proved herself so easy to get around, it was almost a joke.

Besides, she thought as her taxi zoomed out into the traffic and got on its way, look at everything that Sarah Keyes had been handed on a plate in her life. A fine home to call her own. A fabulous job, even though she hardly deserved it; she spent so much time working on that ridiculous free legal aid programme. It was actually astonishing that she still expected to represent heavy-duty office clients on top of that.

What Sarah really needed was to toughen up a little, to be a bit more like that monstrous friend of hers, Liz. For all that Liz was a bitter pill to be around, she was tough. Able. No-nonsense. Unafraid to be direct. This woman would almost have relished going head-to head with Liz in a legal meeting or even in a court of law; she seemed like a worthy adversary. Albeit that she was a complete horror story to try to win over. The type who was unreachable, untouchable no matter what sob story she was peddled. Best written off.

Sarah, on the other hand, was one of those people who seemed to have got into the law out of some ridiculously outdated and misguided notion about 'helping others'. So if that's what she wanted, then that's what she could have. Sarah's mission in life was to help those around her, so in actual fact, the past few months for her had probably been like all her Christmases coming at once.

Banishing all thoughts of Sarah Keyes clean out of her head, she fished her phone out of her handbag and got straight back to answering the long list of emails that had come in while she'd been at her meeting. Getting back to work, in other words. As efficient, calm and professional as ever.

*

The first sign that something was amiss was when she stepped out of the lift on the fourth floor for Sloan Curtis and realised that the place seemed a lot quieter than usual. Deadly quiet, in fact. She checked her watch, in case it was lunchtime, but even that didn't make much sense; there was supposedly a policy of taking staggered lunches here, so that the office was never fully deserted.

Then Lucy at reception flushed red in the face, the minute she saw her stepping out of the lift.

'Oh, emm . . . hi. You're back then,' she said flatly, tossing her a cold look. Which again, was odd. Normally she and Lucy were on excellent terms and would at least pass the time of day with each other and have a bit of a chat. Not that Lucy had much conversation; 'did you see *Celebrity Big Brother* last night?' featured strongly, or else, 'what do you think of this bandage dress on Kourtney Kardashian?'

But so far, she'd never betrayed how boring and inane she found Lucy. Instead, she'd usually smile warmly back and chat a bit and entertain her ridiculous small talk. Mainly because the Lucys of this world were easily won over and had uses in lots of ways, she'd always found. Keep the office minions onside, she'd always found to be a good maxim. You never know when you might need them.

Not this time though. No idle, stupid chit-chat, nothing. Instead, Lucy just glared up at her and said, 'they're waiting for you in the conference room. Can you please go there right away?'

She did a double take. That in itself was strange. Because there was no meeting scheduled; if there had been, she'd have known all about it. Efficiency was her watchword. The one thing that marked her out from her co-workers was that she never, ever made mistakes. She flipped out her phone to triple check her schedule for the day, but, no, there was definitely no meeting.

'I'm sorry, Lucy,' she said, smiling very sweetly, 'but I think you must be mistaken. There's no meeting booked in for this afternoon.'

'Oh, didn't I say?' said Lucy icily. 'This is an emergency meeting that's just been called. Bernie is in there already and specifically requested you to go there straight away when you arrived.'

'Fine, in that case I will.' She smiled again, picked up her briefcase and swished briskly through the office – which again, was worryingly empty. Where was everyone? At this meeting, she guessed, although she was utterly at a loss to know what it could be about.

But she soon snapped out of it. After all, she was the resident office Golden Girl, wasn't she? As far as Bernie was concerned, she might as well walk on water. In an astonishingly short space of time, she'd come such a long way. She'd even heard rumours they were thinking of her as a potential partner in due course. And let them. She was a woman who'd been undervalued and undersold for quite long enough, thank you. Now it was time to cash in her chips and move onto bigger and better things.

No, she thought, fixing a bright confident smile on her face as she walked through the huge, heavy double doors that led to the conference room. Whatever this meeting is about, it can only mean good news for me.

To her surprise, there were just four others waiting ahead of her in the conference room. Bernie, of course, looking ridiculous with his red, puffy face, bloated from decades of having one whiskey and soda too many.

Beside him sat Harry. Ahh, poor Harry, she thought, almost pitying him. He was so clearly going nowhere in this company and, at the end of the day, who did he have to go home to only that harridan of a wife of his?

Opposite Harry at the giant conference table sat Sarah, but there was something different about her today, though it was hard to put a finger on. She could sniff it a mile off. Outwardly Sarah looked exactly the same, doll-like and waifish, in that awful suit from Reiss that she'd worn to death. So what was it about her that had changed?

And then, with a tiny jolt, she realised. There was a quiet confidence about Sarah this afternoon, a quality the poor woman had always been lacking. She normally sat at this very conference table looking like what she was; a scatty, ill-prepared, overloaded lawyer, constantly being distracted by her phone ringing, then pulled in twenty different directions over some crisis or other, usually concerning that spoilt, over-privileged Darcy.

But Sarah seemed emboldened this afternoon, as if she had some card up her sleeve that she'd yet to play. And not only that, but there was a guy sitting right beside her, mid-forties at a guess, with one of those long, lean, ectomorph builds. Thick, dark hair and trendy square-ish glasses.

Attractive, she thought, assessing him at a single glance. A new client, clearly, though hardly a big fish, like the McKinsey's were. Small potatoes, she thought, weighing him up. But still, a client was a client and an attractive guy was an attractive guy.

'There you are,' Bernie said crisply as she took a seat at the opposite end of the table and prepared herself for whatever this was about. 'There's someone here who'd like to speak to you and ask you a few questions. Can I introduce you to Mal Evans?'

She stood again and stretched across the table to shake hands. Funny thing, she thought, he didn't make eye contact with her. Unusual; normally men couldn't take their eyes off her. It was a reaction she'd been provoking since she was about fifteen years of age and she was so used to it that she pretty much took it for granted.

'Mal,' Bernie went on, 'I'd like you to meet Lauren Cunningham.'

Chapter Thirty-six

Sarah

If Lauren betrayed the slightest sign that she was caught off guard when summoned to the conference room, then she certainly didn't let on. How she kept her cool though and actually managed to look composed was beyond me; the tension was practically ricocheting off the four walls.

'We understand you've had quite a busy morning, Lauren,' Bernie said calmly, from his usual chair at the top of the table.

'Yes,' she said, eyeballing him and without even as much as a giveaway blush as she slipped gracefully into a seat opposite.

'Down at the Records Office,' I prompted, hoping to steer her towards a good, juicy lie. 'Wasn't that where you said you were going?'

'I had intended to,' Lauren answered calmly, 'but then I was called to another meeting en route.'

'With the Simpson Hotel Group, I understand,' said Bernie, steepling his fingers and eyeballing her directly.

There was the tiniest pause while she took in the subtext of what was really being said.

You lied. And not only that, but then you went and met with a client behind our backs. Now why would you go and do something like that?

'Yes, I was just about to tell you,' Lauren said, again betraying absolutely nothing. A real sign of a practised liar, I thought, glaring coldly across the table at her. That she could convince herself that her whole web of deceit was actually the truth. Jesus, who exactly were we dealing with here?

'Tell us what, Lauren?' I said.

'I was actually troubleshooting a potential problem with Simpson Hotels this morning,' she said, glaring right back at me. 'A last-minute emergency that arose. Naturally I didn't like to bother you with it, Sarah. I know how busy you are with all your free legal aid work just now. Plus I know how difficult you find it to multi-task.'

Oh, you utter bitch, I thought, as my heart rate began to pound. You saunter in here after everything you've done and now somehow you're trying to shift the blame onto me?

Right. That was it. As far as I was concerned, it was gloves off.

'It's curious that you use the word "emergency", Lauren,' I answered, determined to keep all emotion out of my voice, 'when in fact we've been told this particular meeting with Simpson Hotels had been planned since yesterday.'

It did my heart good to see the confusion written on her face at the curve ball I'd just thrown her. You could almost see her thinking, how do I lie my merry way out of this one?

'You'll understand our concern at this development,' said Bernie from the top of the table. 'Particularly in light of the fact that you met with George McKinsey only yesterday too.'

For the first time I think in all the months I'd known her, I actually saw Lauren look flustered. A highly gratifying sight, believe me.

'Excuse me?' she said. '*What* did you say?'

'You were seen, Lauren,' I said, God forgive me actually relishing my moment. I'd certainly waited long enough for it. 'It's pointless denying it.'

'I'm sorry, but have you been spying on me?' she said, fighting fire with fire. Like an animal who's wounded and whose only way of retaliation is to keep on fighting back.

'If we have been, we're perfectly justified in doing so,' I retorted. 'You were seeing getting into the back of George McKinsey's jeep at exactly ten to three yesterday afternoon.'

'That's crazy!' she started to say, but I didn't give her a chance to finish.

'There's no point in trying to put a spin on it Lauren, we've already got all the proof we need.'

'Plus we have a right to know what that was all about,' said Harry. 'McKinsey is our single-biggest client after all. And you lied to get out of here so you could meet him – all that about having to make an emergency dash to the dentist. Remember?'

'I happened to be meeting George on a personal basis,' was her comeback, 'which is absolutely none of your concern. After all, what I do in my private life isn't anyone's business but my own, now is it?'

At that I almost guffawed.

'Oh, come on,' I said to her. 'Seriously? Do you honestly expect us to believe that you were going on a *date* with George McKinsey? Are you for real?'

There was a stilted silence with every eye in the room focused on Lauren. Then Bernie spoke, taking control.

'Lauren,' he said sounding authoritative, 'if there's anything you'd like to come clean to us about, then now would be a good time. Before I hand the floor over to Mal.'

Lauren looked across the room at Mal, in much the same way as you'd look at a lump of dog poo stuck to the sole of your shoe. Meanwhile, Mal folded his arms and sat right back in his chair, looking like he was actually starting to enjoy all this.

'I'm afraid I don't know who Mal is,' said Lauren, 'or what exactly his presence at this meeting has to do with me.'

'Then sit tight,' I said, 'because you're about to find out.'

'I'm throwing you a lifeline here,' Bernie added. 'Far better for you to tell us everything now, Lauren. For your own sake.'

There was a knife-edge silence and I found myself involuntarily clenching my knuckles. I looked up and caught Mal's eye and could have sworn he gave me a tiny half wink, as much as to say, stay cool. We're almost home and dry.

But I of all people should have known by then that Lauren was a brinkmanship player.

'Once again,' she said, 'I must reiterate that I have absolutely no idea what any of you are insinuating. I've done nothing wrong. I've worked myself to the bone for Sloan Curtis; you all know that. And I'll continue to do so.'

Bernie shrugged as much as to say, well, you had you fair chance and you just blew it. He almost looked a bit regretful, but I wasn't allowing him to wallow.

'Of course you can appreciate the alarm bells that rang

here when you were spotted with George McKinsey,' I said. 'Not to mention your rendezvous with Simpson Hotels on top of that. Poaching clients is a very serious offence.'

'And a sackable one,' Bernie added.

'Which is where Mal came in,' I said, indicating him. At that, Mal took off his glasses, rubbed his eyes and addressed her directly.

'I should begin by telling you,' he said in that calm, even voice, 'that I'm an investigator specializing in IT technology.'

'I'm afraid I don't quite understand what any of that has to do with me,' Lauren replied.

'Don't worry, you're about to,' I couldn't stop myself saying. This moment had been a very long time coming and I was determined to savour every lovely minute of it.

'As soon as I gained access to your desktop computer earlier,' Mal began, referring down to a mound of computer printouts that were neatly stacked on the table in front of him.

'You did *what*?' Lauren interrupted, blanching. 'Do you realise what a violation of my privacy that is?'

'It's not actually,' I said.

'Sarah is quite right there,' said Bernie, backing me up. 'Under the company's house rules, any computer can be accessed with my authority at any time. Such as when I strongly suspect an employee of violating the terms of their contract.'

'I can assure you I did no such thing,' Lauren began to say, starting to look rattled. There were actual beads of perspiration on her forehead that she had to dab away with a tissue.

'You know what?' I told her, waving my hand for her to

373

shut up. 'Save it. Just save it, OK? And have a listen to what Mal has to tell us.'

'On the twenty-fourth of May,' Mal began, sounding utterly in control as he referred down to a printout in front of him, 'you had a series of email exchanges with Jim Simpson of Simpson Hotels. So let's cut to the chase and read you out this particular one.'

'You can't do this!' Lauren began to say. 'I refuse to give you permission . . .'

But Mal read on regardless. I could see that he'd even gone to the bother of using a bright yellow highlighter pen on the particularly juicy bits.

'"As we've already discussed at length",' he read out as Lauren squirmed – actually squirmed – in the chair opposite as her own, incriminating words were read back to her. '"I've been headhunted by the Whites and Company legal firm and will shortly be taking up a post with them as an executive junior partner."'

'Which certainly came as news to me,' said Bernie frostily from the top of the table. 'Very big news.'

Whites and Company were huge rivals of ours and it was well known that James White, the head honcho there, and Bernie had been locked in mortal combat, pitching for clients for years now. Let's just say inter-firm competing for clients between the two companies was at *Game of Thrones* levels by then.

'Look . . .' Lauren stammered, 'I can explain all of this – it's absolutely not what it looks like.'

'If you'll allow me to read on,' said Mal, blankly, going back to the printout in front of him. '"Further to this development, I strongly feel I should advise the Simpson Hotel Group to be newly represented by Whites and Company.

As we've discussed, not only are Whites a considerably larger firm with a firmer foothold in European territories, but from my new post there, I could continue to oversee your activities and guarantee you the highest possible service. Sloan Curtis are a fine firm, but a small one, and I feel the time has come when you and I have both outgrown them."'

There was a silence around the table, as Mal slowly put the printout down then fiddled about with his glasses. All eyes were on Lauren who sat across from me, like a rat cornered down a hole. I swear to God, you could almost see the cogs of her brain whirring into overdrive as she desperately tried to claw her way out of this one.

'This is ridiculous,' she said, trying to pull together the threads of her dignity. 'That was obviously a private email which has now been completely taken out of all context—'

'So how come when I spoke to Ali at Simpson Hotels not half an hour ago,' I said, taking great care to lock eyes with her, 'she told me you'd just attended a meeting out at their Ballsbridge hotel, where you clearly outlined how the firm Whites and Company could represent them from now on. Explain that, if you can, please.'

'May I reiterate,' said Bernie, 'that poaching clients is a sackable offence.'

'But I can explain all of this!' said Lauren, losing her cool.

'No explanation is necessary, Lauren,' I said crisply, determined not to blow it. 'Furthermore, it seems that Simpson Hotels weren't the only client of ours that you intended on poaching. Which brings us neatly to George McKinsey and your impromptu meeting with him yesterday evening.'

'When you were suffering so badly from toothache,' Harry prompted sarcastically.

'I told you,' said Lauren hotly, 'that meeting was private and confidential and I'll thank you to stop trying to ruin my good name and reputation here, Sarah.'

'Excuse me, did you just say "your good name and reputation"?'

'You're jealous of me,' Lauren snapped back at me. 'And you have been for months now. You even had to stoop to bringing in some kind of detective to snoop through my private correspondence, just so you could get rid of me. I found you snooping through my bedroom at home yesterday and now you're doing the same on me in work! You're pathetic, Sarah Keyes. Do you hear me?'

'I'm afraid that's not how I see it at all,' said Bernie from the top of the table. 'Both Sarah and Harry have done this firm a great service, in fact. Naturally after I was alerted to your meeting with George McKinsey yesterday, I contacted the man himself straight away.'

Lauren went snow-white at that. Even under the perfect, caramel skin, she actually looked like she was about to pass out cold on the floor.

'And George confirmed everything for me,' Bernie went on. 'Apparently he took you to dinner yesterday evening and you urged him to move all his business interests to Whites and Company, without delay. It's QED, I'm afraid.'

'But . . . but . . .' she stammered uselessly.

'It's all here too,' said Mal, referring back down to the printouts in front of him. 'Your email correspondence with Whites and Company leaves no room for doubt that you intended joining the firm as soon as you'd served out your notice here.'

'Bernie,' said Lauren in one final appeal to him, like a gambler shaking the dice for the very last time. 'You have to believe me, this isn't what it looks like at all. Yes, I've had discussions with Whites, but I hadn't mentioned it to you or handed in my notice because I haven't made up my mind whether to accept a job with them or not.'

'Oh please.' I almost wanted to laugh at that. 'Do you really expect us to believe that? You mightn't have officially accepted the job with Whites, but it still didn't stop you from trying to poach two of our biggest clients from here and taking them with you, did it?'

Then there was a silence, and all eyes automatically drifted up the top of the table to where Bernie sat impassively. After all, he was the boss-man. We'd all done our bit, now the final decision rested with him and him alone.

'I want you to listen to me very carefully, Lauren,' he said after a long, thoughtful pause. 'Because I'll only say this once. I want you to go to your desk, where I'd like you to clear away the last of your things. Then security will escort you out of the building and off the premises. And that's pretty much the last that I'd like to see of you here at Sloan Curtis.'

'And when you're finished doing that,' I added, 'you can go back to my house, pack up your things and be gone by the end of the day.'

Lauren went to speak, but with an imperious wave of his hand, Bernie shut her up.

'Nor would I even think about asking for a reference from this firm either,' he said. 'Because unlike you, I'm not a compulsive liar. I'd only tell the truth about who you are and exactly what it is that you've done.'

As we were all dismissed and everyone clambered up to leave, Lauren sat there alone, utterly defeated. I had to walk right past her to leave the room and, God forgive me, I couldn't help myself.

'Your mother says hello, by the way,' I said.

It was worth it just to see the look of confusion and disbelief wash over her pale face.

'What did you just say?' she demanded.

'Oh, I think you heard me. Lovely lady, your mum. And she looks remarkably well too. Considering she's been dead for the last seven years.'

Chapter Thirty-seven

Darcy

Ding dong, the witch is dead.

She was really going then. Going, going, gone.

Darcy and her mum sat in the kitchen of the house listening to Lauren upstairs, flinging the last of her stuff into the same, tatty, stuffed suitcases she'd arrived with. Neither of them could speak, or eat or do anything except hold hands and wait for her to be gone.

'Won't be long now, pet,' her mum said reassuringly. 'Just a few more minutes and then we're rid of her. She'll be out of this house and out of our lives for good and that's a promise.'

More clattering noises from the top of the stairs, followed by the sound of heavy, stuffed bags being dragged down to the hall, one step at a time.

'I really can't believe it, Mum,' Darcy said, feeling the weirdest mixture of relief and exhilaration at the same time. 'I can't believe that in just a few minutes, we'll have the house to ourselves again. We'll have peace. Finally, after all this time.'

Her mum squeezed her hand feelingly and nodded, like she was feeling exactly the same thing.

'You don't even have to watch her go if you'd rather not,' Mal said quietly, from where he stood over by the kitchen window, hands shoved deep into his pockets. 'Might be better not to, in fact.'

'No,' said her mum quietly with a firm shake of her head. 'I'd actually like to see this for myself. I want to see her physically walk down my driveway for the very last time. I need to hold that image in my mind.'

'Me too, Mum,' Darcy said loyally.

'Whatever you say, ladies,' said this guy Mal, with a quick, understanding nod. 'In the meantime though, why don't I make myself useful and help her load her things into a taxi? Get her out of your hair that bit faster.'

He went out into the hall and Darcy heard him lugging more heavy bags out the front door.

'He's nice,' she said. And she really meant it too. Mal seemed gentle and kind; she was glad he was here, glad to have him around.

'I don't know what we'd have done without him today,' her mum said. 'He really was incredible. So calm and unruffled in spite of Lauren's trying to worm her way out of everything. He just kept backing up every single point he made with cold, hard, printed evidence, until there was absolutely no way out of it for her, none.'

'And then he drove you home?'

Her mum winced a bit.

'I know, I'm pathetic,' she said, taking a sip out of the mug of sugary tea in front of her, 'but after everything that happened earlier, I really didn't really feel up to driving home through all the traffic. So Mal offered to drop me off, which was lovely of him.'

Darcy allowed herself a tiny smile. Because this was

good, this was a step in the right direction. After all, if her dad thought the time was ripe for him to move on, then why not her mum too? And she'd liked the way Mal treated her mum; holding a chair out for her, insisting on making her a cup of tea . . . basically being the perfect gentleman.

Her mum spent so much of her time looking after everyone else, from Darcy herself to all the free legal aid prisoners she devoted herself to, not to mention her clients in work. She was a minder, that's all she ever seemed to do. So wouldn't it be great if someone came into her life who actually took care of her for a change?

And, OK, this Mal guy could easily turn out to be married or living with someone or maybe even gay – although Darcy prided herself on having a fairly accurate 'gaydar' and Mal didn't seem to register on that at all. All she knew was that a sweet, intelligent, kind man was under their roof for the first time since her parents had broken up and that she was absolutely OK with it.

Better than OK, in fact.

'How are you feeling now?' Darcy asked her. 'You've had an emotional rollercoaster of a day. You all right?'

'It's the weirdest thing, love,' her mum said quietly, with an understanding smile. 'Because I think this is the first time in as long as I can remember that I actually feel relief – with a tiny bit of euphoria thrown in there too. Do you know what I mean?'

Darcy just smiled back at her. Yes, as it happened. She knew exactly what her mum meant. To a T, as it happened.

*

'Looks like she's finally ready to go,' Mal said a few minutes later, sticking his head around the kitchen door. Darcy and her mum gripped hands tightly and walked down the hallway together. There was a taxi right at the garden gate and Mal strode on ahead of them to load up the boot of the car with the last of the heavy-looking bags and baggage.

And there was Lauren, just about to get into the car. She turned back to take one last, final look at Darcy and her mum with a cold, flinty look; a look that seemed to say 'you may have won this round, but I'll be back'.

Her mum didn't bother even wasting another word on Lauren though. Instead she just stared back at her, giving as good as she got. Moments later, Lauren slipped into the back seat of the car and in the blink of an eye, she was gone.

'She's really out of our lives then,' Darcy whispered half to herself.

'For good,' her mum said, slipping her arm around Darcy's skinny little shoulders. 'That I faithfully promise you, love.'

Mal strolled back up the driveway to join them, hands in his pockets and a smile on his face.

'So, how does it feel?' he asked them both, 'to finally be rid of her? Do you feel like doing a little jig out here in the driveway singing "Hallelujah"?'

Darcy grinned warmly back at him. He seemed really sound, this Mal guy. This all felt good, somehow.

'The funny thing is,' her mum said, as the three of them stood in a little huddle together on the porch, 'I thought I'd want to dance on Lauren's grave after everything she's done, but it's not like that at all. I'm just . . . oh, glad to have my life back again, really.'

'Me too,' Darcy seconded. 'Although maybe we won't get any more lodgers in again for a while.'

'I think that's a very sound idea, love,' her mum replied. 'So now, anyone for a bite to eat? How about a takeaway, my treat?'

'Sounds cool,' Darcy said, suddenly aware that she'd been in such a ball of tension all day, she'd actually forgotten to eat. 'Maybe from Indie Spice? With garlic naan bread to go with it too?'

'Whatever you like,' her mum smiled.

'And here's another thought,' Darcy added, looking tentatively over at Mal, who seemed in absolutely no rush to go anywhere. 'Maybe you'd like to stay and have a bite to eat with us?'

Mal smiled at that and as Darcy looked from one of them to the other, determined to give the two of them an extra nudge in the right direction. After all, elderly people needed all the encouragement they could get, didn't they?

'Come on, Mal, you've got to try Indie Spice,' she added warmly. 'Trust me, their spinach and lentil tikki is to die for.'

Chapter Thirty-eight

Liz

'Now this I have to see for myself,' I said jubilantly as Sarah let me in through the front door. 'I have to stand there in her empty bedroom and see the cleared-out wardrobe and drawers before I can really believe it! Has this happy day actually come to pass? Or am I dreaming?'

'It's absolutely true, babes,' Sarah laughed, giving me a huge, warm hug. 'Lauren left just over an hour ago.'

'Did she cry? Cause a fight? Was there a big scene? Did she try to bitch slap you across the face? Come on, I need details!' I said impatiently, handing over a bottle of celebratory Prosecco, which I'd stopped off to buy on the way there. But then this was a Big Day. A red-letter day. Days like this needed to be celebrated and marked.

'None of the above, I'm sorry to tell you,' Sarah said as I followed her down through the hallway and on into the kitchen. 'It was all over quite quickly, really. She had her things packed up in a flash and was gone. And Mal was here, of course, so he was able to speed things up and get her out of here that bit faster.'

As she swung the kitchen door open I realised Mal was

384

in fact still there, sitting beside Darcy with the remains of the most divine-looking Indian takeaway, half-eaten and spread out in serving bowls all over the kitchen table.

'Hey Mal,' I said, a bit taken aback to see him, but still. Mal was one of life's good people and it was always great to see him, 'I heard you played a blinder today.'

'Team effort,' he said, grinning back modestly.

'Glass of fizz, anyone?' I said, pulling up a chair and waving the Prosecco about.

'Oh God, yes please!' said Sarah, bustling about the kitchen cupboards looking for champagne flutes. 'Mal, will you join us? Ahh, you will, go on, one little glass.'

'You twisted my rubber arm,' he said looking nicely relaxed, in absolutely no rush to go anywhere.

Just then, Darcy's phone made that annoying whistling noise that teenagers all seem to have their mobiles pre-set to, as a text alert pinged through.

'Guess what, Mum?' she said, brightening, 'that's Sophie texting. She's invited me around for a sleepover this evening, just to hang out with a few of the other girls from our class. So is it OK if I go? Sophie lives so close by and I can easily walk there.'

'Well, I don't know, love,' said Sarah wavering, 'you've got your exams looming.'

'Oh go on, *please*, Mum? It's been a rough day, and it is a Friday after all. I promise I'll spend the whole weekend studying to make up for it. Is that a deal?'

'Go on, let her go,' I said. 'Rosie's already there and all the girls are doing is chatting and messing about with each other's make-up. Besides, I've got to collect Rosie in the morning, so I can drop you home at the same time, Darcy.'

Yet another recent development that I was very grateful

for. Rosie had always been so studious and diligent, that I was always worried she didn't have as many close friends as I'd have liked. But lately, she'd grown a lot closer to both Sophie and Darcy and it did my heart good to see.

'All right then, you can go,' Sarah smiled. 'Just this once.'

'Fab, you're the best, Mum!' she beamed, skipping up from the table and making for the door. She hugged Sarah on her way out, gave me a quick peck on the cheek, then turned back to Mal.

'It was really cool meeting you,' she said, and I knew by her that she really meant it too. You could always tell with teenagers. Then with a sly sideways giveaway glance over at her mum, she added, 'and I hope we'll be seeing you again, Mal. Very soon.'

Jaysus, I thought. Was Darcy trying to do a bit of very unsubtle matchmaking here? Now I had absolutely no idea what Mal's status was, whether he was gay, married, single, divorced, whatever. He was a professional colleague who I'd worked with from time to time in the past and somehow our private lives just didn't seem to come into the equation.

Yet as the evening wore on, the thought lodged in my head like a wasp under a jar and once it was there there was no budging it. I looked over to Sarah and she seemed happier, more relaxed and there's no other word for it – *lighter* – than I'd seen her in months.

And as for Mal, well he was such a laid-back type, so relaxed and chatty, he'd be at ease anywhere. Yet, I noted, as the time ticked by and the evening drew darker outside, he seemed in absolutely no rush to go anywhere. If he had a wife, or a girlfriend or kids, wouldn't he have checked in with them by then? Or rushed away much sooner?

As it worked out, with Darcy out for the evening, Mal,

Sarah and I settled in for a chat over a lovely, civilized glass of fizz and somehow, without realising it, hours had passed by and I'd barely even noticed.

'So what do you think will happen now?' I asked, more out of curiosity than anything else. 'To Lauren, I mean.'

There was a thoughtful pause as both Sarah and Mal digested this.

'If it's one thing I'd bet good money on,' Sarah eventually said, 'it's that she'll land on her feet. Somehow the Laurens of this world always do, don't they?'

I could only agree.

'But she certainly won't get a reference from Sloan Curtis,' Sarah added. 'Bernie made that much perfectly clear to her.'

'What do you think?' I asked Mal. He sat back, took off his glasses and gave them a little wipe, clearly really giving it some thought.

'Well,' he said, 'you both know as well as I do how small and tight-knit the legal community is in this town. It's like a pinhead. Everyone knows everyone else. And word travels fast, lightening quick in fact. Sooner or later it's going to get out that Lauren worked for Sloan Curtis and tried to poach their two biggest clients before she jumped ship to a rival firm. It's purely a matter of time. Even Whites, the firm she's aiming to work for, are going to get wind of it and I can tell you, they won't be impressed. Chances are they'll drop her quick as anything. And what other firm would go near her, with that hanging over her?'

Silence around the table at that. But then his words really did ring true.

'It's the Law of Karma in action,' I said, crisply, nibbling on the remains of a bit of naan bread. 'Lauren had absolutely no compunction in shafting everyone around her and now it's come back to bite her in the arse. That's what happens when you're a thundering wagon.'

'Still and all though,' Sarah said thoughtfully, fingering the stem of the glass in front of her.

'What?' I asked her.

'It's just that—'

'For feck's sake, Sarah!' I said, prodding her in the ribs. 'Don't tell me your conscience is at you now, after everything Lauren put you and your family through? Don't tell me you're actually feeling sorry for her? As far as I'm concerned, I hope she ends up back in that dingy salon you first discovered her in. Good enough for the aul' wench.'

'No,' she replied, taking another sip of the Prosecco, 'it's just – I feel like such an idiot. That's what I can't stop beating myself up over. Lauren marked me out as an easy, soft touch and then played me like a violin. After all, you saw right through her from day one, Lizzie. So why did it take me so long?'

'In a strange way, it's no bad thing, when you think about it,' I said.

'How do you mean?'

'Lauren is a user,' I explained. 'An out-and-out user. She doesn't see people as regular human beings, she sees them wholly in terms of what she can get out of them. Like a commodity. The fact that you didn't recognise it when she sauntered into your life is a sign that you'd never had to deal with anyone like her before.'

She smiled back. 'Only a good pal like you, Liz, could make my complete and total blindness over the past few months actually sound like a virtue. Bless you for that.'

'Thing is,' said Mal, sitting forward, 'I come across a lot of Laurens in my line of work. You'd be stunned at just how many of them there are out there. And in a way it's heartening to know that there are still a few Sarah Keyes left in this world. People who look for the good in others, and who genuinely what to help where they can. It's a lovely trait – and a rare one at that. So don't you go changing. Just stay as you are.'

He looked warmly across the table at her and I could see Sarah glowing at the attention, unused to an attractive man giving her a bit of a compliment.

At that point I judged it tactful to say my goodbyes. After all, I still had the boys to get to bed and all that jazz. So I made my excuses, pleaded tiredness and got up to go, promising Sarah I'd call her first thing the next day.

As Sarah walked me down to the front door to let me out, I noticed Mal's eyes following her.

And I don't know why, but it just made me smile.

Chapter Thirty-nine

Sarah

'So . . . umm . . . I'd say you must be exhausted,' Mal said. 'It's been a really long day for you.'

'And for you too.'

'I should probably, you know, make a move. To go home, I mean. That kind of move.'

With that Mal thumbed vaguely in the direction of the hall door.

'Yeah, of course'

'Let you get to your bed, I mean.'

'Sure . . . and thanks so much again. For the lift home, for everything . . .'

'Are you kidding? I'm the one who should be thanking you.'

'What for? I did nothing!'

'For the dinner, I mean. Darcy was right, it was great. Really good.'

'Indie Spice really are the best . . .'

'Yeah . . . I'll definitely use them again . . . Fantastic. Right then. Better be off.'

Why was I being so bloody awkward around this man?

We'd had a perfectly relaxed evening and yet, the very minute Liz left, the two of us completely clammed up with each other and could only speak in half-broken sentences.

Very irritating.

*

And it was the exact same thing when Mal called me two days later.

I instantly perked up when I saw his name flash up on the phone.

'Hi,' he said.

'Hi!'

'Just . . . you know . . . checking in with you, that's all.'

'That's good of you . . . ehh . . . thank you.'

'I mean, I wanted to make sure that . . .'

'That what?'

'Well, that you hadn't heard anything more from Lauren for one thing . . .'

'No . . . thank God!'

'Because it just occurred to me that she might try to contact you again.'

'Trust me, Mal, she'd be wasting her time.'

'In fact, if it were to happen, I'd nearly suggest . . .'

'Yeah?'

'That you just don't take any of her calls.'

'Exactly what I was thinking too.'

'And maybe blocking her number too?'

'Yes. Absolutely. Great suggestion.'

Then there was a long drawn-out pause while we both racked our brains around for something else to say. And neither of us could.

'Well, I'd better let you get back to work then,' Mal said.

'And you too. Thanks for the call.'

'Any time.'

Jesus! I thought hanging up. What the feck was wrong with me?

*

'He fancies you and if you ask me, I think you clearly like him too,' Darcy said briskly, playing with a tendril of her hair as she sat barefoot on the sofa watching rubbish on TV. 'That's the only reason why you're both being so weird around each other. God, Mum, what are you like?'

'I do not fancy him.'

'Yes, you do. The other night you actually flushed once when he looked at you; it was hysterical. I was this close to Instagramming you. And I think he wouldn't mind seeing you again either, Why else do you think he keeps on calling?'

'Rubbish,' I said doubtfully. But if the truth be told, I couldn't figure out what I really felt about Mal. He was sweet and kind and attentive, that was as far as I was prepared to go. Plus he was easy to spend time with. And how long was it since a sweet, kind, attentive man had come into my life?

'You're just totally out of practice, Mum, that's all,' said Darcy. 'It would be so much easier if you were my age.'

'Why? What would I do if I were your age?'

'What everyone else does,' she shrugged. 'Get bladdered drunk and just go for it.'

Delightful.

*

As it happened though, in the end I didn't have to do anything at all. The following Sunday morning I was home alone, as Darcy was off with Tom for the weekend.

Now as any single woman will tell you, Sundays are by far the trickiest day of the week to get through. It's primarily a family day, after all, so what are you supposed to do if you're, ahem, "a woman of a certain age" with the whole day stretching out ahead of you and little to fill in the long hours till Darcy came home again?

Right then, I thought, resigning myself. Might as well catch up on a bit of work as I'd nothing better to get on with. And there was certainly plenty to do; not only was I reinstated back on the McKinsey case – with a full and flowery apology from Bernie for ever having taken me off it in the first place – but the mighty George McKinsey himself had decided in light of recent developments to carry on as a client of Sloan Curtis.

Just like that. Like nothing ever happened. And Lauren's name was completely airbrushed, as though she'd never existed.

It was coming up to midday when my mobile rang. It was beside me as I worked away at the kitchen table and I answered without even glancing down at the number. Darcy, I figured, ringing to tell me there was something urgent she'd left behind her and could I possibly drop it over to her? Probably worth noting that the last time she had a 'dire emergency' like that was because she'd left her mascara behind.

Give me strength, I thought, answering the phone.

'Darcy, whatever it is, the answer is no. Now I love you very much and I'll see you later.'

'So the answer is no then?' said a man's voice, catching me totally off guard.

'Mal? Is that you?'

'Yeah, is it a bad time?'

'Yeah . . . sorry . . . no! I mean no. Not a bad time at all!'

'So what are you up to?'

'I'm just working my way through a pile of tax returns, which has to be the most boring activity known to man. How about you?'

'I'm home,' he said, yawning lightly, 'with the whole day ahead of me. God, don't you hate Sundays?'

'Despise them. Great to know that I'm not the only one.'

'I actually use the word Sunday as an adjective now. As in, 'yeah, I saw that movie and it was really *Sunday*, if you ask me."

'I'm with you there,' I smiled. 'Deeply overrated as a weekend day.'

'But do you know the one good thing about a Sunday?'

'Ehh . . . no traffic on the roads? Good, thick, juicy supplements with all the papers that I can spend the week ahead reading?'

'Nice try, but no. Brunch, I think you'll find, is the correct answer I was looking for.'

'Oh yeah?' I said, wondering where this was leading. And also wondering if I'd time to wash my hair, if he was about to suggest what I thought he was.

'Ah, not just any old brunch though,' he chatted away easily and totally without any awkwardness this time. 'Brunch in Sophie's at the Dean. Have you ever been there?'

No, but I'd heard of it, of course. Sophie's was a rooftop restaurant in the trendy Dean Hotel on Harcourt Street, just a stone's throw from our offices, as it happened.

Bernie was forever talking about it and how fabulously fantastic it was, with its stunning aerial views overlooking the entire city, though of course he was far too much of a tight-arse to ever take any of his co-workers along with him. Lucy and Ruth at the office though often went to the bar there, as Lucy said, 'because where the cute, single guys go, we follow. On a Friday night at least.'

'No, I've never been,' I said, 'but I've heard only the most wonderful things about it.'

'Oh, Sarah Keyes,' he said, 'are you really a Sophie's newbie? You've no idea what you've been missing out on. Their Sunday brunch is a thing of beauty, whether you're into healthy crap like granola and all that birdseed, or the full heart attack on a plate like me. Trust me, there's something for everyone.'

'Is that right?' I said, starting to flirt a little now, amazing myself at how easy it was – like riding a bike really. It may well have been twenty odd years and a marriage break-up ago before I'd actually flirted with an actual guy, but it was actually astonishing how fast it all came back.

'So can I persuade you to join me?' Mal said after a long, long pause. 'Come on, it's only brunch.'

He's right, I thought. It's not a date, it's not dinner or anything scary. It's just brunch. No need for me to be nervy or anxious. All I had to do was be myself.

'See you there in one hour,' I told him.

'Till then, Sarah Keyes.'

It's funny, I thought, hanging up the phone, how you can hear a smile over the phone. And just then I knew that Mal was smiling.

SIX MONTHS LATER

Epilogue

Sarah

'Just hang on for me, I'm coming!'

'Running late again?'

'I know, I know,' I said apologetically, 'but it wasn't my fault – a meeting ran over—'

'Oh, Sarah Keyes,' he said in mock exasperation, 'I am so buying you a watch for Christmas. Whether you like it or not.'

'I'm running, I'm actually running out the door now . . . don't worry, I will make it!'

'Wouldn't it just be easier if I collected you at the office? It's no trouble, I'm in the car anyway and it would save you driving.'

Typical of him, I thought warmly, always putting himself out for other people. And without complaint too, which, as Liz was always pointed out – not a little enviously – to me, made him a rare gem amongst men.

So how lucky was I, that my love life had upended itself so perfectly? Not in a thousand years, and after everything that I'd been through with Tom, did I ever think that things would work out so Hollywood-ending-perfect for me?

'That's sweet of you, Mal,' I said warmly, 'but I promise, I'm just leaving the office now and it would be so much faster if I walked there. It's barely ten minutes away anyway.'

'You'll freeze, it's bloody arctic out there.'

'I'll be fine. See you very shortly . . . and keep me a seat!'

Six months. It had really been six months since that first brunch we shared together back at Sophie's at the Dean, which had by default, had become 'our place' ever since then. Dinners, my birthday, nights when we just felt like pushing the boat out; we were at the stage where the two of us knew a lot of the staff by name.

'Jammy bitch,' as Liz often quipped, 'look at the pair of you, love's young dream.'

'That's a laugh; love's middle-aged dream, more like.'

'And "your coupley place" is a fancy restaurant in town. Can I just point out that on the rare occasions when Harry and I get to do out, our "special place" is the Pizza Hut down in the Stillorgan Shopping Centre. That's *reality* for you, babes.'

And now Mal and I were about to face into another milestone together, our first Christmas as, dare I say it, an actual proper couple. Not only that, but we were due to meet up that evening for a Christmas concert that Darcy was singing in, along with a gang from her class. It was to be held in the Pepper Canister Church, a gorgeous Victorian building with amazing acoustics, according to Darcy, which was just a short-ish walk from the Sloan Curtis office.

We were all going and, because I was running late, the chances were everyone else was already there ahead of me; Liz and Harry, and even Tom, were coming along to cheer on our gal.

I'd already introduced Tom to Mal and while Mal was

his usual easy, affable self throughout the whole ordeal, Tom on the other hand seemed a little more iffy about the whole idea of my moving on. Particularly as he himself was still single. But then as far as I was concerned, there was only one person who mattered in my private life. And she was due to sing Christmas carols on stage for the evening ahead.

'Hey, you guys, that's the BEST news!' Darcy had said feelingly, when Mal and I first came out to her as a couple. God spare me, it was all nerve-wracking stuff, but by some miracle she had completely taken it in her stride.

'We're like an episode of *Modern Family*, if you think about it, Mum,' she'd added, twinkling away at me from under a new fringe she'd just had cut in, 'where you're Claire and I get to be Hayley, the stunningly beautiful daughter.'

For the first time in as long as I could remember, I thought, racing down the canal bank to the church just as it started to sleet rain, I had genuine reason to believe that it really was going to be a happy Christmas. Wherever I looked, all was well: it really was one of those rare, wondrous times you sometimes get in your life where you just want to burst into some class of a big musical production number, just for the hell of it.

I pulled up the hood of my heavy cashmere coat against the worsening sleet and clipped as briskly as I could down Herbert Place, beside the canal.

And then I stopped dead in my tracks.

No. No, no, no, no, no.

It couldn't be, could it?

I squinted through the rain and had a good, long stare.

Sweet Baby Jesus and the orphans, it was. It actually fecking well was.

She was just tripping down the stone steps out of a nondescript Georgian building and into a taxi waiting outside. Wearing a bright scarlet-red coat and huddled against the cold, briefcase in hand.

Lauren.

Definitely one hundred per cent Lauren. There was no mistaking her. The jet-black swishy hair, the walk, the super-smart way she dressed – it was her all right.

I stared at her, transfixed, momentarily forgetting about the icy cold, forgetting about the concert. In that moment I forgot everything.

She must have felt my eyes burning into her because, just as she was about to get into the cab, she glanced to where I was standing transfixed on the pavement opposite.

Our eyes locked and the icy cold glare she gave me would have turned a lesser woman to stone.

She was completely wasting her time though. Instead of even acknowledging her, I pointedly turned my head away and calmly walked on towards the church, just around the corner.

The Laurens of this world somehow always land on their feet, I remember predicting all those months ago. And it looked like I'd been right. Maybe she had got another job and maybe she hadn't. Maybe she'd found herself another Sarah Keyes to sponge off like a leech.

All I knew in that moment was that it was absolutely nothing to do with me and my lovely, happy little life, thanks very much.

'Hey, there you are!' said Mal with a big wave, as he spotted me from a distance clipping up the stone steps to the church. 'Come on, I saved you a seat; it's almost show time. Everyone is here ahead of you.'

'Sorry about being late—' I went to say, as he slipped his arm around my shoulder, kissed me lightly, then stopped for a moment to scan my face up and down properly.

'You OK?' he asked. 'You look like you've just seen a ghost.'

I turned back in the direction of the street where I'd just seen Lauren.

'I did see someone I used to know,' I said thoughtfully. 'But it was no one of any importance. No one that need ever concern us ever again.'

With that, he pulled me tighter to him and as I snuggled into the crook of his warm arm, together we made our way inside.

THE END.

Acknowledgements

Thank you, Marianne Gunn O'Connor. For absolutely *everything*.

Thank you, Pat Lynch for your kindness and friendship all these years.

Thank you Vicki Satlow, for all your tireless hard work abroad.

Very special thanks to the lovely Phoebe Morgan, who worked so hard to edit this book. It's really been a joy to work with you Phoebe.

Thank you Eloise Wood and Helen Huthwaite, for your incredible kindness and tireless hard work.

Thank you Charlie Redmayne, for making your authors feel so special. The annual summer party is always one of the highlights of my year.

Thank you Oli Malcolm, for everything you do for authors across the board.

Thank you Helena Sheffield, for all your fabulousness across digital media.

Very special thanks to the wonderful team at Avon and to all at HarperCollins too, who I've had the pleasure of working alongside with all these years. Special shout out to Louis Patel, Natasha Harding, Kate Ellis and Hannah

405

Welsh. I love coming to see you all in London and only wish I could get you over to Dublin more often!

Thank you Donna Hillyer, for the terrific job you did in copy-editing this book.

Thank you Mum, Dad and all my lovely family, for everything. Special thank you to my Aunt Lilla for being such a rock.

Thank you Clelia, for being the kind of pal I can call at 7am to talk rubbish down the phone to. And thank you even more for putting up with me in the dressing rooms at Fair City. Thank you Pat Kinevane and Frank Mackey for being like brothers.

Thank you to all my pals – some of whom go back decades. I'm looking at you, Karen Finnegan, Susan McHugh, Marion O'Dwyer, Fionnuala Murphy, Fiona Lalor. And special thanks to my writer buddies, especially Sinead Moriarty, Liz Nugent, Monica McInerney, Patricia Scanlan, Sheila O'Flanagan, Carmel Harington, Martina Devlin, Sarah Webb, Caroline Grace-Cassidy, Fionnuala Kearney and Hazel Gaynor. A night out very soon, I think. . .

Thank you to all at RTE and Fair City and special thanks to Isobel Mahon and Caroline Fitzgerald for getting me back onto a stage for the first time in ten years. Thank you Maria McDermottroe and Rose Seymour for being such rocks. Both onstage and off.

And in case you think there's anyone I've forgotten, huge and heartfelt thanks to the most incredible team, who between them somehow make any author's job an utter joy. Thank you, Tony Purdue, Ann-Marie Dolan and Mary Byrne.

Superstars, all three of you.

And this one's warmly dedicated to you.

**Marriage. It's a dream come true.
Isn't it?**

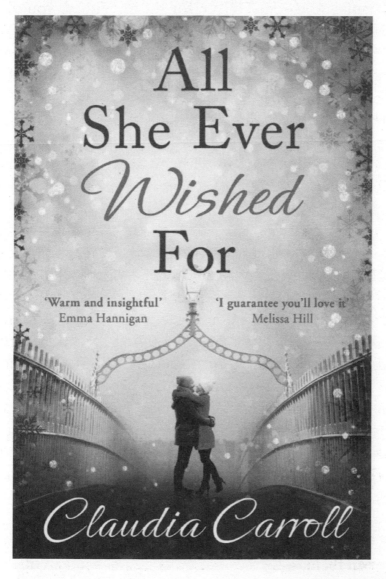

**A gorgeous story of chance meetings and
unexpected friendships. Because sometimes
what you've always wished for isn't necessarily
what life has in store . . .**

A sparkling, feel-good romantic comedy
to whisk you away . . .

What if *the one* isn't who you think he is?

The Number One Bestseller

Meet Me in Manhattan

Claudia Carroll

What should be a dream come true is looking a
little like a nightmare. But Holly is determined
to get her New York happy ending!

**True love lasts a lifetime.
But sometimes, life just gets in the way . .**

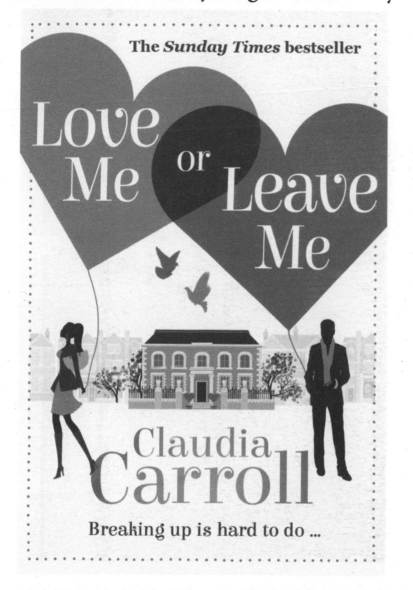

The *Sunday Times* bestseller

Love
Me or Leave
Me

Claudia
Carroll

Breaking up is hard to do ...

Get lost in this gorgeous bestseller today.